PRAISE FOR THE
OAKWOOD BAY SERIES

"A glittering small-town romance, delightfully angsty and heartfelt, packed with sizzling tension, heat, and sweet, swoon-worthy moments. Wilde's voice is fresh, authentic, and wonderfully charming."
—Peyton Corinne, *USA Today* bestselling author of *Unloved*

"Achingly tender and deliciously sexy, *Only in Your Dreams* is everything readers are looking for in a brother's best friend romance! Wilde's writing is brimming with palpable tension and deeply relatable characters, and my heart was completely enthralled by every moment."
—Jillian Meadows, author of *Give Me Butterflies*

"All at once tender, funny, and charming, *Only Between Us* delivers everything I love in a romance: undeniable chemistry, page-turning tension, and authentic emotions. I loved every moment! Fake dating, football, and yards of delicious chemistry—what could be better? Wilde's voice leaps off the page in this charming, sexy sports romance."
—Grace Reilly, *USA Today* bestselling author

ALSO BY ELLIE K. WILDE

OAKWOOD BAY Series
Only in Your Dreams
Only Between Us

SUNSET LANDING Series
The Sixty/Forty Rule
The No-Judgment Zone

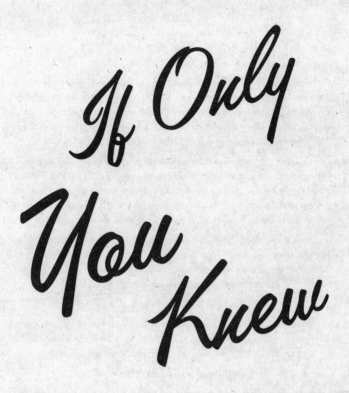

A NOVEL

ELLIE K. WILDE

ATRIA PAPERBACK

New York   Amsterdam/Antwerp   London
Toronto   Sydney/Melbourne   New Delhi

ATRIA
PAPERBACK

An Imprint of Simon & Schuster, LLC
1230 Avenue of the Americas
New York, NY 10020

For more than 100 years, Simon & Schuster has championed authors and the stories they create. By respecting the copyright of an author's intellectual property, you enable Simon & Schuster and the author to continue publishing exceptional books for years to come. We thank you for supporting the author's copyright by purchasing an authorized edition of this book.

This book is a work of fiction. Any references to historical events, real people, or real places are used fictitiously. Other names, characters, places, and events are products of the author's imagination, and any resemblance to actual events or places or persons, living or dead, is entirely coincidental.

First Atria Paperback edition February 2026

ATRIA PAPERBACK and colophon are registered trademarks of Simon & Schuster, LLC

Simon & Schuster strongly believes in freedom of expression and stands against censorship in all its forms. For more information, visit BooksBelong.com.

For information about special discounts for bulk purchases, please contact Simon & Schuster Special Sales at 1-866-506-1949 or business@simonandschuster.com.

The Simon & Schuster Speakers Bureau can bring authors to your live event. For more information or to book an event, contact the Simon & Schuster Speakers Bureau at 1-866-248-3049 or visit our website at www.simonspeakers.com.

Interior design by Lexy East

Manufactured in the United States of America

1   3   5   7   9   10   8   6   4   2

Library of Congress Control Number has been applied for.

ISBN 978-1-6680-9385-6 (pbk)
ISBN 978-1-6680-9386-3 (ebook)

 Let's stay in touch! Scan here to get book recommendations, exclusive offers, and more delivered to your inbox.

For anyone who took a little longer to figure out life.

If Only You Knew

Chapter 1

Summer

"So, how do all these big college athletes feel about a pretty little thing like you attempting to train them in a gym?"

Cory H., the dirty-blond veterinarian brought to me by one of the dozens of dating apps that've been letting me down for years, winks across the table as though he's just paid me the compliment of a lifetime.

I try to decide which part of that I'm supposed to swoon over. Perhaps it's being called a *thing*? The fact that he deigned to remember that I *attempt* to work as a physical therapist when I'm not suffering through this date?

Either way, I pull a face around the lip of my glass—tragically down to ice cubes and badly diluted remnants of margarita—hoping the sad sip absolves me from answering.

My sense of humor fled the premises around the time Cory casually grazed my ass when he hugged me at the start of our date.

I gaslit myself into believing it was an accident. Rationalized that he'd been perfectly normal when we'd texted after matching on the app. And now, I have no one to blame but myself and my expert ability to ignore the bouquet of red flags he must have been waving at me since the moment I swiped right.

I've been in the dating trenches for a while. Still, all of my carefully plotted strategies—born and evolved through copious years of painful first dates—inevitably led me here. Sitting across a table from a man whose hot factor took a nosedive with the very first syllable out of his mouth.

Cory's phone trills, loud enough to hear over the bustling sounds of Oakley's Pub around us. He silences it right away, which would be a point in his favor if he didn't proceed to scroll through the litany of notifications that've appeared on his phone over the course of this short nightmare. It rings again.

I tip an ice cube into my mouth, shamelessly crunching on it. "Do you have to take a call? It won't bother me if you do."

Cory sneers at his phone. "Nah, it's just some chick I went out with a couple days ago. I've been trying to dodge her, but she doesn't seem to understand the concept of silence."

I've never been so envious of another woman in my life.

As one of only two restaurants in Oakwood, the small town where I've lived my whole life, Oakley's is packed to the brim this Thursday night. Locals occupy the mahogany tables and booths upholstered in fading tartan. The fact that none of them—usually so keen for a hint of viable gossip—are paying us any mind is an indication that they've had a front-row seat to so many of my dating fiascos, they're as unfazed by them as they are by the sun setting at night.

"You're way hotter than she is, by the way." Cory nods to his phone. "No way you'll be getting silence from me. I'll be all over you until you agree to see me again."

Ah, so we've graduated to stalking.

I crunch another ice cube. "That's . . . very sweet of you, Cory."

Seriously, *how* didn't I see this coming? We texted for days leading up to tonight, and—Cory's face splits into a wide smile, bright and crooked and . . . right. *That's* how I didn't see this coming. I was blinded by the very pretty man in the collection of pictures on his dating profile.

"You want another drink?" Cory takes a deep swig of his own. "Let's get you another drink. You're nowhere near lubricated enough, if you know what I'm saying."

Yeah . . . screw this guy.

I've had no trouble simply strolling out of dates in the past, but I've been out with enough Corys to know exactly how he'd take that. Fortunately, after years of finding myself in these undesirable scenarios, I've implemented a fail-safe: a way to divest myself of these boys without awkwardness or argument, or endless follow-up texts.

Discreetly, I slide my foot out from under our table and tap the toe of my four-inch heel.

Cory leans in, a smirk stretching his mouth. "It's a double entendre. Lubricated as in drunk . . ."

My gaze drifts to a man sitting solo in a booth at the very back of the bar. Legs stretched out on the bench seat, broad shoulders resting against the wall, facing out into the restaurant. He's wearing a truly obnoxious Hawaiian shirt, sky blue and bright green, and frowning down at a book. Light brown hair thrown messily over the pull of concentration in his brows as he reads. He reaches to his right until his fingers close around a sweating glass of radioactive-yellow liquid and takes a long sip, all without breaking eye contact with his book.

". . . but also as in your panties." *Tap, tap, tap.*

"How charming." *Tap, tap, tap, tap, tap, tap—*

"Summer? Summer Prescott?"

The man in the Hawaiian shirt now strides across the bar, staring me down with wide, dreamy eyes. Like he's been toiling over that book for years—*decades*—trying to fill the gap left by missing pages . . . only to find all the answers in my face.

Cory's gaze follows mine. "Who the fuck are you?"

I gasp. "*Parker*? I haven't seen you in years."

Parker's face falls at that. He turns an apologetic look on Cory. "I hate to interrupt, but do you mind if I steal your date for a second?"

There's a flush rising up Cory's neck. "You can fuck right off, buddy. We're in the middle of something."

I really hate to agree with this moron, but I shake my head at Parker. "I'm not coming with you. You've had *years* to come find me. *Years* to come talk to me." My voice rises, and I jump to my feet. "Years to explain why you up and left town—left *me*—without so much as a word. And suddenly you're here, wanting to talk in the middle of my date? How dare you do this now?"

Parker stuffs his hands into the pockets of his dark jeans. "Summer, I'm sorry—I've been praying to bump into you every day since."

"Why? What could you possibly have to say to me now?"

"I've . . . God help me, I've missed you. I know you've missed me, too. Please, just give me a minute to explain."

I sniff hard, wiping a nonexistent tear. We're properly hitting our stride now, and I can practically taste my sweet, sweet freedom from Cory. Parker will quote a couple rom-coms, I'll fake a few more tears, and—

"You went out with *this* guy? In the ugly Hawaiian shirt?"

Damn it, Cory—not the shirts. If there was ever a way to get Parker Woods going—

His eyes narrow on Cory. My stomach pangs, starts to sink. "Yes, she went out with me."

"Really?" Cory gives Parker a scathing up and down. "I don't see it."

"She did. And she still calls me." His tone is pure outrage and I'm officially losing him. "Every day. She's obsessed with me. *And* my Hawaiian shirts, which she loves."

I widen my eyes at him. "I don't think—"

He widens his right back. "Come on, Summer. The private number that keeps calling me? Hanging up when I answer? We both know it's you."

My jaw drops. "Cory, did you know that Parker gifted me his great-grandmother's engagement ring on our two-week-iversary? Talk about obsessed."

"Oh, yeah?" There's a half-second twitch at Parker's mouth, but he wrangles it quickly. "I found a shrine she had for me in her closet. She had my hair in a jar and my boxers in a frame."

"He's slept with a picture of me under his pillow since our very first date."

"She cried like a baby the first time we made love."

"Tears of epic disappointment, I assure you."

"Oh, Summer." Parker's mouth stretches in a smirk, dimple popping in his right cheek. "I highly fucking doubt that."

"Can somebody explain what the hell is going on?" Cory practically shouts. "We're on a date, buddy."

I widen my eyes at Parker. *Land the damn plane, Woods.*

He gets the message. Parker clears his throat, winds an arm around my waist, and sweeps me into his chest. "The point is . . . I still love you, Summer Prescott. And I'm sorry that it took seeing you with another man to knock me to my senses. But . . . I'm just a boy standing in front of a girl, asking her to love him."

I force a sob, spinning in Parker's arms to give Cory a tearful look. "I'm so sorry, Cory. But I can't have that drink. And I can't see you again."

"Seriously, who *is* this guy?"

"He's my best friend. And the love of my life."

"I'm sorry to do this to you." Parker produces his wallet and tosses some cash onto the table, enough to cover our drinks. "But what can I say? It's serendipity . . ."

"Seren-fucking-*what*?"

"And you don't mess with serendipity," I finish, sighing up at Parker.

"You're both insane." Cory jumps to his feet so aggressively he sends his chair skittering across the worn hardwood. He storms across the bar, throws open the door, and disappears into the night.

Parker and I stare at each other for one long, loaded moment filled with love, lust, and—

"I had your boxers in a *frame*?" I sweep my purse off the back of my chair, trying so hard to be mad at him even as my body shudders with laughter. "Really, Park?"

Parker laughs. "It was that or the used tissue I—"

"*Okay*. We're done here."

He throws an arm over my shoulders, steering me to our regular booth at the back of the pub—the one he'd been reading at prior to the rescue mission. There, he settles into his seat, facing the bar, legs laid out on the bench as I do the same across the table. I wave at Lisa Parsons, who owns Oakley's with her husband, and with a nod she moves to pour my usual Diet Coke.

"So, what was wrong with Mr. *Seren-fucking-what*? That barely lasted twenty minutes."

"I wouldn't even know where to begin." My head hits the wall behind us. "These guys keep getting worse and worse, I swear."

Parker hands me my Kindle from under his book, proof that at least *he'd* seen the writing on the wall with tonight's date. "Was he worse than the one who spent the entire date trying to convince you that the moon landing was faked?"

Jeremy. He blinded me with his abs. "Worse."

"Worse than the one who kept trying to lure you to the washroom for a quickie?"

Stephen with the bright blue eyes. "Worse."

"What about the one who dined and dashed while you were getting another round of drinks at the bar?" Parker asks darkly.

I grimace, remembering how I'd come back to our table to find a furious Parker forking over cash to cover our bill after witnessing Garrett's vanishing act. He'd then plied me with Diet Coke and Thai food from my favorite place in the next town over to cheer me up. I'd actually been hopeful during that date—thought it had been going well for once.

But I've been trapped in a string of bad first dates for the last three years.

Three years without even a glimmer of hope for a second date. Three years of navigating a slew of hook-up-type, moon-landing-denying men that seem to look at me and think, *Yep, she's the one.*

My last boyfriend, who dumped me when I started feeling him out on an eventual engagement after four years together, was normal, at least.

Well, normal adjacent.

His idea of quality time involved me watching him drive tricked-out cars through video game streets, hitting innocent pedestrians along the way. He broke it off, then turned around and got engaged to his next girlfriend a year into their relationship.

The wedding bells in my life didn't stop there. Our friend Zac and Parker's twin sister, Melody, who split their time between Oakwood and the city, got married just last month. Brooks, who we met in college, and his fake-girlfriend-turned-real-fiancée, Siena, shipped across the country when he signed with an NFL team out in Los Angeles. Even our newest friend Shy has a husband and three-year-old daughter.

I stare over our table at Parker taking a deep sip of his soda. It's an undeniably pretty view that's evolved plenty over the years—from preschooler with a perma-smile to baby-faced teen to this nearly-thirty-year-old man with his mess of thick hair, a subtle bump on the bridge of his nose from taking a bad tackle in his college football years, and a jaw dusted with stubble.

Even he's started dating more seriously after years of happily living the single life, and seeing as he's pretty much the best person I know, it's only a matter of time until he's paired off, just like the rest of them.

I'll be happy for him once he finds someone. *Thrilled.* The first to champion their relationship, celebrate their eventual engagement. Because he's my best friend, deserving of all the love in the world.

But then . . . it'll be me. Single, thirty-year-old only-child-of-her-practically-estranged-parents Summer Prescott.

It's hard not to feel like I'm constantly chasing after a high-speed train, scrambling for a foothold, trying not to get left behind. Trying to silence the voice in my head that points to all the departures in my life and concludes that I'm the problem. It's not just my friends who've left me behind, after all.

"Serious question. What is it about me that says, *Weirdos, nymphos, and grown men with mommy issues welcome here?*"

Parker squints at me from over the top of his book. "That felt like a personal attack."

Lisa appears with my soda. "Another bad one, hon?" I pull a face in reply, and she pats my outstretched calf. "I've been saying it for years. That picker of yours gave up on you a long time ago."

I give her a look over the rim of my Diet Coke. Lisa is withholding her favorite, incorrect caveat about said picker.

According to her, it did its job when I met my true love at the ripe age of three. When he barged into the pillow fort I'd built on my first morning at day care in Oakwood, and announced we were now friends.

Worst meet-cute ever, but it was the perfect introduction to the mischief that would go on to follow me for twenty-seven years in the form of a blue-eyed, dimple-smiled, Hawaiian-shirt-wearing tornado of a man.

It followed me all the way through high school, when we, plus Melody and Zac, would let Parker pull us from our homework and into some middle-of-the-night misadventure we'd get grounded for later. Through college, when our passion for biomechanics meant we shared an identical class schedule that led to our physical therapist jobs at the University of Oakwood Bay's athletic rehabilitation center. Even after, when Parker moved into the apartment above this very bar, only to find me moving into a place directly across the street just a few months later.

Parker huffs a laugh across the table, but Lisa turns a sharp look on him. "You're in no shape to laugh given your own track record with ladies."

"Lisa, please. Tonight's about Summer." Parker reaches over the table to lay a hand on my arm, giving Lisa a reproachful look. "She's just been through a terrible ordeal—shockingly, the guy whose pictures she spent a week salivating over turned out to be all chiseled jaw, no decency."

Lisa cinches her graying ponytail, looking back and forth between us. "Don't you think you two should cut to the chase already?"

"What chase is that?" Parker asks around a sip of his Mountain Dew.

He's being difficult on purpose, and the blank look I give her is just as phony. We know exactly which chase she means—the one where we supposedly wake up after almost three decades of platonic friendship to realize it was more than that all along.

Never gonna happen, for a multitude of reasons.

We've never kissed. Never had a sleepover, not even the kind with sleep involved. The most we've shared are friendly hugs and humiliating secrets I'd never dream of telling a guy I was trying to win over. And while I'm perfectly aware that my best friend is wildly, ask-me-to-join-his-cult-and-I'd-happily-sign-on-the-dotted-line attractive, inherent awareness and a desire to act on it are entirely different things.

"The chase. The *chase*." Lisa waves an impatient hand at us. "There's a reason all your dates keep failing, isn't there?"

"We know exactly why my dates keep failing," Parker says darkly.

We've all heard the rumors about Parker, the excited chatter among Oakwood's female population. And the things they say he's into in bed . . . Well, there's a reason women keep cutting their dates short to proposition him instead, eager to see if the rumors are true.

Lisa's nose wrinkles. Meanwhile, I shift on my bench as an image of Parker breaches its confines inside my brain, where I've actively buried all thoughts of the small-town rumor since the first time I heard it. It's not even a real image—just a synthesis of the different versions of him.

The way he looks when he focuses on a book. The way the tight pockets of muscle over his stomach flex when he works out. How his hair turns to waves when it's damp with sweat, how his chest moves while he pants from exertion. That smile of his—tilting slightly to the left, the long, shallow dimples bracketing plump lips. How it exudes endless reserves of playfulness, but the wholesomeness is completely offset by the mischievous spark in his deep blue eyes, telling you exactly which kind of adventure you're in for in his hands. Illicit. Middle of the night. Either waking up behind bars or butt naked and sore as hell.

And all of it pointed at the woman sprawled underneath him, squirming into his sheets, French braids turning more dishevelled by the thrust—

For fuck's sake, Prescott. Stop picturing your best friend naked.

I shove the thought back from whence it came. It's not even that I *want* to see my best friend naked. It's that godforsaken rumor, putting crazy thoughts in my head.

"Perhaps it's the universe trying to tell you something," Lisa tells Parker.

"What, that my dating life is so dire I may as well join a monastery?"

"Good grief, you're both hopeless." Lisa heaves a resigned sigh. "Keep on going like this and you'll end up alone."

With those awe-inspiring words, Lisa heads back to the bar.

"Thanks for that, Lisa. Excellent pep talk. Truly life-changing," Parker calls after her, before giving me a look that says, *Can you believe her?*

Except . . .

Lisa is dead wrong about me and Parker, but it's not as though she doesn't have a point—there *is* a reason our dates keep failing. I eye Parker's profile as he returns to his book, the very beginnings of an idea forming in my head.

As much as Parker's dead-end dating life brings relief to my co-dependent heart, it makes me a little frustrated on his behalf. He's incredibly funny. Self-deprecating. Smart and supportive. And he can weave a damn good French braid, too.

It's not as though he was the one to spread that rumor about himself, but he is the one who keeps asking out the wrong women.

Distractedly, I rub my nose, wincing when it jostles my tiny hoop piercing. "You know what? I think Lisa's right."

Parker's gaze darts to me. "About which part?"

"About us being hopeless."

He returns to his book. "You, of all people on this earth, are not hopeless."

"No, hear me out. I think we're the problem. Well, not *us*—our pickers." I swing my legs off the bench and under the table so that I'm facing him. "I bet I could find you a girl who at least finishes her drink before trying to strip for you."

Parker's eyes narrow in thought. "To be clear, she *will* strip for me eventually?"

"See, that's exactly what I mean—you're letting your dick do the picking. Maybe this requires a woman's touch." I laugh when Parker opens his mouth. "Don't. Do not joke about my touch in the context of your dick. You wish, Woods."

"Harsh, Sum." Parker's hand slaps over his stomach, exaggerating as though I just punched him.

"*Focus*—I figured it out. How to remedy the train wrecks trying to pass for our dating lives. No monasteries required." The more I think about it, the better the idea becomes. We know each other better than anyone. Have each other's best interests at heart. This idea isn't just good—it's brilliant.

Parker sobers the longer he stares at me, squinting over the top of his book. "You're scheming. I'm officially worried."

"Don't be. It's genius." I sweep my Diet Coke off the table and toast my increasingly skeptical best friend. "I'm going to become your picker. And in return, you're going find me the love of my life."

Chapter 2

Parker

Minutes later, an avalanche of pastel-colored pens and spiral-bound notebooks hits Summer's coffee table. She doesn't waste any time before reaching for one of each and scribbling *Parker's Dream Woman* at the top of a page.

Just the sight of those words has my stomach sinking.

I drop next to her on the worn-in blue sofa, rubbing my thumb over my brow and willing away the headache that tends to build whenever I read for too long. "Summer, we've just established that our pickers are broken. Why do you think we'll suddenly be able to find each other people to date?"

"Not *people to date*. We're finding each other's soulmates!"

I squint at my best friend through the recent fuzziness in my vision that feels like the cold hand of death lying on my shoulder, reminding me of the impending end of my twenties in just a few months.

She's grinning happily, cheeks rounded and pink, the way they get when she's excited. Eyes crinkling, still dusted with the soft purple stuff she wears on dates that makes the green in them sparkle even more than they usually do. Brown hair tousled around her shoulders, permanently wavy from the daily hours she spends surfing in salt water. Nose ring glinting under the overhead light. She changed out of that little number she wore for that dipshit Cory—the tiniest dress I've ever seen—and into a matching light-blue tank top and Lycra shorts, her signature gym outfit.

She's stunning, both looks suiting her beyond comprehension, and it's almost enough to distract me from the insult she just dealt me.

Here's the thing about me and Summer: We've been teased to no end about our friendship, how close we are. Since we hit puberty, people have been obsessed with the idea that we've spent years pining, battling jealousy, and sighing over all sorts of *what-if*s.

I can't speak to any of that.

But it came to me years ago, reading Campbell Ackerman's auto-biography. The happily married Hall of Fame quarterback spoke at length about his teammate Zander Larson, the tight end he'd played with his entire career, won a handful of Super Bowls with. They'd been a dynamic, once-in-a-generation pair. The way they could read each other with half a glance, always managed to find each other through a sea of bodies, knew exactly how to push each other's buttons or talk the other into stillness . . . They existed on a wavelength that defied normal human connection. He'd called Zander Larson his soulmate.

I'd known then, without a doubt, that Summer Prescott is my soulmate.

"Think about it, Park," she says now. "I've been falling victim to pretty boys with charming smiles for years. A trap you won't fall for, given your preference for boobs. And seeing as *my* appreciation for boobs mostly revolves around the way they look in a cute outfit, I'll be finding your dream girl in no time. I don't know why I never thought of this before."

"I don't know," I groan, already exhausted by this side quest. I feel like a jerk for the lack of enthusiasm, but nothing's ever sounded less appealing.

"Come on," Summer needles me. "Please? I don't know how much longer I can keep doing this on my own. The swiping. Coming up with a cute pickup line. Trying to sound all fun and sexy and intellectual over text, only to end up wasting layers of my favorite lipstick on another dud date."

"Not the lipstick!" I give an exaggerated gasp. She doesn't play along; just stares back at me with those wide, twinkling green eyes. Her lip trembles and I know for a *fact* that it's fake as hell, but I crumble like a dry cookie anyway. "Fuck, fine. I'll matchmake you."

"You're so damn easy." With a happy bounce in her seat, Summer thrusts a pen and notebook into my hands.

"This requires note-taking?"

"It requires thoughtful planning and careful strategy. I'm not going to set you up with just any woman. We're going for . . ." She assesses me. "What *are* you looking for, exactly? A long-term girlfriend with the potential for marriage, kids, a picket-fenced house?"

Again, it's that sinking feeling—one I can't quite put my finger on.

I nudge Summer's knee with mine, trying to buy time to get my thoughts straight. "Let's fix your hair first."

Patting at the waves on her head, Summer slips off the couch and settles on the old parquet between my outstretched legs. I get to work, splitting her hair in half, then in threes, and twisting it all together in the two French braids I perfected as a teenager when she adopted the hairstyle for her surf sessions at sunrise.

The guys tell me it's kind of weird. But she can't French braid on her own, and this nightly ritual has always felt meditative after a long day. Just running my fingers through her hair stills me. Helps me breathe a little deeper.

"Would you judge me if I said I've never really thought about it?" I say slowly. "Marriage, kids, and picket fences—it always felt like some nebulous thing I had years to figure out. And then I blink, and I'll be turning thirty in a couple of months. My twin sister married our childhood friend, and Brooks wins a Super Bowl and proposes to his fake girlfriend, all within a year. Everyone has it all figured out, while I still get stuck coming up with what I want for dinner."

I know these things have never been nebulous to Summer, but she hums a thoughtful sound anyway. "I'm still here. Still just as single."

"But you know what you're looking for. You know what you want out of life." I slip an elastic band off my wrist and tie off the second braid, smoothing my fingers along her hairline and smiling at the tiny freckle hidden under the unruly baby hairs. "And it's not just about picket fences. It's my apartment, my job. Rewind about ten years and I'm in exactly the same place I am today." She peers over her shoulder as I sit back on the couch, staring at the ceiling. I wave vaguely toward the window overlooking Oakwood's main street. "Is this it for me? All there is?"

"Maybe you need a break from work. Get your mind off it and the spark will come back?"

"But that's the thing—I fell into that job because it's what made sense for me at the time, and then I never stopped to think whether it was what I really wanted." I gesture at the pile of pens on her coffee table. "And now you're asking me to describe my dream woman, someone I'm supposed to marry one day, and . . . I can't. I have no idea what I'm looking for."

She reclaims the seat cushion next to mine, a teasing smile pulling at her full, glossy lips. "Not even a hair color? Shoe size?"

I shake my head, gaze drifting to the bookcase on the far wall piled with Summer's favorites—books about blue aliens bedding human women, and men who shapeshift into all kinds of mythical creatures. My own face stares back at me from several of the framed pictures scattered between the spines.

"You have to give me *something*. I can't promise you a hole in one with finding you a wife if I'm going in blind."

A wife. Jesus, it feels like I was in college just a minute ago—how the hell did I get to the point where we're talking about my future wife? I haven't even had a girlfriend in years. Not since Lainey, who dumped me when I told her I wasn't ready to move in with her.

I was twenty-two. Hardly ready for adulthood, let alone a live-in girlfriend.

When—*how*—did I get here?

I feel Summer's eyes on me as I fiddle with the hem of my T-shirt. "Park, are you okay?"

I don't think so.

It's a conclusion I've been drawing for the past few months, as I recognize myself increasingly less. Things that would've made me laugh then, barely faze me now. A job that used to have me excited for the next day keeps me paralyzed in bed long after my alarm goes off in the morning. A simple conversation about what I'm looking for in a woman makes me sweat more than it should.

I'm constantly on edge. Constantly exhausted. I feel like I'm approaching a cataclysmic event with no idea where it'll come from, but terrified by what it'll do to me.

"Parker?" Summer's hand comes down on my knee, pulling me out of my head. The shift is instantaneous. The fog in my head recedes as quick as it came, the weight falls off my chest, the tightness in my stomach unravels. Like she's just injected me with sunlight from the palm of her hand.

"Sorry." I breathe a genuine, sheepish laugh and uncap the bright pink pen she handed me. "Let's . . . let's hit pause on my wife and talk about you. *Summer's Dream Guy.* What do you have for me?"

It takes her a beat, but then Summer hops to her feet, her earlier enthusiasm returning full force.

"Dream *man.*" She disappears into her tiny galley kitchen. I catch a glimpse of her through the rectangular opening in the wall before she bends into her fridge. "I've dated boys and bros and guys, and I'm done with them all. I won't settle for less than a grown man, with goals and ambitions. Who's steady and predictable, and wants exactly what I want out of life: marriage, kids, and picket fences."

I scribble in my notebook as she speaks. "Steady and predictable? You really had the right idea with this matchmaking thing. You need all the help you can get."

She peeks through the opening in the wall. "What's wrong with steady and predictable?"

"Summer, you throw yourself into the ocean—willingly—with just a piece of plastic for safety, every single day. As dangerous a hobby as it gets. I think there's a whole lot more you want out of life than steady and predictable."

"Maybe that's why it works. I'm not looking to swim for my life at home, too." She scoffs when I shake my head. "Go ahead, then. Tell me what I really need, matchmaker."

I tip my head, studying the pink pen between my fingers. Drawing on my decades of Summer. "You need . . . someone to shake you up. Dishevel you a little."

"I don't need disheveling."

"You do. You used to have all these big ambitions that would've taken you out of this town years ago. But you're still here. Summer Prescott, town darling of Oakwood. Friendly and neighborly with everyone, happy face on no matter how bad someone hurts you."

Her gaze shoots left, through the kitchen doorway to where her surfboard leans against the wall by the front door. She knows I'm right. Knows exactly what I'm talking about. But she made me forfeit that particular line of questioning a long time ago.

"You want all the regular stuff, too," I continue. "Someone who makes you laugh, lets you cry, rages with you when you're angry at the world. Someone who'd match the effort you'd put into the relationship. Who showers you with affection, is so out of his mind for you that he can't ever stop touching you. But who wouldn't be afraid to put you in your place when you deserve it—and yes, Prescott. There'll be times when you deserve it." I break into a grin when her mouth opens. "Can't have a smart mouth like yours and not deserve it sometimes."

She hums, eyes narrowed, unconvinced on that last point. But the teasing fades from my face, my voice, everything, as I stare back at her. My best friend, my soulmate, who's poured her heart into finding a family for years. Who puts on a smile every time it goes wrong, clinging to optimism I know isn't really all there anymore.

She's been through so fucking much. Her mother blowing up what everyone had thought to be a happy little family of three, then vanishing from Summer's life. Her dad fleeing town the second Summer came of age, and starting a whole new family without her.

"Most importantly"—something in my tone has her expression thawing—"you want someone who stays. Permanence. A home, no matter where life takes you."

"Something like that," she says quietly. She holds my gaze through the hole in the wall. Blesses me with the softest smile. My favorite Summer smile—the one that makes something shimmy in my stomach, like I've done something right for once.

When I resume scribbling in my notebook, Summer's soft laugh fills the apartment. "Hey, Park? D'you think it's time to get your eyes checked?"

I grunt noncommittally and try to relax my eyes, but my writing goes too fuzzy. "What does he look like? This dream man."

"Dark hair. A nice smile. This should go without saying, but after the dates I've been on, I feel the need to make it clear that he should shower regularly. Put actual effort into planning dates and alone time together. And keep a job. Have a five-year plan. Wants to own a home. Oh, and he better cook, considering . . ." I hear a creak as she opens her oven, which doubles as shoe storage. She and I have this in common—we're both hopeless in the kitchen. "Bonus points if he's got big hands, if you know what I'm saying."

Pardon me?

The pen falls out of my hand. I stretch out my fingers, frowning down at my palm.

I don't notice Summer has returned to the living room until her snort breaks the silence. "Are you trying to figure out if you have big hands?"

"No. What does it matter how big my hands are?" She's holding two soda bottles—Mountain Dew for me, Diet Coke for her—and I hastily take mine.

Obviously I know that Summer has . . . I can't even bring myself to think the words.

It's that the thought of her with a guy makes me want to break something. Or, like . . . strangle anyone who's touched her.

You know, the usual kind of thing.

I just don't need to hear about it, is all. It's like how I don't want to hear about my sister's nighttime activities. Same thing.

"Are you looking to apply for the job? Summer's Dream Man?" She sips her drink, shoulders bouncing with laughter.

"That would make me the world's worst matchmaker, considering I don't cross a single thing off this list. Aside from the showering and the job I hate."

Unless . . . I glance at the notebook in my lap, then break into a grin.

Summer tips her head to examine me. She makes a wishy-washy sound. "Seven out of ten."

My jaw drops. "*Bullshit.*"

Her brows go up. "I know you're not questioning the integrity of the scoring committee."

"Yes the hell I am. I demand a recount."

"Recount granted. I'm afraid you've lost a point for insolence."

My grin returns, twice as wide. "I've been told insolence is part of my charm."

"Parker, we talked about this." She pouts. "Your mommy will say that about anything."

I poke at her cheek, pulled taut in a wide smile. "You think you're real funny, don't you?"

"That's never been up for debate." She bats away my hand, trapped in a breathless laugh, and I tuck it under my thigh because a laughing Summer has always been my weakness. Always makes me a little lightheaded.

For a moment, it occurs to me that we've missed a crucial point about *Summer's Dream Man*—that whoever she ends up with has to be man enough to accept our friendship, just the way it is. Because I wouldn't give it—*us*—up for anyone.

But that's unnecessary. She and I have endured decades together. Never turning on each other, never wandering out of sight. Nothing's ever disrupted us, flipped our friendship upside down.

It never will.

"So, we're really doing this? Blind dates at Oakley's, in exactly a week?"

"Why not?" I toss my notebook onto the coffee table and reach for the remote. We quit watching *Serendipity* halfway through last night, and I cue it back up on her TV. "Summer's dream man, coming right up."

She settles into the couch, lying all the way across with her legs over my lap, feet skimming my arm along the way. I'll never understand how they always manage to be ice-cold, even in the summer, but I throw a blanket over us both and clench her toes in my hands to warm them up. And then a cacophony of honks from the street below filters through the open living room window, vaguely to the tune of "Stayin' Alive" by the Bee Gees.

My stomach sinks. Low. All the way out of my body. "No."

I beeline to the window with Summer at my heels. There's a silver RV now parked haphazardly across the street. The side door bursts open. Two suitcases fly out of it, bouncing off the cobble-stone, shortly followed by my mother's distinctly disheveled blond head of hair.

Summer winces. "Suitcases?"

My forehead hits the window. "Fuck my life."

Chapter 3

Summer

"Team, we've got about two more months to pull off the best Surf's Up series the country's ever seen. Who's with me?"

Grant, the head volunteer for Surf's Up—a qualifying series within the World Surf Organization held annually in and around Oakwood Bay—claps his hands together in a way I'm sure is meant to galvanize the group around the cluttered table at the Pine Point community center.

It seems only half of us were paying attention, because the other volunteers startle at the sound, guiltily looking up from the phones they'd been covertly using under the table.

The murmur of agreement is vague, hardly enthusiastic, but in typical early-thirties surfer dude fashion, Grant circulates an unfazed grin around the table. He gives an extra nod of approval when he lands on me beside him, with my pen still poised over my notebook, then launches into an animated project update.

I've been a frequent inhabitant of this room since I retired from competitive surfing and took up this volunteer work. Surf's Up is a three-event competition series spread out over the summer, bringing in seasoned surfers from along the coast who hope to qualify for the

WSO's Champions Tour, which surfs some of the world's most elite waves over the course of a year.

As far as growing up in a small town goes, Oakwood's proximity to the ocean and prime surf spots is one of its few highlights. The waves in this part of the country aren't as colossal as you'd find on the West Coast or abroad, but, as a competitive-turned-hobby surfer myself, I know just how challenging they can be, requiring athletes to show off major endurance and skill.

The delinquent texters return to their phones, all smiling or silently giggling at their private conversations. I tap my own phone to life. Not a single awaiting message.

Swallowing my disappointment, I return my focus to Grant. Across the table, Tristan Thomas stifles a snort at his screen. I slide my phone closer and fire off a text to my dad as discreetly as possible.

SUMMER: Are we still on for family dinner this Sunday?

Minutes later, it sits unanswered below two similar texts I sent earlier in the week. Dad's a general surgeon at his local hospital and is always tending to some emergency, which makes seeing him a luxury, especially after he fled Oakwood in my late teens. These days, my best bet is the monthly family dinners with him, my stepmom, and twin toddler half-brothers—whenever they don't get canceled.

To Dad's credit, I haven't heard from my mom in years.

I give it a minute before firing off another text, this time to my friend Shy.

SUMMER: Still up for our shopping date on Saturday?

Her reply, at least, comes quick.

SHY: Sum, I'm SO sorry. Rosie just came down with something and doubt it'll clear up by then. Rain check?

SUMMER: Totally! Let me know when you're free and give Rosie-Wosie a big kiss from me.

I can't help sinking in my seat a little. Grant catches my eye and gives my phone a pointed look as someone runs through their sub-committee update. "Everything okay?"

"Totally fine!" I whisper back. My phone lights up several min-utes later with another reply that has my heart sinking.

DAD: The boys caught a bug at day care. Sorry, Sunshine. Gonna have to cancel dinner.

SUMMER: No worries, I hear there's something going around!

SUMMER: Should we reschedule for next week?

I stare at my screen for several long seconds, even knowing I won't hear back for a while. I know I shouldn't take it personally; that the world doesn't revolve around me. My dad, my friends, they're all perfectly entitled to have other priorities. But it'd be nice to have just one person whose attention I don't have to constantly compete for, only to come up second, or fifth, or tenth in line.

Which is why this matchmaking has to work.

This plan with Parker isn't about finding me a boyfriend for the sake of it. It's about finding someone who can't live without me just as much as I can't live without him. Who'd think I'm the best part of his day, like he'd be the best part of mine.

I scramble for my phone when it lights up again, this time with a text from Parker.

PARKER: Is there such a thing as human exterminators? Some kind of pest control for humans?

I snort a laugh that has Grant looking over again. Parker's been in a particularly foul mood all week, since his parents showed up un-announced and made themselves right at home in his two-bedroom apartment.

Caroline and Brian Woods have always been eccentric at best, chaotic at worst, and a nightmare for someone like Parker, who needs routine and structure to keep things straight. They're nomads to their core and sold their family home in Oakwood years ago to travel the country in an RV, making pit stops in town whenever the mood strikes.

SUMMER: I believe human exterminators are called hitmen, and I'd advise you to stop leaving a paper trail if you sincerely intend on hiring one.

PARKER: I don't need a hitman. Just someone who can get unwanted human inhabitants the hell off my premises.

SUMMER: Alive?

PARKER: Yes.

SUMMER: Are you only saying that because of the paper trail?

PARKER: Maybe.

"Summer?" Grant's voice pulls me away from my phone. This time, every pair of eyes around the table is fixed on me. "What's the status on the local business market?"

With a pang of guilt, I bounce to my feet to deliver my subcommittee update. "It's moving along as planned! We'll be opening registration this week, and we expect the highest numbers to date, given last year's success. Most of the businesses sold out of their stock, as you know."

I sweep a loose sheet on top of my notebook, indicating the wrap-up figures from last year. A couple of years ago, I convinced Grant to let me take over half the parking lot at each Surf's Up event, inviting small businesses around Oakwood Bay to set up shop for the day. The local business market has become a staple of the series since. People love browsing through the farmstands and kitschy boutiques, and businesses eagerly fight over the few spots we're able to offer.

It's the highlight of my year—I love seeing the locals I've known all my life thrive, love that I had a hand in it.

Movement in my periphery draws my attention to the door, where a familiar tall woman with long, sun-bleached hair and a deep tan has appeared. Harriet Young, the lead judge for Surf's Up, lifts her sunglasses on top of her head. She leans against the wall, grinning when she catches me looking. We first met way back when I competed in the junior division, but in recent years our interactions have centered around my volunteer work.

Waving at her, I return my attention to my fellow volunteers. "I was thinking, though, that this year we could charge a small entrance fee to help raise funds for the repairs to Sheffield's Diner." I look over the smiling faces around the table. Last fall, a rough storm had a tree collapsing onto an incoming car, sending it crashing into Oakwood's beloved diner. "Most of you will know that Wynn Sheffield's had trouble with his insurance, and . . . Well, seeing as the local business market is all about community to begin with, I thought it might make sense! Thoughts?"

"Excellent idea." Grant makes a note in his notebook. I can barely keep myself from preening under his praise. "I assume you'll want to lead this part of the project, on top of everything else you're running?"

There's a laugh around the table. Across me, Danica Klein, who I've been friendly with since we started volunteering around the same time, shoots me a teasing look. Possibly, I might've spent the past few years participating in . . . *all* the planning activities.

But I like it. It keeps me busy, when the alternative is hanging out at home alone, or encroaching on my friends' time. And there's always been something so magical to me about Surf's Up.

"If you insist," I joke with a sigh. "I already took the liberty of running the idea by a few locals, who seemed supportive of an entrance fee."

"Of course, you did." Grant smiles down at his notes. "Your zest truly is contagious, Summer."

I take a moment to bask in the murmurs of agreement. This is why I love Oakwood Bay, the reason I could never bring myself to leave it. After my parents shipped out of town, this group's support has meant the world.

Eventually, Grant breaks us into our various subcommittees and waves Harriet over for their private meeting. She touches my shoulder as she passes me.

"You're quite the star planner, Prescott." She smiles in a way I can't decipher, tipping down her chin to bring us eye to eye. "But there's one thing I know you're even better at."

Her words are meant to be kind. But my smile falters anyway.

By the time the meeting is done, Dad still hasn't replied.

Chapter 4

Parker

"*Mom*—how much longer do you need in there?"

I rap at the door to the single bathroom in my apartment, then again even louder when I'm only met with the warbled sounds of my mother singing "The Tide Is High" over the running shower.

Maybe I should be happy to hear her dulcet tones through the door. Glad to have had my parents move in with me this week, while the Airstream RV they've called home since they sold my childhood house gets much-needed repairs after years of nonstop travel.

I might've felt those things . . . if my free-spirited parents hadn't spent the last seven days turning me, my routine, and this two-bedroom walk-up apartment completely upside down.

The logical thing to have done when they arrived, ready to move in without so much as a conversation, would have been to hand them the spare key to my sister's empty mini-mansion on the water, just minutes away. They'd have the run of the place until she comes back from her honeymoon.

But by the time I made heads or tails of what they wanted, they'd already dumped out their clothes in my spare bedroom and cleared enough space in my fridge for copious bottles of the trailer-made kombucha they've apparently become addicted to.

I pound on the door again, glancing down the hall only to be informed by my microwave that I'm running severely late for work.

"Goddamn it, Mom," I mutter.

In the living room, I lift my phone off the coffee table to find a stream of texts from Summer. I don't bother answering. Instead, I throw open the window overlooking the street. The lights are off in Summer's apartment right across the way, and I find her on the sidewalk below leaning against the side of my Wrangler, dressed and ready for work in well-worn sneakers, black leggings, and a UOB-branded polo.

"Give me five minutes." With a start, she lifts her chin to find me partially hanging out of my window. "These guys are driving me up the fucking—"

"Language, Giggle Bear," my mother calls from the hall. Maybe it's the frustration from being late for work, but the nickname she's called me since I was a newborn—when I supposedly started giggling and smiling far ahead of my moodier twin—grates on me more than it ever has.

I find Mom dressed in a colorful poncho with a towel on her head, while my dad follows her out of the bathroom wearing a towel around his waist and a nausea-inducing look of satisfaction on his face.

It's my childhood all over again.

"Come *on*," I groan as they head into the spare room. "We talked about this. None of that needs to happen in the bathroom, which is a communal space."

I regret saying anything when my mom's head pops out of the doorway. "There's no need to be so uptight about it, Giggle Bear. We've always told you that sex is a very normal, very *natural*—"

"Fucking hell." I power walk to the bathroom and shut the door before I get roped into another one of the *sex is beautiful* lectures I grew up hearing.

Inside the steaming bathroom, I brace my hands on the counter and duck my head to take several centering breaths. Despite the lectures and accusations of uptight behavior, I'm a lot more like my parents than they probably realize. A lot more like them than I want to be.

I may have a permanent address and a long-term job that neither of them currently have, but I've spent the past several years indulging in the very normal, very natural sex they seem to be having at every turn. Have put off the thought of a relationship, or a family, or a home away from my favorite bar until a date in the future, because I had youth on my side.

Plenty of time to think about it later.

Planning ahead has never been my strong suit, and certainly nothing my parents instilled in me growing up. And then *later* started hitting me in the face.

I think this is it. Why my parents' out-of-the-blue appearance has put me in this uptight mood. Why the sound of my childhood nickname incites pure bitterness inside me. The clock's run out on my optimistic *I'll figure it out later* mentality.

I'm turning thirty in exactly three months. Living in the town where I was born and never left. Working the same job I've had since graduating college. With that godforsaken rumor running rampant, attracting women whose interest in me starts and stops with the hope of panty removal. And now I'm living with my parents.

With another long breath that does nothing to save my mood, I yank my toothbrush out of its holder and finally get ready for work.

～～～～

"Why did Summer just invite me to a party to *plan* a party?"

Noah Irving—star quarterback for the Florida Hornets,

surrogate brother to my sister and her husband, and my pain-in-the-ass client—eyes my reflection in the wall of mirrors at the gym facility at the University of Oakwood Bay, where he's come to train during his off-season.

The squat rack sitting on his shoulders doesn't seem to faze him any, which is a sign that either I'm not pushing him hard enough or that he's just that scandalized by the so-called planning party that Summer issued invitations to this morning.

"It's for our joint thirtieth birthday—mine and Melody's. Summer and Zac are putting something together, I guess." I nudge Noah's sneaker in a silent command to get to squatting.

"So, to be extra clear on this . . . I just got invited to a party taking place a month from now . . . to plan a party taking place *three* months from now?"

"You know how it is, man. Everyone's always got something going on." *Aside from me.* "Planning anything requires several weeks' notice and a robust scheduling software."

A party to plan a party is a little weird, I'll admit. But I've learned over the years not to question Summer when it comes to these things. She loves planning a social event—makes some of the best cocktails I've ever had, too. This is pretty on-brand for her.

I do wish it wasn't yet another uncomfortable reminder of the looming end of my twenties, but who am I to deny her the joys of double party planning.

"And why do you sound like they're ushering you to the gallows instead of throwing you a birthday party?" Noah grits out between reps.

"You wouldn't get it." The words come out as a sigh, though I don't mean for them to. I do my best to keep my increasingly shitty mood in check, at work most of all. But it's harder to do the longer I stay stuck on this hamster wheel. Even harder when I'm being asked about it by a twenty-two-year-old star professional athlete.

Today is yet another day at UOB, where I move from the training facility to the adjoining rehab center depending on the client. Since training my friend Brooks to a triumphant return to the NFL last year, every new assignment has felt like scaling a molehill after conquering Kilimanjaro. But I have no idea what I'd do instead.

How do other people simply . . . *know*? What they want out of life, a partner?

And how am I supposed to figure it out with the incessant swirling vortex of anxiety that comes with *not* knowing? I'm constantly on the edge of calling it quits and relocating my existence to my queen-size mattress.

Summer floats out of the open doors of the rehabilitation center. She's with Quentin Moore, a junior on the UOB basketball team who'd stuck around Oakwood after suffering a dislocated shoulder this past spring. She's saying something to him as they walk toward the facility's exit, gesturing emphatically with her hands in the way she does when she talks, brown hair swishing in tousled salt water waves.

She's not looking at Quentin, but he's got his full attention on her and whatever instructions she's giving him. Pride blooms at the sight; she so easily commands the attention of this six-foot-six, two-hundred-and-twenty-pound star athlete, who I'd put money on getting drafted to the NBA this year pending his recovery. And with Summer on his team, there's no way he won't be ready for the first tip-off of the college season.

If there's any kind of positive to be found in this job, it's spending the day with Summer. Watching her kick ass with her clients. Sneaking in early workouts together before our first appointments of the day. Lunch and unsanctioned donut breaks.

I couldn't survive this without her.

"Last one," I announce to Noah, who grinds his teeth in anticipation of his final squat. He's struggling now, legs trembling.

Once he finishes, he slumps onto a workout bench. "New business idea for you: Sell walking canes at the door for all the poor souls you torture for money, you fucking sadist."

"I wouldn't be doing you a favor by taking it easy on you. Not if you want to keep playing the way you did last season."

Noah wipes his face with the hem of his shirt. "I need to play better than I did last season, seeing as it was your buddy who won the championship—not me."

"Think you just gave me permission to dial up the torture."

Across the gym, Summer blesses Quentin with that pretty smile of hers, the one I can feel all the way from here.

"Look, I've never understood the kind of long game you seem hell-bent on playing there. But if you're shooting for any kind of subtlety at all, I'd probably pick your jaw up off the floor."

I glance over at Noah. "The hell are you talking about?"

His gaze travels slowly over my face, filling with increasing fascination the longer he stares. "Ah. I see."

Irritation prickles. "See what? Spit it out."

"I *see*. I get it now."

I roll my eyes. "You see nothing."

"Trust me, I do. Clear as day." He laces his fingers behind his head of sandy hair, unperturbed by my increasing impatience. "See, I always thought you were playing the long game, you know?"

"I *don't* know."

"But now I get it. You have a thing for Summer—"

I groan. "For fuck's sake."

"Hang on, that's not even the best part. You're not playing a long game for her at all. You have a thing for Summer, and you don't even *know* you have a thing for Summer." Noah snorts, and this conspiracy is apparently worthy of a deep-belly laugh they can probably hear in the next state.

But he's only embarrassing himself with all this, because I

absolutely, unequivocally, categorically do not have a thing for Summer Prescott.

Seeing as I've had her in my life for the last twenty-seven years, I'd like to think I would've noticed if I was in love with her. But I've never felt it once. The big punch in the gut you hear people talk about when they fall in love. That one, life-altering moment you can point to without a shred of doubt. When your world shifts from underneath you, leaving you all hot and jumbled and incapable of stringing together words. Twenty-seven years and none of that.

My words never have any trouble coming out with Summer. She's my favorite person to talk to.

I'm with her and the ground feels steadier than ever. Not a hint of a tremor.

There's no punch in the gut when she's around—exactly the opposite. She makes the inside of my head, lately so loud and mean, sound like a serene summer evening at the lake. Sunset, warm breeze, water gently lapping up the shore. Loons singing in the background.

A whistle draws our attention to find her approaching our bench. "Cool it with the pumping, Irving. You're about to bust out of that T-shirt."

"Think she just gave you permission to dial *down* the torture." Noah blows a kiss at Summer, getting to his feet. "And on that note, I'll leave you two to . . . I don't know. Ignore reality?"

"Ignore which reality?" She looks back and forth between us.

"Ignore *him* altogether."

She takes Noah's spot beside me, unclasping her hand to show me a miniature paper plane folded from a bright pink sticky note I left on her desk. The same kind I used to send flying at her from across our high school classrooms, passing her notes without our teachers seeing. This one is half opened, with my messy scrawl inside it.

"Thanks for the donut." With a smile, Summer tucks the note in her pocket. Then she drops her voice, giving a shifty glance around the gym. "Much better than those muffins Kendra was circulating this morning. Which, by the way . . ."

She leans in closer, and my thoughts are promptly derailed by the floral scent drifting off her skin. I've never smelled this one on her—it's sweet, floral, somehow a little musky.

It hits me right in the common sense, knocking it over, and for a moment I'm gripped by the urge to run my lips along the side of her neck. Douse myself in that scent and the satisfactory way she might shiver at the touch. If scents were tangible, this one would be the satisfied cuddle after a marathon fuck. Pure, hedonistic bliss.

I blink through the feeling. "Did you get a new perfume?"

Summer nudges me. I realize she's been speaking for an unknown number of minutes. "*Focus*, Park. I'm telling you, something weird is going on here."

"About . . ." I clear my throat when the word comes out grainy. "About the perfume?"

"With Kendra and Don," she hisses, eyes darting across the gym. Squinting through the mild fuzziness in my vision, I find Don, our boss, chatting with Kendra, another trainer. "You know those muffins she was handing out? I found an entire container of them on Don's desk."

"Muffins?" I shake myself mentally, try to focus on her words and their implication, but that perfume is ruthless. All my brain seems capable of at the moment is picturing the two of us. Naked. Sweaty. Her cheek on my chest, lashes grazing my skin as she drifts to sleep, exhausted from coming over and over, and— "What . . . what's in this perfume, exactly? Which flower is that?"

"Why? Is it bad?" She lifts her shirt to her nose and inhales deeply. "I'm trying something different for our dates tonight."

Something niggles at me as I fight her perfume for sanity. "Dates?"

"Our blind dates!"

And my stomach just leaves my body.

Summer beams at me. "Parker, I'm so excited. I really think you're going to love her. I spent all week *scouring* town for the perfect person for you. You've got so much in common, and . . ."

The rest of her words are drowned out by a ringing in my ears, and the panic quickly raising my body temperature. Because I forgot.

Between my impromptu tenants and the brain fog that I've barely been able to keep at bay . . . I fucking *forgot*. Our blind dates, tonight at Oakley's. I find her a guy, she finds me a girl.

And I don't have anyone for Summer. I'm going to have to reschedule—

"Just wait until you see the dress I'm wearing tonight. Or, wait until *he* sees the dress I'm wearing tonight. I bought it specially." Summer bounces happily and I wipe the rapidly growing panic off my face. "I woke up this morning with such a good feeling. I mean, you know me better than anyone! If someone's going to lead me to the love of my life, it'll definitely be you. I can't wait to meet him!"

I open my mouth to say something.

To confess. To apologize. To ask for more time. But Summer continues chattering excitedly and I can't do it. I can't disappoint her like that.

I need to fix this. Now.

Chapter 5

Parker

Wicked guilt propels me into Oakley's the minute I'm showered and changed after work.

I couldn't even bring myself to wait until my hair dried, as my amused mother pointed out. It drips onto whichever T-shirt I threw on before barreling down the steps of my walk-up to fix this absolute screwup before Summer shows up in the next twenty minutes, expecting her future husband.

Only to find her future ex–best friend with a piss-poor memory, begging for forgiveness.

It's Thursday night, thank fuck, so Oakley's is busy, tables loaded with people. I scan each of them for options, glossing over the married and elderly men, for obvious reasons. The local guys I know already fumbled their chance to date Summer.

But the joy of a small town means it's slim pickings in here.

I forge ahead, walking past occupied tables like I'm browsing for a new car. A luxury car, obviously, because like hell am I going to stick Summer on another bad date. But by the time I make it to the bar at the back, I've come up empty. Maybe sensing that I'm on the verge of a meltdown, Jim, the owner of Oakley's, slides a Mountain Dew across the counter at me.

"You look like you need this." He goes back to drying pint glasses with a towel.

"You have no idea. I'm about to have my ass handed to me so hard." I take a deep gulp, letting the harsh carbonation punish me. I squint around the pub again for a viable option I might've missed.

"Looking for someone?"

"Yeah." I rub my face so roughly it sets off a waterfall from my hair. "You happen to see a decent-looking guy in his thirties? Big hands, employed, and no mommy issues to speak of?"

Jim stares down at the glass in his hand, and it's a mark of how long he's known me, how long I've been a thorn in his side here at his bar, that he doesn't even look fazed by the request. "Don't know anything about mommy issues, but do you mean the guy at the table by the door? Up against the window?"

I zero in on who he means. Some shaggy-haired guy I've never seen before sits at a table for two, typing quietly on his phone. He's probably got decent height on him, by the length of his legs. He's wearing cargo shorts, which is definitely a strike against him if I know Summer. But he's deeply tanned, the same kind of sun Summer gets when she spends a whole day surfing out in Crystal Cove.

"Who is he?" I scrutinize every inch of him. He's blond but looks athletic enough, which means he has something in common with Summer, at least.

"He came in a few days ago with a crew of guys. Sounded like they were in town training for Surf's Up."

Halle-fucking-luhia.

I dart to the table by the window, where my target continues staring at his phone. "This seat taken?"

The guy startles as I pull up the chair across from him and drop into it without waiting on an answer. His gaze floats out of the window overlooking the main strip as though searching for clues about my arrival. "Can I help you with something?"

I cut to the chase. "What's your name?"

"It . . . it's Denny."

"Are you single, Denny?"

Denny's eyebrows shoot up his forehead. "Sorry, man, I'm not interested—"

I huff impatiently. "Not for me. Though you should count yourself lucky if I did give you the time of day, because I'm a fantastic date and an even better lay." I untuck my phone from the pocket of my jeans, find what I'm looking for, and set it on the table between us. "Fortunately for you, I'm here with an even better proposition."

Tentatively, like he's afraid of what he might find on the screen, Denny leans over my phone. It's Summer staring at my camera mid-laugh—rather, staring at me beyond the camera, as though to check that I was listening to whatever insane story our friend Siena was telling. I remember looking at her and feeling like I couldn't *not* capture that moment. She looked so damn happy.

"It's your lucky day, buddy. How would you like to treat this woman to the best date of her life?"

He stares at her picture. "Wow."

"Tell me about it. You interested?" Denny stays silent. With an annoyed *tsk*, I flick to the next picture on my camera roll: Summer beaming after beating her personal best at the squat rack a few months ago. When that doesn't seem to inspire him, I flick through the next few photos. "Well?"

Denny's gaze finds me slowly. "Your entire camera roll is pictures of this woman."

"So?"

"So, you're asking me to take her out?"

"In ten minutes, to be exact."

Denny blinks away his confusion. "She's hot."

"Stunning," I correct. It took me years to finally land on the word that best encapsulates Summer—the fox-like quality to her facial features, with high cheekbones and shrewd, mischievous eyes that tell you she'll make you pay for every inch you give her and have you begging for seconds.

I swipe away from the picture on my phone—Summer blushing furiously behind her Kindle here at Oakley's, reading what I suspected to be some kind of blue alien mating ritual. "You interested?"

Denny seems to think on that for a beat—for which reason I couldn't say, seeing as I just dropped the gift of a lifetime in his lap. But then he's nodding, and . . . okay. Smart guy. Another point in his favor.

"Yeah, I'm interested. What's she like? Is she a good time, or—"

I lift a hand to cut him off. "I'm the one asking the questions here, bud. Do you have a job?"

Denny fingers his phone, flipping it over and over. A fidgeter. Might drive Summer crazy. "I used to be a teacher—I quit to focus on competitive surfing."

"Good with kids, then?"

"I hope so. I taught fifth grade for years."

"You own a house?"

"Yes, it's—"

"How's your relationship with your mom?"

"I call her once a week."

I sit back, silently thanking whichever god looked down upon me with favor and delivered me this cargo-shorted *Dream Man*. "Congratulations, Denny. You just won the opportunity to date Summer Prescott."

I get to my feet for this next part, using my full height to my advantage. Denny's face flashes with alarm. "And so we're on the same page, I'll be sitting in this bar watching your every move. You will be polite. Charming. You'll ask her about herself, laugh at all her jokes, and tell her how beautiful she is every chance you get. You'll pay for her drinks, and dinner if she wants it. And if I get even a hint of miscreancy, if you so much as *sniff* the wrong way, I'll be over here snapping your little neck faster than you can say, *I'm sorry.* We clear?"

The glass door swings open behind him as Summer walks in. Heads around the pub turn in her direction, making me straighten with pride.

She's wearing her signature date look, the one with a subtle dusting of purple on her eyelids. Her hair is perfectly tousled in that effortless, mind-numbing way. And then there's that pink glossy stuff on her lips that makes her mouth look that much plumper. Her soft pink dress is fitted over the body she's spent years toning to perfection, and she's wearing a pair of heels I've never seen before.

And then she spots me just a few feet away and smiles, and I swear, this girl brings the light with her wherever she goes. It lifts my mood, melts away any of the irritation I'd been pointing at Denny, who's a little slow on the uptake.

"Stand up. Make the first move, for fuck's sake," I mutter at him. He scrambles to his feet.

Summer's gaze slides onto Denny. She gives him a quiet up-and-down and I do the same, checking again for anything amiss. He's shorter than me, six feet if I'm being generous, but he'll have to do.

He extends a hand toward her. "Hey, I'm Denny. It's great to meet you." I clear my throat. His smile goes brighter. "You look beautiful."

"It's nice to meet you, too, Denny." I hold my breath as Summer lingers on the cargo shorts. The corner of her mouth twitches. "How do you guys know each other?"

Shit. "Actually, we just—"

"You surf?" Denny says suddenly.

Summer nods at him. "It's a bad day when I can't. How'd you guess?"

"You have a leash tan." I follow his gaze down her sun-kissed legs to her right ankle, where a band of pale skin sits underneath the strap of her shoe. Denny looks on with more light in his eyes than I've seen since I met him. "I'm out here on and off for the next few months for Surf's Up."

I think I actually did it. Pulled it off, without a second to spare.

It's subtle, nearly invisible to the naked eye, but I've spent the last twenty-seven years knowing this woman in and out. Summer's body vibrates with so much excitement that it gives off fumes of joy. They lick at my skin, soak in deep, fill me with the kind of intense satisfaction that only ever comes with making her smile like that.

"Looks like my job here is done. You kids have fun." They beam at each other and something odd scrapes inside my chest, a rather unpleasant feeling I chalk up to that perfume she's still wearing.

Summer's takes hold of my arm as I head for the door. "Where are you going? Trinity will be here any second."

Trinity. My date. Right.

For some reason, the thought of spending the night in this bar—usually one of my favorite places in the world—feels even worse than dragging my ass into work in the morning. Right now, all I crave is the dark of my bedroom, letting me wallow in the pressing *grayness* of my life.

But I couldn't let Summer down like that. So, I go find me and Trinity a table.

~~~~~

As far as dates go, Trinity Tate is as good as I've had in a while.

She's . . . cute.

Into sports, coaches the women's volleyball team at UOB. Summer clearly put in the effort when she chose Trinity. Which is why I'm choosing to ignore the fact that I'm partial to darker hair on a woman, rather than the bright blond strands tickling Trinity's elbows. Also, that most sports outside of football and surfing tend to bore me to tears.

But it's just a date. Not like I'm signing up for a reserved seat on Trinity's volleyball court once the school year starts.

"And you know what? You should totally come to our games when the school year starts."

Fuck.

Trinity drops her chin into the palm of her hand, fingers toying with the rim of her empty cocktail glass. She's doing that thing, tucking her chin and looking up at me through fluttering lashes, and it's . . . fine. Cute.

A familiar, raspy laugh drifts over the noise around us. I find Summer at the table by the window, head tipped back in mirth, strands of wavy hair dancing around her shoulders. The way the setting sun pours through the window creates a halo of soft light around her.

Stunning.

Denny is making her laugh. And it's great. Looks like a picture-perfect date.

Except for the odd prickle of . . . *something* at the back of my neck. This feeling of *wrongness* I haven't been able to shake since I left them to it. Denny's got his phone on the table, flipping it over and over the way he did when we met. Even from where I'm sitting, I can see the growing, unsettling number of notifications on his screen.

"Are you okay?" I'm pulled out of it by Trinity, who gives me a dejected look that incites a flood of guilt.

"Sorry, I . . . It was a long day at work." I rub my face, willing myself to get it together. Trinity breaks into a happier smile when I wave at Jim, indicating her empty glass. "I have to confess something, Trinity. I don't know much about volleyball other than the gnarly ankle injuries I see more than I'd like. But I'm always happy to learn."

There. Nice and pleasant.

"At least we keep you busy at work. You're welcome."

I nod into a sip of beer as Jim drops off Trinity's fresh gin and tonic. "Not that I enjoy seeing our athletes injured."

"Of course not." Her cheeks flush. "It was a . . . dumb joke."

"No—not at all." Fuck, I'm blowing this so bad. Across the bar, Summer's fingers meet Denny's forearm for half a heartbeat. I suck down another long sip of my drink. "I, uh . . . Actually, you did keep me tied up pretty good last year. The player with the mallet finger?"

The relief in her face is evident. "Cara. Huge loss to the season."

"I bet. She was almost my height."

Trinity leans in. "Which is . . ."

"Huh? Oh. I'm six-three."

"And gorgeous. But I'm sure you get that all the time." She's staring me down, starting from the crown of my damp head, lingering on my shoulders, before drifting as far down my body as she can.

"Sure. Thanks." I damn near squirm in my seat. Ever since that stupid rumor started making the rounds, it's been impossible to make it through a date without—

"I hear you live upstairs, Parker."

Damn it.

"Mhm." I lift the drinks menu off the table, pretending to peruse it like I don't know it back to front just to shield myself from her increasingly brazen stare. "What about you?"

Something brushes against my calf. Trinity hooks her foot around my leg; it drifts upward, and with it goes every meager shred of enthusiasm I managed to scrounge up for this date.

"I live in Baycrest. Not nearly as convenient as your place. I wouldn't mind if you kept *me* tied up a while. Pay me back for last season?"

Fuck me, this rumor has oozed across town lines?

At her table by the window, Summer catches my eye and mouths, *going to the beach. I'm in love!*

I find Denny settling up at the bar. The excitement is rolling off Summer in waves, and it's the only reason I'm able to muster a smile as Trinity keeps drawing lines up and down my leg.

Summer and Denny move toward the exit, with that phone still in his goddamn hand. But then he opens the door for her, and at least there's that.

My date might be a bust. But at least Summer's happy.

Chapter 6

Summer

Denny kisses me that first night on the beach, with the shore at our toes and the sunset drawing pinks and purples above us.

The next morning, and every morning since, he surprises me by moving his surf session from Pine Point—the toughest of the three Surf's Up event locations—to where I surf at Crystal Cove. It's the first time I'm not surfing alone since my dad left town.

That next Friday, just over a week in, he's genuinely understanding when I turn down a date and tell him Friday nights are for me and Parker and our weekly tradition called Summer Friday—born last year, when I resolved to no longer spend my Friday nights on disappointing dates—where we sit in our booth at Oakley's, people watching over my romance book du jour and whichever autobiography Parker is on. But Denny comes over afterward, arms laden with grocery bags, and cooks me a late-night dinner that has me stuffed for several days.

On the weekend, he makes the three-hour drive back to his hometown to relieve the neighbor who watches his dog while he trains for Surf's Up. I resolve to play it cool, determined to let him do the chasing.

My phone pings not a minute after he makes it home.

DENNY: Is it crazy that I miss you?

SUMMER: After knowing me just a week? I'd call you a liar if you didn't.

DENNY: Best week of my life.

He sleeps over that next Monday. And Tuesday.

On Thursday, when he leaves my text unanswered all day and I brace myself for disappointment, he picks me up from work with his back seat loaded with takeout and our surfboards strapped to his roof. We eat on the beach, watch the sun set on our boards, and he sleeps over that night, too.

And that's how it goes for the week that follows. Denny wishes me a good weekend after this morning's surf, once again texting me the moment he arrives home to his dog.

DENNY: Best three weeks of my life.

I barely manage to sit still in my seat. To reel back the excited shimmy dying for release, audience be damned, as I swipe away from Denny's text and back to my four-way video call with the girls.

"She's back and she's blushing." Melody beams at me through the phone. Siena's and Shy's excited sounds fill the darkening inside of my car where I've parked it outside Oakley's after tonight's volunteer meeting.

Friday nights are as lively as it gets in Oakwood, as people pop into Oakley's early to secure a table before the evening dinner rush. Tables have been especially in demand lately, with Sheffield's Diner still shuttered. Down the street that's crowded with milling locals, the diner's lavender-painted bricks are still lined with yellow caution tape, flapping in the breeze.

I've been bombarding the group chat about Denny for weeks, but between kids and jobs and honeymoons, it's the first time I've been able to properly connect with my friends since he and I started dating.

It's also the first time in ages that we're gushing about *my* life. After years of being happy for my friends, it's nice to have my turn.

There's every chance I'm getting ahead of myself.

After all, I've been known to be tragically color-blind to any and all shades of red. But if there's one person in this world I trust, it's Parker. And seeing as he was the one to bring me and Denny together . . .

I've got visions of white dresses, beach houses, and water babies in my head. It's probably delusional. But what's life without a little delusion?

Siena's voice snaps me out of my fantasy just as Denny gets down on a knee, ring in hand. "Of course she's blushing. You've seen the pictures, girls. The guy's got an ass on him—must be all that surfing."

"Oh my God, Cee." Shy shakes her head with a laugh. Her bright blond three-year-old daughter, Rosie, waves obliviously at the camera, smiling in her mom's lap. "Do you ever *not* say whatever pops into your head?"

"Pretty sure you know the answer to that." Melody's dirty blond hair shudders with her laughter. I can hear Zac chuckling off-camera.

"What can I say? I'm an ass girl." Siena twirls her index finger in a *turn around* motion, presumably to an off-camera Brooks, if her barely contained bedroom eyes are anything to go by. Whatever his reaction is, it elicits a nod of appreciation from Siena. "I've always believed you can tell a lot about a man by the firmness of his behind. Brooks's says *Meet me upstairs for a very important meeting in five.*"

"Okay, so in five minutes or less, tell us about Denny, Summer." Mel shifts on her couch and half of Zac's body appears, apparently a willing participant in the gossip session. Behind them is a window with a view of a busy, town house–lined street, definitely not in Oakwood. They've been sticking around their place in the city since the honeymoon.

"By the way," Zac cuts in. "My mother-in-law heard about your new guy and asked when you and Parker opened up your relationship."

I cough. "Pardon?"

Brooks's frowning face materializes over Siena's shoulder. Melody shakes her head. "My mom, from the bottom of her heart, thinks that you and Parker have been dating since high school, and that you've now added a third to the mix."

"Caroline Woods." I press my face into my hands. "I know your mom's been out to lunch since . . ."

"Since she was born, probably."

"But shouldn't she know who her son is dating? They only just lived in his apartment for two weeks. Without even asking if they could."

Four out of six faces on the screen stare back, amused by the whole thing. And while Rosie grins at someone off-screen—her dad, maybe—I notice that Shy's gone suspiciously quiet.

I know exactly what her smirk's about. Parker admitted she's been grilling him about our friendship since they met, convinced that it's something . . . else. That smirk tells me she hasn't taken his denial to heart.

And it's making me grateful for the lack of light inside my car, as a flush blossoms in my cheeks. Maybe it's obvious to her how often my mind drifts to that godforsaken rumor. I might hate it more than Parker does.

"Where *is* Parker tonight, Sum?" asks Shy.

"Holding our table at Oakley's. It's . . . Summer Friday." I clear my throat, knowing I'm doing very little to dissuade her suspicions by bringing up the Friday ritual. *Date night*, she likes to call it. "Well, now that we've wasted precious seconds on Caroline Woods's nonsense . . . I know it's crazy, but I've never felt this good about a guy before. We have so much in common. And he cooks. Cooks *well*, which you know is crucial for me, seeing as I can't toast bread without catastrophe."

"He's already cooked for you? Three weeks in?" Mel asks.

"Try three *days* in." I bask in the rosy glow that descends upon me whenever I think about it. "I mean, that's a good sign, right? I'm not just blowing that out of proportion?"

"Amazing sign. Brooks won me over with his baking." Siena gathers her mane of dark hair and twists it into a messy bun on top of her head, which Brooks watches with an inordinate amount of concentration.

Mel nods enthusiastically. "Zac's made me breakfast every morning since the first time I stayed over at his place."

"Well, let's not get ahead of ourselves. There's no need to book the wedding caterers just yet," I say. The girls sober up. "Just kidding! I'm thinking French cuisine."

"Summer's getting married!" Siena shimmies her shoulders. Melody starts humming the bridal march. I pretend to clasp a bouquet to my chest, bouncing in my seat as though I'm traipsing down a petaled aisle. The boys shake their heads . . . and Shy stays uncharacteristically silent, damn her.

"Well, when do we get to meet the future Mr. Prescott?" Mel asks.

"We're home next weekend to visit my mom, if you want to set something up, Sum?" Siena adds.

I gasp. "Why didn't you say anything? Could you squeeze us in on Sunday night, maybe?"

"Done deal!"

"Consider us there," Mel adds.

"Shy?" I prompt, raising a *don't fuck with me* eyebrow.

"I'll be there." She gives an innocent shrug.

With a satisfied sigh, I jab at the ignition on my car, killing the engine and the AC already badly needed this early in May. "Well, I'm off! Summer Friday awaits."

I hurry into Oakley's after a round of goodbyes. While Parker is plenty used to my tardiness, I really do look forward to our solo nights. It's nice being able to fully unwind—to sit in easy, comfortable silence without constant pressure to engage the people I'm with.

Parker perks up the moment I slide into our booth in the lively bar.

"You'll never guess what happened." He sets down his half-finished book, swings his legs underneath the table, and leans over. "Check it out. Don's here." He tips his head toward the rest of the pub, and a quick scan shows our boss sitting solo at a table near the hall leading to the washrooms. "And . . . so is Kendra. Sitting at the bar."

I spot our coworker Kendra with her friends, wearing a frilly dress so unlike the casual attire I always see her in.

Parker's fingers curl around his book. "I've been thinking about what you saw a few weeks ago, about Kendra leaving a full container of homemade muffins in Don's office? And the next day, Don chose her to pick up Harley Deangelo's training program, when his own schedule got too busy for it?" Harley Deangelo, a minor league baseball player, had been working with Don to rehabilitate a knee injury. "I assumed Kendra won Don over with the muffins, because, well . . ."

"She's blatantly incompetent and a total suck-up?"

"Yes—you were onto something, but I don't think . . ." Parker wrestles with a smirk. "I mean, I do think she's been enticing him with muffins. But . . . of a different variety."

I gasp. "*No.*"

"*Yes,*" he hisses. "They keep shooting looks at each other, and—Oh, shit. Here we go."

I turn my head as far as I dare without making it obvious. Kendra splits away from the group of women she's with, then makes her way past Don's table and into the dim hall beyond it.

A beat passes. And another. And then Don gets to his feet and follows her.

"Oh my *God.*" I grip Parker's arm, nails digging into his skin as he gives me a wide-eyed *told you* look. "He's totally eating her muffin!"

"That's what I'm saying!" With a shake of his head, Parker reorients himself into his usual position lounging on his bench. "Fucking hell, Sum. I couldn't believe it when he handed her Deangelo. She's only half as qualified as either of us."

"You'd think the work you put in with Brooks would earn you a little recognition." I rip my Kindle out of my bag. I'd helped out with Brooks between my own clients, but there was a point where Parker was working seven days a week to get our friend back into playing shape. Somehow, though, Don spun the success story as a team effort.

"Why would it, when I have neither a literal nor figurative muffin." He opens his book, flipping through the pages. He glances at my Kindle. "What are you reading today? The dragon shifters?"

I wag my eyebrows. "They're minotaurs."

With a nod, Parker returns to his reading. His eyes don't move across the page, though, and after a beat he turns a frown across the table. "How does that work, with minotaurs? Anatomically speaking."

"Carefully, and with a lot of lubrication." I jab at the screen of my tablet with a flourish. "There's a ton of dirty talk in this one, which I'm certain helps. All that growling, you know?"

"Do minotaurs growl?"

"These ones do." I shrug. "It's hot. Possessive. *Animalistic*." Denny's not much of a growler. Not much of a talker at all when we're getting frisky, but a girl can't have it all.

With a contemplative *hum*, Parker returns to his book. This time, my own eyes stall on my e-reader. Drift across the table at Parker's profile.

Are you a growler?

The unbidden thought has my face heating. I'd do anything to go back in time, to the moment I overheard Sammie Waters's hushed whispers about Parker. I'd . . .

Well, I'd probably charge over there and demand precise details. And then lecture them all for spreading around Parker's private business in the first place.

I clear my throat. "So, how was your lunch date? Claire was bombarding me with excited texts all week, leading up."

Parker pulls a face. "She's not the one."

"*Again*? I thought for sure a day-date would make a difference." My shoulders fall. Three weeks and another five blind dates later, it's clear that matchmaking Parker won't come as easy as I thought. First, it was Jenny Heath spilling an entire drink on herself apparently as an excuse to insist they head up to Parker's to dry her clothes. Then it was Portia Kenney—who I'd hoped would demonstrate at least *some* restraint at the age of thirty-seven—coming to their dinner date with a pre-written list of personal kinks she'd like to explore with him. And on and on it went.

Claire, who's new in town and teaches yoga at the studio across the street, had seemed sweet. She'd happily agreed to a weekday lunch date, which I hoped would convey a clear message of *No sex will be had today. Please behave accordingly.*

"She didn't proposition me," Parker mutters. "It was just . . . off."

"Off how?" I sort through my bag for a pen and the *Parker's Dream Woman* list, which I've been adding to after every date. *Doesn't wear vanilla perfume, must enjoy reading* . . . I've never known Parker to be so choosy, but if there's one benefit to these failed attempts, it's him figuring out what he *doesn't* like. In addition to propositions.

Parker rubs at his brow. "She's very touchy."

"You just said she didn't proposition you."

"It wasn't like that—she kept casually touching my arm while we spoke. I hated it."

I shift awkwardly. "I touch your arm all the time. Why didn't you ever tell me it bothers you?"

"Because it doesn't bother me. You're completely different." He flips a page in his book while I frown at my sheet of paper, trying to figure out how I'd determine whether a woman is *touchy* before setting them up. "How're things going with Denny?"

"Good." I hesitate, guilt weighing on me for failing Parker while his very first blind date for me was a winner. "Great, in fact. He's home visiting his dog for the weekend."

Parker squints at me. The man really needs his eyes checked. "His dog?"

"He relieves his dog sitter on the weekends. Why do you look so suspicious?"

"Surprised he'd give up whole weekends with you."

"His dog's important to him. I get it." Parker makes a noncommittal sound, delivered into the pages of his book, and my heart stalls for more beats than comfortable. "You think that's a red flag?"

"Caring about a dog? No." Parker doesn't say anything more, apparently absorbed in his book.

It takes him several long minutes to flip to the next page, though.

Chapter 7

Parker

Denny Peterson.

It's the first time I've laid eyes on that mop of unkempt hair since the night I discovered him in this bar and bestowed upon him the role of a lifetime: Summer's new . . .

Guy.

Elbows propped on the mahogany bar behind me, I squint at the table our friends have occupied in the middle of Oakley's. Brooks and Siena flew in a couple of days ago to visit her adoptive mom. Zac and my sister made it down, too, and they, plus Shy, all sit happily surrounding Summer. Listening avidly to Denny's talking.

I swear, there's something off about him.

I can't put my finger on it—the reason for this scrape in my chest whenever Summer gushes about him. That prickle at the back of my neck when I watch him too closely. He's a decent conversationalist, if a little reserved—like he's sitting in a job interview, trying not to say the wrong thing. But then, he's being introduced to Summer's closest friends. Maybe I'd be nervous, too.

Denny tugs his phone out of his pocket and flips it face down on the table once he's checked it. His arm drapes over the back of

Summer's chair and he absently strokes her bare shoulder with his thumb. I'm glad he's paying her the attention she's owed, but I wish he'd just quit it for a minute so that I can properly think.

It's been nagging at me for weeks, and I really need to figure out what it is about this guy that isn't sitting right.

"She really likes him." Shy sidles up to me, smoothing down her ponytail as we stare at our table. Her words do something so . . . strange to me. Incite a dull ache in my throat—a tug of something uncomfortable deep in my gut.

"Isn't that a good thing? She deserves to be happy."

"Yes, except we all know there's something critically wrong with him."

I whip around to face her. "You feel it, too? What is it?"

To my annoyance, Shy's mouth tugs into the smirk she's haunted me with since she first accused me of harboring feelings for Summer. "The problem with *him* is that he isn't you, Woods. Want to know what the problem with *you* is?"

The fact that I'm literally standing in the same place I was as a teenager, with no prospect for anything greater for the rest of my life? The fact that, lately, my head keeps cycling between the normal, happy me, and some guy who can't figure out why he should bother getting out of bed in the morning?

Even if I had the feelings that Shy's been accusing me of, I'd have so little to offer Summer, it would be comical. I'd laugh in my own face.

Shy continues unprompted, "What's wrong with *you* is that, at this rate, you're not going to realize what you want until she's signing a marriage certificate in front of her closest family and friends."

I shake my head, because she's got this one wrong. "I'm telling you, there's something off about him. It has nothing to do with me." At our table, Denny fiddles with his phone. "Do me a favor and just . . . keep an eye out."

Two glasses appear between us, a Mountain Dew and Diet Coke, and I lead Shy back to our table. I slide Summer's refill in front of her, catching the flash of annoyance in Denny's face.

It only occurs to me then that it probably isn't my place to get her a fresh drink anymore. But Summer shoots me a smile in thanks. And just like that, I don't care what the cagey dickhead thinks about it.

"All I'm saying is, too many sights to see and it ruins the honeymoon," Siena is musing, thoughtfully combing her fingers through her hair. The meteor-sized diamond on her finger sparkles in the dim light. "I want somewhere warm enough for a nighttime skinny-dip, and without so many sights that we'd feel guilty for staying in and doing it the whole time."

Brooks scoffs around the rim of his beer. "You, of all people, would feel guilty about that?"

"Absolutely not. But it'll save me from admitting to the people at work that I was too busy riding your Eiffel Tower to check out the real thing." Across the table, Zac hangs his head, which only makes Siena grin wider. "Don't give me that, Mr. Gets Down and Dirty in This Very Bar's Bathroom." She flicks her hand in my sister's direction.

Zac rounds on Mel. "You told her about the bathroom?"

"Summer makes a stiff drink, what can I say?"

"Maybe let's tone down the sex talk about my twin sister while I'm at the table." I pinch two fingers until they're almost touching. "Just a bit disturbing."

"Try swapping a minotaur into the story," Summer says. She coughs on her sip of Diet Coke when I dig my elbow into her ribs. "Parker's recently unlocked some monster fetishes."

"I was in Hawaii a few months ago," Denny chimes in. "If you're looking for honeymoon ideas."

There's an awkward beat as we switch gears back to Brooks and Siena's upcoming honeymoon.

Summer gasps at Siena. "You can get lei'd in Hawaii!"

"Absolutely terrible," I mutter. "You're made of funnier stuff than that."

Her knee bumps mine under the table. From two seats away, I can feel the heat of Denny's gaze on the side of my face. "It's not a bad spot for skinny-dipping," he continues. "Not that . . . I was there with friends. Annual surfing trip, all clothes stay on type of thing."

It's there again, that prickle. *Thou doth protest too hard about the naked swims, buddy.*

"Boring," Siena stage-whispers to Brooks. My sister rests her cheek on Zac's shoulder, chuckling to herself.

For the umpteenth time tonight, it hits me square in the chest— this flood of unbearable envy, followed by the familiar pang of misery. I'm surrounded by happy couples. Even Shy, who's out alone tonight, has the comfort of knowing she's got a husband and daughter at home, and not the empty apartment waiting for me upstairs.

And now there's Summer and Denny. She's leaning slightly toward him, and that there is enough to mess with my head. I don't think we've ever sat so far apart while sitting right next to each other. I feel robbed of those inches. Worse, by a guy setting off wailing alarms in my head.

After a few minutes, Denny excuses himself to the washroom. Summer perks up in her seat the moment he's out of earshot. "Well? What do we think?"

He's dull, shifty, and—

"He's so sweet," Mel tells her.

"And *really* cute," Shy adds.

"And you two?" Summer gestures at the guys. "Parker already co-signed on him when he set us up, but what do you think?"

"This one seems to shower," Brooks says. Zac nods his agreement.

Siena leans over the table. "It really doesn't matter what we think. You're *glowing*, Sum."

I study Summer for myself. Her green eyes are bright, smile is wide, soft sun freckles dot the slope of her nose. She *is* glowing, but . . . is that any different from usual? Her skin has always done that shimmering thing. I don't know what everyone else has been looking at over the years, because it's kind of hard to miss.

"Someone please tell me I'm getting ahead of myself," she says. "There's still so much I don't know about him."

"When you know, you know." Siena shrugs. "Took Brooks two seconds exactly to become obsessed with me."

Brooks seems to take offense to that, but the protest fizzles by the time he opens his mouth. "Yeah, all right. That's accurate."

Summer's cheeks go pink. "Do you think he's obsessed with me?"

"Summer, the man cannot stop touching you," Melody answers. I don't manage to rein in the *ick* in my face before Shy notices. "He's completely obsessed."

"He *is* very touchy." Summer buries her face in her hands. I chase a sigh with a long gulp of soda. "I mean, he's not . . . you know. Tying me to his bed all night and edging me within an inch of my sanity, or anything. But maybe one day."

My body snaps in her direction so fast my drink sloshes, dribbles into my lap.

Summer doesn't seem to have noticed her slipup, but a quick glance around the table tells me everyone else did. The near-identical *what was that* looks Zac and Mel level at Summer's hidden face. The *oh shit* stare Brooks and Siena exchange. Shy sinks her teeth into her lip, shooting me a pointed *say something!* with her eyes.

And then it seems to click in Summer's head. The fact that she just did *that*—volunteered this personal fantasy, an exact replica of the things I know women say about me behind my back.

Her hair whips as she turns horrified eyes on me. "That's not . . . It's the first thing that came to mind."

My instinct, always, is to tease her mercilessly. But not a thing comes out of my mouth.

All I seem capable of is staring. At her flaming cheeks, the way her throat works as she swallows. The deep intake of air that has her breasts nearly bursting out of the low neckline of her shirt. The way she can't seem to look away from me, either.

I can't figure out this energy. Have no idea whether she fantasizes about *that* or that with *me*. I've thought about her like that plenty myself. I mean, this is *Summer fucking Prescott*—it's only natural.

Someone across the table clears their throat. Brooks, I think. It does enough to draw Summer's attention, and the moment I lose her gaze I re-enter my own body. Recall exactly who I am, who she is, what we are to each other.

"I'm gonna go dry off. Give you a second to figure out how to walk that back," I say.

Summer flips me off as I get to my feet, and I give a genuine laugh. All that odd tension already a distant memory.

My best friend just slipped up in a major way, and by the time I'm in the washroom, I'm deep into a list of ways I plan to hold this over her head until old age regretfully wipes this from my brain.

It's not until I'm standing in front of the mirror, drying off my jeans with paper towels, that I notice a voice coming from inside an occupied stall. A hushed conversation happening over the phone before goodbyes are apparently exchanged.

Denny emerges from the stall.

His smile slips when he catches sight of me, but he recovers quickly. "Hey."

I nod and we stand silently at the counter doing our own thing. Another nod and he heads back into the bar, leaving me in the empty washroom. I'm ripping more paper towels from the dispenser when a flash of light on the counter catches my eye. It's a phone sitting in the corner Denny had just occupied. He must have forgotten it.

I pick it up. And I swear, my last intention is to check it.

I couldn't care less about what he and his surfer buddies talk about. But then text notifications appear in quick succession from a contact named Allie. With a heart emoji next to it.

I blink, hoping it's my dwindling vision playing tricks on me.

I'm perfectly aware that he and Summer have only been dating for three weeks, two days, and fifteen seconds. Perfectly aware that unless conversations have been had about monogamy, it doesn't matter that he's the kind of idiot who'd spend a moment of his life on another woman when he's got Summer Prescott in his grasp.

But hell if the hairs on the back of my neck don't rise anyway. Allie sends him text after unanswered text. The phone goes silent. And then it lights up, her name appearing over the display. Without thinking, I answer the call.

A woman's voice fills my ear without waiting on a hello. "Babe, I forgot to mention the photographer wants a list of family portraits for the wedding. What do you think? Do we cap it at our immediate family?"

My body goes still. And that thing at the back of my neck is no longer a prickle. It's a blanket of dread, slowly crawling over my skin.

"Hello?" Allie says when I don't speak. "Denny, you there?"

Fuck. *Fuck.* "Sorry, this is uh . . . Parker. I'm on the surfing circuit with Denny. He left his phone in the bar bathroom."

She gives an easy laugh. "That man would find a way to lose the shirt off his back, I swear."

I swallow. "I'm gonna head back to our table. Who . . . who should I tell him called?"

"This is Allie," the woman says with a touch of surprise. "His fiancée."

My stomach drops.

I'm glued in front of the mirrors, heart pumping furiously, staring in horror at my own reflection. Allie—Denny's fucking *fiancée*—is saying something else, but I don't register a word of it. I cut off the call, feeling sick to my stomach.

"Jesus fucking Christ." I grip the edge of the counter. This is going to destroy Summer. She likes Denny, but that's not even the half of it.

At sixteen, I spent months watching her sob over the demise of her parents' marriage—they were high school sweethearts whose seemingly perfect family life imploded after her mother's yearlong affair with a neighbor came to light.

It was the inescapable town gossip for months when her parents' split went public. And after Summer sided with her dad, her mother picked up and moved from the entire continent with her lover. Leaving Summer and any chance at repairing their relationship behind.

There isn't a chance in hell Summer knows about the fiancée.

She's going to kill me for setting them up. For roping her into this, the very thing that ruined her family.

But not before I kill him.

Chapter 8

Summer

With a parting wave at our table, I let Denny lead me across Oakley's and onto the busy main street. It's warm outside even with the sun setting, and every few feet the cobblestone sidewalk is occupied by someone I know.

I wave at Callie, the silver-haired boutique owner benefitting from my shopping addiction since I earned my very first teenaged paycheck.

"Headed home already, Miss Life of the Party?" she says as we pass on the way to the crosswalk. "I've never known you to quit on a night out this early."

"It's my fault." Denny tucks me into his side. "It's hard to resist her sitting next to me."

"Well, isn't that sweet." Callie's eyes widen in delight. She's had a front-row seat to the many retail therapy sessions needed after crappy dates. "And what are your intentions with our Summer, young man?"

"Cal!" I shoot her a warning look, but she only gives me a teasing smile in return. "This is my friend, Denny."

"Friend?" Denny nudges me. "Do you let all your friends whisk you out of a bar for . . ."

"A gentlemanly kiss at her front door, and absolutely nothing else?" Callie supplies.

Denny shoots her a wink, Callie laughs, and I'm trying to keep myself in check, trying to play it cool. But I can't remember the last time I've been happy like this.

"Well, don't let me keep you. You lovebirds have a good night." Callie squeezes my shoulder before heading for a small group gathered in front of Oakley's. They all wave happily when they spot me. Lisa, who owns Oakley's with her husband, clutches her chest when Denny presses a kiss to my temple.

"This town loves you," Denny muses as we cross the street to my apartment.

I smile. "I've lived here all my life. Callie's wife used to babysit Parker, Mel, and me."

"You ever think about moving out of here?"

"When I was younger, definitely. But I love it. Love the people. Love being near the water." And when my parents up and left, building new families without me, people like Callie and Lisa rallied around me. Made me feel like I still had a home.

Denny pulls me into his chest outside of my apartment building. I feel like someone else. Someone who hasn't been bloodied by years on the dating circuit, hasn't wondered if there was something so fundamentally wrong with her that it drove men away, her father included, then drove her toward the worst kind of them.

For once, I'm basking in real possibilities, beyond the delusional fantasies. I'm feeling wanted and longed for, and I don't want it to end.

"Get your keys out. I think I can actually hear your bed calling our names." Denny leans in for a kiss. Quite possibly, I might be the happiest girl in the—

An angry shout echoes around us, bouncing off the brick buildings lining the street. I jolt away from Denny like I've been slapped by it.

Parker marches across the street. His hair is a mess, standing up at odd angles as though he's spent hours tugging at it, though I barely saw him a few minutes ago. The closer he gets, the clearer I can see the absolute, terrifying fury in his eyes.

For a silly moment, I assume he's ticked off I headed home without saying goodbye. He'd still been in the washroom when we left, and I'd been relieved to have a reason to avoid him after the things I said.

"Parker," I say when he's close. Strangely, I register a faint *fuck* from Denny. "I'm sorry we snuck out—"

"*Get your hands off her.*"

Too late, I realize his attention isn't on me. It's on Denny. And my horrified gasp is overshadowed by the grunt of pain out of Denny as Parker grabs his shirt, slams him into my building, and drives his fist right into Denny's face.

"Parker, what the *fuck*?" I take the back of his shirt and try to heave him off a winded Denny. But Parker doesn't budge, barely even registers me. I've never seen him this incensed. It's like he's been sucked into a vortex of rage, just him and his prey.

"Parker, stop." I take his arm instead, tugging, pushing, trying everything I can to get his attention. "Have you lost your damn—"

Parker reaches into his back pocket and pulls out a phone I recognize as Denny's. And that's all it takes for my heart to stall. For that familiar sinking feeling to take hold of me. That *I'm an idiot* moment I inevitably get at some point during a date. The *I should have seen this coming*.

My arms fall limp at my sides. I suck in a breath as I take in Denny's face, the one that's been buried in my hair, my neck, whichever part of me he could reach for *weeks*.

"Come clean," Parker seethes. "Come clean right now and I'll *consider* letting you leave with your life."

I swallow. "Parker. Maybe we should do this inside."

"Summer, he's getting married!"

Getting married.

Getting married.

Parker's voice bounces in my head, over and over. There's a sob, or maybe vomit, crawling up my throat. My mouth snaps shut in an effort to stop it.

Parker's expression flickers from fury to concern to regret. That's where it stays, his shoulders deflating, brows pulling together, fingers falling from Denny's shirt as he faces me.

"He has a fiancée back home," he whispers. "Summer, I'm so sorry. She called his phone and I picked up. He's getting married."

"I heard you." For the first time since he stormed across the street, I become aware of our audience. Callie, Lisa, and her husband, Jim. Wynn Sheffield, the owner of the shuttered diner. Four people I've grown up knowing, all gaping at us from across the street.

That's Ken Matthews, a football coach at UOB, and his wife, Gina, staring at me from just a few yards down this sidewalk. She leans into him, and even from here I can hear the word *affair* she whispers to her husband.

My eyes burn. "I think everyone in town heard you."

Even if they didn't, they'll all know by sunrise. It's how it went with my mother's affair, why she only lasted here a few months before fleeing across the Atlantic.

Free of Parker, Denny straightens off the brick wall. "Maybe we should head upstairs and talk, Summer."

Parker's face snaps right back to fury. I take hold of his arm before he can get his hands on Denny.

"Why would you . . ." I swallow hard, losing my words. "Is this an affair?"

Denny gives me a funny look. "Summer, come on. We're having fun, aren't we?" *Do not fucking cry.*

My mouth opens as though to say something more, and I scream at my brain to cooperate. To release the *how could you* and *fuck you* and *tell her I'm sorry* I want to throw at him. But that thick sob surges again, and it's all I can do to head for the door to my walk-up, searching through my purse for keys with violently shaking hands.

I'm vaguely aware of Parker saying something behind me—to me or Denny, I have no idea. But the moment I'm through the open door he's right there, taking my bag from me, steadying me when my knees almost give out, helping me up the stairs as I shove air into my lungs in short bursts. Trying so hard to keep it together.

I'm used to this. Crying over a man or the lack of a man. Done it plenty of times.

I've always been able to see the end coming, whether at the tail end of another long night pretending to give a shit about video games, or two minutes into yet another dead-end date.

This one, though? This one has me stumbling down the hall, gutted and empty. Winded by the neck-breaking shift in gear. One second zipping through the final stretches of a dark tunnel, blinded by the bright lights of possibility at the end. Only to come crashing into a wall of pain and humiliation, crippling loneliness, and pure defeat.

Parker is speaking but I don't register any of it. Because I give up. *I fucking give up.*

I'm done clinging to optimism only to discover it's really delusion. Done opening myself up only to come out of it with my heart chipped even smaller than the state in which the guy before left it. Done dusting myself off and throwing myself back into the fray, pretending every ending doesn't ache more than the last.

I'm so done being hurt by men.

The man who ruined the perfect marriage I thought my parents had. The man who got himself a fresh new life without me, new children and all. The man standing right in front of me, unlocking my apartment with the spare key I gave him the day I moved in.

A flame erupts deep inside me, shoving anger through my veins.

I'm grateful for it, the way it dulls my urge to cry. Of course, I'd wondered where Denny had come from, the night Parker introduced us. But we connected so quickly I hadn't thought to question the fact that I know all of Parker's friends. All his coworkers and clients.

Parker opens the door and ushers me in first, dropping my purse on the small table in the hall. "The guys are downstairs wanting to be let up. I guess people in Oakley's heard the commotion."

"Tell them to go home. I don't want to see anyone." Fury races through me. Of course news has already spread. He should've known better than to make a scene in a town like ours. "I've put so much effort into trying to vet dates for you for weeks, and this whole time . . . Who is he, Parker?"

Parker turns slowly to face me. "Summer . . ."

"Who is he? How do you know him? Why did you think to set us up?" I take step after step toward him, and my rage must be palpable because he lets me drive him backward, through the open front door and out into the hallway. Dread and anxiety occupy every inch of his face—this face I trusted with everything, for years and years of my life. Parker, the one guy I thought would never dream of hurting me. Who's always been careful with me, the same way I've been careful with him. "Who did you let into your so-called best friend's life? Who did you trust with my heart? Who did you let me waste my time on? *Answer me.*"

An eternal pause. Finally, Parker's shoulders lift and fall in sheer resignation. He looks miserable, but manages to look me in the eye. "I met him right before I introduced you."

I slam the door in his face.

Chapter 9

Summer

I hate him.

It's the sole thought bouncing in my exhausted brain as I stare at the shadows on my speckled ceiling.

The morning sun pours through the slatted blinds I didn't bother shutting last night. I'm wrapped in a towel still damp from the 3:00 a.m. shower I took when I couldn't fall asleep. The pillow under my head is still soaked with tears I've long since stopped crying.

By this time on a regular Monday, I'd have already made it home from a sunrise surf session, showered the salt water out of my hair, and thrown together two breakfast smoothies before heading out to meet an awaiting Parker, no less than fifteen minutes late for work.

But I couldn't stomach the thought of surfing today, for obvious reasons. I consider blowing off work altogether. But then I'm reminded that the alternative is to continue lying in this bed, thinking about how much I hate Parker Woods.

And I really need to stop thinking about him.

So, I bounce off the bed. Don't even bother righting the peach-colored comforter thrown around during hours of tossing and turning, and head to my closet to get dressed for work. I debate the merits of makeup before catching sight of my tired, blotchy face in the mirror above my dresser, and then reach for the most heavy-duty concealer in my possession. The brightest blush. The shiniest gloss.

I'm looking for a hairbrush when my eyes catch on the floating shelves next to the mirror. They're a cluttered mess, like everything else in my apartment. Too many picture frames and fading Polaroids. An old, sparkly green party hat. Mason jars filled with colorful, mini paper airplanes covered in years' worth of teenaged secrets and jokes and stories flung at me from where Parker sat several rows toward the back of our classrooms.

Every inch of those shelves is covered in him, and it fills me with rage all over again that he, out of everyone, would have been so damn careless with me.

I consider launching the jars out of my window as hard as I can, hoping at least one of them shatters against his own window across the street. But my aim's always been shit, despite the years my football-playing friends tried to remedy it. Odds are, it would hit an unsuspecting pedestrian below, giving this town even more reason to gossip about me after last night's street-side display.

Humiliation wells inside me, threatening tears. Instead, I layer on another coat of my darkest, least waterproof mascara.

Because I will not cry today.

I will be the happy employee I've always been. The most dedicated trainer to my clients. I will not give anyone a reason to pity me, or hate me, or judge me even more than they already must for a transgression I didn't know I was committing.

I don't bother with the smoothies this morning, seeing as I'm down both an appetite and a best friend, so I bypass the kitchen and head straight for the front door. Plaster on a bright smile as my hand closes around the knob.

I will not cry today. I will not—

The door swings inward, a large shape falling at my feet. Parker startles awake as his head bounces off the ground. He blinks, disoriented, still in yesterday's clothes.

God damn this man. The sob that'd been stifled by anger somewhere around dawn breaks free, tears falling.

"Summer." Parker scrambles to his feet. He reaches for me but pauses with his hands in the air when I step back.

"What are you still doing here?" The mirror by the door shows black streaks already running down my cheeks, and I wipe them away angrily. "I thought slamming the door in your face was sending a pretty clear message."

"Please, give me two minutes. Thirty seconds. Let me explain, apologize—"

"I'd have liked an explanation weeks ago, before I spent my time helping a scumbag cheat on his innocent fiancée." Giving up on my face, I brush past him out of my apartment. He hurries after me. "You want to know the worst part? What *he* did, what he roped me into? It probably makes me a prime candidate for intensive therapy. And, yeah, odds are pretty low that I'll ever date again. But I'll get over it eventually."

I pivot to face him. It's so abrupt, Parker's momentum carries him several steps past me. "You, though? You weren't thinking about me when you forgot to find me a date. You weren't thinking about me when you set me up with a stranger off the street. Didn't think of me at all when you put me in a situation where a nearly married man touched me and kissed me and made me all kinds of promises I was desperate enough to believe. And you sure as fuck weren't thinking about me when you made that scene in front of the entire town last night. *You*, the person I'd have trusted with my life, put me here. *You* got my heart broken. *You* humiliated me in front of people who watched me grow up. And that's something I'm never getting over."

I don't wait for a reply. I stride down the stairs and onto the busy street, trying to scrub Parker's shattered look out of my head and hoping it's just my imagination when people turn to stare in my direction.

~~~~

People do stare.

All day, they stare as my car drives through town. When I'm in the gym, setting up for my next client. They stare whenever, despite myself, I scan the rehab center for the head of pale brown hair I've never gone a workday without.

Parker never shows up to work. But every time I start to feel guilty for letting him have it, I catch another glance in my direction. Another couple of people whispering as I park my car outside my place at the end of the day.

Charity Reynolds, whose son Cameron was in the grade below mine in high school, wanders down the sidewalk just as I step out of the driver's seat. It must be the years I've spent chatting up the other locals whenever I bump into them, because a smile breaks over my face out of habit.

"Hey, Charity. Haven't seen you in a while!" Charity acknowledges me with a minuscule nod though she doesn't stop walking. For some reason, I persist. "How's Cameron doing these days? He was thinking about moving back to town, right?"

The disdain in her eyes is blatant as anything. "He's married. *Happily.*"

I hear a snort from somewhere behind me.

"That's . . . that's great." Charity has already meandered across the street but I flee into my apartment before anyone else can catch a glimpse of me.

Inside, the stifling silence takes me by the throat. It presses into me from all angles until it physically hurts. Like I do every time this happens, I sit on my sofa and force my gaze across the apartment, over the shelves and walls covered in frames.

That picture at the very top of my bookcase? That's me and my former client Merrill Hunt, after his first NBA game. On the gallery wall surrounding the TV, the time Parker broke us into our old high school for a midnight pool party with Melody and Zac when we were sixteen. Me and my co-volunteers, on our boards after last year's final Surf's Up event. Me and Callie at her sixtieth birthday down at the pub. My dad and Estelle, with me sandwiched between my half-brothers in front of a lit-up tree, two Christmases ago.

Long minutes pass as I try to let the pictures do their job: remind me I'm far from alone whenever the loneliness creeps in.

Tonight, though?

When I'm single again—if those weeks with Denny could even be called a relationship—and getting shunned and judged by the people who became my family when my parents left town . . . With this morning's unanswered text to my dad, asking if he had a minute to talk . . .

I allow myself a single quick glance out of my window. The blinds are open at Parker's, and though the sun has long passed a spot in the sky that brightens his apartment, there's not a single light on.

I'm not sure I can get through even a text conversation without laying into him right now. And I'm terrified I've already done irreparable damage to us this morning. We've fought plenty over the years, but never like this—never in a way that felt like I put a flaming torch to our friendship and walked away while it crumbled.

A knock at the door pulls me out of my head, away from the last, broken look Parker gave me this morning. "Summer, it's us!"

I close my eyes at the sound of Melody's voice. I've been avoiding my friends all day, not wanting to get into the events of last night and having no energy to talk about much else.

Dragging my feet down the short hall, I pause at the mirror by the door when I catch sight of my haggard appearance.

Get it together, Prescott.

I wipe tears, comb hair, slap on a smile. They've got husbands and a kid and enough to contend with without concerning themselves with the pit of despair inside this apartment.

The door swings open to reveal Mel and Shy wearing identical pitying looks. I pop a hip, leaning against the doorframe. "Why the long faces?"

Awkward silence stretches several beats before Shy indicates the paper bags she's holding over each hip. "Siena sent provisions—they had to fly home late last night. There's wine in this bag, hard liquor in this one. And she asks that you please answer her calls."

I gesture to the box in Melody's arms. "Who sent that one?"

"Parker left it for me to pick up."

His name is a boulder plummeting in my stomach, disturbing the momentary peace that's come over me at the sight of my friends. I pluck a paper bag out of Shy's arm and head for the kitchen. They watch in silence as I uncork a bottle of wine and lift it to my mouth, guzzling liquid until coming up for air becomes a critical necessity.

"I appreciate you coming to check on me. But, as you can see, I'm absolutely fine." They stare pointedly at the bottle I'm cradling to my chest. "All right, so my feelings got a little dinged up. And, sure, I probably won't date again until . . . well, probably until I die. But if you're going to be here, it can't be a pity party. I need feminine rage. The Fuck All Men Brigade."

Shy winces. "I'm more of the let's-talk-about-our-feelings type."

Mel leans back against the fridge. "I always find that greasy food and a rom-com helps."

I blow out a breath. As grateful as I am for the ungodly amount of alcohol now in my possession, I'd have really preferred for Siena to be here. She's got that unhinged, let's-slash-his-tires-in-the-middle-of-the-night attitude I need. And seeing as I still have the keys to Parker's car, we'd be able to do exceptional damage.

I pour more wine down my throat. "Fine. But *not* a rom-com. That used to be our thing."

"You and Denny?" Shy asks.

Mel shakes her head. "Her and Parker. It started at my parents' house when we were kids. They let us watch them earlier than we probably should've. Look, Sum—"

"Can we not talk about him? For the rest of the night."

"Denny?"

"Oh, no. He was dead to me the second I found out about the future wife." I take another long swig of wine. The alcohol is already hitting me divinely hard after not having had a single bite of food today. My brain feels delightfully fuzzy, arms pleasantly tingly. "Parker's worse than dead to me."

"Is that even . . . possible?" Shy asks.

"Trust me. It's possible. And you know what? I'm done letting men fuck around with my emotions. Making me trust them one second, only to introduce me to lying, cheating scumbags the next. I'm *done*." With the bottle at my lips, I stride into the living room and throw open the window, hanging my upper body over the street below. "You hear that? I'm done! Hope you're happy with your—your solo donut breaks at work! And your stupid Mountain Dews and all that rope and the shackles and whatever else you pretend isn't hiding under your bed—"

"Okay, let's maybe do the yelling indoors." Melody tugs me back inside. "You've got people staring from the street."

I throw myself on the sofa, clutching the wine. "They were already staring. Everyone thinks I'm a homewrecker, thanks to your brother. Like mother, like daughter, right?" My chin wobbles and I clench my jaw.

Shy attempts to pry the bottle from my grip, but I need it now. It's a lifesaving buoy, just like this anger, sparing me from the depths of my darkest feelings. "Do we think that you're maybe misdirecting your anger on Parker? I mean, how was setting you up with Denny any different than you picking a stranger on a dating app? Denny was the one who—" I glare. She lifts her hands in surrender. "The Fuck All Men Brigade. Got it."

I bounce off the sofa, stumbling my way to the kitchen. I can feel their eyes on me through the opening in the wall as I pry open the box Mel brought. There are several packs of Diet Coke, in both can and bottle form—which *do* taste different, no matter how much Parker disagrees. I crave one or the other depending on my mood. There's a sleeve of blueberry donuts he's been paying Wynn Sheffield to home-bake for us since the accident at the diner, to keep feeding the addiction we've shared since we were fifteen. I sort through the rest of the snacks contained in the box, none of them doing a thing to whet my vanished appetite.

Then I catch a flash of color buried under a bag of salt and vinegar chips. It's a miniature paper plane folded from a neon pink Post-it note. I rip it up without reading it.

Much as I hate to admit it, Shy's right. I'm using my anger at Parker as a crutch. But right now, hating him is easier than thinking too hard about the truth that's been staring me right in the face for years—mean and insistent, no matter how many times I've tried to bury it.

All signs point to there being something so wrong with me that I only attract the wrong kinds of people into my life. And chase away the ones who should've stuck around.

I slide down the cabinets until my ass hits the worn kitchen tiles. By the time Melody and Shy join me, I've dried my tears.

Shy links an arm with mine. "Summer, what Denny did to you isn't a reflection on you. You know that, right?"

You're wrong. "I looked for her online. The fiancée." I stare at the scuffed white fridge opposite me. The ripped-up paper plane digs into my palm. "I kept thinking I'd want to know what he was up to, if I were her."

Mel's shoulder touches mine. "Did you find her?"

"Couldn't. I don't have him on social media, and I know nothing about her other than she exists. He claimed he wasn't online, but it's obvious now that he was hiding his real life from me." And I was the love-starved idiot who fell for the relentless attention he paid me just to get in my bed. My chin wobbles. Again, I shut it down. "Could we please stop talking about it?"

Mel grabs the wine bottle and takes her own swig. "Would it help to hate on my brother some more?"

I sniff. "Tremendously."

"Does anyone else think he needs a haircut? He looks like he's just stepped off a hockey rink, when I'm pretty sure he's never laced a pair of skates in his life," Shy says.

I couldn't disagree more. I love Parker's hair, the way it's permanently tousled. It suits him. But I make myself nod in agreement.

"Can confirm. The man can't skate." Mel passes the wine over to Shy. "And what kind of person goes to a bar to read? It's weird. Antisocial."

"I do it, too. But he started it." I love how much he loves to read. And I love that it became our Summer Friday ritual. In our own bubble, even surrounded by people. "He's so stupid and ridiculous."

Simultaneously, their heads rest on my shoulders. I'm the sad brunette, being buried by her feelings in a blond sandwich.

"So stupid."

"*So* ridiculous."

"And I hate him."

Chapter 10

Parker

Guilt tears at me as Summer tugs the black baseball cap down her forehead, obstructing nearly the entire top half of her face from view. She's all the way across the gym putting away the equipment she'd been using during Quentin's session, lifting and racking his hundred-pound weights with impressive ease.

On a typical day I'd wander over to help her, making noise about the weights being too heavy for her, too rough on her delicate hands. Pushing and prodding at her until she inevitably challenges me to the bench press contest that she always loses, but attacks with the kind of gusto that says she truly believes today might be the day she beats me.

Instead, I remain stuck to the workout bench I'm sitting on. I found my peace offering donut in the trash in the staff offices, along with yesterday's donut and the accompanying apologies written on our pink Post-it notes.

I fucked up, in a multitude of ways.

Donuts and paper planes won't do a thing to fix the town gossip I started, nor Denny's treatment of her, but I hoped they'd entice her to speak to me. Look at me. Acknowledge me in any way.

I've got a best friend who pretends I don't exist, while the very thought of laying eyes on her is the only thing that makes dragging myself to work in the mornings worthwhile.

Between school and work and the vacations we'd take with the rest of our friends when we were younger, I haven't spent more than a few hours without her in . . . as far back as my earliest memories.

I've never had to miss Summer, and I envy the me from before. Blissfully unaware of this agony.

"She's still icing you out? It's been . . . what?" Over my shoulder, Noah's face is screwed up in thought. I hadn't even noticed him arrive. "Two days?"

Two days, fifteen hours, and thirty-three minutes to be exact.

I don't bother correcting him. Instead, I count to three, then five, then twenty, and force myself off the bench to get our session started.

Noah shakes his head. "People really think she'd go after an almost-married man on purpose?"

"You know how it is here. Small town with nothing better going on." I've been snapping the truth at anyone I overhear talking about it. Not that it's helped. The gossip seems too salacious to part with, especially with Summer's family history. More entertaining than the truth. "It was the same with the bullshit they were spreading about me."

Noah looks amused. "That was bullshit?"

"Hey, Prescott." Don's booming voice travels across the gym. Summer peers at him from under the brim of her hat, shoulders hitching toward her ears as though bracing for impact. Every head in the vicinity turns to look at her.

Don points to his own head. "What'd I say about hats while you're on the clock?"

"What the hell's with that guy?" Noah mutters.

"There's not enough time in the world to explain Don."

Summer peels the hat from her head. She avoids any and all eye contact as she heads to the offices.

I hurry after her, sucking down the trail of floral perfume she leaves behind. "Summer."

She doesn't stop walking. Doesn't even look at me. Changes direction and slips into the women's washroom, swinging the door shut in my face.

At three days, fourteen hours, and sixteen minutes, my stomach growls with hunger, drawing Noah's eye.

He gestures to the sleeve of donuts in my lap. "You can take a minute to eat if you need to. I can go warm up."

"They're not for me." I tried filling the growing pit inside me with any food I could get my hands on a couple of days ago, but the realization came quick that it wasn't going to help me.

Help *this*.

The mounting soreness in my shoulders, and the thickening fog in my head. This feeling like I'm both empty and so full of lead I can barely make my limbs function the way they should. I've been fighting this growing pit for weeks, months, only for it to be dwarfed by the Summer-shaped crater now inside me.

"Then I'll have one if you're offering," Noah says. "I only had time for a quick breakfast, and—"

Summer waves goodbye to her client, and I bolt off the bench. The sudden movement in the wall of mirrors catches her attention, and the way she glances at my reflection is as close to eye contact as we've made in days.

"Summer—"

She tucks her chin, fiddling with the rack of free weights lining the mirrors.

I thrust the box of donuts toward her. "If you're hungry, Wynn baked them fresh this morning. They're still warm."

"Noah?" she calls over her shoulder. "You in the mood for donuts?"

He strolls over. "The better question is, am I ever *not* in the mood for donuts?"

Summer plucks the box from my hands, pushes it on Noah, and walks away. He shrugs, downing half a donut in one bite. "At least she didn't toss them in the trash this time."

At four days, fifteen hours, and forty-eight minutes, Noah plants his hands on his hips. "I've been given strict instructions from your sister to make you answer your texts by any means necessary. She and Zac are worried about you."

"My phone died." Last I checked, it wasn't just them texting. Brooks has been calling me nonstop. But I don't have it in me to answer. I'm exhausted, barely able to keep it together at work, let alone long enough to entertain a dozen questions about my questionable well-being.

"So . . . charge it?"

"Can't find my charger."

Across the gym, Don emerges from his office with a pair of men in crisp suits I've never seen before. He walks them to the exit, shaking their hands, exchanging pleasantries, looking pleased with himself. I find Summer where she's spotting her client. She's noticed the suits, too—I catch her frowning in the mirror.

And then she looks for me, probably out of habit, but it's enough to cast a spotlight of warmth on me. I'd known I was cold without her, but it takes her looking at me to know just *how* frigid I've been. That same feeling when I emerge from relentless AC in this ice-cold gym and into the summer sun. The way my skin prickles with relief, sunrays sinking deep.

Her gaze falls away the moment she finds me staring. Just like that, I'm drenched in shade again.

I feel like I've been hurtling down this path for months. Colors turning increasingly dull and then gray. Destinations dwindling, navigation system flickering. Directionless. Ambitionless. Now without the glue that held me together.

Noah looks me up and down, not a speck of his usual amusement to be found. "Are you all right?"

At five days, twenty hours, and eleven minutes, I leave yet another draining day at work. And for the first time in years, instead of heading down to Oakley's early to save our Summer Friday table before the dinner rush, I crawl into bed.

~~~~~

I moved into my apartment on the day I turned twenty-three.

By then, my parents had sold their house and left town. Zac had been avoiding me at every turn after we'd disagreed over his high school feelings for my sister, who was off in the big city she'd dreamed of living in since we were kids. Brooks was in LA for his first stint in the NFL. I didn't see any of them that birthday, but I never felt their absence.

I'd finally rented this brand-new, adult apartment after years of roommates in college. And I had Summer in a sparkly green party hat, sitting across from me on the empty living room floor. It had been my hat originally, but the shimmering pink one she'd brought herself fell apart the moment she put it on. She'd looked so miffed over that stupid broken hat. And then so elated when I'd slipped my own on top of her head.

We ate too much cheap pizza, drank even worse prosecco before switching to more reliable soft drinks. Then she led me around the empty apartment, describing in precise detail exactly where I should put the couch once I got one. Which color curtains would match the pale gray walls I couldn't be bothered to paint over. I followed her down the hall toward the bedrooms, the pom-pom on her hat bouncing as she went.

She'd hemmed and hawed over the two bedrooms before deciding that I should take the smaller one to the right, because it had a view of the main street. She joked that one day she'd rent a place right across, and we could wave each other goodnight every day before falling asleep.

The waving thing never happened when she eventually moved into her place. But I did take that bedroom. I suspect it was a kid's room in a previous life, given the pencil lines marking measurements inside the closet door, growing higher with the years, and the glow-in-the-dark stars still stuck across the ceiling. I've never thought about these stars too much, other than finding it mildly charming that a child had once stared up at them, pretending he was under the limitless sky outside.

Tonight, though, with the streetlights shining through the open curtains and the sounds of the busy street filtering in through the shitty soundproofing in this old building, that star-covered ceiling feels like it's slowly inching down on me.

Has been, for the day or days or months since I got into bed.

There's a buzzing in the hall alerting me that someone's on the street trying to come up. I don't get out of bed, though. Anyone who matters has a key. I called in sick at work a while ago and haven't seen anyone since. Haven't managed to choke down more than a slice of plain bread here and there, whenever I get too lightheaded.

Another buzz and I turn over, pressing my face into the pillow. After a minute the sound ceases, leaving me in the relative silence of my bedroom. I picture that sparkly party hat, the bouncing pom-pom, willing myself to fall back asleep.

A deafening crash sounds somewhere in my apartment. Then rhythmic banging that I realize are stomping feet approaching my room.

I lift my head off the pillow, hoping for Summer. I don't care if she's come to forgive me or yell at me. I'll take it all.

But it's Melody barging into the room, flicking on the overhead lights with no regard for my retinas. She looks furious, though I can't imagine what I've done to her seeing as I haven't seen her since that night at Oakley's.

"Good evening." My voice is scratchy. "Make yourself at home, sis."

Her glare is withering. "Zac's been buzzing you downstairs for days. You're ignoring my texts, and Brooks keeps getting your voicemail."

I rub my face. "Zac's been camping out on the sidewalk for days, waiting to be let up? You didn't give him your key?"

"He has my key—confiscated it when I threatened to come set you straight last week. Something about giving you space if that's what you need, and that you'll come around when you're ready." She plants her hands on her hips, standing at the edge of my bed. My twin sister is tiny, almost a foot shorter than me and probably half my width. But she's got the most threatening scowl I've ever seen. "I'm not nearly as patient. Get up. Zac's holding us a table downstairs."

I flop back down on my pillow. "I don't want to get up. It's dark out. Nighttime. *Sleep* time."

"It's been *sleep time* for days, Parker. Six days, to be exact, and after you practically bullied me into a camping trip with our friends shortly after my last breakup, you can call this retribution."

"Retribution? I was setting you up with Zac—who you *married*." My head pops off the pillow. "Is this a setup? Will Summer be there?"

Mel's expression flickers. It's just a flash of pity before settling back into its stern mask, but that's all I need to know. I tug the comforter higher up my body. Mel reaches over and flings it off me. I pull it back up. She flings it off again.

"Seriously, Mels?"

"*Yes*, seriously." She looses a breath, and her body deflates. "Parker, you're officially scaring me. All this sleeping, skipping work. Your apartment's a mess. This isn't ... . *you*."

Little does she know, it *is* me. Me lately, anyway.

"Please, just come downstairs with me. Let's get something to eat. We won't even talk if you don't want to."

My sister's eyes go pleading, and guilt whacks me over the head. It takes several long breaths to get me there, but eventually I manage a gravelly "okay."

Chapter 11

Parker

Twenty minutes later, I'm showered and shaved at Mel's insistence, and sitting at a corner table in Oakley's.

Unfortunately, it's Thursday night and stupid loud. After six days of existing in the quiet of my apartment, the noise has my head pounding. All I can think about is how much I'd rather be upstairs, alone. Anywhere but here.

But the relief in Melody's face grows with every French fry I swallow. Meanwhile, Zac's been trying to play it casual, making conversation about things that don't matter, only to look way too engrossed whenever I interject with so much as a grunt.

"I'm thinking of getting one of those tractor lawn mowers. You know, the ones you ride? Since there's so much grass out back and I—"

"For fuck's sake, since when do you give a shit about the state of your lawn, Porter?" My words are impatient but Zac's eyes actually light up.

"Since never." He and Mel exchange a thrilled glance. Probably because it's the most I've said since sitting down. "Couldn't care less about my lawn."

I run my hands over my face. "So, let's stop talking about it."

"Sure. What would you like to—"

"Where's Summer tonight?"

Their hopeful smiles slip. Mel picks at the pile of fries in the middle of the table. "She's at Shy's house."

I never knew this kind of jealousy was possible. "And—what's . . . Is she okay?"

"She's Summer." Mel shrugs. "I thought for sure she'd break down by now, but you know her. She bounces back like no one else."

I nod, chest swirling with hurt and relief. She's okay. She's out there smiling and laughing and fine without me. While I'm here. Paralyzed by the way I miss her.

I blow out a breath, propping my head in my hands. "Should I go over there? Try to talk to her?"

"I think the space helps," Mel says gently. "She'll get over it eventually, Park."

"Then why does it feel like there's no going back?" It's like I'm mourning a death. The end of our friendship as we knew it. This perfect, untarnished one, where we've never done more than roll eyes at each other's nonsense.

Even if she stops icing me out, what do we look like once she does?

After a moment, Zac clears his throat. "Mel, I think we need fresh drinks. Mind going to the bar?"

Too slowly, I recognize how out of character it is for Zac to send Mel to fetch her own drink, when he spends 99 percent of his life catering to my sister's every whim before she's even *whimmed* them. I catch them mouthing something to each other before Mel disappears into the crowd.

"Fucking hell, what now? You both wanted me out of bed, so I got out of bed. You wanted me to eat"—I reach for a fry and shove it into my mouth—"so I'm eating. I don't need some kind of bullshit therapy session on top of it, about how to repair my friendship with Summer. I'd rather talk about your fucking lawn."

Zac shakes his head. "You're a jackass when you're miserable."

"So let me be miserable in peace."

"Let me save you some time: I've been where you are. Tried being miserable in peace and it doesn't work. I was a right moody asshole after your sister left town."

I shove too many fries into my mouth to spare him a moody asshole response. I have no idea what he's getting at, but I do remember that phase. We didn't know it at the time, but he'd just screwed up his chances with my sister who'd moved out of town before he could make it right. He'd gone from the happy-as-hell guy we grew up with, to a broody-as-hell prick. It took Mel coming home to get the old Zac back.

"I'm going to open this conversation once, and then never again. Because I know you get all pissy whenever it's brought up." Zac's words are so ominous, they finally draw my gaze. There's no mirth or accusation in his face. He looks genuinely curious. "But it seems to me that the way you think about Summer—the way you're sitting here like a sad sack without her—it's a lot like the way I was without your sister."

My head falls forward, hair flopping over my face. "You're really begging me to be an asshole. And I'm trying real hard not to be, on account of the whole *sixteen years of friendship, brothers-in-law, groomsman in your wedding* thing."

"Just humor me for a few minutes, and I swear I'll let this go forever." I flick my hand in a *get on with it* gesture. "You love her."

"Of course, I love her. You've known Summer as long as you've known me. Don't *you* love her?"

"Yeah, I love her. But it's not . . ." Zac sighs, toying with a salt shaker. "You miss her."

"Wouldn't you?"

"Sure, I would. Would I also become a shell of myself without her? Probably not."

"Sounds to me like you need to appreciate your friend a little more, Zac," I say darkly.

Anyone who'd go on smiling in the streets after a falling out with Summer is straight up off their gourd. I'm trapped in a therapy session with a fucking quack.

"Let me say this once and for all," I say. "Matter of fact, why don't you get out your phone and record this, send it to the whole group. You can all replay it whenever you wander back down this rabbit hole: Summer and I are friends, just like you are. I love her, same as you do. I like being around her, just like you do. Sure, I sometimes think about her naked. But it's not like you don't, too, and—"

Zac splutters beer all over the communal fries. "*Pardon me?*"

"What? What now?"

His eyes are watering from a coughing fit. He wipes an arm over his face, then takes several sips of Mel's water to soothe his throat. "What the fuck did you just say? You think about her naked?"

This conversation is officially unbearable. "It's *Summer*."

"*So?*"

"So, it's Summer. Everyone thinks about her naked. Have you seen her?"

Zac blinks. Slow, like he's buying himself time to dig into the reserves of his patience. "Parker, I have never—*not once*—thought about Summer naked."

There's a strange, sudden niggling in my brain. I shake my head, dismissing it along with Zac's words. "That's because you've been obsessed with my sister since you were a child. You don't count. Just wait."

I pull the phone from my pocket, and after the dip of disappointment at not finding a single notification from Summer, I video call Brooks. The ringtone cuts off and his face fills the screen. He's sitting in his LA kitchen, the lights bright around him, wearing a look of acute relief.

"Hey, I've been trying to call you—"

"Tell Zac you think about Summer naked."

The pause on his end of the line is fleeting. One second, it's quiet. The next, Siena is shouting, "*What did he just say?*"

Brooks's panicked gaze darts beyond his phone. "I don't! Siena, I do *not* think about Summer naked. I swear to God!"

Siena's head of dark hair appears over Brooks's shoulder. She looks about ready to strangle me. "You're lucky I'm relieved to see you alive, Parker Woods. Or I'd hop on a flight just to—"

"*Before*," I say quickly. Across the table, Zac howls with laughter. "I meant before he met you. When he was single, he thought about Summer naked."

Siena regards her fiancé expectantly.

"*No.*" Brooks shoots me a death glare through the phone. "She's my friend—why would I think about her naked? That's weird as fuck."

"But . . ." I'm trying to focus, trying to keep up with the conversation, but that niggling inside me grows more insistent by the second. "You're trying to tell me you've never noticed her?"

There's something clinically wrong with him, if that's the case.

Brooks stares back, baffled as hell. "I know she's good-looking, in a general sense. But if you're asking me if I've ever sat there ogling her or—or *thinking about her naked*? That's a hard no. I've never thought about her that way. We're *friends*."

The niggling becomes more of a hard tug. Like a leash has wound itself around me with an excitable hound on its other end, sniffing and pulling me along an unchartered path it's desperate to explore.

"Why are you asking me this, anyway?" Brooks is frowning at his screen. Meanwhile, Siena presses her lips together, trying not to laugh, all animosity apparently forgotten. He glances at her, back at his screen, and— "*Holy shit*, you think about Summer naked?"

Siena bursts into laughter, wanders off-screen, and I am officially mortified.

"I . . ." I scramble to find words. Any words. "Is that not— Am I not supposed to do that?"

I've never once questioned my desire for Summer. It seemed to me a complete no-brainer, given the way she looks, the way her mind works. The way her smile draws the light, rendering her the only viable point of focus in the room.

"Whenever I've thought about people naked—and by *people*, I mean my loving fiancée, who is the only person I have ever thought about naked. Ever." Brooks glances past his screen. "But whenever I've thought about people naked, it's because I wanted to fuck them. And I can say with full certainty that sleeping with Summer has never been on my wish list."

I blink at Brooks. Glance at Zac.

Zac snorts. Siena is laughing again. Brooks wipes a hand over his face. "How long have you wanted to fuck Summer?"

"Jesus Christ, I don't know," I burst. My body temperature is spiking, mind going into overdrive trying to make sense of all this. "I thought everyone did!"

"As in you genuinely believed that every single person who laid eyes on Summer wanted to fuck Summer?" Zac looks completely baffled. "That it was some kind of mark of humanity, like . . . people believing in a higher power?"

Brooks laughs. "Eat, pray, think about fucking Summer."

I stare. "Well . . . yeah. Who *wouldn't* want to sleep with Summer?"

Both guys hang their heads. "Parker, I think it's time to seriously consider the possibility that your feelings for her aren't as perfectly platonic as you think."

"But . . ." This doesn't make any sense. She's *always* been beautiful. Always been my favorite person, since before I even knew *love* could mean something different than the way I felt about my sister. "You're saying that just because I want to sleep with her, I'm . . ."

I can't even say it.

"Not necessarily," Brooks concedes. "But she stopped talking to you and you dug yourself a hole to live in. You look like *death*. And I love the hell out of Summer, but . . ." He fixates on something off-screen again, presumably Siena. "There's only one person who could leave me and have that kind of effect on me."

Zac gives me an *I told you* half shrug.

I scramble through years' worth of memories, all my moments with Summer. And I come up with . . . nothing. No pivotal moment where the platonic love I had for her as a child transformed into whatever everyone seems to think has befallen me now.

She's my best friend. The one who gets my humor and makes me laugh in return. The one who keeps me steady when things feel bleak and impossible. Not a day has passed since we met that I didn't want to see her happy. I'd do anything for her. And these are all qualities of a friendship I've always felt so unbelievably lucky to have.

If that's also what romantic love is supposed to feel like, then how the hell does anyone ever tell the difference?

"Give me this, I'm about to save you all some effort." Siena plucks the phone from Brooks's hand. She's barely keeping a straight face. "Hey, Parker? When was the last time you thought about me naked?"

There's a shout from Brooks, but I'm shaking my head even before his narrowed eyes are back on screen. "I don't ever think about you naked. That's ridiculous. We're just frie—"

Every single person seems to hold their breath, watching reality slam into me like a wrecking ball. "*Fuck*."

Chapter 12

Summer

I sink deeper into my seat at the very far end of the table of volunteers. When I showed up to this morning's Surf's Up planning meeting, it had been with the hope that, since these typically take place in the evenings, I'd be spared the vicious stares from a full committee.

No such luck.

Even with the baseball cap pulled low on my head, I can feel their eyes on me, teaching me the very same lesson I'd learned at sixteen when my mother imploded my world: In a small town, scandal travels fast. And it kills you slow. Twelve days later, yesterday's news remains today's news, and I'm still the woman who dated an almost-married man.

"Summer? Did you have something to share?"

I chance a glance out from under my hat. Grant looks at me expectantly from the head of the table, while every other face is pointed at me. Across from me, Danica, who's never given me less than a friendly smile, now stares me down with disgust. She'd confided in me a few months ago that her live-in boyfriend had left her for someone else, and I seem to have become a lightning rod for her anger.

"The pop-up market," Grant clarifies. "How many businesses do we have registered so far?"

"Um . . ." I sit up, flipping through the notebook in my lap. "We're quite a bit behind on the projected numbers. It—I . . ." I close my eyes, fighting the inner defeat, but it's futile. "I've been thinking a lot about it, and it might be best to hand this project to someone else, on account of the whole . . ." Somebody snickers. I hear not-so-subtle whispers of *married* and *homewrecker.*

"Are you sure, Summer? I know how much you enjoy running this," Grant says kindly. News must not have traveled to wherever he lives. I wonder where that is. Whether they have apartments for rent.

"I think it would be best. I don't want it to suffer," I say quietly. Registration has never lagged like this, and as much as it kills me to give up the program I built from the ground up, I have to accept that it's now better off without me.

"Do we have anyone who'd like to take it over?" The words are barely out of Grant's mouth before Danica's hand shoots into the air. And the moment Grant claps his hands in his signature dismissal, I'm hustling out of the Pine Point community center.

Waves crash in the distance, my favorite sound since Dad first took me surfing as a five-year-old. I haven't had it in me to take my board out since Parker's confrontation with Denny, and my body throbs as though protesting its own momentum away from the ocean.

I avert my eyes from the beach and head straight for my car, adjusting my hat for maximum coverage. All that remains is my lower periphery, flip-flops and sneakers moving around me as I hurry along, late for work.

I wonder if Parker will show up today. Where the hell has he been, anyway?

It's taken everything in me to refrain from grilling our friends and colleagues on his whereabouts, settling instead for the conflicting crumbs they let slip. He's off sick. He's taking some vacation days. He hasn't been seen in days. He was in a fun mood at Oakley's tonight. Meanwhile, the lights are never on at his place.

I'm still too angry to see him. Livid that he'd skip work this week, when all I want to do is see him. And mad at myself for being this irrational headcase to begin with. But if he even thinks about skipping the planning party tonight for his and his sister's birthday, I will march across that damn street and—

"Summer. Hey."

I stumble to a stop mere feet from the safety of my car. Denny stands just ahead, hair soaked, with his forest green surfboard tucked under an arm. The dam holding back the tears inside me buckles, threatening irreparable destruction at the complete *ease* in his face. Like we're old friends meeting again after years apart.

When I don't say anything, Denny's eyes wander to my car. "What happened to your Jeep?"

"It's Parker's Jeep. He lets me drive it when I surf. It fits my board better than my car." My voice sounds raw, weak, nothing like the cold hard bitch I'm trying to be. "How's your fiancée?"

Denny gives a smile. "She's good. I'm headed home for the weekend now."

"She was the dog you visited on the weekends?" *Great job, Summer. You had a real winner with this one.* I don't wait for his confirmation, pulling out my car keys and stepping around him.

"I'd still be into . . . hanging out. If you are."

His words have me pivoting on the spot. "You're asking me to be . . . what? Your piece of ass on the side? Why would I agree to that?"

He shrugs like it's the world's most reasonable request. "We had a good time, didn't we?"

"So everything you said and did—all the dates and the cooking. You were just laying the groundwork to get me in bed?" His loaded silence is all the answer I need. "You really think I'm desperate enough to keep that going?"

I don't wait for him to say anything. I wrench open the driver's side door, jabbing at the ignition once I'm seated.

In which dimension of this universe does he think I'd ever *knowingly* enter into an affair?

But my hand pauses on the door, stopping before it forms a barrier between me and this man whose actions have made me feel more worthless than all the men that preceded him combined. Who's so thoroughly broken me that I've been hating my own best friend to distract myself from what Denny's done to my insides.

It's so stupid and twisted to care what he thinks about me. He ceased to matter the moment I found out he was engaged. But part of me still wanted to believe that there was something in me worth falling for.

"Just tell me why it was me," I call after him. I swallow the lump in my throat before stepping out of my car. He made it a few steps away, but Denny turns, board swinging with him. "If you want to fuck around on your fiancée, that's your problem. But why did it have to be me? I told you on our first date that I wanted a serious relationship. You knew I was in it for the real deal, and you strung me along anyway. Why?"

Denny releases a long sigh. "You said it yourself, Summer: You've failed at dating for years."

My heart picks up speed, slamming into my rib cage, sensing danger. Still, I press him for more. "What's that supposed to mean?"

"Honey, come on. What do you expect? With all those tiny outfits you wear, ass practically hanging out of your shorts? All that weird sex shit you read about in books? You use your oven as shoe storage—I had to teach you how to scramble an egg." With a small laugh, his gaze fixes on my nose ring. I have a sudden itch to take it out, to drape myself in thick fabric rather than the fitted leggings putting my every curve on display. "You need a *vibrator* to get off—do you know how emasculating that is?"

My lip trembles and I hate myself for it. "I don't know how to fix that."

"And I'm sure there's a guy out there who could live with it. But when you want to be a wife and go years without any takers, then maybe it's time to accept there's something wrong there. Hell, your dad avoids you, your mom wants nothing to do with you. You've been following this guy Parker around all your life, and not even *he* wants you that way. Never made a single move on you." He gives what I think is meant to be a sympathetic smile, but it's all poison-tipped sharp edges, carving into me, bleeding me out right here in this parking lot. "You're the good-time girl. The one you laugh with, mess around with before it's back to reality. And that's completely okay. Honey, not everyone's wife material."

For some reason, I nod. And the quiet words out of my mouth are "Okay. Thanks."

That makes him smile wider, even as tears gather on my lash line. I try to gesture to my car, but my arm is made of lead. "I need to . . . I have to go to work."

I manage to shut the car door before the tears fall, but only just. They trickle, then pour. Harder and faster the longer Denny's words cycle in my brain.

Tiny outfits, good-time girl. Dad avoids you. Never made a single move on you. Nothing to do with you, back to reality.

Never made a single move on you.

I rip down the driver's side visor. In the mirror, my eyes are bloodshot, lips puffy, face soaked. With badly shaking hands, I pick at my nose ring until it falls free, and launch it into the back seat.

My teeth dig into my lip painfully hard; I'm trying to stifle my sobs but also make it hurt enough to forget—to offer a distraction from the words twisting and tearing inside me. When that doesn't work, I reach into my purse for my phone, thumb hovering over Parker's contact.

But I can't make myself do it. We've gone weeks without speaking after the awful things I said to him, and I couldn't withstand parsing through our fight only to hear that our friendship is over. Not ever, but especially not in this state.

I hit a different contact.

The phone rings, and I put everything I have into gathering myself. I hold my breath, shove the tears off my face. It rings and rings, and I grip the steering wheel with my free hand, willing my fingers to stop trembling. I wipe my nose on the back of my arm.

It rings and then cuts off, my dad's voicemail recording filling the inside of the car. I close my eyes, listening to his voice, but it brings me none of the peace I'd been searching for. I cough a breath into my lungs in a last-ditch effort to calm down before the tone sounds.

"Hi, Dad! I was hoping you had a minute to talk!" I barely sound like myself. I clear my throat, hoping it helps.

But could he even tell the difference?

When was the last time we spoke—truly spoke, without rambunctious toddlers distracting him or my stepmother in the room? When did he last ask me about something that wasn't work, or my friends, or—ironically—the latest town gossip?

"I just wanted—" My breath catches, and I swallow it down.

But what does it matter what I want?

I want my family back, but I get sent straight to voicemail. I want a partner, but I'm too defective to attract one. I'm . . . me. *A good-time girl. Not wife material.*

"Never mind, Dad, I . . . I totally forgot I need to be somewhere." I hang up, dropping my phone into the passenger seat.

Denny might be a monster, and I might hate the things he said. But it doesn't make them untrue, does it?

For years, I've tried to convince myself that I wasn't the problem—that sooner or later, my life would fall into place. A little longer, and I'd find the right person. A little longer, and my dad's life would slow down. A little longer, and my mother would start missing me. A little longer, and I'd have a proper home again.

So, I've kept at it.

I've dated. I've called, I've attended every family dinner. I've built friendships throughout my small town. I've dated more, and thrown parties, and smiled, and tried harder, and hoped harder, and all for what?

Here I am, crying alone in my car.

Wiping my face with the back of an arm, I yank open the glove compartment. Pull out an ancient, mangled notebook, and a pen that takes several aggressive scribbles to get the ink flowing again.

It's about damn time I see myself for what I am.

Chapter 13

Parker

The clink of heavy weights hitting a rubber gym floor used to bring me peace; it's been part of the soundtrack of my life since my football days in high school and here at UOB, and then training athletes after I graduated.

Now, though, that sound is the backdrop to the steady thrum of anxious energy coursing through me. After enduring Melody's gleeful laugh when she returned to our table last night, I made my friends swear they wouldn't tell Summer about . . . any of *that*.

I then spent the night restlessly tossing in bed, trying to figure this out. Toiling over their accusations and the very real possibility that I might be . . .

Shit, I can't even bring myself to say it.

I woke up overcome with the need to see Summer. Convinced that, now that the door has cracked open to the possibility that I might . . . I could lay eyes on her and simply *know*. One way or another.

Do I, or do I not?

My chin whips around every time the doors swing open at the other end of the training facility, expecting the bounce of Summer's hair, the soft clap of her sneakers on the floor, that bright grin as she lays eyes on her client. Always so approachable and ready to go, no matter what she's feeling that day.

But she doesn't show up, and I'm the most miserable prick on the premises because of it.

My mood is made even worse by the fact that I have absolutely nothing to do here today, seeing as I showed up unannounced. Don split my client list among the team during my absence, and after a quick talk about my possible full-time return next week, all I've done is sit on the workout bench with the best view of the doors, waiting on Summer's arrival.

"Nice to see you're alive." Noah strolls toward me, freshly showered after the session I watched Don put him through all morning. "I had Zac and Mel breathing down my neck all week, asking whether I was back on your schedule." Noah pauses, takes a better look at me. "You look rough as hell, man."

"I've been off sick," I tell him, resuming my vigil. "How's it been training with Don?"

Noah glances over his shoulder. "He has me on two-a-days."

I make a face. "Why? Training camp isn't for a while."

"He kept insisting. I agreed just to shut him up."

"Great." I'm sure the Hornets are going to love hearing that idiot's trying to exhaust their star quarterback in his off-season, after a deep playoff run.

"At least I got a muffin out of it." Noah happily unpacks one from his gym bag. "What's-her-name brought some in this morning."

A laugh bursts out of my mouth, surprising us both. "Kendra brought in muffins?"

Out of habit, my gaze bounces around the gym, looking for Summer. Noah breaks a piece off the top and offers it to me, shoving it into his mouth when I decline. "So, are you going to this planning party tonight? Summer threatened my balls if I skip it. Which I won't, obviously. I quite like my balls."

"Was this today? She texted you today?" I hadn't heard a peep from anyone about the planning party Summer put on everyone's calendars last month. I suppose it's a relief, knowing that she still plans on organizing a birthday party for me and my sister.

Noah gives me a look. "She texted me yesterday. Are you two *still* not speaking?"

A loud clapping draws our attention across the gym, where we find Don standing in the doorway to the adjoining rehab center. "Team meeting, everyone. Can I see you all in here?"

I give an irritated sigh. I saw the block in the team calendar when I showed up this morning, but had hoped to have made my exit before it came around. Noah hikes his bag up his shoulder, still munching on the muffin as we move across the gym.

"Are you back to work on Monday?"

"Maybe. I'll make sure you're on my schedule if I am."

The team is already surrounding Don by the time Noah and I part ways. Some sit on the ground, others prop themselves up on treatment tables. I stand at the very back of the group, with a perfect view of the doors. Just in case.

"I've got some exciting news," Don starts. "Obviously things have become busier than ever these last few months. We've had pro athletes from every major league wanting to work with this team after our effort in getting Brooks Attwood signed and winning his first shot at a Super Bowl after his injury."

My snort draws a fair share of stares, but I couldn't care less. He says *our effort* like Brooks hadn't specifically hired me for the job. Not a single one of them touched his training program other than Summer, and I wouldn't have let them near it if they'd tried.

Instead of correcting him, I pull out my phone and eye my dormant text thread with Summer. I wonder whether telling her I plan to skip tonight's planning party might get her to talk to me for the sole purpose of threatening my balls.

"Things are about to get even busier," Don continues. "We've just signed a deal with the Boston Sabres, to support their trainers with the recovery of players on their injured reserve. They were impressed with our work with Attwood and believe we can do it again."

My head snaps up. The Sabres are the top MLB team in their league. A deal like that would bring athletes of the highest caliber to our facility, and we—*I*—would be focused on recovery rather than running regular training routines. Again, I find myself looking for Summer.

"We've already got our first major client," Don says over the collective murmur. "As I'm sure you're all aware, Alfie Norton has suffered repeat injuries to his Achilles tendon, and—"

Alfie Norton? Fuck it. I'm texting her. She'll *have* to talk to me once she hears this. My fingers fly over my phone.

"That said, I'll be leading the program myself." My fingers freeze. "And Kendra here will be assisting me."

And that spark, that gasp of life inside me, fizzles out to nothing.

"Is that a joke?" The words slip out before I can stop them, and everyone, Kendra and her muffins included, turns to stare at me. "You're assigning Alfie Norton to yourself just like that? The rest of us don't even have a shot at it?"

"There will be opportunities in the future—"

"Opportunities bigger than *Alfie Norton?* The face of Major League Baseball?"

"I'm sensing some frustration."

"No shit you are." There are more than a few gasps around the room. I can feel my mind spinning out of control, all reason leaving the building. Can feel the threat of self-destruction coming, and coming fast. But I can't get it to stop, let alone make myself shut up. And the one person who'd have had a fighting chance at talking me down didn't make it to the show. "I've spent all year listening to you take credit for the work *I* put in with Brooks, like you even lifted a fucking finger."

"Parker." There's a warning in his tone, but I don't give a damn. This is the last drop in a bucket of bullshit, and I can't take it anymore.

"Yeah, *Parker*." I jab my thumb at my chest. "The guy whose work got you that deal to begin with. You have no idea how many hours out of my day it took to get Brooks into winning shape. I gave up my weekends for *months*. And I was the only reason he trained here in the first place. But hey"—I give a dry chuckle while Don silently stares—"maybe I didn't need to do all that. Maybe all I had to do was offer you my muffin."

Don's arms fall limply at his sides. There's a death sentence in the glare he sends across the room. "My office. Now."

"Let me save you the trouble." I move past the training staff littered around the room, all staring in varying degrees of shock, and head right for the exit.

～～～

"You quit your job?"

Melody's cocktail glass claps down to the countertop in her kitchen, color draining from her face.

I turn an irritated look on Noah, who felt the urge to announce my employment status barely thirty seconds into his arrival at Zac and Mel's waterfront house on the outskirts of Oakwood. Apparently, Don hadn't wasted any time letting my clients know I'd be permanently unavailable. "Thanks for that, Irving. Nice to know you can keep things to yourself."

He winces and retreats out of reach of Mel's scowl.

"That's it." My sister hops off the stool she's been perched on at the island. "Forget party planning. This is now an intervention."

"I don't need an intervention. Things just . . . got out of control, all right? But I'll figure it out. Get another job."

"Because Oakwood is rife with training facilities." I ignore Zac's sarcasm but accept the glass of water he hands me.

Obviously, the fact that there's only one gym in the whole of Oakwood Bay wasn't part of this morning's thought process. But, to be fair, there hadn't exactly *been* a thought process.

In fact, I'm not sure the reality has hit me quite yet. Since heading home from my untriumphant return to work, I've been a fidgety mess. I'm so close to laying eyes on Summer for the first time in a week.

The anticipation is eating away at me so bad, it hasn't been hard to ignore the watchful looks from Zac, Mel, and Shy, all likely wondering what kind of show they're in for after last night.

I wave a hand, dismissing Mel's concern. "Let's shelve this conversation. This night's about us, Mels. Planning our thirtieth birthday party."

Mel grimaces. "Neither of us care about a party. This is all Zac and Summer's doing."

I study my glass. "And . . . where is Summer exactly? Out of curiosity."

Noah snickers.

The front door swings open and goddamn, my heart almost gives out. It forgoes several beats and catapults into my throat, cutting off my air supply. I'm fairly certain Zac tries to make eye contact, but I can't return it. My gaze is stuck to the kitchen doorway.

It's been a long, drawn-out starvation, and I can't waste another moment of my miserable existence not looking at Summer.

Not knowing for sure.

"Oh my God, I'm so sorry I'm late! I totally lost track of time." Summer hurries into the kitchen, carrying a large white box in her arms.

I take her in like the greedy fucker I am. Her hair dances in her signature beach waves, skin glows with rosy cheeks. Toned, mile-long legs are covered in pale gray leggings, and a tight-as-sin tank top hugs every rise and dip of her upper body—over the swell of her tits, curving along her waist, showing off the hint of abs I've watched her work so hard for.

But am I . . .

Then Summer grins, lighting up the room, the entire hemisphere. Growing brighter as she lays her excited gaze on Melody. And dear God, I've never known jealousy like this. It claws at me, nearly gutting me of my sanity, and for a wild moment I truly consider shoving my own sister out of the way to have that smile all to myself.

Just like that, a mental dam comes crashing down, blinders come flying off. Because not within a single stretch of anyone's imagination is that a standard reaction to seeing a platonic friend smile at your relative, and . . .

Sophomore year of high school.

We were at a party, sitting around an empty spinning bottle of cheap vodka, stolen out of my parents' unmanned liquor cabinet. It had been my turn to play, and that bottle spun and spun around that circle of underagers, only to land pointing at my best friend.

She'd turned those sparkling green eyes on me and it was like clouds parting, rabbits pulled out of top hats.

Not love. But possibilities. Maybes, yeses. *Definitelys*.

Summer was always simply Summer to me. A constant, favorite presence in my life. It'd never occurred to me that I was allowed to *want* her that way. Until that bottle made her an option.

Made her *the* option.

For the first time in my life, I couldn't stop thinking about how very . . . *kissable* she was. How close together we were sitting, knees touching. How I'd come up with every excuse under the sun not to kiss the other girls at that party when that same bottle dared me to.

We'd stared at each other for one long moment, with my heart nearly bursting from my chest. To this day, I swear she stopped breathing, too. At least for a second. And as quickly as I thought *do it*, she'd laughed.

Full-on *laughed* at me.

Said she had a hard and fast rule against messing around within the friend group. And she'd ordered me to spin again.

I buried that *what-if* as quick as it came—filed it under *never gonna happen*. Snuffed it out before it got the chance to ignite into something else. Something big and unruly. Overwhelming. Something I couldn't undo.

I lived by the rule she'd made clear, almost to the point of obsession—our guy friends knew never to look twice at my sister, and I lumped Summer into that hands-off rule as best as I could. *No messing around within the friend group.* And I moved on with my life.

So I thought.

Now, in my sister's kitchen, with a full-blown audience, my head spins with years upon years upon *years* of Summer. Words and actions and little moments rearrange themselves in my head, telling an entirely different story than the one I held as truth.

The way I've spent my entire life tailing her like a happy puppy. Following her to college, staying in the town where she was, applying to the same job as her. I've built my entire life around this woman like it was second nature—how the hell had I never noticed?

I've never once braided another woman's hair.

Summer Fridays?

Summer fucking Fridays? I mean, come on.

"Don't look so tense, Mels. I know you're not a fan of parties but I came with ideas! All very *you*." Summer drops the box onto the island and sweeps Melody into a tight hug. My throat dries the longer I stare at them. The way Summer puts her whole body into delivering affection. The way my sister, who'd been stressed over the state of my life mere minutes ago, melts into Summer in response.

It's pure Summer. She's so present, perceptive. Gives you exactly what you need without even waiting on the full story. She's always been like this. Has done it for me countless times since the moment we met in that pillow fort, and . . .

There's not a damn question about it.

I am absolutely, unequivocally, categorically in love with my best friend.

That overflow of affection for her? Devotion in disguise. That constant craving for her company? Yearning. And then there's the lust. So much pent-up lust suddenly rushing through me that I feel like I'm on fucking *fire*. Needing to touch her and hold her and pin her down and—

My lovestruck spiral comes to a screeching halt.

A line forms between Summer's eyebrows, and she momentarily buries her face in Melody's shoulder before releasing her. She graces Shy and Noah with their own smiles. Conveniently, she ignores me and Zac in our corner of the kitchen. I'd be more upset by it if I weren't suddenly preoccupied with the nasty feeling that . . .

There. Her grin droops for half a heartbeat before she wrangles it back in place. She's clasping her hands together so tightly her fingers are pale. She's missing her nose ring.

What the fuck happened to her?

"Wow." Shy lifts the lid off the box Summer deposited on the counter and pulls out a cupcake. "Did you bake these yourself?"

Summer's grin wobbles again. "No, I don't . . . I don't cook, as you know. They're from the bakery in Baycrest."

"What were you doing in Baycrest?"

"Just . . . felt like hitting the boardwalk. Getting a change of scenery. All that ocean air really . . ." Her wandering gaze finally settles on me. "It's good for the system, you know?"

"Yeah." I nod, answering the question as though it weren't rhetorical. And it feels so good. Saying even a single word to her. Feeling her eyes on me for the first time in weeks. "Hi."

She doesn't say anything, just rubs her lips together while maintaining eye contact. The room is blanketed in heavy silence, every single person fixed on our wordless exchange.

Then I notice the pink in her eyes. But when I open my mouth to demand answers, Summer gives a minute shake of her head. And finding myself on the receiving end of her silent, secret signals again has me heeding the warning.

"Anywho!" Beaming once again, Summer flings an arm across the island, making room for the pink folder she places there. I hurry to catch the box of cupcakes before it falls to the ground. "Shall we dial in the LA crew?"

A moment later, her phone is propped up on the island with Brooks and Siena filling the screen. She claps her hands, calling to attention the uneasy looks being exchanged around the kitchen.

"Okay!" Her voice is several notches too bright, even for Summer. "As you know, Zac and I have been entrusted with organizing this joint birthday weekend—"

"Summer, are you all right?" Mel takes a tentative step closer to her. "You're acting a little . . . manic."

"Me?" Summer laughs, laying a hand on her chest. "You're so sweet for asking, but I'm great. Now, I took the liberty of investigating activities we could book for the weekend." Summer flips open her folder and plucks a sheet off the top. "What do we think about—"

My attention catches on the mangled piece of paper now on top of her pile. It's a bulleted list in her handwriting, dotted with dried-up splotches. *Tears?*

Mel's noticed it, too, and she slides it toward herself while I skirt around the island to get a look over her shoulder. Summer chatters away. "Of course, we can always do the typical nightclub thing, but that wouldn't be very *Melody and Parker*, you know? Thoughts? Questions?"

"'Can't cook,'" my sister mutters, reading off the tearstained paper. "'Clothes too short. Mom wants nothing to do with me.' Summer, what is this?"

I tug the list out of her hand, stomach sinking further with every line. *I'm the good-time girl.*

The room's gone dead silent. Miraculous, considering the racket my heart is making. Red blotches bloom on Summer's cheeks when she spots the paper in my hand.

She forces an airy laugh. "Oh, that? I thought it was about time for a mental reset. A fresh perspective! Given all my recent . . . turmoil." She reaches for the page but I yank it away.

"What. Happened?"

She feeds me a snarky little smile. "Growling, Parker, really? Those minotaurs really did pique your interest, didn't they?"

I shake the paper in my fist. I can't help how my voice comes out when I'm clutching a list of cutting, poisonous things she's written about herself. "Who said this?"

"I did." She makes a grab for the paper. Her fake-as-shit enthusiasm clouds over when I don't let her have it. "Cut it out, Parker. I mean it."

"Did you run into him? You ran into him, didn't you? I'm going to kill him."

"Don't you think maybe you've made enough rash decisions for one day?" Noah cuts in.

"What's he talking about?"

"He quit his job today," Noah supplies, helpful as ever.

Summer's eyes nearly bug out of her head. "Parker, are you insane? It's the only gym within a two-hour radius!"

"Tell me where he's staying." I fume, crumpling the paper in my hand. "Tell me now."

"Okay, that's enough," Mel snaps. It takes a whole lot of effort to drag my gaze off Summer's furious face and onto my sister's. "You two need to leave. Now."

"What?" Summer squeaks. "We haven't even settled on—"

Mel slices her hands through the air. "We've got an entire two months to figure out what we want to do for our birthday. But you two? You need to go figure out your shit before you're both disinvited."

Summer gasps. I scoff. "You can't disinvite us. It's my birthday, too. And she's my best friend."

"Yeah—what he said. You can't kick us out!"

"Try me," Mel says flatly.

"I wouldn't try her," Zac mutters from somewhere behind me.

I look around for support, but Shy and Noah are busy fighting laughter. On Summer's phone, Brooks and Siena sit chewing on gummy worms, fixated on us like we're primetime entertainment.

Melody's arm swings toward the hall. "Get. Out."

Chapter 14

Summer

My slow clap breaks the dead silence on Zac and Melody's front porch.

"Nice work, Woods. Really outdid yourself tonight."

The murder in Parker's eyes hasn't dimmed. He raises his fist with the stupid list I'd scribbled down this morning and spent the rest of the day rereading—making sure it sunk all the way in so that I'd never forget the words, could never again mistake who I am.

"Where did you see him?" Parker demands. "Was it while you were surfing?"

"No. I haven't been out in . . ." Holding back tears physically hurts at this point, but I try anyway. "I had a committee meeting. He was surfing."

"I will *end* him." I've seen Parker pissed off on several occasions. He's always led with impulse. Felt his emotions so deeply, never shied away from them. I've always envied him for that kind of vulnerability and courage, even when it drives me insane.

Tonight, though? He's never looked more prepared to commit vicious crimes on my behalf. Parker uncrumples the sheet of paper and jabs a finger somewhere near the bottom. "'Not wife material.' What does that mean?"

Humiliation forces heat up my neck. I make a grab for the paper, managing to take it back this time. "We're not even within the realm of discussing this, after the crap you've put me through."

"So, let's talk about *that*. You were the only reason I even showed up to work this morning."

"And, what? I wasn't there so you quit? God, Parker, do you ever just use your head?"

The porch lights cut off. We watch a figure about Melody's height walk away through the window in the front door, leaving us in the pitch black. The sun and moon are the only sources of outdoor light this far out of town, and neither are visible with tonight's cloud coverage. All I can see is the shape of Parker's body, large and tense.

"Great," I mutter, patting through my purse for car keys. "Now my best friend is pissed at me."

"I'm a little annoyed, but I'll get over it."

An unintentional chuckle blows past my lips, but I'm still unprepared to make nice. I move around him for the porch steps.

"I missed your laugh. Summer, you have no idea."

Goose bumps erupt over my skin despite the warm spring night. Parker's words are a whisper in the dark, feel like a caress to the back of my neck. Spoken so softly, devoid of frustration, and like nothing I've ever heard out of him. They catch me like a lasso around the knees and I buckle, start to teeter off the porch steps, until Parker's hand closes around my wrist. He tugs, and I stumble into the hard wall of his chest.

Home.

It feels like I've arrived home after a hell of a time away. Banged up and bloodied but so damn relieved to have returned somewhere I know.

"Please be careful," he whispers. "Need you in one piece."

"Okay." The word comes out sounding like a question, though I haven't got a clue what it's asking. His arms shift, and I expect him to circle me into a hug. Instead, his fingers brush down the length of my spine—a single soft pass, almost tentative, exploratory—before his palm settles on my hip.

And just like that, I feel anything but at home. I know nothing of being touched this way, not by Parker.

I blink, trying to get my eyes to adjust to the dark, but all I can make out is the shape of his eyes, the dip of his chin as he stares back at me. Stares *into* me.

"What are you doing?" I mumble.

"I don't know. What am I doing?"

It seems like an honest question. Like he's hoping I can fill in the blanks for him. Explain why we're standing so close, why his eyes haven't come off me, why his palm feels so damn possessive on my hip. Why his body feels this hot through his T-shirt, and why the familiar peppery scent lifting off him coils around my brain, rattling me, dulling the anger I've clung to for twelve too-long days without him.

A warm breeze flutters by, sweeping my hair over my cheek. "You're looking at me."

"Yeah. I'm looking at you." He hooks a finger around a strand of hair stuck to my lip gloss. His skin grazes my cheek as he tucks the mess behind my ear and my throat goes inexplicably tight.

My brain scrambles to catch up, to slot this moment into the mental scrapbook of me and Parker, and the way we are together.

Playful. Comfortable. Frustrating. This doesn't fit anywhere.

"I . . ." My fingers fumble around my car keys. We both start, stumble apart as a *beep* breaks the silence. The headlights on my car flare, bathing the porch in light.

"Fuck me." Parker runs a rough hand over his face, through his hair.

A sharp edge digging into my palm has me realizing I'm still holding my list. The weight of this day presses down on me. Between giving up my pop-up market, Denny's words, and Parker's . . . whatever that was, it has officially become more than I can bear.

I follow the light from my car down the porch steps. "I'm going home."

"Let me come with you. Let me talk to you." I've reached my car, but he hurries over, looking more frantic than I've ever seen him. "Summer, I'm sorry—"

"You made a scene in front of everyone," I burst, spinning to face him. "Do you understand how humiliating it was to find that out at the same time as the rest of town? To have them find out at all?"

"I wasn't thinking. I saw red—I just wanted him away from you." His lips move, struggling around more words. Parker throws out his arms as though urging them to appear from thin air, make their way to him. "I tried to vet him before I introduced you. I swear to you, I asked him if he was single, but . . ." He gives a helpless shrug. "I should've dug deeper, asked more questions."

"That's not the point. If he was willing to cheat, no amount of questions would've changed that. What you should've done is bring it to me privately."

"I know—I'm sorry," he says again. "Summer, you don't have to stop punishing me for it. But I need you to let me back in now. Please, invite me over."

I study him under the glare from my headlights. He's wearing a T-shirt that brings out the dark blue of his eyes and his usual backward hat, hair just tickling the back of his neck. There's nothing amiss with the outfit, but he looks . . . down to the bone exhausted. His face is thinner. Somehow, he's managed to lose weight in the twelve days since I've properly seen him.

He quit his job today.

And he's begging for me the same way my stinging insides beg for him, despite the carefully cultivated anger I've clung to since that night.

"Fine," I say at last. "But we're going to your place."

~~~~~~

I stand at the end of the hall, taking in the destruction of Parker's apartment.

Clothes strewn over his couch, food containers covering his counter, and stacks of water glasses in his sink. It looks like *my* apartment.

Parker fusses around the living room, tidying up. Shoulders tense under his shirt, avoiding eye contact. Even if I hadn't decided on a ceasefire before arriving, his evident shame at the state of his usually pristine home would have backed me right down.

Without a word, I collect the half-empty Styrofoam containers scattered over the kitchen island, then set them back down to empty the overflowing trash.

I blink back tears, overwhelmed with guilt. He's been struggling for months, and the last thing I told him was that I'd never forgive him. He needed me, and I was sitting across the street hiding behind anger.

"You don't have to do that." Parker stands in the middle of his living room, tightly clutching a pair of socks.

"I know I don't." I throw out the last of the containers before blowing out a steadying breath. "Parker, I'm sorry."

"I'm sorry, too." He comes around to help with the dishes. We work silently, arms brushing, shoulders bumping. There's more than enough space for both of us. But maybe, like me, he finds the contact reassuring. Whatever dark place he went to while we were apart, he's here now. And that's a relief beyond any I've felt before.

Dishes done, I pull out my phone and order a pizza from the shop a couple towns over. I load it with his favorite meats and the dairy-free cheese he needs, hoping it will entice him to eat.

"Thank you." Parker's fingers brush my lower back, punctuating his appreciation. My skin pulls taut with awareness, same as it did on his sister's front porch. Again, my brain struggles to make sense of it. "Go sit. I'll bring you a drink."

All I muster is a nod, folding a T-shirt tossed over a plushy sofa arm before taking a seat. I feel flustered in a way I've never been in Parker's company. Like coming back to the home you grew up in, and it looks the same as it always does, but not really. There are small, tiny things out of place. Not necessarily in a bad way, but just jarring enough to shake you.

"So, am I really stuck alone with Don and Kendra from now on?" I accept the Diet Coke Parker hands me, making room for him beside me. "How bad was it?"

He pulls a face. "I ripped him a new one during a team meeting and maybe, sort of, definitely insinuated he's been fucking Kendra."

I hang my head. "I'm gone for *one day*."

"I know," he groans. "See what happens when you're not around? I'm falling apart."

"And as lovely a sentiment as that is, you cannot keep doing this. I can't be the one saving you from destruction, Park. You need to own that. Take charge of your life." I linger on the dark circles under his eyes. "You can't stay so . . . *reactive*. It didn't do me any good with Denny; did you even less good with Don. And, look, you know I love you—"

Parker fumbles the Mountain Dew he'd been reaching for on the coffee table. "Do you?"

I clutch his arm. "Of course I do. We've been friends all our lives. A couple weeks apart can't change anything."

Parker takes a prolonged sip of his soda, glancing at where I still hold him. "Don signed a partnership with the Sabres because they saw what you and I did with Brooks. And then assigned himself and Kendra to Alfie Norton's recovery team."

My own soda can claps down on the coffee table, fizzing furiously. "*What?*"

"It drove me over the edge. But I shouldn't have quit. Not before having a plan, anyway." He rubs absently at the arm I'd just been holding. "I'm a mess, Summer."

"So am I. I've been avoiding town since your blowup with Denny. I guess I know how my mom felt." I hug a throw pillow to my middle. "Except that these are people I grew up with. They babysat me, I babysat their kids. And suddenly, I'm nothing to them. Maybe I shouldn't let it get to me, but I don't have very many *people* as it is."

Shame casts a shadow over his face. "I'll fix it, I promise. I'll knock some sense into them."

"No—no more knocking. I need you to stay out of it."

"I meant it figuratively. I'll speak to them, and I won't let you down this time—"

"I'm sorry, Park, but I don't believe you."

Parker flinches, his body pressing deeper into the sofa. The fridge across the room starts to hum noticeably loudly, drawing further attention to the tense silence as though my stomach wasn't already twisting because of it. Parker's anxious gaze sweeps the space, landing on the crumpled, tearstained paper on the kitchen island.

"Will you tell me about the list?"

Suddenly, Denny's words are a welcomed distraction. I deepen my voice, drawl it out the way Denny's sounds. "'Honey, not everyone's wife material.'"

Parker's expression darkens. "How much money do you have saved up? I've got a few thousand at least."

"Why?"

"I'm calculating my bail money. My parents would be useless, but d'you think Mels would contribute?"

"She just kicked us out of my own planning party."

Parker grunts. "We should've taken the cupcakes."

I huff a laugh, the first real one I've managed in a while. But then

Parker's gaze falls to my mouth and . . . heats? Again, I'm plucked straight from the familiar comfort of our friendship. Dropped somewhere a whole lot more restless, charged, and confusing.

A little . . . thrilling?

Good grief, what is wrong with me? This is Parker. And I've apparently become desperate enough to look for thrills where there aren't any.

I slap his shoulder, shuffling onto the next couch cushion. "Come on, you gotta stop looking at me like that."

Parker rubs at his face. "Denny had one thing right. You aren't meant for him."

"I know. I'm not meant for anyone."

"Summer, that's not what I'm saying."

"No, it's okay. There's only so long I can go on ignoring the signs." My gaze travels over his living room, landing on the pile of clean clothes now neatly folded on the dining table. "Do you ever think back to when we were younger?"

He nods. "Lately especially."

"I miss what I thought my life would be, you know? I keep thinking about the me of back then, eighteen and about to graduate high school. I had all these big plans for myself. How I'd finish college, travel for surfing, meet the guy that was my perfect fit. We'd get a house on the beach, have Sunday dinner with our families . . . I wasn't even dreaming that big, but it all turned out to be the stupid wish of a dumb kid anyway, with no idea what was really coming for her." For a moment, it looks as though he might reach for me. But Parker slots his hands underneath his thighs. "Part of me wishes I could go back and warn myself not to get my hopes up. And the other part just wants to be that girl again, so fucking optimistic."

I get to my feet, venturing to Parker's fridge just for something to do. It's empty but for soft drinks and beer.

Beer. That's what this day calls for.

I reach for a couple of bottles and hand one to Parker, taking a long pull of mine. "But you know what? This was the wake-up call I needed. I deleted all my dating apps today and it actually felt . . . liberating." I shake my head and my vision *whooshes*, the alcohol already taking effect. "And then I thought, you know what I should do?"

Parker reaches for my beer. "Slow down, for starters. Let's wait until the pizza gets here."

"Forget food." I snatch up my drink again. "I should be more carefree. Spontaneous; living in the moment."

Parker makes a face. "Trust me, unless you've got some kind of nomadic gene like my parents, that's not all it's cracked up to be."

A nomadic gene. Inherently built to exist in solitude, wandering and exploring the world without pressure to return home—or to find yourself a home to begin with.

"That sounds nice," I whisper. "What's the point of the alternative when I can"—I snap my fingers—"lose everything just like that. Hell, even your sister—my so-called best friend—kicked me out of her house tonight." Parker clears his throat. "Best friend after you, obviously. My point is, it's time I stop chasing a life that isn't meant for me."

"What does that entail?"

Another long sip of beer, and I place my bottle on the table. "I don't know—playing the field, no strings attached, for starters? Maybe . . ." I glare up at the ceiling, thinking hard, ignoring the feel of Parker's stare.

And then the metaphorical clouds clear above my head, sunrays beam around the brightest, *best* idea that's ever come to pass. "I'm going to enter Surf's Up."

Parker bobs his head. "This I can get behind. You used to compete all the time. It'll be fun."

"Not fun. I'm going to enter Surf's Up. *Win* Surf's Up. And I'm going to qualify for the Champions Tour."

I think of Denny and his friends, who travel the world chasing waves on the competition circuit, living off their winnings and spon-sorships. I'd have to place in the top two of Surf's Up to make it onto the tour. But then I'd be . . .

Gone.

The Champions Tour runs for a whole year, starting at the end of the current surf season. Even better, if I place high enough by the end of it, I'll qualify for the Masters Tour after that—the elite level above it. I wouldn't be forced to wallow in my silent apartment day in, day out. It wouldn't matter that all my dates are dead ends. Wouldn't matter that I barely have a family.

For years, I've been trying to make a home for myself. I thought I had one here, even after my parents left. But then my friends started leaving, too. The one person who made work tolerable up and quit today. I've got no partner tying me down, no matter how hard I've tried to find one who'd do just that. The people around town won't give me the time of day.

What am I sticking around for?

"What do you mean, you're going to qualify for the tour?" The quiet panic in Parker's voice draws me out of my nomadic fantasy.

Shit. He's in enough of a rough place without adding this to his pile. This will require easing him into. Making sure he's in a better place before I make my triumphant exit.

"Easy tiger." I pat his knee. "I only meant I'd qualify by default. Consider this an exercise in . . . revenge."

That doesn't seem to assuage his alarm. "I'm scared to ask what that means."

"It means I'm going steal that twenty-grand prize right from under the nose of the guy who's favored to win it this year: Denny. Someone needs to show him he can't toy with people's emotions. That there are twenty-thousand dollars' worth of consequences. I'm going to take it from him, and then spend the money on . . . shoes. Twenty grand worth of shoes."

I lift my phone off the coffee table and open the Surf's Up webpage. This is it. Exactly what I need. Making it onto the tour would be the perfect fresh start. A low-pressure lifestyle. Add in the shoes and revenge, and this plan sounds better by the second.

"When did you get a petty streak? This sounds like something I'd do." Parker watches my thumbs fly across my screen, entering my information into the online registration form. "Do you think that maybe you're using this revenge scheme as a way to avoid dealing with the contents of this list?" Parker gestures at the crumpled sheet on the coffee table. I shoot him a look. He sinks back into his seat. "Never mind. Do you think you can win it?"

"At the moment? No. Hobby surfing is completely different from competitive surfing. I've got the skill set, but my body is nowhere near primed for competition anymore. Which is where you come in, seeing as you now find yourself with plenty of spare time and happen to owe me several large favors after Denny-gate." Parker turns those deep blue eyes on me. "If I'm going to win—to teach that lying, cheating scumbag a lesson—I'm going to have to build some serious endurance in the water. The first of the three events is in a month. I need you to get my ass in gear, and fast."

Form complete, my thumb hesitates over the red SUBMIT button at the bottom of the screen. I meet Parker's wary gaze. "Should I do it?"

There's a pinch deep inside me, knowing I'm asking for his approval without giving him a clear picture. That if he knew what I was really in it for, he'd snatch away my phone. Tuck it out of reach until he knocked sufficient sense into me. Parker wouldn't get it—not with a family who loves him, the women around town clamoring for him. He's not on the outs with pseudo parental figures—doesn't need pseudo parental figures to begin with.

And it's not as though I'd just up and leave once I qualify for the tour. I'll tell him, as soon as it feels right.

Parker sits back, tips his beer to his mouth. He doesn't look at me, doesn't say a thing, clearly concerned for my sanity. I can't blame him. I've gone from wounded bird to vigilante surfer in the span of twenty minutes. But he's been the Thelma to my Louise since we were practically in diapers. There's no way he'd let me plummet off a cliff solo.

Squinting at my screen, Parker hits the SUBMIT button for me. His hand skims mine on the way, and I barely have a moment to contemplate why it's accompanied by a rush of heat to my face before he says, "Let's kick some adulterous ass."

Chapter 15

Summer

The mattress underneath me is rock-hard. Nothing like the plushiness I've grown accustomed to since I got it years ago.

I'm not strictly uncomfortable. The bed is pleasantly warm, smells heavenly, and the pillows I must have arranged around me feel like a cozy cocoon. It's so comforting I could easily fall back asleep, were it not for the strange, rhythmic *thump thump thump thump* in my ear, slowly bringing me to full consciousness.

My eyes flutter. And they wrench all the way open when I realize I'm not in my bed.

This is Parker's living room. Parker's couch. And that's Parker lying underneath me. His hair is a mess over the throw pillow he's using, eyes squeezed tight against the morning light filtering through the curtains. He's got one arm flung up over his head, and the other . . . wrapped around me. Holding me tight to him, with his massive hand tucked underneath my tank top, cupping the curve of my waist.

What the hell happened last night?

And how is he so *firm*?

The second question is a stupid one—I know exactly how he got this way. I've watched him work out every day for years. But I didn't *know*.

Remnants from last night litter Parker's living room. Soft drinks were eventually exchanged for copious beers. He agreed to train me for Surf's Up, we sealed the deal with too much alcohol, popped on a rom-com, and worked through a training program that'll occupy the entirety of my spare time this summer. Help me win the series. Qualify for the tour. And ship me out of the town that's let me down so deeply.

Or, as far as Parker is concerned, exact my revenge on Denny.

The night passed like plenty over the years—constant teasing and so much laughter my abs are sorer than if I'd powered through hundreds of sit-ups. And yet, it had been nothing like before. Because there'd also been touches lingering just a *smidge* past the point where they could pass as accidental. And then the staring.

Parker's going through something—obviously, given the impulsive unemployment and the state of his apartment when I arrived. I've never known depressive episodes to lead to touching and staring at childhood friends, but if that's what he needs to do . . .

I watch my fingers spread out over his soft T-shirt with deep fascination. The way they don't dent him in the slightest when I press down, testing the firmness of his body.

Parker shifts underneath me and the movement has me sliding farther down his body. The leg I had hooked over him knocks against the TV remote that somehow became wedged between us as we slept. Perhaps the right thing to do would be to get up, go home, let him have his rest. But he's still gripping my waist. And I'm comfortable. So, careful not to wake him, I slide a hand between us, looking to dislodge the remote.

My hand closes around the offending object and two things happen simultaneously.

First, Parker moans. A thick, loaded moan that hits me right between the thighs. Sends lava rushing through my veins.

Second, I realize I don't have my hand around a TV remote at all. It's *him*. I've got my fingers curled around Parker's hard-as-nails, *thick-as-fuck*—

"Oh my God," I whisper-shriek, yanking back my hand. "Why is it so fucking big?"

And then things go from bad to worse. Parker releases a sigh, this soft sound I feel in every inch of my body, before mumbling, "*Summer*."

Oh my God.

I'm paralyzed on top of him, my body cycling furiously through its options: fight, flight . . . wake him up and see if he'll let me touch him some more. Wait, no—

"Get a grip," I command myself in a whisper.

Carefully, I peel myself off Parker. Deliberately avert my eyes, because I am a *gentlelady* who'd never think to objectify my closest friend, and . . . My jaw actually drops.

Good *grief*. What does a man even do with a dick that big, anyway? It's absurd. As is the sexual prowess that surely accompanies it—a man can't simply go around stabbing that kind of thing into women, willy-nilly. That kind of package requires serious skill.

I wonder if anyone's ever needed a vibrator to come with Parker. Probably not, but it would be just my shitty bedroom luck that I'd be the one to break his toy-less streak.

Hypothetically, of course.

Parker gives a satisfied *hum*, and I should really get up. Get out of this apartment and pretend I never saw, felt, heard any of this. Instead, my lust-addled brain shouts silent questions at him.

What am I doing to you?

What gets you moaning like that?

What makes your abs tense under your shirt like this?

A heartbeat blooms between my thighs, and I squeeze them together against the sudden demand for relief. I've gone my entire post-puberty life without going there with Parker. Maybe I've been curious about him after the things I've heard lately, but I've never once touched myself thinking about him.

It's always felt . . . not *wrong*, but against some cardinal rule of friendship. Crossing a line I could never come back from. But fuck if it doesn't take everything in me to stop from reaching down my leggings at the sound of his sighs.

And then his hand wanders down his own body, blindly looking for—reaching for—Parker's fist closes around the shape of his cock. He groans. And I momentarily black out.

One second, I'm kneeling over him, soaking him in. The next I'm falling off the couch with a yelp. I smash into the coffee table. Beer bottles clink together, topple over. Parker jerks awake at the racket, eyes springing open, finding me crumpled on the floor.

"Summer?" His voice is thick with sleep but all I can hear is the way he moaned my name. I scramble to my feet, shoving my hair behind my ears.

"Good morning!" I flap my hands, frantically searching the room for my purse. "I was just leaving!"

"Why? It's Saturday." He runs a hand over his face, propping himself up on an elbow. "Stay. Let's get breakfast."

"Oh, no. That's . . . No." My bag lies under a discarded throw pillow and I toss the strap over my shoulder, looking anywhere but at him. I jab a thumb toward the door. "I'm going to go. Thanks for the visual—the *visit*! Thanks for the visit."

Screaming inside my own brain, I shoot across the apartment and swing open the front door. Parker's arm darts over my shoulder, snapping the door shut before I can escape.

"Summer."

"Yes?" I squeak.

"Turn around, Summer."

My forehead falls against the door. He's standing so close I can feel his body heat. "I can't."

"Was I talking in my sleep?"

"Why would you think that?"

His exhale dusts over the back of my neck. My eyes fall shut. "I was dreaming about you."

The shock of his brazen confession has me spinning around. Parker stares at my mouth, the way my teeth dig into my lip. Against my wishes, my own gaze falls down his body. He's clutching a cushion below his waist, as though the damage hadn't already been done. As though I'll ever be able to scrub the sight of his absurdly enormous, utterly *ridiculous*—

"Looking for something?"

"No!" My stare zips up to meet his. "What on earth would I be looking for?"

His head tilts ever so slightly. "What indeed."

"All right, fine." I force a bright smile. An easy smile. Breezy as hell. "Look, we're all adults here. There's no need to feel awkward about this."

The tilt of his head deepens. "Awkward about what?"

"The . . ." I can't even say it. "You know what."

"I assure you, I don't. I was dead asleep until you made a racket." His teeth scrape over his lip. "Feel awkward about what, Summer?"

"You might've . . . said . . . done . . . some things with . . ." Why? *Why* did I just gesture at his— "But as I said, it's nothing to be embarrassed about. These sorts of dreams happen to the very best of us."

"I'm not embarrassed," Parker says unflinchingly.

"Oh?"

"It's my favorite dream." My back presses against the door, head falls back to look up at him. He conducts his own assessment of me, gaze bouncing over my face. As though he's given me an opening with that confession. And he's waiting to see what I'll do with it.

What the hell does he want me to do with it?

"Do you . . ." I clear my throat. "Have it often?"

"If I'm lucky. Why are you blushing so hard?" That head tilt goes even deeper. "Are we talking about the same thing?"

I hesitate. "We're talking about the dream you just had. The one where you and me—"

"Go to the zoo and—"

"Have sex!" I finish at the same time. *No.* My hands fly up, clasping my cheeks. "What?"

"That . . . that time in the tenth grade when we went to the zoo. You dragged me to the insect pavilion and dared me to volunteer to have that tarantula crawl over me. I was so mad I let you talk me into it." Parker's brows pull together. "Wait. You thought we were—"

"Oh *God*, I'm never living this down, am I?" I wail, face heating furiously. I nudge at him, trying to create enough space to back off the door and make my escape, but he doesn't move. "You were dreaming about the *zoo?*"

The shallowest of dimples appears in his left cheek. "Nah, we were definitely fucking. Just wanted to see you blush again."

My breath audibly catches. I've heard him use the phrase before, but never about . . . us. It forces awareness into my skin. Of *him*, his size, his body heat. The teasing spark in the depths of his eyes that truly never goes away. His hair is charmingly disheveled, and he has faint pillow creases on his cheek. He still clutches the pillow to himself. It's so bashful and at odds with his words about *us* that something fizzes happily deep inside me—this delicious twinge in my stomach I've never felt before.

You've been following this guy Parker around all your life, and not even he wants you that way. Never made a single move on you.

The fizzing fizzles at the memory of Denny's words, a harsh but evidently needed reminder that Parker has never thought of me that way. Has never wanted me. Surely, whatever's gotten into him is nothing more than a bizarre side effect of his delayed quarter-life crisis.

"Parker, this is not . . . I know we took a mini friendship break, and your memory might be a little fuzzy on the particulars. But this isn't us." I'm saying the words to us both. "We should endeavor to return things to normal. The way they were before."

He's quiet another long, drawn out moment. "Is that what you want?"

"Is there another . . ." I blow a frustrated breath through my nose. "Of course, that's what I want. We're friends."

"Friends." The word ping-pongs between us. Bouncing off my confusion. Lobbed right back at me by Parker's steady stare.

Then he blinks. Shakes his head as though clearing it of fog, before breaking into an easy smile. "Of course we are. I'm glad to have you back, Sum."

Chapter 16

Parker

My freshly washed hair soaks the seat cushion when I flop back onto the couch a while later, head full of Summer.

Specifically, what to *do* about Summer, and these feelings that've suddenly decided they're done living in silence. It's as though years of repression strengthened their resolve to throw my insides into disarray. Unleashing this incessant chant of *mine mine mine* in my brain whenever I look at her. Frying all rational thought.

Daring me to test the waters, to see whether she's been repressing it, too.

Except she demanded friendship and normalcy. Fled my apartment. And I guess it's my lot in life to die a slow, painful death, crushed under the weight of these feelings for her.

Blowing a breath at the ceiling, I tug my phone out of my sweats.

PARKER: How'd you do it?

The reply comes several long minutes later.

ZAC: FYI, if you're trying to deliver context through telepathy, it isn't working.

PARKER: You were in love with my sister for years. How'd you keep it to yourself for so long?

This time, the gray dots at the bottom of my screen flicker right away, his answer appearing just a breath later.

ZAC: If I could do it all over again, I'd tell her the moment I realized how I felt.

With a groan, I toss my phone onto the coffee table. I don't know why I bothered. There's one glaring difference between our situations, which is that my sister had been pining for Zac just as hard, and just as long. When I got my head out of my ass and realized what was going on between them, there was no question that they belonged together. Fit together perfectly. He was exactly the kind of guy she needed. He made her life better.

I can't be the one saving you from destruction, Park . . . Take charge of your life.

Summer's words hit me square in the stomach, same as they had last night. Of course she doesn't feel the same way. She's *Summer*. The fantasy of fantasies. A dream you write off as being too far-fetched, but can't help hoping it comes back around the next time you close your eyes. She's a woman deserving of castles and shrines erected in her honor. Not some guy who can barely keep his head on straight these days. Who's unemployed. Living above a bar, without drive or ambition.

I'm a dead end. If I ever encountered a guy like me supplicating at Summer's altar, I'd drag him away. Tell him to hit the bricks. Try his luck elsewhere.

At least I don't have to worry about her shipping out of town anytime soon, like my sister did to Zac.

The buzzer goes off at my front door. I force myself to my feet and hit the intercom button.

"What?" I bark.

There's an awkward pause before a voice I faintly recognize fills the hall. "Is this Parker Woods?"

"Yeah, it's me. Who's this? And how did you figure out where I live?"

"Uh . . . Everyone in this town knows where everyone lives."

Fair point. "And who're you?"

"Right, yes. This is Colin Nowak. I taught you and your sister history in high school?"

I frown at the intercom. "Pretty sure I don't have any homework due."

He chuckles, undeterred by the dickishness that can't stop pouring out of my mouth. "No, you don't. But I'm hoping you might be able to help me—*us*—with something else. Specifically, my son River—"

Colin is cut off by someone in the background, words that sound vaguely like *fucking pointless*. What draws my attention most is the absolute bitterness in that voice.

Then it clicks.

Late last year, seventeen-year-old River Nowak got stuck driving through the worst thunderstorm I've ever witnessed. I'd been sitting it out in this apartment with Summer, playing board games over candlelight after the power cut off. And the sound of River's car crashing into the diner on the street below had startled us worse than any clap of thunder before it. The destruction had been visible from up here, even through the rain and fog: an ancient oak tree split by lightning, lying across the road and crushing the roof of the Nowaks' old silver Chevy, which was partially buried inside the diner.

Word around town was that it'd taken River a couple of days to wake up in the hospital he'd been airlifted to. The bones in his right leg had broken in several places, putting the kid—who'd been quarterbacking the local high school's football team—on crutches ever since.

Colin clears his throat from down on the sidewalk. "The thing is, we've tried several physical therapists, all the ones at the hospital in the city. But unfortunately, they didn't . . . They weren't a good fit."

"It wasn't my job to maintain their precious feelings, Dad. I'm the one on fucking crutches."

Again, I'm struck by the kid's voice. It's not just bitterness. There's defeat in there, too. And my heart goes out to him, it really does, but . . .

"What do you want from me? I've got things to do today." My bed's calling my name.

"I heard you were let go from your job," Colin rushes to say. "And I'm here to offer you a new one, working with River."

Oh, hell no. Don's telling people he *fired* me?

I wrench open my door and march down the steps leading to the street below. Colin Nowak startles when I throw open the door. Aside from the graying ginger hair and faint lines on his face, he looks exactly like he had as our history teacher. Tall and lanky.

"The Oakwood rumor mill, man. It truly never rests," I say.

He retreats a step. "Pardon me?"

"I *quit* my job. Sure as fuck wasn't fired."

"Guess that makes him slightly less useless than he was five seconds ago." River stands a little farther down the sidewalk, propped on a pair of silver crutches. Despite his height and the spotty red facial hair, he's still just a baby-faced kid. If babies were capable of shooting that much hate from their eyes.

"You got something to say to me, big guy?"

All he does is scoff, but his father seems to have recovered from my abrupt presence. Colin steps closer, drops his voice. "The thing is, Parker, River here is a big fan of Brooks. And seeing as you trained him back to the NFL, I'm hoping that working with you encourages my son to . . ."

I stare expectantly, without saying a word.

"To *try*," Colin says quietly. "He's driven away everyone else who's worked with him. But I'm hoping that your experience—"

"I don't have experience with this." River turns his back on us, staring down the street in the direction of the decrepit diner. "Pediatric therapy isn't my area."

"He's almost eighteen. Isn't it close enough?"

Colin's desperation manages to dim my growing impatience. Technically, I've worked with UOB freshmen barely older than River.

"Are we done wasting our time yet?" River says. "We've tried fifty different people, and none of them have fixed me. The football season starts in three months. *Scouts* show up in three months. And there's no college on this planet that wants a quarterback with a limp."

"Please," Colin begs. "If this doesn't work I don't know what else to do for him."

River is still staring down at the diner. His shoulders are tense, hands tight around his crutches. I can't see his face, but I'm not sure I want to, convinced it's manifesting emotional pain worse than any of the physical kind he must've endured after his accident. I can imagine exactly what he's thinking: He's an athlete—a good one at that—who had an entire career snatched away by a fallen oak tree.

And how unfair is that? He's just a kid.

I heave a sigh. "What's going on with the recovery?"

Hope flares in Colin's eyes. "I've got his scans in the car—the bones healed. But there's a nerve that pinches whenever he puts too much pressure on the leg."

There's a pillow and glow-in-the-dark stars calling my name upstairs. I should probably get something to eat. Summer will get over this morning eventually—maybe I can convince her to spend the day with me. Distract me from the fog in my brain.

I can't be the one saving you from destruction, Park . . . Take charge of your life.

I bid a sad farewell to the prospect of sleep. "Fine. I'll agree to an assessment. But I'm not making any promises."

~~~~~

"Try it. I said *try*, River."

"Why don't you say it again? Maybe then I'll be able to do it."

At some point during my break from work, all semblance of professionalism has departed my body. Because the look I level at the moody kid suddenly in my charge would've gotten me fired from UOB long before I'd have had the chance to expose my philandering ex-boss.

River sits on one of the workout benches lining the massive garage Brooks converted into a gym at the home he and Siena keep here in Oakwood. He sent me the code to the doors without even questioning why I wanted access to his house.

Meanwhile, I'm seriously questioning all my decisions.

Half an hour into this physical assessment, it's clear that River Nowak has a long way to go before he's back on a football field. He's not in physical shambles, exactly. The alignment of this leg and hip is out of sorts, and he's lost a ton of strength after the injury and the months of failed therapy. But it's fixable. Workable.

What's going to do him in is his defeatist mentality. And here's the thing about having trained athletes for as long as I have: It became obvious real early in my career that half the battle happens in the mind.

I could do only so much to get Brooks back to peak physical shape last year. If he hadn't wanted it, been willing to fight tooth and nail for that comeback to the NFL, he'd still be here in Oakwood.

River grinds his teeth, working to shove the foot of his injured leg against the resistance of my hand. His palms find the edge of the bench and he shoves harder.

"Hands off the bench. I told you, it doesn't count if you use leverage."

"And I told you I can't fucking do it," River snaps. He yanks his leg out of my grip.

I straighten out of my crouch, ripping the backward hat off my head just to wrench my fingers through my hair. This kid is gonna make me lose my damn mind.

"It's an assessment," I say for what's got to be the fiftieth time since we arrived. I expect I'll have said it another fifty by the time River's dad comes to rescue me from this miserable decision. "I don't need you to be able to kick my arm out of my socket. I only need to know what I'm working with."

River sneers up at the raftered ceiling. "You saying I'll eventually get to knock your arm out of your socket?"

"At this rate, you'll be lucky if you ever lay eyes on me again."

River shoots me a glare that very clearly wishes fire and blood upon me. "My dad's on his way back. We can lump this in with all the other failed experiments since I got this way." River reaches for the crutches propped farther down his bench, yanking them closer as though preparing for a swift exit.

And that there—the glimpse of defeat that leaks through the bitter armor River wears—is the only reason I haven't called Colin to demand his early return. Apparently, the dark pit inside me hasn't spared me from my sense of sympathy.

I drop onto the bench across from River. "What the hell *did* happen to you that night?"

River looks at me like I'm an idiot. "Raging storm? A tree crushed my car?"

"We were all warned to stay inside during that storm. What were you even doing out there?"

"Who cares? It happened. No point revisiting it."

"Whatever, man. Just making conversation." I fiddle with the yellow resistance band sitting next to me, fingers skimming the rubbery surface. "Your leg isn't that bad—"

"Fuck you," River mutters. "You have no right to say that."

"Actually, I'm exactly qualified to say that. And when your dad asks, I'll tell him the truth: that if you spend the rest of your summer working with me, you'd have a solid chance at making your high school team. Just in time for those college scouts to watch you play."

River's wandering gaze flies to my face.

"When your dad asks," I continue, enunciating carefully, "I'll also tell him the other truth. Which is that if you don't work through what's going on *here*"—I tap my temple—"you won't see the inside of a locker room for the rest of your life."

My words go down about as well as predicted. River looks like he's been sucker punched in the mouth, visibly working to salvage his mask of teenaged indifference. "What do you even know? You got fired from your job."

Irritation spikes inside me, grabs me by the throat. I open my mouth to tell him he can fuck right off with that . . . and I shut it again. River stares at the blue socks on his feet, dejected as hell. As good as it would feel to let him have it, it won't do *him* any good.

"Like I said, I *quit* my job," I say once I've got a handle on myself. River doesn't deign to respond, so I pull out my phone and stare down at my message thread with Summer.

Maybe I should apologize for this morning.

"Why'd you quit?"

River isn't looking at me. His eyes wander around the gym like he doesn't care about my answer. But he still bothered asking.

I turn my phone over. And I really think it through, for the first time since quitting. Yes, I hated my job. Yes, Don is an incompetent asshole and the favoritism he showed my colleague was way out of bounds. But there's another truth I haven't voiced, even to myself.

There's no point hiding from it in this empty home gym, with a kid I'll never speak to again.

"Because I was tired of feeling like shit about myself. And my bedroom felt safer from disappointment."

River is silent for a long time after that. He stares down at his socks again, apparently deep in thought. Meanwhile, I'm struck by the relief of saying those words out loud. Acknowledging how unhappy

I've been, and the fact that I haven't had it in me to do anything productive about it.

Telling River Nowak, of all people, feels like a first, shaky step in
digging myself out of the mess I've made of my life.

Finally, River stretches out his leg. Winces as he points and flexes
his foot. "Pussy."

I snort. "Takes one to know one."

He shoots me another moody glare. But I swear, I see something resembling a laugh in his eyes. The sound of tires running on
asphalt breaks the silence, and we watch Colin's car pull up the driveway through the open garage door. I don't bother getting up, already
contemplating an afternoon nap.

River makes it all the way outside before turning his chin over his
shoulder. "Are you free tomorrow?"

Chapter 17

Summer

"Hey Dad, you'll never guess what I did—I entered Surf's Up! Crazy, right? I always thought I was done competing for good, but . . . the itch came back, I guess. So, listen, I know you've got lots going on, but maybe you could come out with me again, like you used to? Not . . . not the daily surfs, obviously. I know you're busy. But maybe competition days? I always surfed better when you were there. And bring Estelle and the twins, too! I'd love to have them there—friendly faces in the crowd and all that. Then maybe we could—"

Beeeeeeep.

The tone cuts me off.

I hang up, knowing that my words will likely collect digital cobwebs in Dad's voicemail inbox, which he never seems to check. Still, I couldn't help a last-ditch effort to salvage whatever's left of our relationship. And what better way to do that than to reconnect over the thing that made us so close to begin with?

Dad had grown up in the ocean as a West Coast kid, and I fell in love with it just as deeply after he taught me to surf. He registered me for my first junior surf competition at thirteen, but it wasn't until a couple years later that I really started hitting my stride, placing in the top three of every single junior event I competed in. Surfing was ours—mine and Dad's. He'd train with me, never miss an event before our life fell apart.

I toss my phone into my bag, sitting in the sand next to my freshly waxed surfboard, legs outstretched toward the water.

Crystal Cove is quiet this morning, just a couple of surfers dotting the ocean. It probably has something to do with the lackluster waves currently flowing toward shore. And while I love the comradery of a busy ocean, I'm glad for the relative quiet. It's exactly the kind of practice I need—learning to embrace solitude, my own company, before hopefully embarking on a year's worth of it.

Making the Champions Tour became the dream as soon as I learned of its existence. It was ultra cliché, really—I was a small-town girl with an appetite for the great big world. And the idea that I could see it while competing in a sport I loved . . .

The plan had always been to compete locally while fulfilling my promise to my dad to get a college degree. Then, I'd be free to qualify for the tour that would take me to the world's dreamiest surf locations—from Hawaii to Portugal to Australia, and everywhere in between.

But then Dad announced he was moving out of town to live with his then-partner Estelle. He stopped showing up to watch my local events. And I could never again muster the desire to compete, let alone leave Oakwood.

It's ironic that the loneliness that kept me rooted at home has set me right back on the path I'd given up on because of it.

Far down the shore, a row of bungalows with washed-out blue siding sits higher up the beach, their weathered picket fences lining the edge of the sand. Years ago, there'd been a version of my future where I stepped out the front door of one of those bungalows every morning to surf. It'd be my home base between tours, and then the place where I'd eventually teach my own kids to surf, the way Dad taught me. Now, though . . .

Not everyone's wife material.

A *thump* to my left coaxes my attention off the bungalows. A navy surfboard now sits on the sand next to mine, along with a pair of familiar, athletic legs.

"There you are. Don't you usually leave home at six?"

I drag my gaze up those legs to find Parker frowning at me. He's wearing swim shorts and a T-shirt, hair so thoroughly disheveled it's clear he hadn't stopped to tidy it before leaving his apartment.

I snort a laugh at the sight of his Hawaiian shirt, the horrendous highlighter orange and murky brown pattern coaxing me out of my misery. "Nice shirt, Park. You look like a hot suburban dad trying his *very darndest* to let loose on vacation."

"You mock, yet all I heard was *hot*." His mouth tilts up at my flush. He jerks his chin toward the bungalows I'd been staring at. "Still pining over those houses, huh?"

I brush a dusting of sand off my thigh. "What are you doing here?"

"Surfing."

"Parker, you've never surfed in your life."

"You're going to teach me. I'm your trainer, I need to get a feel for the body mechanics."

"I'm working with a future NBA star and I've never sunk a free throw in my life. That's what textbooks are for."

"Fine." Parker drops into the sand beside me, spreading his legs, bent at the knees. "Then you'll teach me because I want to surf with you. Come here, let me do your hair."

With a burst of pleasure and a touch of confusion, I settle between Parker's open legs, letting his fingers run through my hair. I missed this ritual more than anything.

Except, much like everything since our reunion, it's just different enough to unsteady me. The way his fingers move, stroke through the short lengths of hair. There's no efficiency. It's slow, like we've got hours ahead of us, and he plans to spend every second of them tangled in my hair. It's gentle, like each strand is some precious length of the rarest silk. Indulgent, like he's gone years forced to rush the job, and he's finally letting himself take his time.

He skims the back of my neck for no other apparent reason than to make my breath hitch. Brushes my shoulder just to make my heart gallop.

I should stop him. There's no *friendly* to be found in any part of this. But it's feeding the parts of me that crave attention. I like it too much to stop him.

"I miss your nose ring. Have I said that yet?" Parker ties off the second braid with the hair ties he keeps around his wrist. The uncalled-for proclamation has me laughing uncertainly. I feel him shrug, like it was perfectly placed commentary. "It's part of you. It'd be the same as if this freckle disappeared." The tip of Parker's finger lands by my hairline, on the tiniest freckle that blends with the baby hairs along my forehead.

"I have tons of freckles."

"That one's my favorite. It's your secret freckle. You can only see it close up." I don't know what to say to that, but Parker saves me the trouble when he gives one of my braids a tug that elicits a strange, giddy flash inside me. "So, will you teach me to surf?"

"You're really serious about it?" I don't know why I'm fighting it so hard—the idea of having Parker out there with me has my stomach twinging pleasantly.

"Definitely. Just show me enough not to end up at the bottom of the ocean. And if that fails, just promise me you'll give my collection of Hawaiian shirts to Brooks if I die. I need him to have it."

I turn a frown over my shoulder. "You're leaving it to Brooks? I thought I was inheriting them."

Parker's collection is embarrassingly large. He'd bought his first Hawaiian shirt on an out-of-town shopping trip we'd taken in the weeks following my parents' split—a ridiculous yellow-and-hot-pink combination that had me cackling when he tried it on. Every pattern since has been increasingly ridiculous. It always guarantees a good laugh whenever I see him in one.

"Nah, you'd just keep them in the back of your closet. They'd never see the light of day."

"But Brooks hates your Hawaiian shirts." Honestly, I'm a little miffed about this. Why does *Brooks* get Parker's prized collection? I was there from its inception.

"He does hate them. But he has such a guilty conscience that he'd force himself to wear them just to honor me. Prime afterlife entertainment." I stay quiet as the tip of his finger traces the length of my shoulder. "Summer, are you mad you're not getting my Hawaiian shirts?"

I know that he's teasing me. But damn him, I'm mad I'm not getting the Hawaiian shirts. It's a matter of principle. "I'm not mad. I'm disappointed."

"You can inherit my shirts if you want them," I grumble. Parker tugs at a braid again. It makes me feel strange—all fluttery and hot, even worse when he starts quietly laughing and I picture the dimples in his cheeks. "Summer, if I sink to the bottom of the ocean, I want you to inherit my shirts."

I grin. "Thank you."

With another laugh, his arm drapes across my chest, drawing me back into his body. It's comfortable. Familiar, the way it feels to be hugged by Zac or Brooks.

But it's also not. There's tingling over my skin. A maddening uncertainty. Between the braiding and the favorite freckle and the tugging, he's making my head spin. Acting like himself, but *just* out of character enough to make it impossible to predict his next move.

And I can't stop thinking about it—the way he moaned my name in his sleep yesterday.

He's gone and put that damn idea in my head, worse than that town rumor ever had. Made all the more frustrating knowing that it'll never, *ever* happen.

Aside from the fact that I've never considered anything more with him—our friendship has always been such a perfect fit, it's hard to imagine it differently—he's going through a tough time. Saying and doing things that aren't him. And when he's feeling like himself again, all this staring and dreaming about me will dissipate. It's up to me to make sure we stay the course of this friendship.

Nah, we were definitely fucking.

He'll thank me in the end. We'll have a nice, friendly laugh about all the morning wood and staring, and settle back into our normal.

With a squeeze of his forearm, I extricate myself and shuffle around to face him. His expression is unreadable. "What do you know about how surf competitions work?"

"I watched you compete for years, at this exact beach." Parker lifts an eyebrow and he's not so unreadable anymore. "You'll be in the water for thirty-minute heats, leading up to a two-way final round between the top scorers."

I nod. "Assuming I make it to the final round."

"You will."

I wish I had half of Parker's confidence. Waves are scored by judges based on their level of difficulty and on the maneuvers a surfer performs. I'll be able to catch as many waves as I can during a heat, but only my two best will count toward my ability to move to the next round.

Scores from each of the three events are tallied to decide the final series standings. And each event is weighed more heavily as the series progresses, and the surf spots become more challenging. Rocky Ridge is weighed lowest, as the easiest spot—if you can even call it easy— then Crystal Cove, and Pine Point as the hardest.

Pulling the wax out of my bag, I kneel by Parker's board and ready it for our lesson. It's brand-new, clearly purchased just for me—just for *this*. Training together.

His fingers dust over a strip of skin below my shorts, brushing away the sand sticking to me. Again, I'm infuriatingly aware of him. He's not even that close, isn't even looking at me, and all I feel is *him*.

And then the man loses all mercy when he reaches behind him and pulls off his shirt.

We were definitely fucking.

"We'll head to Brooks's gym right after this, get a session in before you go to work," Parker says, meeting me at his board. "I brought a waterproof camera to record you while you do your thing out there. We can study the footage after, see what needs improving before your first event."

"Good idea." I avert my eyes from the solid plains of his upper body and sweep his board's leash off the sand, strapping it to his right ankle.

As I walk Parker through the basics of reading waves, I manage to stay decidedly focused on the lesson, my board, the sand around us, anything and everything but the shirtless man beside me. Until I'm walking him through the mechanics of a pop-up.

I've been surfing for decades, surrounded by highly experienced men and women performing this exact move out in the water. And yet, I've never seen something as simple as the prone position look as pretty as Parker's.

Parker pushes his upper body off his board, revealing six perfect abs bunching to help carry his weight. Tanned biceps flex, the muscles over his shoulder blades ripple. He's staring down at himself checking his form, so his hair falls over his face in thick, messy waves, damp from humidity.

I've never had a hair fixation. Then again, I've never met another man with a head of hair as inviting as Parker's. Despite the perpetual mess, the pale brown strands always look soft enough to bury your face in. Long enough to get a good handful, twist around your fingers. Use it to pull him in, and—

I don't have a real sense of what he's like in bed, but I do know Parker. He might not be a big-picture guy, but no one is as attentive and dedicated as him when he's got a job in front of him, something to achieve. All he needs is a little direction, and he takes off running.

I can easily imagine that intense focus translating to the bedroom. Can see his gaze raking up my body, assessing, teasing me in that way he loves to do, drawing it out until I'm an aching mess below him. The way his hands would move over me, the cocky grin he'd wear when he discovered exactly the right tempo and pressure to make me squirm. The way his cock would fight against the front of his jeans as he toys with me until I'm begging for him.

Parker executes another pop-up, ass flexing against his blue swim shorts. "That one felt better. Did it look good to you?"

"So good," I whisper without thinking. Parker whips his hair out of his eyes to get a look at me, quite possibly catching me in the act of admiring his backside, but I can't tell from the quiet, contemplative way he stares back.

I don't want him to know I've been looking and thinking about him in wildly inappropriate ways. I don't want to encourage the new possessive touches, or the quiet stares, or the way his blue eyes spark with something teasing the longer he looks at me now.

Don't I?

With just a hint of a dimple, Parker takes pity on me and steps off his board. "I think that's good enough for a lesson. Let's get you in the water."

Chapter 18

Summer

"Oh, fu—"

I'm weightless. Flying through the air, sucking down a breath as white ocean spray hits me in the face.

A split second later, I'm underwater.

For the length of a heartbeat, the world around me is blue-green and serene. Deafeningly silent, the way it gets at home when the music is off and the noise from the street below has died down.

Then I'm being flung around, clinging to my last breath as the water works me like I'm in a washing machine's rapid spin cycle.

I kick for the surface, so exhausted by the last hour that my limbs feel ready to fall off, lungs just seconds from collapsing. I'm one wave away from my entire body atrophying so bad I get swept into the depths. Which is an alarming reality when going the distance in a surf event will have me in and out of the water all day.

I surface in white, foamy water and slide back onto my board, disoriented, searching for Parker. He's floating a ways away, squinting over the top of his waterproof camera. His body relaxes when he spots me, the same way it has every damn time I've wiped out this morning.

"What happened there?" Parker says when I'm within earshot. I push up to sit on my board the way he is, our feet dangling off the sides.

"Kicked out late. Again." I shove a strand of wet hair, loosened from my braids, off my face. Waves don't get too big here at Crystal Cove—six-to-eight-foot walls of water that never form a barrel quite big enough to stand upright in. But the second one of them comes, and I start to fit behind the falling curtain of water . . .

I tried to bail, did it late, and paid the price.

"Why are you kicking out at all? You'd get barreled by waves twice that size at Pine Point all the time, even in the junior league." Parker squints at the tiny screen on his camera. "I could break you in half with all the tension you're carrying in your back. We'll build some yoga into your program. It might be that's the problem."

"Maybe." I don't mention that this morning has felt off in a way that transcends the stiffness in my body. I haven't felt so out of sorts in the water in years, so disconnected from my board. And the barrels . . .

Well, no manner of picturing Denny's demise, my triumphant exit from town, or the looks on its gossipmongers' faces as I win Surf's Up could motivate my ass to stall into a barrel. The second the water falls over me . . .

"You're exactly where you need to be in the early stages of training. This is where the work starts." Parker's using his reassuring trainer voice, the one we wield in the face of athletes feeling down on themselves.

I nod because he's right. I should know better than to count myself out on day one. I've got weeks to go before the first event at Rocky Ridge, then two more events to pace myself through.

And hopefully an entire tour after that.

The morning sun has made its way higher in the sky now. We bob on our boards, mere feet apart, legs brushing underwater though there's an entire ocean of space up for grabs.

"We'll have to get you swimming laps, too, which . . ." Parker wipes off his camera lens, but it's doused in water by the next rolling wave.

"Which is a little complicated seeing as you're now banned from the only aquatic training center in a three-hour radius?"

Parker pulls a face. "I'll think of something. Let's call it for today and head to Brooks's for a workout before you go to work."

I nod. "What time is your session with River?"

He'd grumbled about it, but listening to Parker tell me about his impromptu meeting yesterday had been a relief. I'd been so worried about what I'd be coming over to when I went back to his place for a rom-com last night. But Parker had his nose in a textbook, deep in planning for their next session. Maybe he'd gone the entire day without eating a meal, but he'd filled the time with something productive. Hell, just the fact that he let Colin Nowak convince him to leave his apartment was a triumph.

And he got up before dawn today. For you.

I flip a mental middle finger to the desperate girl inside me, trying to lead me down a fantastical path where that means something it doesn't.

"I have my doubts River will show up at all." Parker snorts. "Might be for the best. I'm pretty tired."

I twist around to get a better look at him. He stares into the distance with unfocused eyes, and more than anything, I wish I could exist inside his head with him. Keep all the nasty thoughts at bay, the ones that have him looking for safety in his bedsheets.

"Do you like it out here?"

Parker nods. "I can see why you do this. It's not a bad reason to get out of bed."

"No, it's not. I missed this. After everything that happened with Denny . . ." He took a lot away from me. My desire to surf. My self-esteem. "It was hard to get out of bed for a while, between not coming here and fighting with you. But I found other reasons to do it."

Parker hesitates, then asks, "Like what?"

His question cuts into me deep. I know it's not rhetorical—it's his way of asking for help.

"Like . . . the next day was a Monday. Which, according to my carefully crafted schedule, meant my newest cans of Diet Coke had been sitting in the fridge for exactly two days. And you know what that means." I wiggle my eyebrows and Parker shakes his head, failing to kill a smile. "Perfectly crisp soda awaits."

"You do realize that's all in your head, right? It tastes the same on day one as it does on day fifty."

"You're wrong. Second-day Diet Coke is worth getting out of bed for." I shrug, watching beads of water drip from his hair onto the back of his neck. "Your turn."

"Something worth getting out of bed for?" Parker's grip tightens on his board when the edge of a small wave pushes us toward shore. "Honestly? I'm drawing a blank."

Those words cut me even deeper. What I wouldn't give to bridge the watery distance between us, wrap him safely in my arms and never let go. "Well, today I'm looking forward to my morning blueberry donut."

Parker's head whips around. "I haven't asked Wynn for those all week."

"Me neither, for obvious reasons. But you're going to procure me a few when we get back to town, as a thank-you for teaching you to stay alive in the water."

His eyes spark, and suddenly he's here. My Parker. "Wait until I tell him you were tossing them in the trash a couple weeks ago."

I gasp. "You wouldn't dare! Resident Homewrecker has nothing on Donut Trasher. I'll have my face plastered on *wanted* posters on every light post within town lines."

"Then we'll leave town. Fuck 'em all."

My stomach pinches uncomfortably because that's exactly the plan. And I'll tell him. Soon.

"Sheffield's donuts," Parker says after a while.

"Worth getting out of bed for?"

He holds my gaze, and we grin at each other while bobbing on our boards. "Worth getting out of bed for."

Chapter 19

Parker

"*Strange Love Under the Hidden Moon.*"

In the wall of mirrors across the bench I'm sitting at, I watch Summer weave through the training equipment dotting Brooks's home gym.

She's dressed for a day of work after our post-surf workout, designed to build muscle everywhere she needs it, increase her stamina, and make me drool at the sight of her tight-as-hell ass moving in figure-hugging leggings.

Stop staring at her.

Summer's polo shirt hangs unevenly over her hips, one side skimming the waistband of her leggings and revealing the smallest sliver of tanned skin as she approaches. I swallow hard.

Stop. Fucking. Staring.

Now.

I drag my eyes off her and jab at my tablet, pausing the footage I've been studying. "Come again?"

"*Strange Love Under the Hidden Moon.*" Summer widens her eyes like I'm supposed to have a clue which hidden moon she's talking about. "The book I'm reading! They've been getting real touchy-feely the last few chapters, and I'm sensing some good old-fashioned double-dicked-alien fornication coming my way." She throws her arms out. "Something worth getting out of bed for."

I frown. Her hair is still wet from the shower she'd taken inside, as though she rushed through her routine just to come here and make me wonder about the mechanics of alien sex. "Aliens have two dicks?"

She gives a conspiratorial nod. "Awesome, right?"

And now I'm thinking about Summer getting double-dicked by a mythical creature, which leads to thinking about whether she'd ever let my single appendage near her, and . . . *Please pull it together.*

Easier said than done. I couldn't be more aware that she doesn't return my feelings, but I can't for the life of me forget the slip she had at Oakley's weeks ago, parroting the town gossip about me. Add to that the moments I catch her staring back at me, and it's all starting to mess with my head.

I'm becoming increasingly concerned that I'll end up doing something so stupid, it'll mean a real end to our friendship.

"Still watching that?" Summer has caught sight of the tablet in my lap, paused on this morning's footage.

I hit play. The small figure in a hot-pink wetsuit paddles hard for an incoming wave, pale-yellow surfboard gliding through the water.

Summer looks . . . good. Strong. Fearless while the wall of water grows and builds momentum as it catches up with her. She pops up on her board, grabs rail, and plummets straight down the face of the eight-foot wave. The water curls into itself, forming a barrel over her.

And that's when it all goes to hell.

I spent several hours studying competition footage yesterday, watching the best of the best ride barrel, trying to get a feel for where she's been going wrong. She hasn't managed a single one in the five straight mornings that we've surfed together.

She'll carve up a wave, land aerials no problem. But the second she comes up against a barrel . . . she bails on the wave a touch too late for a clean exit and gets flung underwater.

Every single time.

And if she can't pull this off during an event—particularly at Pine Point, where surfing barrels is the bare-minimum expectation—then this won't be much of a revenge.

"The way you're surfing . . ." I pick my words carefully, same as I would with any client—aside from River, who seems to respond best to having his own moodiness mirrored back at him. "You keep bailing late. Like you want to get barreled but talk yourself out of it at the last possible second."

She glances at me. "Sounds like you're trying to say something."

"I'm waiting for you to fill in the blanks for me. Why is it that you haven't completed a single barrel this week, when I've seen you pull them off plenty of times?"

"I'm out of practice. It'll come to me when it comes to me."

"You wouldn't lie to your trainer, would you, Summer?"

"Wouldn't dream of it."

With a hum, I lean in closer. Just enough to hear her breath catch, get her cheeks to flush. There's a drop of water running from her hair, down the side of her neck, and it's all I can focus on now. I'm jealous—*jealous* of a bead of water touching her the way I wish I could. The urge is so strong to lick it off her just to see what she does about it.

Like I said—I'm gonna do something stupid one day.

In the end, I don't lick her. But I do stroke the back of a finger over her pink cheek. "When did you become such a blusher?"

Summer scoffs. "It's makeup."

"The makeup you put on while leaving your hair soaking wet?" I hold her wary gaze. "Do I make you blush, Summer?"

Do I? my brain shouts at her. *Do you want me? Because I'm a single nod away from kissing the life out of us both.*

But Summer juts out her lip in a mocking pout. "Oh, sweetheart. Is the arrogance flaring up again?" She touches the back of her hand to my forehead. "We talked about this. Your mirror time is supposed to max out at *fifteen minutes*. Otherwise, look what happens."

I round my eyes. "But I'm so pretty to look at." Summer laughs, flush gone, eyes bright, and I can't help reaching out and thumbing her chin. "Don't laugh. I know you think so, too. I've seen you staring."

She shoves away my hand. "Arrogant *and* delusional. Truly a winning combination."

"It's okay to admit it. It can be our little secret. I'll even tell you one of mine to make it even."

Her eyes narrow. "I already know about the life-size cutout of yourself you keep in your closet, Park. I do have to ask, though: Does it ever get old, orgasming to your own face?"

"Shockingly, it did. But then I added yours to the rotation, and all's right in the world again."

"*Parker.*" Summer tries to smack my chest, but I catch her hand before she can.

"Oops." I wince, squinting at her cheeks. "I think I set off all that makeup again."

She scoffs but doesn't say anything. And then we simultaneously realize that I never let go of her hand. That, at some point, our fingers laced. The space between us shrunk so that we're just a foot apart.

And when our eyes meet again, neither of us moves away. Every single cell in my body demands *more*. More proximity, more contact. More of that blush. And a lifetime's worth of her laugh.

"You wanna know my secret?"

"Is it better than the cutout?"

"Probably not. It's not even a secret. Everyone knows."

Irritation clouds her expression. "Everyone knows your secret but me?"

"Does that bother you?"

"*Yes*," she admits after a split-second debate. "Tell me."

I lean closer, leaving barely an inch between the tips of our noses. "You, Summer Prescott, are the most stunning girl I've ever laid eyes on."

Her lips pop open. She stares at me with those perfect green eyes, long lashes skimming her skin. And she still doesn't move away.

Would she laugh at me this time?

We're short a house party and a spinning bottle, but if I tried to close the gap between us and kiss her . . . would she let me?

A throat clears from somewhere nearby. Summer's fingers slip from mine and she retreats several steps—several *large* steps—as River makes his way through the gym wearing the mask of disdain he's worn since we started our sessions.

"I have to get to work." Summer fiddles with the strap of her gym bag sitting on a nearby bench. "I'm going to stay back after my last client to swim laps in the pool."

"Don't. I've got you covered tonight." Her eyes narrow suspiciously, and rightfully so. She's going to *hate* the idea—and that makes me really damn giddy. I slip her bag over her shoulder and turn her around toward the garage door. "I'll text you the details. Say hi to Don for me. And grab me a muffin if Kendra offers."

She shoots me a look that plainly says *shut up, you big idiot*. And just like that, the tension evaporates. Summer shoulder-bumps me goodbye, grinning at River on her way out of the gym. He scowls back at her.

I wait until she's gone before turning to River. "Nowak, act like a dick with me all you want. But when she smiles at you"—I jab a finger at the now-deserted driveway—"you smile back. Got me?"

River pauses his progress toward me for the sole purpose of flipping me the bird. "Someone's gotta balance out the doe eyes you make at her. It's sick."

"I don't make doe eyes at her."

River drops onto a bench while I gather some equipment. "Yes, you do. Everyone in town knows about you and Summer Prescott."

I fumble a roll of athletic tape. Fucking hell, how is it possible that everyone clocked my feelings before I did?

Does . . . does Summer know? Has she known all along?

But then I remember those looks she gives me whenever I stare, like she genuinely thinks I've hit my head, and I sigh my relief internally. There's no way she knows.

"Everyone in town is wrong. There's nothing going on between me and Summer."

River's mouth curls into as much of a grin as I've ever seen on him. With a dreamy sigh, he clasps his hands to his chest. "'Summer Prescott, you're the most stunning girl I've ever laid eyes on.'"

My face goes furiously hot, he smiles wider, and it's official: I will never, ever, tease Summer about the way she blushes again.

~~~~~

"How'd your walks go yesterday?"

River's reflection in the mirror grimaces as he follows me to a treadmill on his crutches. He does well without them in short bursts after a decent amount of work on loosening his joints, but any sustained weight on his recovering leg still sets off that pinched nerve. In addition to the home exercises, he's supposed to take a couple of short strolls around his neighborhood a few times a day, to keep building strength.

"Good. I made it all the way to the—"

"You're a shit liar. How many walks did you take?"

"One," River says morosely.

"You mean none?" I heave a sigh when he rolls his eyes. Swear to God, this kid was brought here to test me. "River, there's only so much we can accomplish in the time we spend together. There are a whole other twenty-two hours in the day where you have to take ownership of your own recovery."

When River doesn't answer, I point him to the nearest bench. It's a mark of how little he was looking forward to that treadmill that he sits without protest. "At the risk of inciting another eye roll, I'm gonna ask you an honest question: Do you *want* to play football again?"

Cue the eye roll. "It's the only reason I'm here."

"Well, that's messed up. What if you can never play again?"

"A few days ago, you were telling me you could get me there."

"But what if I'm wrong?" I insist. "All I'm saying is that maybe you should have more than one reason. More than one plan. Or before you know it, you'll end up like me. Almost thirty, unemployed, and living over a bar." *And harboring unrequited feelings for your best friend.*

River is quiet a long while after that. We're killing valuable session time, but I let him have his moment.

"You're forgetting that you're also single as fuck and making sad puppy eyes every time Summer Prescott leaves the room." *Never mind.* River smirks over at me. "Might be even worse than the doe eyes."

"Shut it, Nowak. And if you don't think Summer Prescott is the most stunning girl *you've* ever laid eyes on, then you've got bigger issues than your leg, my guy."

River shakes his head. "She's not."

"Yes." I narrow my eyes. "She is."

"Trust me, she's not."

I'm ready to argue this to the death, but River's eyes wander wistfully, as though seeing something that isn't there. I take a seat at the end of the treadmill. I've seen that look before, on Zac and Brooks whenever their girls stroll into the room.

"What's her name?"

"Who?"

It's like pulling teeth with this kid. "The girl who's allegedly more stunning than Summer. And let me tell you, that's a big *allegedly*."

Several long seconds pass before he says, "Macy McAdams. She tutored me in math last year. We got close."

"And . . ." I struggle to find the right words, wishing Summer were here. She always knows the right thing to say. "Have you asked her out?"

"Wanted to. Never did." He scrapes at nothing on his athletic shorts, buying time before looking at me again. "I was going to see her that night."

I go still. "The night of your accident?"

He does a funny head-tilt-shrug move I'm going to interpret as a yes. "She's afraid of storms. But after the crash . . ." He kicks at a crutch with his injured leg.

Shit. The puzzle piece slips into place, and the complete picture is a sad but familiar one. He's down bad for a girl he thinks is way out of his league, unable to get out of his own head long enough to do something about it.

Well, maybe that needs to end.

I stand and tap at the settings on the treadmill. "I'm gonna make you a deal, River. I'm gonna get you off these crutches in a month flat. And when I do, you're going to ask Macy McAdams on a date."

I prepare for another frustrating round of eye rolls, evasive answers, and moody responses. To my surprise he looks at me with more hope than I've seen since we met. "You think I'll be off these crutches in a month?"

"I think it'll be hard as hell and take every bit of mental and physical effort you can muster. But I wouldn't promise you that if we couldn't do it." I point at the treadmill. "Are you in?"

Eye roll. I think that one's supposed to pass for another yes. Then River turns a sneer in my direction. "What about you? If I have to do something about Macy, then you need to do something about Summer. And by *something*, I mean a little less making eyes, a little more growing a pair."

"Fuck off, my pair's fine. I like my pair."

I'm only half kidding, but River laughs.

A real laugh.

And damn if I don't feel like I've just won some sort of medal. This miserable kid, who's still on crutches and feeling down about himself, his college prospects, and his dating life—even if it only lasted a heartbeat, I made him look past all that long enough to laugh. I got him showing up here, six days in a row, when he'd sworn up and down that our work together was pointless.

Maybe I'm not as much of a dead end as those glow-in-the-dark stars tell me I am at night.

Maybe I do have something to offer people. To River. And Summer, too.

"Okay," I tell River, squinting at myself in the wall of mirrors and then moving closer until the blurred image comes into focus. I study my reflection, from the top of my mess of hair, to the sneakers on my feet. "We've got a deal."

~~~~~

Back at home two hours later, I dig through the textbooks and notebooks piled on my coffee table until I find what I'm looking for.

If I'm really going to do this, I'm going to do it right. No more messing around or hiding beneath plastic stars.

I stare at the spiral-bound notebook in my hands, at the words Summer dictated last month.

Summer's Dream Man: Dark hair. Showers. Nice smile. Has a job and career aspirations. Plans dates and alone time. Has a five-year plan. Owns a home. Cooks. Has big hands.

If I'm going to ask Summer out, it'll be for the long haul. With plans and stability and big dreams for our future. As the kind of man she wants—the kind she deserves.

Some way, somehow, I'm going to become Summer's dream man.

Chapter 20

Summer

"Hey, Dad! It's me. I got your text about rescheduling this week-end's family dinner. Of course, that totally makes sense with the twins' birthday party! Except, I actually had a little something to give them. Nothing huge—just some new soccer gear for them to play with. I'd be happy to come to their party? Even just to help out? Or I can drop off their gifts at your house sometime? Or . . . I could totally hang on to it until the next dinner. Do you have any dates in mind?"

~~~~~

PARKER: Show up at ten thirty, bring a swimsuit, and park your car as far back from the building as you can.

In the dark inside of my car, I stare down at the text like I haven't read it a dozen times since he sent it this afternoon.

I do have an inkling as to why I'm currently parked in the very corner of the deserted lot of Oakwood High. All signs point to the kind of shenanigans Parker used to pull in our teens, but I'm really hoping I'm wrong.

I jump in my seat when my car door swings open and Parker ducks down to look at me. "Took you long enough. Let's go."

"Parker, I'm begging you." I let him help me out of the car and then reach for the backpack in the passenger seat. "Tell me we're not doing what I think we are."

After some fumbling, the flashlight on his phone comes on, pointing at our feet but illuminating his proud grin just enough. "If you're thinking we're about to sneak into our old high school to use the pool, then . . . yes. This is our only option."

"Breaking and entering is our only option?"

"Something like that." His hand comes up between us, palm side up. "Do you trust me?"

I stare at the dark outline of our old school. The sensible answer to all this would be a swift *hell no*. But the thing is, we've done this before.

At sixteen, it had been one of Parker's not-so-bright ideas that led us, plus Zac and Melody, to our high school pool in the middle of the night during a summer heat wave. My irritation at him for dragging us into such a reckless excursion had evaporated the moment my toes dipped into the water.

Yes, we'd totally gotten caught. But Parker got us safely out before turning himself in to the security on patrol. He got off easy, and the entire night had been the most fun I'd had all summer given the nightmare I'd been living at home. My mom's affair had come to light only weeks prior.

"I swear, you're going to land us in jail one day." I drop my backpack into his waiting hand. He stares down at it long enough to make me pause. I . . . don't think he wanted the bag.

Still, he hitches it on his shoulder and flashes me a small smile.

The side door swings open without struggle—Parker must have unlocked it before I arrived—and then we're quietly tiptoeing through our old high school. There was a security guard's car parked out front when I pulled in. But the building feels deserted, lit only by dim lights at the mouth of every long hallway. We pass several open classrooms without stopping, headed in the direction of the gymnasium and adjacent pool.

Parker's hand trails over nondescript lockers along the way. "Mine," he whispers with his hand over one before moving to the next. "Yours."

My gaze lingers on the lockers as we pass them. They'd been assigned alphabetically by last name. "It's funny to think we had no idea why Zac insisted you trade spots with him. He wanted the locker next to Mel's."

We creep along the hall for a quiet beat before Parker looks over. "It was me. I was the one who asked to trade."

Oh. I don't know why that confession hits me the way it does, and *where* it does. Right in the chest, making my heart squeeze then take off in a gallop.

His words still reverberate in my head by the time he opens the door to the pool. The overhead lights are off, the massive room bathed in blue light from within the pool, giving it an ethereal quality. Like we're wandering in a dream.

"Come here," Parker says once we're at the water's edge. For a silly moment I think he's asking me to step into his arms, to let him hold me just because. The way my heart leaps is downright humiliating. I'm so starved for romantic attention that I'm looking for it in two simple words uttered by my best friend.

Parker twirls his finger in a *turn around* motion and starts working braids into my hair. My eyes close, chest swells at the feel of his fingers.

You've been following this guy Parker around all your life, and not even he *wants you that way.*

Denny's words are a mean but welcome reminder. Parker's out-of-the-blue flirtation is getting to my head, and it's bound to leave me in emotional shambles if I can't keep a tight leash on these delusions.

That's my friend, who hasn't shown a crumb of desire for me in twenty-seven years. Who's trying to find himself, and acting out of character.

"Do you want me to set you up again? Another blind date?"

Parker's hands pause in my hair. "Where the hell did that come from?"

"You seemed keen on dating before." I rub my lips together. "They've brought in a new trainer to fill your spot at the clinic. Her name is—"

"She's not my type."

"I haven't told you a single thing about her."

"I know enough."

"Is it because she's a trainer, too?" I stare at the far wall as he resumes braiding, my stomach inexplicably sinking. Then spiking with frustration when he stays silent, declining to shed any kind of light on the situation. "I thought you didn't have a type."

"I have a type. Just took me a while to figure it out."

"Well?" I throw out my arms. "What is it?"

With a soft chuckle, he turns me around by the shoulders. Smooths down the unruly baby hairs along my forehead with faint dimples in his cheeks. "I love it when you're annoyed."

"Sadist."

He strips off his shirt, leaving him in his swim shorts. I follow his lead. Because I'm getting into the pool, obviously. Not at all because I need a distraction from his half-naked body.

"It's not sadistic," Parker says. "I love that you *get* annoyed with me. Not everyone gets the full range of Summer. I love that I do."

I huff a breath, dropping my denim shorts. "Do you want another setup or not?"

Parker shoots me a look on his way to the very edge of the pool. "Not sure if you noticed, but I'm a bit preoccupied these days."

He dives into the water headfirst, without even dipping in a toe. I chew the inside of my cheek watching him swim to the surface with a few powerful kicks and push his soaked hair off his face. He zeroes in on me the moment he opens his eyes. Drapes his hot stare over my body, lingering on my hips, breasts, before meeting my eye.

"You're a knockout, you know that?"

My stomach swoops. "I'm the same I've always been."

His eyes soften. "I should've been telling you every day. I'm sorry it took me so long."

It takes enormous effort to redirect the conversation. "I know I've been sucking up a lot of your time lately. If you want to scale back the training, or write out a program I can follow on my own . . ."

"Summer, who else would I spend all my time on?" He treads water, his smile amused. "What about you? You want a setup?"

"Not sure if you noticed, but I'm a bit preoccupied these days," I say in a poor imitation of his deep voice. I dip my big toe into the water. "*Fuck.* Why is it so cold?"

"School's been out for a while. Get in."

"No way. Park, it's freezing."

"Get in anyway." He swims for me, climbing out and dripping streams of water on the tiled ground. Holds out his hand again. "You're thinking too hard. Give me your hand. Jump in with me."

He's always been so good at it—leaning into whatever he's feeling at the time. I know he sees it as a fault, but I couldn't be more envious of him and his ability to jump—to act without overthinking every tiny step along the way, trying to predict minutes, hours, years down the line and how I might come to regret the simple decision in front of me.

His grin doubles when my hand drops in his.

I squeal when I surface from the water, muscles locking together in a shiver. "How is it worse than I thought?"

"You'll get used to it. I'll keep you warm until you do." Parker anchors his hands on the edge of the pool, caging me in. In this lighting, the deep blue of his eyes looks stormy. Like the raging sea, no land for miles. His wet hair is curling at the ends, tickling the backs of his ears. It strikes me that I've gone my entire life without ever running my fingers through it.

Suddenly, it's all I can think about doing. And it's so absurd a thought that it makes me laugh out loud. A nervous-but-excited kind of laugh. The same exhilaration that has me dissolving into uncontrollable laughter on a roller-coaster ride, even as people shriek around me.

Oddly, some kind of light goes out in Parker's eyes.

"Did you really ask Zac to trade lockers so you'd have the one next to mine?"

One corner of his mouth lifts and drops. "Every year."

Those two words do some real heavy lifting inside me. They push aside any thought of who we are, the precious, longtime friendship between us. They dim my common sense, futilely shouting that this isn't really Parker. That he's just confused, saying and doing things he never would in his right mind. They let me want what I want—him, his indulgent stares, and knowing things about him I never thought I would.

His eyes spark again when I reach for him, pushing a strand of hair off his forehead.

But before I can make sense of what it means or what I think I'm doing, Parker jerks his chin toward the far end of the pool. "Let's get to work, Prescott."

Chapter 21

Summer

We spend a good half hour swimming laps before Parker's need for mischief flares.

I've got a towel wrapped over my swimsuit. He's just in his shorts, dripping water behind us as we move through the deserted school with our backpacks slung over our shoulders. That dripping water is a very obvious trail for any lurking security guards, but in true Parker fashion, it doesn't seem to worry him. He pokes his head into an open door to the left of the hallway we're exploring.

"I think we had English class in here."

"It was biology." The desks are newer, not the beat-up ones we worked at. I'm almost certain the plastic backs of our chairs had been a paler blue than this one. But I recognize the view from the windows on the far side of the room. It's a wall of pine trees illuminated by the moon.

What made this classroom so special, other than the fact that it was pivotal to my future, was the deer we'd sometimes see poking out from the forest's edge during class.

We drop our bags by the open door and Parker sits in the front row of desks facing the whiteboard—which had definitely been a chalkboard in our day.

"Fuck me, we were tiny back then." I laugh at the sight of him wedged behind the desk. He's always been tall, but his bare upper body puts all the extra muscle he's put on as an adult on glorious display.

I move around the teacher's desk by the whiteboard and toy with a red dry-erase marker. "This is the room where I figured out what I wanted to be when I grew up."

"Yeah?"

I nod. "Senior year. Our college applications were due any day and I still had no idea." I'd been so stressed about it in the summer leading up to our final year. The fear of choosing poorly and setting my life on the wrong course before it even got started. I turn to face him, slapping the marker against my palm. "It was late October. We spent all week presenting our midterm research projects. Pretty sure I got an A."

Parker grins. "Typical you."

"You bet it was." I point the marker at him. "But then you got up here at the front of the class, the last to go on account of the *W*."

"I always hated going last."

"That one was perfect timing. The rest of us researched all this avant-garde science. The kind of stuff that's fascinating, but totally useless day-to-day unless you work in a lab, you know? Then you got up here and did a whole twenty minutes on the science of sports. And things clicked into place for me. That stuff was *interesting*."

"That's how you chose your major?" His thumb traces lines along his desk. I find myself wishing I was in its place. "I'm pretty sure I chose kinesiology because you did. I didn't have any other ideas."

I laugh. "It was *your* idea. Subconsciously, at least. I chose it because of you. Haven't regretted it a day since."

He makes a face as he thinks on that. I hop on the front edge of the teacher's desk just to resist the urge to go over there and . . . I don't know.

Smack the back of his head. Wrap my arms around him. Kiss away the line between his eyebrows. He thinks he's a tissue aimlessly blowing in the wind, but Parker's always underestimated himself that way. I hope it means something to him to know he was the one to give my life direction.

"How are things going with River? He seemed less angry this morning. Actually returned my smile."

"He's still a moody little shit." Parker pauses. "He made it fifteen minutes on the treadmill without a nerve pinching today. Only snapped at me three times. That's a win, right?"

"A big win." I smile at the thought of these two lost boys snipping at each other every morning. "And you? What's going on in my favorite head?"

"Being with you helps," he admits, setting off little bursts of satisfaction in my stomach. "And the morning donuts. I bought Juliana Bekker's autobiography today—the surfer? And . . . River made it fifteen minutes on the treadmill without a nerve pinching."

"Look at that. Reasons to get out of bed."

Seconds pass where all we do is stare at each other. Eventually, Parker clasps his hands over the desktop, sitting up straight as though class were in session. "You got anymore lessons for me tonight, Miss Prescott?"

"What would you like to learn?"

"How about an anatomy lesson?"

My head falls back in a laugh. "I have it on questionable authority that you know plenty about anatomy."

Parker's eyes narrow playfully. "Summer Prescott, you seem positively gripped by this rumor. Have you ever stopped to think about why?"

"Not particularly." I cross my legs and my towel inches up my bare thighs. He drags his gaze up my legs. Over my towel-covered middle, the dip in the fabric where it drapes over my breasts.

It's so addicting, watching him watch me. The way his jaw tenses, chest rises with deep, steadying breaths. I find myself wishing it'd been this way all along. That he'd been feeding my confidence, my heart, and hell, my ego with that look, for as long as we've known each other.

I could live off the new way Parker Woods looks at me.

You, Summer Prescott, are the most stunning girl I've ever laid eyes on.

"Parker, you're staring again."

"You like it."

"Says who?"

Parker gets to his feet, lusty blue eyes on me as he moves toward the desk. My legs uncross, fall open when he reaches me. He notices, and he's smirking, and I'll never live this down.

"Says you, love."

I don't even have it in me to fight him on it.

"Why are you shaking?" He takes my hand, watching my fingers tremble. It's a bit of fear but a lot of adrenaline. And it surges when he glances up at me and says, "I don't bite unless you ask for it. Guess that part didn't travel."

Ask, my brain commands. *Ask ask ask.*

"Tell me why you think about the rumor."

"I'm jealous." The confession shoves past my lips, unable to deny him when my hand feels so good in his. "It makes me jealous that other people know things about you that I don't. Have done things with you that I haven't. I like being the person who knows everything about you."

"A little possessive, don't you think?" he asks. I shrug, because what do I say to that? "Okay, Summer. Anatomy lesson. You ready?"

Parker's eyes are on mine, trapping the air in my lungs as heat rages inside me, scorching me, making everything it touches smoke and sizzle. I'd put money on us regretting this in the morning. Still, I loosen my arms at my sides, and my towel unravels down to my hips.

He chuckles softly. "You're reading ahead, Miss Prescott. You wanted to know things about me." Parker raises my hand to his hair. It's soft, still damp from our swim. My fingers tangle in the thick strands I'd longed for in the water.

"That's my hair." My fingers comb through it under his guidance, then run down the back of his neck. I can't help but curl them, graze his skin with my nails. With a soft breath, he places my hand on the side of his face, letting me feel the light stubble there, the sharp angle of his cheekbone. "My cheek."

I brush my thumb over his skin and Parker's hand falls away, leaving mine free to explore. So, I do. I let my fingers drift, skimming his plush lower lip.

"Your lips," I whisper. He nods, eyes on me. Then he parts them, licks the pad of my thumb, and I go up in flames.

How many women have kissed him?

That senseless, irrational jealousy surges. There are people out there who know what it's like to kiss *my* Parker. It's unfair. Maddening.

I push the tip of my finger just past his lips. "Bite me."

He grins around my finger and nips at it. The sting sends a shock-wave through my body, down my arms and legs to settle between my thighs. This hot, throbbing bundle of energy just inches from where Parker stands. I can't remember ever being this dizzyingly turned on. Rational thought has gone straight out the window.

I take back my finger, loving the scrape of his teeth on my skin. My hand trails down, over his jaw just to feel it pulse beneath my fingers. Down his neck to his bare chest, feeling it rise and fall so rapidly, it gives away that he's just as turned on as I am.

Parker watches my hand trail along his upper arm, squeezing, testing the muscle. His massive palms grip above my knees. Squeeze, slide up, squeeze, and up again until his fingertips skim the edge of my towel.

"Your skin's so soft." Parker leans into me. His lips touch the side of my neck, press a kiss under my ear. I whimper. Feel that kiss turn into a smile against my skin. He does it again, and I arch my neck, giving him more room to play while my hands roam his body. Over his shoulders, past his racing heart. Down his stomach, counting six flawless pockets of muscle that tense under my touch.

Parker stays put on my body, hands still gripping my upper thighs. Lips and teeth teasing the spot that earned him that first whimper until I give him another. But when my fingers reach farther down, all ten going still right above the waistband of his shorts, he releases a ragged breath. He's hard and pushing his cock into my inner thigh.

My breaths come out in shallow bursts. How ridiculous is that? He's barely touched me, and not at all where it counts. His hands have stalled just inches from my pussy and it pulses furiously, demanding attention.

His attention. No one else's would do it.

Parker pulls away, breathing hard. His eyes have gone hazy, blinking slow, staring right at my mouth. I read the question there clear as day. *Should we?*

A storm swells in my head, warning of mistakes and broken friendships and hurt feelings. But it feels so good. So damn good to have this kind of effect on him.

I want it. I want him. Fuck it.

I reach for his hips, tug him closer, so close there's just a sliver of air left between our lips. Parker cups the back of my neck. Brushes his lips with mine.

And we both gasp, spring apart, at the devastating sound of footsteps marching down the hall. Coming closer by the second.

"Goddamn it." Parker's head tips back so he can glare at the ceiling. "I'm going to kill him."

"What? Kill who?" My nails dig into his sides. The footsteps seem to be coming from the direction of the pool, tracing our exact path down the hall. I peer down between us. Parker's bulge is absurdly obvious. Impossible to disguise. "Should we hide? We should hide."

Parker calmly tugs my towel back into place, wrapping it over my swimsuit top before adjusting his shorts. "It's okay. Summer, it's fine."

I leap off the desk. "It's *fine*? It's fine that we're about to get caught breaking into our high school?" I clap my hands over my cheeks. "Oh my God, we're going to prison. This is so not ideal."

Parker laughs. I really thought he'd been doing better mentally, but it's clear now he's got several loose screws. The footsteps outside stop. I tense, grip Parker's arm, say a little prayer that the local jail has a two-for-one bail special so that our friends are less likely to murder us when they get our phone calls.

"Parker," a male voice hisses. A security guard I recognize as Herbert Ambrose, who's lived in town for as long as I can remember, pops his head into our classroom. He lifts a hand in . . . *greeting*? "I'm afraid you're out of time. My replacement arrives in fifteen minutes."

"What the hell's going on?" I mutter to Parker, letting him adjust my towel to make sure I'm fully covered up, though Herbert has politely diverted his gaze to the far wall.

"Thanks, Herb." Parker goes to sort through his backpack and hands Herb a handful of cash. "Same time tomorrow?"

Herb flips through the bills. "You bet. You two have a good night. Head back out through the side door."

"Parker," I whisper once we're alone again and hurrying through the silent school. "You're bribing security to let us use the pool? I thought we were breaking in!"

Parker tosses me a smile over his shoulder. "That's what I call personal growth, baby."

I let my laugh bounce off the lockers, all kinds of dangerous, fizzy feelings swirling inside me. Only Parker freaking Woods would proudly evolve from breaking and entering to bribing authorities.

I wouldn't have him any other way.

Chapter 22

Parker

"I can't believe you actually got your eyes checked." Melody squints through her phone, frowning when I fiddle with the new pair of glasses sitting on my nose. "You look like a miscreant masquerading as a professor."

"Excuse you. I am an upstanding citizen of this town." I eye myself in the rearview mirror of my Jeep, ruffling the hair on my forehead. Trying to convince myself that I chose a good pair. A pair Summer will like. "The appointment was overdue, really. And Summer's first event is tomorrow at Rocky Ridge. We're going up there now, staying overnight because of the early start time."

I peer through the window at Summer's building across the street. She texted that she'd meet me at my car once she finished packing. I've already got a couple of her surfboards loaded in the back, and a sleeve of donuts ready for the two-hour drive. I sit back in the driver's seat, nudging up the frames. They're gonna take some getting used to.

"Not sure what that has to do with you finally getting your eyes checked, but it's nice of you to accompany her." The amusement in my sister's voice pulls back my attention in time to catch her exchanging a look with Zac, who's sitting next to her. "What's inspired the act of chivalry?"

I narrow my eyes at the screen. "What's inspired that look you're giving each other?"

"Oh, I don't know. Maybe the fact that you're in lo—"

"*Don't say it.*" As if I need the reminder of how far off my feelings are from Summer's.

Melody smirks. "Do you happen to be sharing a hotel room?"

"We have two rooms. Summer booked them herself." She proudly announced it earlier in the week. Trying, I think, to put me on notice that what happened in that biology classroom wasn't to be repeated. That almost kiss. The way her hands roamed my body, setting me on fucking fire. The way she stroked my hair, melting something inside me.

Apparently, it was all a temporary lapse in judgment. At least on her part.

Meanwhile, my lips touched hers, just barely, and it's all I've been able to think about since. It defied all logic, but she seemed interested enough sitting on that desk. I woke up the following morning more than ready to talk about it, only to be met with news of our sleeping arrangement at Rocky Ridge. And then the respectable few feet she kept between us while we paddled in the ocean. And again, when we trained in Brooks's gym. Swam more laps during Herb's night shift. Rinse and repeat, all week long.

So, I've taken the hint and backed off.

"You sound thrilled about those two rooms," Zac says with a laugh.

"I am. I'm fine. It's fine. Me and Summer, we're . . ." *Almost kissing and then pretending it never happened.*

"Fine?" Mel supplies.

I go to rub my face but end up knocking the glasses askew. "This is your fault. Everything was great before you went and got involved."

"Parker, you were living in denial about being in love with Summer. How was that *great*?" I flinch at Melody's use of the *love* word, embarrassed all over again. "So, how come you're going to this event, anyway? Isn't it just her volunteer gig?"

I peer at my sister. "What? It's not a volunteer—"

I damn near jump out of my seat at the sound of a knock at my window. Lisa stares at me from the sidewalk. Beyond her, her husband, Jim, hauls a stack of cardboard boxes into Oakley's, the inside of which looks quiet between lunch and dinner hours.

I lower my window. "Hey, Lisa. I should be pulling out in a few minutes if Jim needs this spot."

For some reason, she grins at me with a wide, knowing smile. "Nice glasses. You look like a naughty professor." Zac's and Melody's laughter fills the car, growing louder when I shoot them a searing look. "We haven't seen you at the bar lately, other than to pick up your take-out orders."

There's a very simple reason why Lisa hasn't seen me in our usual booth at Oakley's, but I promised Summer I'd stay out of the way the members of this town have so carelessly discarded her.

"Been busy," I say politely.

"Seems so." Lisa's eyes twinkle, for some reason. Her graying hair slips over her shoulder as she leans in, dropping her voice. "I couldn't help but overhear your conversation. Going on an overnight trip with Summer, are we now? I just knew there was something going on there."

Damn this town. Can't anyone mind their own business?

Zac and Melody go quiet, watching this unfold like it's a high-speed car chase on the news.

"We've got separate rooms at the Rockford Inn. And there *isn't* something going on."

"That's not what Herbert Ambrose said at the bar the other day."

I force my face to stay perfectly smooth. Pointless, considering the way my hands wring the steering wheel. "I'm not sure what you mean. What would Herb Ambrose know about it?"

If Herb's been running his mouth about our midnight swims, it's only a matter of time before I'm paid a visit by the county sheriff. It'd taken some real finessing to dodge a criminal record the last time he caught me breaking into that school. Not sure he'd take as much pity on my twenty-nine-year-old ass.

My only consolation is that I'll surely avoid jail time. Summer will murder me before I even get booked.

"He says he's recently spotted you two getting . . . *familiar*."

Two gasps fill my car from the phone on the dash, loud enough to have Jim looking around at us, box in hand. I end the call before those vultures can get started on me. "Herb is mistaken. Don't believe everything you hear on these streets, Lisa."

Lisa doesn't appear convinced. But Jim calls her over to help with the last of the boxes, leaving me free to roll up my window and groan in the nonexistent privacy of my own car.

Just what I need. The entire town reminding me of my misguided feelings for my best friend.

Chapter 23

Parker

"Canceled?"

The word squeaks out of Summer's mouth. She stares wide-eyed at the woman at the reception desk of the Rockford Inn. "What do you mean, the second room's been canceled? How does something like this just happen?"

The woman continues to calmly tap at her keyboard, colorful nails *clacking* off the black keys. "I've just started my shift, so I'm not quite sure. But it's only possible if someone on the reservation calls it in."

Our gazes clash. *Well, well, Prescott. Are we angling for another anatomy lesson, after all?*

"Parker." Summer nudges me a few feet away from the counter, eyes narrowing until they're barely more than slits. "Tell me you didn't do this."

"I didn't do this. But I'm highly interested to know what you thought might happen tonight, when *you* canceled the room."

"I did not cancel the room," she hisses. "If you think this is some cute or clever way to make me feel you up again . . ."

I bark a laugh. "*Make* you? Let's not pretend you didn't beg to feel me up, love."

"I begged, really?" Summer smirks. "You're the one who demanded an anatomy lesson. Real subtle, Park."

"You dropped your towel."

"You kissed my neck."

"You almost kissed *me*."

Guess there's no more dancing around it. Summer glares up at me, lips parted like she can't believe I had the balls to bring it up. As though the feel of her lips hasn't haunted my every waking minute since.

"Trust me, this wasn't my handiwork," I tell her. "The next time you feel me up, it'll be your own doing."

"You'd love that, wouldn't you? Admit it: You're on your knees at your bedside every night, praying I'll lose my mind enough to fondle you."

"I'd settle for you asking me to bite you again." I shrug. "But I'll take that fondle if you're offering."

"There won't be a fondle, I assure you."

"Oh yeah?" I step forward, bringing us so close our fronts nearly touch. "Then why are you so damn afraid to share a room with me, Summer?"

She's breathing heavily, like she's just swum a half-hour's worth of laps at the high school.

"How many beds?" Summer asks the clerk without looking away from me. "In the room we have. How many beds are there?"

"One." I have been *blessed*. "The second room got snapped up almost immediately. I believe there's some sort of event taking place locally . . ."

"Surf's Up." Summer digs her teeth into her plush bottom lip, still staring at me. "I suppose we don't have a choice."

I smirk. "How convenient for you."

Fuming, Summer returns to the counter, digging her wallet out of her bag. I get my credit card out and toss it there first.

"You don't have to." She almost sounds resigned, though I'm not quite sure what she's resigned herself *to*.

"I want to." The room sharing, the sleeping in one bed. I don't know how or why this happened. Whether Summer really made that call, if someone else did, or if it was just a fortuitous glitch in the system.

But I definitely want to.

~~~~~

We spend the rest of the day avoiding the tiny room.

Take a drive out to Rocky Ridge, spend a couple of hours there walking the beach and taking our boards out to give Summer a feel for the water. We take our sweet time eating street tacos on a picnic table by the boardwalk. Watching the sun set. Holding conversations that feel like ours, but for the undercurrent of tension coating each word.

Now, Summer messes around in the bathroom of our room. Has been for the past twenty minutes: showering, then running a hair dryer; pausing for a good thirty seconds, as though straining to hear what it is I'm doing on the other side of the wall, before continuing to rummage around the bathroom. Then pausing again to listen.

She's trying to run out the clock. Hoping to come out here and find me sound asleep.

Joke's on her, though. I've never been more awake in my life.

I flip the page in Juliana Bekker's autobiography. I picked it up last week, figuring that if I was going to train Summer to be the best, I should study the best. She's a two-time Olympic gold medal surfer, and it really is a fascinating read. But I'm getting through each page at a glacial pace, anticipating Summer's arrival.

It's a cozy room. A decorative stone fireplace with a wrought iron grate faces the queen-size bed. Rustic sconces fill the room with pale, warm light. There's no TV, but there is an oversized armchair, with cushions so soft and worn-in they look like they'd swallow you up the second you touched down on them.

Notably, I haven't offered to sleep in it. Equally as notable: Summer hasn't insisted I do so.

Finally, the bathroom door squeals open. Summer's floral scent gushes into the room, more intoxicating than usual as it's accompanied by steam from her long shower. Her hair sits in loose waves. She's wearing a fitted T-shirt and tiny shorts to bed, definitely no bra by the looks of her straining nipples. She crosses her arms over her chest as she contemplates my very deliberate choice to forgo a shirt tonight.

I close my book, carefully placing it on the nightstand before nudging the frames up my nose. "Good shower?"

She nods, lingering on me. "I still can't believe you got your eyes checked."

I shrug. "You'll be farther out tomorrow than I could've seen without them."

"Oh," she whispers, arms falling limp at her sides. "Parker, that's really sweet."

She gives me a small smile, looking less tense by the second. I sit up, stretching out my legs. "Braids?"

"Hm?" Her brows rise, then fall as she figures out what I mean. "Oh. Yes, please."

She crosses the small room and climbs into bed. When I start working braids into her hair, her shoulders rise and fall in a deep, lung-filling breath. "All right, I think we officially need to talk about it. Parker, we almost kissed last week."

I keep my focus on her hair, twisting the strands together. "We did almost kiss last week."

"But then we didn't. So there's no reason to be weird about it, is there? And anyway, friends kiss all the time."

My hands pause mid-braid.

This is exactly opposite to the *no messing around within the friend group* rule she made clear in our teens. The rule that, coupled with her laugh, had humiliated me so thoroughly I erected military-grade mental barricades against anything resembling romantic thoughts about my best friend.

And just like that, she's cleared the blockade?

"Do they? Kiss all the time, I mean."

"Sure. All the time." Summer smooths the comforter underneath us, worrying over a wrinkled edge. "And ours was just an almost kiss. No reason to be weird about it. Nothing happened."

Ah. I see what's happening here. I'm being gently ushered back into the friend zone, just in time to share a bed. I should've seen this coming.

But I'm feeling petulant tonight. Those tense minutes at the reception desk proved that there's something happening between us. Something beyond friendship, no matter how much she wants to deny it. And I've got a spiral-bound notebook burning a hole in my duffel bag right across the room, commanding me not to retreat. Same way it did in that classroom.

Summer's dream man would fight for her, take risks for her, chance a broken heart just to show her how much she's wanted.

"Good to know," I say when I finish up the braids. "I'll keep that in mind the next time we almost kiss."

Summer whips around to look at me. I smooth the baby hairs along her forehead, unable to restrain a smile at the freckle hidden underneath. My freckle. "That's not—I didn't mean there would be a next time, Parker."

"Why not? Friends kiss all the time. You said it yourself."

"Yes, but . . ." She shakes her head, mouth opening and clos-ing. Gaze bouncing over my face. Eyelashes fluttering. "Parker, you can't . . . I can't . . ." With an impatient sound, she reaches for my glasses and carefully pulls them off me. "I can't think straight when you smile at me, wearing these things."

She glares when I smile bigger, so delighted by the confession. I should've gotten my eyes checked years ago. Summer folds the glasses and places them on her nightstand.

"Better?"

Her gaze falls to my dimples. Her lips purse. "Not really."

When I laugh, she slides under the covers and hits a light switch on the nightstand, unceremoniously plunging us into darkness. "I'm glad you're enjoying this."

"You finally admitting that I fluster you? Highlight of my life." I join her under the covers, and she wastes no time delivering a swift kick to my shin. I grab her leg before she can retreat to her side of the bed, sliding my hand over her soft skin, the toned muscles in her thigh.

Summer settles on her back, staring at the ceiling. "And yet you're the one who can't keep his hands off me."

"Not true. I kept my hands off you for years." I drift up her thigh and over, resting my hand on her far hip, arm stretched across her stomach. Her shirt's ridden up as she settled in bed, skin so warm and soft against mine. She shifts, the tip of my pinkie slipping under the loose waistband of her shorts. I can feel the edge of her panties and I really might fucking combust tonight.

Her cheek meets her pillow as she looks me over. "So, what's your excuse now?"

"Can and want are two very different things, Summer."

"What does that even mean?" She bristles, glaring at the ceiling again. I know the non-answers frustrate her. But I've got a long way to go before she'd ever agree to date me, so she'll have to get used to it.

"How're you feeling about tomorrow?" I ask.

"You've seen me surf. You know exactly how it's going to go."

She still hasn't managed a single barrel, and it's making us both nervous. Her, because of the revenge scheme. Me, because there's not a single thing worse than seeing her get dragged underwater like that and gasping for breath when she surfaces.

"You might get away with it," I say. "Rocky Ridge isn't known for its barrel waves."

"Which is why our scores here are weighted lower than in the rest of the series."

"So you'll just have to maximize every wave. Put yourself in as good a position as you can before the next event." She bites her lip. Her irritation has dissolved into stress, and that's the very last way she should enter the water tomorrow. "Talk to me, Sum. What's going on with your barrels?"

She swallows hard, hesitating around something. Then, with a shaky breath, she says, "I can't stop thinking about how I used to come to these things with Dad. It was half the fun of competing, you know? Being around him. We always talked about me qualifying for the tour after I graduated, how he'd come traveling with me. We'd have all these amazing adventures together, just me and him. Made it hard to miss my mom when it was us against the world."

I'm not sure what this has to do with the way she's surfing, but I nod anyway. "Did you tell him you were competing again?"

I watch as her eyes fill with tears. "He doesn't answer the phone."

"Love," I whisper, because what the hell do you say to that— which words could I give her to repair this kind of wound?

"I keep thinking about his twins, and how he comes home to them at night. And makes it to their soccer games, and has dinner with them, and talks to them through more than just words sporadically typed on a screen. I used to have all that with him, and he was . . . he was a really great dad to me, before everything."

She drags her fingers over her cheeks, smearing away her tears. I'm suddenly wishing I was a few hundred miles south, laying into David Prescott for causing her these tears and the hundreds more she's cried over him for years. She might have it in her heart to welcome him back, to keep trying for more with him, giving him chance after squandered chance. But I'll never forgive him for it.

"All I want is a phone call that he can't find the time to give me. And I know he's busy with work. He's—he's saving lives every day, and six-year-olds need their parents more than a thirty-year-old does—"

"Don't do that, love. Stop making excuses for people who aren't sorry. He fell short. You're allowed to say it, and you're allowed to be angry about it."

She eyes me, cheek pressed into her pillow. "The last time I competed, he was supposed to be there but didn't show. Our friends had their own things going on. It was you and me. Just like this."

"You and me." I squeeze her hip. "Minus your completely unsubtle attempt to get in my pants tonight."

"You wish," she says, chuckling wetly.

"I'm not complaining. It's pretty hot that you'd go for what you want like this—"

She claps a hand over my mouth, shuddering with laughter now. "You should be studied. Your delusions truly know no bounds."

I kiss her palm. She glares, but it's half-hearted. "Parker, I hope you know how grateful I am. I don't take it for granted that you're here for me. I'll never forget that, no matter where I go."

"And where are you going?" I ask gently. She only sniffs, though. "Summer, I know you took it to heart, the things Denny said to you. But you have no idea how much you attract people to you. You're the kind of light that draws people in, makes them thirst to be around you."

"And yet, an entire town turned on me a few weeks ago. And then there's Dad."

"You're surrounded by love, Sum. Don't let a few bad eggs take that away from you."

Summer closes her eyes, fresh tears leaking onto her cheeks. I reach for her face, wiping them away. I expect her to flinch, maybe make a dig at me. She doesn't.

"I've always wanted to do that," I admit.

She opens her eyes. "Have you?"

"It hurts when you cry. Makes it hard to breathe."

"But you've never wanted me like that."

"Summer, the things I want with you . . ." I stroke my thumb over her cheek, wishing I could do so much more than that. "If only you knew."

A crinkle of disbelief appears between her eyebrows. I never could stand to see Summer like this—feeling small and insignificant. The very opposite of the gravitational anchor she's always been for me.

"I've been embarrassing myself wearing Hawaiian shirts since I was sixteen," I say.

She bursts into laughter. "The first step is admitting you have a problem. Well done."

"You want to take a guess why I've been doing that?"

"Don't tell me you're suddenly renouncing the shirts. I don't buy it."

"Come on, Sum. Do you understand how thick and itchy they are? The colors don't even match. I know I'm of questionable sanity, but to *that* degree?" The playful derision in her face morphs to confusion. "D'you remember the first time I wore one?"

"My first day back at school after my mom's affair came out." She rubs her lips together. "Are you saying you hate Hawaiian shirts?"

"I'm saying that, despite hating Hawaiian shirts, I've been wearing them since I was sixteen. And I'd wear one every day for the rest of my life if it still made you laugh."

She blinks fast, warding away more tears but not taking her eyes off me. Deciding to push my luck, I slide across the sheets until we're just inches apart.

Her entire body calls to me but it's her lips I focus on, chest going painfully tight at the very thought of feeling them. I'm not sure I've ever needed—just *needed*—something so damn badly.

"What are you doing?" she whispers.

"Almost kissing you."

"*Why?*" The word comes out like a plea.

"Because I really fucking want you. More than I thought it was possible to want someone." I sweep her lower lip with my thumb. "Tell me you want me, too."

She closes her eyes. If I know anything about Summer, it's that she's currently conducting an entire conversation in her own head. Playing tug-of-war with herself. Analyzing every possible outcome of every possible decision.

I think my entire sanity might rest with that decision.

My heart thunders in my ears, a frantic, unsteady beat, waiting to see on which side she lands, taking me with her. Reliable friendship. Or something entirely different.

It stops dead, mid-beat, when Summer takes a breath, wrenches away from me. Scrambles off the bed and runs for the door.

Chapter 24

Summer

I fly down the dim, carpeted hall toward the grand staircase at the front of the inn, furious with myself and doing my best to be quiet as I pass rooms on either side of me.

I'm supposed to be keeping my head while Parker's clearly lost his. And I'd been doing a fine job of it since the first night back in our high school, until some sadistic being canceled the second room I'd been counting on.

Until he went and got those stupid, utterly ridiculous glasses. Just to watch me surf.

Until he confessed . . .

It'd been one of the hardest times of my life, the first time I ever saw a Hawaiian shirt on him. Trying to come to terms with my mother's affair while also enduring the relentless whispers around town. I'd been bursting into tears at random intervals all week long, alternating between fury on Dad's behalf, crushing disappointment in my own mother's behavior, and mourning the end of life as I knew it. I'd skipped school for days, trying to escape the curious eyes of my peers. Eventually, it sunk in—*really* sunk in—for Dad what she'd been doing. And the tension at home exploded into shouting matches and tears and slamming doors, to the point that being around my parents felt even more unbearable than the gossiping.

So I dragged myself to class. And there Parker was, waiting for me by the school's front doors, wearing a Hawaiian shirt I recognized as his dad's—a truly incomprehensible pattern of lobsters, lightning bolts, and bananas that had me crying laughing when I first saw it on Brian. It's probably, to this day, the hardest I've laughed in my life.

And on that miserable morning, I saw Parker wearing that stupid shirt and couldn't keep a damn smile off my face.

Why is it that I never noticed it until now? On my worst days, my hardest days, my most confusing days. For as long as I can re-member, he's shown up wearing one of those shirts. And it always makes me smile.

I touch my cheek, right over the place Parker just held me. The last thing I want is to ruin the only stable relationship in my life. I still don't understand where any of this is coming from for Parker; why he's gone years not looking at me twice—not in *that* way, at least— only to never look away now. Most of all, I'm furious with myself for getting swept up in it.

For wanting him. For the way my heart tugs whenever he touches me. For the question that's wormed its way into my brain, asking . . . *why not Parker?*

I'm walking fast, damn near breaking a sweat, with no idea or care as to where I'm going so long as I locate reserves of the good sense I seem to have misplaced. At the very least, I need to make it out of the door before—

"Summer." Parker's hushed voice carries down the hall. A peek over my shoulder shows him hurrying after me with a dark bundle in his hands. He even had the gall to put his glasses back on. The dark frames bracket his gorgeous eyes, selling fantasies of a hot-as-hell nerd who'll whisper filth in your ear as he fucks you hard, then cuddle you with your noses in a book after you're good and wrecked.

Dream scenario, honestly.

I turn a corner, the staircase now within sight. "Go back to bed, Parker."

"Where are you going?"

"For a walk."

"In your tiny pajamas?"

I pause just before the double staircase leading down to the foyer. Parker drags me through an archway a few feet away, into a dimly lit nook with armchairs, cut off from the rest of the hall. He unravels the mass of fabric and hands me an oversized sweater I recognize as his.

He takes a knee on the musty carpet, holding a pair of sandals, and grips my ankle. "Come on, Prescott."

"Don't." I step away, unable to stand the feel of him. My back hits the nook wall.

"Don't save you from sepsis?"

"Don't do *things*. Don't be thoughtful. Don't almost kiss me. And don't smile at me with those damn glasses on."

Parker rises, dimples out full force. "They really do it for you, huh?"

"Go back to bed, Parker."

His head tilts playfully. "That an order, Miss Prescott?"

"*Yes*. Go. Now, Parker." I splutter, trying to grasp onto anything halfway coherent. A task that becomes increasingly impossible with every slow step Parker takes toward me.

"Come with me." His gaze rakes down my body, from the tips of my braids down to my bare toes, glazing me in warm, sticky honey that suddenly makes it impossible to move. The sweater I'd been holding falls to our feet. "Come back to bed and tell me what you thought would happen when you canceled the second room."

"I did *not*—" I clamp my mouth shut when his twists with renewed mirth. He's teasing me, so shamelessly needling me. Why the hell can't I stop walking into it? I take fistfuls of his shirt and drive him back toward the hall. "You are so damn—"

"Handsome?"

"*Infuriating.* You don't want me, okay? You're going through something." I don't know which of us I'm saying this to. "You—you're confused. And I'm trying really hard to be a good friend to you."

"*Friends kiss all the time.* It's an old saying. Can't remember where I heard it."

"And what?" I fire back, stopping dead. There's no good reason to be breathing this hard. Other than the war waging within me, making my fists clench tighter around his shirt. "We become friends who kiss? Just like that?"

Parker's right dimple deepens, damn him. "Good idea. Let's start there."

He's doing his best to rile me up, get under my skin. Make me lose my goddamn mind over those dimples, and his hair, and his stupid fucking glasses.

I can't stand them.

Can't figure out how to stop wanting him.

How to make my head stop spinning, and my heart stop thumping. How to make my hands stop shaking with absolute, mind-numbing, maddening want for him.

Our noses are mere inches apart. Parker's lusty gaze falls to my mouth, goes a little desperate.

And that's the very last thing I see before surging up on my toes.

Oh my God, his lips are so soft. So warm, so—

I'm so absorbed in the shocking sensation of feeling him like this, this man I've known since we were kids, that I forget what to do. How to do this, how to kiss. I stand there frozen on the tips of my toes, fists braced against his chest, feeling his heart pump wildly beneath them.

Parker doesn't forget how.

His mouth parts just slightly, sucking on my lower lip so softly it startles me. His tongue sweeps the seam of my mouth, gently, seeking permission, and it's not . . .

It's nothing like I'd ever have anticipated it would be to kiss him. Because this is him, bull-in-a-china-shop Parker. Act first, think later Parker. I thought if anyone would kiss with chaos, it'd be him. Hands everywhere, uninhibited sounds. Not a care for who's watching the indecency unfold.

What he gives me, though? It's so much fucking better than that.

I come to my senses, part my lips for him, and he takes the opening without hesitation. He grazes my tongue with his, cups my cheek, brings us closer and kisses me deeper. It's soft and careful and everything my racing mind needs in this moment. He kisses me like only a best friend could. Like he's in my head with me, patiently watching an angry storm of panicked thoughts swirl around us.

For every internal shout of *what have I done?* he gives me a quieting press of his lips. Every *there's no coming back from this* he meets with a soothing brush of his thumb on my cheek. At *you've just ruined the friendship*, he gives a salacious lick of his tongue, answering *isn't this so much better, though?*

The hammering in my chest concurs. So does the way Parker sighs into my mouth when I sink my fingers into his hair. *See?* that sigh says. *So much fucking better.*

That's it. With a gentle nip to my lip, that's all I get before Parker pulls away to rest his forehead against mine.

His blue eyes are as lusty as I've ever seen them. Dark, needy, and staring right into my soul. "*That's* how you kiss?"

I inch away. "Was it bad?"

"For my sanity, maybe."

His eyes search mine and this time, I'm the one to read his mind. *Are we good?*

Good isn't even the half of it. That felt real. Right. There's a fresh wave of thoughts in my head, all of them demanding we do it again. Wondering whether it felt this right for him, too.

Typical me. One kiss and I've dropped the leash, letting my feelings run rampant. Picturing candlelit dinners. Love confessions. Diamond rings and grandchildren. All with Parker.

But damn if it isn't a pretty picture—and such a natural, seemingly inevitable evolution of our existing life together, that I'm wondering what the hell I've been doing *not* picturing this with Parker.

From where I'm standing now, it's the most obvious thing in the world.

A surge of nerves forces a laugh out of my mouth and Parker's face falls, shoulders drop. But then his gaze sweeps over the rest of me. The way I can't catch my breath, haven't let go of his hair.

His brows pull together. "You're nervous. That's a nervous laugh."

Parker places another soft kiss to my lips as though testing a theory.

I moan. He pulls back.

I giggle. He smiles.

And then he rips the glasses off his face, and he's kissing me again, and heat bursts inside me, covering every inch of my body. His fingers inch down, thumb my hips, curl into my ass, and he tugs me up into his body so that my toes barely touch the ground, walking me back into our hidden nook until I hit the wall.

This is it, the chaos. Pure greed and hedonism. And I'm right there with him.

I arch my back, pressing as deep into his firm body as I can. The fingers in his hair twist, tug. He groans into my mouth, and I have no idea where we are anymore. No idea what we're doing and why. All I care about is hearing that sound again, that needy, desperate sound—desperate for *me* in a way I've never felt before.

It's never been like this.

Of the hundreds of kisses I've had in my life, none of them have ever felt this way. Like a million butterflies awakening deep inside me, stretching their wings, pleased to have been summoned at last. Flying upward in unison, jamming the base of my throat, making it impossible to draw a single breath.

My leg hooks around his hip and with a rumble from deep in his chest, Parker lifts me up. Once I'm secured, his hand wanders up my waist, taking my shirt with him as his palm closes around my breast. A single swipe of his thumb over my nipple, and the small room echoes with my moan. My own hands wander over his stomach, lower, until I graze his straining cock.

With a ragged gasp, Parker grabs my wrists and pins them against the wall at my sides. "Fuck, Summer. Go easy on me, please."

"Your dick disagrees." I shift until my clit meets his hard length, eliciting a groan.

"I can feel how wet you are." His lips find mine, and I'm torn. I want to kiss him, but my body now seems to be operating on a power source solely consisting of his groans and I can't help grinding on him, drawing out more of them. "Goddamn, Summer, you're soaking through our clothes."

"So are you." I can feel it, the sticky mess we're making as we move together. I fight against his hold on my wrists, wanting to touch him, but Parker doubles his grip, keeping me trapped to the wall. I moan loudly, and it's silly, embarrassing that something so simple would do it for me like this.

But this feeling—being tied down, being *kept*, it's—

Parker nips my neck. "You ever been tied up, Summer?"

I shake my head.

"You know why I like doing it?"

Another shake.

"It takes away the distractions. Lets me focus on the good stuff." He drags his cock over my pussy and I gasp. "Yeah, that. Do you know how long I've been dying to hear your sounds? To watch you crumble underneath me? I'd get to do that over and over, for as long as I want to hear them. Until you can't take anymore. It's all I want, you know?"

I'm trembling from the in-fighting between my head, my heart, and the pulse in my clit, wanting that—wanting *him* so damn badly. Parker sucks on a sensitive spot on my neck—the one he discovered after our first late-night swim.

And my next words tumble out of me before I have a chance to think them through.

"Show me."

Chapter 25

Summer

A breath gusts out of Parker. His eyes flick over my face.

The man really does have the lustiest stare I've ever seen, in a way that's somehow both measured and intense. It silently threatens to ruin me, and promises I'll love every minute of it. Beg for seconds.

"Parker," I urge, when his silence becomes unbearable.

"Heard you, love."

I blink and suddenly I'm on my feet, the world around me spinning until my cheek meets the cool wall, my back now to Parker. I peek over my shoulder to find him yanking at the waistband of his sweats, freeing the drawstring.

Oh God.

Oh God, oh God, *yes*—

The feel of soft cotton ghosts over me, just a whisper on my skin. Parker threads the drawstring around my wrists once, twice, three times.

The binding is loose, and it's a letdown. I hate that he'd go easy on me when he's supposed to know me better than anyone. He should have a better grip on what I can and can't handle.

And then the thick, excruciating silence is broken by my startled gasp when Parker tugs on the string snapping my wrists together. It bites into my skin, sizzling a path through my flesh, up my arms, down my torso, all the way to my pussy. There's absolutely no give to it. I feel every pinch of it right in my clit, throbbing against the seam of my shorts.

Parker's lips trace lazy lines on the side of my neck and he knots it. "Talk to me. How does it feel?"

"I like it." I'm shaking so hard my knees bounce together, satisfaction filling me the same way it did when he trapped my hands against the wall. Held on to me like he never intended to let me go, wanted to keep me close for good. "Keep going."

Parker's hands travel up my body, cupping my breasts. "And where should I start, huh?" His thumb brushes my nipple through my shirt, drawing out a needy gasp. "Here? I've dreamed about pushing these perfect tits together, sliding my cock between them, more times than you can possibly imagine. Would you let me do that, Summer?"

It should feel weird, shouldn't it? My best friend's hands on me, his voice saying the things he just did—it shouldn't feel so natural. Shouldn't sound so damn appealing.

"I've got something that might feel better than that," I whisper.

Parker's hand trails down my stomach. The heel of his palm grinds over my clit. "Here? This is where you want me?"

I'm panting. "Uh-huh."

"Well, then let's see what we're working with." His fingers slip into my shorts. His thumb slides over my clit in a way that makes me sigh into the wall while his other fingers tease at my entrance. I'm whimpering before he even sinks a finger inside, and close my eyes at the stretch of it.

"That's gonna be a tight fucking fit." His words are presumptuous as hell, but my lust-addled brain doesn't bother fighting him on it. I want him, and every easy, wet slide of his finger in and out of me tells him just how badly I do. "This pussy's gonna ruin my life, I can feel it."

"Is that a good thing?"

"The best thing." With his other hand, Parker turns my chin over my shoulder and kisses me hard and fast. He drags his cock over my ass, groaning into my mouth. "The best, Summer. And if you don't think I'm going to spend all night ruining yours—making sure I haunt you, waking or asleep, until you can't lay eyes on me without begging to be filled? Love, you have no idea what you're in for."

I'm shuddering, my entire body pleading with him to take whatever he wants from me. He's grinding into my ass, finger-fucking me and teasing my clit, and maybe it's not going to get me there—nothing ever does, unless it's battery operated—but it's enough to make my vision dissolve at the edges. I rock my hips and arch my back, trying to take his finger deeper and give him better friction.

"I'm gonna take you to bed now," he murmurs. "You're going to sit this pussy on my face and come on my tongue as many times as I ask you to. And you're gonna be loud as fuck about it. You got it?"

Shit. A storm detonates in head, the same mix of needy demands and anxious questions that flooded me the moment his lips first touched mine.

Me and Parker.

We're about to—we're actually going to—and he thinks that . . . Before I can stop myself, I blurt, "I use a vibrator to come."

"Okay." Parker's voice is thick as he kisses along my jaw, finger-fucking me excruciatingly slow.

I don't think my words registered. The reality that it won't lead to anything but his own frustration when my body refuses to cooperate.

"Parker." My face burns even against the cool wall. "I try really hard. But it's never happened without one."

His mouth stalls inches from mine, hand pausing. I can feel him thinking hard, his jagged breaths hitting my skin. "Do you want to stop?"

Tears of frustration prickle my eyes. Stopping is the very last thing I want. But I need him to understand, to save us both the embarrassment. "I don't have a toy here. I can't come without one. And if it bothers you . . ."

Parker's hand slides out of my shorts. He takes me by the shoulders and turns me around to see the deep furrow in his brow. "Does it bother *you*?"

I fiddle with my fingers, my wrists still bound together behind my back. This has already taken a ridiculous turn. A moment ago, I had his finger inside me, and now . . . what? I'm going to explain to him the pitfalls of my faulty lady bits? I feel so stupid and vulnerable, and I don't know what's wrong with me.

"It feels . . . emasculating."

His confusion gives way to a teasing grin. "You feel emasculated by your own toys?"

"No." My wrists tense against the rope, preventing my impulse to cover my face with my hands. "It makes guys feel emasculated."

Parker's humor falls away. "And how do toys make *you* feel?"

"Oh. Really good. Great, once I get the hang of them."

"I'm . . . so happy and incredibly turned on to hear that. But I meant, how does needing a toy during sex make you feel?"

I hang my head, face positively flaming. "Please, just push me down the stairs."

He laughs softly. "I thought you said we didn't have to be weird about these things."

"Clearly, I was wrong!" I cry, looking anywhere but at him. "I don't know why you listen to me, anyway. I've lost my mind. Completely lost it. I just let you touch my—I'm telling you about my vibrators!"

"Summer." He takes my chin between his fingers and angles me to face him. He's smiling and it's teasing, but it's also unbelievably sweet. "I'm not feeling weird about this at all."

Parker looks at me like . . . Parker. Open and earnest. It's enough to loosen the tension in my shoulders.

"Oh." I swallow. "Well, I can get off without toys when I'm alone. But I think a lot during sex. Like, about body angles and making my boobs look bigger than they are, and whether I missed a spot while I was shaving or if he's having a good time." I hesitate. "Sometimes I think about the snack I'll have after we finish."

Parker bursts out laughing. "What's your go-to postcoitus snack?"

I want to smack him, but my hands are still tied. "Chocolate-covered almonds. And a Diet Coke."

"In canned form?"

"Obviously." I'm smiling now, and we're grinning at each other like fools. For some reason I feel the need to clear the air because I add, "I like my toys. A lot. They're my best friends."

Parker's smile plummets. "Take that back."

"It's true. They make me feel good. Like, *really* good."

"So do I." He's glaring.

I shrug. "It's not the same."

"It could be." He cups my face, thumb stroking my cheek. "I like toys. Toys are fun. And I *really* like your pussy. If you let me, I'll play with it however you need to feel good."

And just like that, I become hyperaware of the rope around my wrists. Of Parker and the things we've just done together. I want to keep chasing the high of kissing him, those ruthless butterflies demanding more of him. Yet, I'm brutally aware that we've just grossly shattered the friendship boundaries that I'm supposed to safeguard.

And that I'm on the eve of my first surf contest in years. That if I get my way, I won't be in town past the end of summer.

And he doesn't even know.

Parker gives me a soft smile, taking in the hesitation plain on my face. "Another time, then?"

"I . . ." *Can't wait.* "It's . . ." *A bad idea.* "You . . ." *Just ruined my life with a single kiss.*

"A tongue-tied Summer Prescott. Never thought I'd see the day." His smile goes a bit smug as he picks up his glasses, apparently accurately translating every fragmented sentence. He turns me around and unties my wrists, then runs gentle lines along the dents left in my skin. "Just imagine what you'll be like when we finally—"

My stomach bursts. "Not gonna happen."

Parker flips me back to face him. He inches closer, still wearing that offensive smile. Those goddamn glasses. He brushes our lips together, and a breathless giggle escapes me.

"You're so full of it," he whispers, pleased as punch by the reaction. "We both know you'll be back for more."

Chapter 26

Summer

I'm jolted awake by the rapid strumming of an electric guitar.

The sound fills our pitch-black room at increasingly deafening decibels, whipping me into full consciousness. An aggressive keyboard sound follows, which I recognize as the irritating tune of "Eye of the Tiger," and before I can theorize about the unfathomable reasons why this particular song is being blasted before the break of dawn, a voice calls over the music.

"Rise and shine, Prescott." Parker's voice is thick with laughter and comes from somewhere near the corner of the room. I didn't even feel him get out of bed. "You've got waves to surf and adulterers to humiliate."

I blindly throw a pillow in his direction before flicking on my bedside lamp. It lands several feet short of where Parker is bent over in laughter.

I want to be mad. I really, really do.

But the big idiot is wearing the most hideous Hawaiian shirt, a truly horrific pattern of aquamarine pineapples and orange hibiscus flowers that drapes over his body and does absolutely nothing for his suntanned complexion. It puts a smile on my face, just like it always does.

Just like he wants it to.

Quickly, I drag a hand over my face to dislodge any crustiness. Run my fingers over my braids to tame them before he gets a good look at me. Casually, I lean back on a hand, and . . .

You dirty little harlot. Are you pushing out your tits?

Apparently, the stern lecture I stayed up giving myself last night was for nothing.

Once Parker drifted to sleep, apparently unperturbed by our near hookup while I stared at the dark ceiling resisting the urge to tuck into his side, I decided I was going to go with the flow, for once.

Unless otherwise discussed, last night was just a kiss. Some casual heavy petting. A little kink exploration between old friends. Nothing to overthink. I'm going to focus on surfing my best today. Qualifying for the tour at the end of this series, getting my fresh start out of Oakwood. Surfing the world. The endless adventure I'd always planned to have, with nothing tying me down.

Drawstrings included.

So, I force myself to hunch. Then Parker swipes at his phone, killing that abominable song before righting himself, and . . . *Why hello, Mr. Woods.*

I completely forgot about the glasses. He nudges them up his nose and, oh my God, I think I almost came just now.

Yep. You're definitely pushing out your tits.

"Check it out." Parker unbuttons his Hawaiian shirt to reveal a white T-shirt with the words TEAM SUMMER written in hot-pink glitter letters across the front. "What do you think?"

Those butterflies surge inside me—the dormant ones that came alive at the touch of Parker's lips last night. "Did you make that?"

"Took some trial and error, and I'll be finding glitter in my apartment until the end of time. But I think it turned out nice."

I cannot stop smiling. "You look ridiculous."

"Ridiculously hot." Parker shuffles across the mattress. His dimples peek through. "Morning."

Those damn butterflies flit and fly. "Hi."

"I got you something." He lifts a package wrapped in pink off his nightstand. There's a mini paper airplane stuck to the front, and I unfold it to reveal Parker's messy scrawl. *Team Summer forever.*

I tear into the package, head falling back with a laugh when it reveals a matching Hawaiian shirt. It's atrocious, in a fabric that feels more like carpet than an article of clothing. "Parker, there's no way I'm wearing this."

"You have to. It's our team colors. And it'll score you extra style points."

"There's no such thing as style points."

"Because they've never seen these shirts." Parker motions to it, bathing me in the wattage from his smile. "Try it on."

He looks so pleased with himself that I do what he says. It's faint, but the shirt smells like him, pepper and safety, and I wonder how long it's been sitting in his apartment waiting to be gifted.

"Smile." Parker tucks me against him and holds out his phone for a selfie. My French braids are disheveled, hair sticking out at odd angles.

"Park, I look terrible."

"You're perfect." He buries his face in the top of my head. I don't know whether he's forgotten that there's a front-facing camera pointing at us, putting his every move and expression on display. Or if he simply doesn't care that I see the way his eyes shut as he draws a breath, looking so intensely content with his face in my hair.

It makes me soften into his side. Makes me smile, and rest my head on his shoulder. Gives me permission to pretend—just for this very second—that the paper plane, and matching shirts, and the photo that he immediately sets as the background on his phone, are his way of staking his claim on me for anyone to see.

Team Summer forever.

～～～

"Hey, Dad. Guess what—I'm at Rocky Ridge! You wouldn't believe how much they've changed the boardwalk here. That ice cream shop we used to love—the one with the huge cow statue out front you'd always make us take a picture with? Do you remember? I went to find it but it . . . it's gone now. Made me a bit sad, you know? We had so many good times there, and . . . it's really weird being here without you, Dad. I really miss you. Anyway. Wish me luck."

～～～

The beach is alive with spectators even this early in the morning; they're laughing and chattering over the music blaring from speakers. It's a steel drum tune that, coupled with the rushing sounds of the ocean and abundant smell of sunscreen, makes me feel as though I should be sipping on a poolside daiquiri.

Instead, I hover to the side of the competitors' registration tent, failing miserably at talking myself through meditative breaths. That was my dad's job, back when I'd compete. He'd take me by the shoulders and then breathe with me. *Big breath in, Sunshine. I love you no matter what. I'll be right here waiting for you.*

Until he stopped showing up.

My lungs fill with nostalgia, rather than air, which does nothing to loosen the tightness in my shoulders. In my earliest competition days, I'd have a small village of people there to support me. A whole family, given and chosen.

A flash of color in my periphery has me looking around at Parker, who stands at the registration tent. He offered to sign me in to save me from facing Danica, my old volunteer-mate sitting behind the registration table. The wind blows his Hawaiian shirt wide open, revealing the glitter letters on his T-shirt.

"Summer?"

The smile that had crept onto my face at the sight of those glitter letters dies.

Denny strides across the beach toward me. For weeks, I refused to linger on what it might be like to see him again, but that was clearly a mistake—I should've prepared for the sight of him, the easy smile he shoots me. As though we're simply old friends reuniting, and I haven't spent the weeks since I last saw him trying to maintain a semblance of the confidence he did his best to shred.

Not everyone's wife material.

You've been following around this guy Parker your whole life, and not even he wants you that way.

"Figured I might see you here." Denny props his surfboard against the side of the registration tent, like he's settling in for a lengthy catch-up.

"What makes you say that?" I'm grateful that my voice is level, even though I swing my board around so that it partially shields me from him.

Denny gestures vaguely at the tent. "You talked about this volunteer thing all the time."

"I'm not volunteering. I'm competing. Hence the board."

Denny contemplates my pink wetsuit and the Hawaiian shirt over it. He shakes his head. "You're not competing."

"What's that supposed to mean?"

"Come on, Summer. Okay, so you can stay upright on a surfboard, but *compete*?" I'm no longer an old friend of his. Denny now looks at me like I'm a pitiful, desperate woman he's been trying to get rid of for years. "If this is some kind of effort to see me, or get back at me for your feelings getting hurt . . ."

Fury races through me. "This has nothing to do with—"

"Do my eyes deceive me? Summer Prescott in a wetsuit, board in hand?"

My eyes close in relief. Even without looking, I know it's Harriet Young approaching, one of the series' judges. I recognize her easy drawl, can practically *feel* Denny straightening at my side.

I plant my board into the sand as she reaches us, taking my unspent anger at Denny out on the beach. "Hey, Harriet, I'm—"

"Harriet." Denny feeds her that happy smile, the one he'd blinded me with for weeks, and sticks out his hand for her. "Denny McCoy. Great to see you again."

My knees give a dangerous wobble. He told me his last name was Peterson.

I am such a fucking idiot.

Harriet gives Denny's hand a quick shake. "Denny, you're in for a real treat if all this means Summer's competing again—I've watched her dominate the water since she was a kid. It was a travesty she ever stopped."

Her singing my praises to Denny should have me smiling. Instead, I pray to the surf gods to get me through at least one barrel today. "I am competing. It feels great to be back."

"And will it be the one event? Or am I seeing you all the way through the series?"

I feel Denny's eyes on me. "All the way through. And then hopefully onto the tour. And then the Masters Tour after that."

"That's what I like to hear." She sets her sunglasses on top of her head and smiles at my board. "I have to say, I'm more than a little envious. My years on tour were some of the best of my life."

"How long did you compete?"

"I made it onto three tours. Each better than the last." She smiles fondly over at the ocean. "It's pure magic. Feeds your competitive spirit as an athlete, while folding you into a tight, sincerely *kind* community. Everyone's in such awe of each other, you know? I met some of my closest friends on the tour. Saw places I never would've without it. In my second year, I started leading surf trips for young women in between events, and that was fulfilling in itself—introducing people to my own first love." Longing and envy coil together, a thread pulling right in the center of my chest. "And then there's the waves. You ever surfed outside the country?"

"Tons of times," Denny cuts in. "The wave at Jeffreys Bay is a favorite of mine."

"It's a good one." Harriet gives him a smile before refocusing on me. "And you?"

"I've surfed some of the classics on the West Coast. But I've never been outside the country, let alone lived outside of Oakwood."

Harriet's smile is teasing, but her excitement is palpable—as though she were in my shoes, on the brink of experiencing it all again herself. It pumps me with this thrilling, buzzing feeling all the way down to my fingers. The one you get when you're, at long last, just minutes away from the thing you've been waiting ages for.

"Oh, you small-town girl. You're going to have your mind blown by what's out there waiting for you."

She's getting far ahead of herself, seeing as I haven't yet surfed a single heat in this series, and I still can't stay on my feet when it counts. But the adventure, the exhilarating waves. The new friendships, self-discovery, and the competitive glory. It's exactly what had driven my longing for the tour years ago.

Until my longing for a home overrode it. And I swept the jagged pieces of that broken dream into a dark corner of my heart, never to be seen again.

Now, with Harriet beaming down at me, those broken pieces shudder to life and inch back together, not as dead and buried as I thought they'd been. For the first time this summer, this series doesn't simply feel like an escape, but a tentative reintroduction to my own first love.

Harriet's gaze drifts over my shoulder, grin going wider. "*Ah*. That boy's still following you around, is he?"

Parker materializes at my side with my red jersey slung over his shoulder. But any fear that he overheard us talking about the tour is squashed when he gives Harriet—who he doesn't seem to recognize—a polite smile, before turning hard, unforgiving eyes on Denny.

"Can we help you with something?"

"Oh dear. Am I sensing some hostility?" Harriet bounces an amused gaze from Parker to Denny. "A little competitive spirit over the girl, perhaps?"

Denny barks a laugh that makes me shrink into Parker's side. "Definitely not."

My throat clogs, face flames in humiliation. And then I realize Parker's entire body has tensed. He's still fixed on Denny, jaw pulsing furiously, eyes threatening hellfire.

Shit. I fist his Hawaiian shirt before he has a chance to lash out. But Parker shocks me to my core when he takes a breath. And instead of throwing punches, he throws an arm around me. Tucks me into his side as though to shield me from the other man, while I stare up at him like he's grown a second head.

"Definitely not," he says, peering down at me with a gentle smile. "She's all mine. I'm not stupid enough to risk fumbling someone like Summer."

My stomach flips, even knowing he's only said it for Denny's benefit.

Harriet grins at us. "How sweet."

Parker kisses the top of my head. "We better go get you ready. You're up in fifteen minutes."

With a parting wave to Harriet, I let Parker steer me toward the competitors' area.

"Are you all right? I looked away for one second, and that jackass was next to you."

"He just can't help himself. It's like he's pissed off I declined carrying on with that . . . *situation*, and all he wants to do is squash what's left of me. I've been pretending I wouldn't see him."

"The guy you're specifically here to embarrass?"

My bare feet slip on the sand. "I was focused on the surfing, really."

Nothing's ever come close to feeling as wrong as withholding the truth from Parker—especially now that I've realized exactly *how* badly I want it. But all I can picture is the way he'd stood clutching that pair of socks like a lifeline in his messy living room the night we made up. The desperation in his voice as he begged me to let him back in. I couldn't live with myself if I caused him to backslide after the effort he's put into himself.

I'll tell him the second I'm sure he's ready to hear it.

Parker stops us a few yards short of the roped-off competitors' area. He sits my board on the sand and places his hands on my shoulders, drawing me just a foot away from his body.

"Close your eyes." I give him a look. "I told you, love. You'll be the one back for more. Now, close your eyes."

I do and he moves his hands up, along the sides of my neck, until he's holding my face, brushing his thumbs along my cheekbones. "Big breath in, Summer."

I do what he says, the same nostalgia as earlier filling me.

"I know we're here on some big bid for vengeance, but we don't have to be." We're standing so close that Parker's open Hawaiian shirt flutters against me with the breeze. "You can be here because surfing is what you love—what you've always loved. Because I never see you smile as big as when you land an aerial. Even when you're just sitting on the beach, waxing our boards, you're at your happiest. And Summer?"

    I open my eyes to find faint dimples in his cheeks. Parker points to his chest, at the TEAM SUMMER glittering back at me. "Win or lose."

Chapter 27

Summer

Lose.

I figure out I'm losing this event about halfway through the day, when the tide turns, waves swell bigger, and the barrels that've eluded us all morning start properly forming. They're small at first, the kind you'd really have to sit nearly all the way down to fit into. And then they grow to the kind you could ride in a comfortable squat— assuming I could ride them at all.

Three-person heats turned to one-on-ones the deeper I got into the event. During the breaks in between, I gulped down water and stretched, trying to stay loose for the next round. And the one after that.

My arms are sore from paddling, fingertips permanently wrinkled, braids weighed down with salt water. I've had near-misses and the kind of tumbles I'd never have had back when I was consistently competing. But I managed to pull through every round to the quarter finals.

And then the barrels came.

My first wipeout? Acceptable—I was just getting a feel for it.

My second? A little embarrassing but nothing I couldn't recover from.

My third? Indicative of a problem I won't be shaking off today.

The giant scoreboard on land lays it out for me: There are six minutes left in this heat. And I'm five and a half points behind Katy Nichols's total score.

After wipeout number three, I've been relying on the smaller performance waves, hoping that showing off my skill set might be enough to tempt the judges into a decent score. The message they've been sending back? *Ride the damn barrels, Prescott.*

To anyone watching me, it's clear that I can't.

To me, it's clear that I *won't*. I just can't make myself do it.

So I've been giving up the waves to Katy, leaving points on the table that she's been effortlessly picking up. The beach is just as busy as it was this morning, the crowd's sounds still just as loud whenever Katy pulls off a good wave.

I rise and fall with the water now, focusing on the stretch of ocean behind me. The incoming ripples, deep blue turning to white as water breaks without fully forming. Katy paddles back toward me after completing her last wave. I've got priority on the next set, and with so little time left in the heat, mine is likely the final wave of the round.

And it needs to be a good one. My best one.

Finally, I spot a decent set coming with only minutes left to go. A fast-forming wall of blue, stormy as Parker's eyes, rising higher as it approaches. If I want to make it through to the next round, this has to be the one.

Paddling hard, I imagine the sour look on Denny's face when I take the top score from him at the end of the series. Picture a delighted Harriet awarding me an oversized check with my winnings.

You're surrounded by love, Sum. Don't let a few bad eggs take that away from you. I let Parker's words wash over me, take hold of me. Let myself believe them and use them to fuel me as I pop up on my board and carve down the face of the wave.

My braids whip behind me as water propels me forward at the kind of pace that requires every single muscle to fire just to keep me upright. I owe Parker an endless supply of Mountain Dew for his training program. Spray slaps me in the face as I slice through the first section of the wave, and I smile to myself when I'm able to get a tiny bit of air off the lip.

This.

This is the feeling that gets me out of bed every morning, has me hauling ass to Crystal Cove despite the hurt of spending hours at the spot where Dad and I shared so many happy memories before our life together blew up. The people on shore, those in the water—none of them exist anymore. Yesterday's shitty day at work? Never happened. I am fearless, untethered. Euphoric. My body working exactly the way it should without my giving it a thought. The forces of nature aligning to offer me, Summer Freya Prescott, the unrivaled pleasure of surfing a perfect wave.

That feeling lasts about a split second.

That damn barrel starts to form, water curling, falling onto itself. And I have every intention of disappearing inside it—I really do. A barrel like this one would get me through to the next round, easy. I lift up at the bottom of the wave, align with its opening. Scramble to hold on to that blissed-out feeling.

I imagine packing my bags and bidding a not-so-sad farewell to my silent apartment and everyone in town. Landing in Portugal and surfing the wave I've dreamed about since I was a kid. Tasting the salt water just to know whether it's different from back home. Meeting new people, making new friends, exploring a different world than the only one I've ever known.

You're surrounded by love, Sum—

I picture my friends at a table at Oakley's on a busy Friday evening while I'm away. Laughing together as they plan a group trip to watch Brooks's first game of the season. One of them—Parker maybe—suggests they dial me in on a video call. But then they're interrupted by Wynn, who's eagerly come to share the latest town gossip, and they forget all about me.

The sound of water thunders in my eardrums. Thick and dangerous panic builds in my throat, threatening to cut off my air supply.

I kick my board out from under me, bailing on the wave before I can't breathe anymore.

Regret hits the second I plunge into the water.

Chapter 28

Parker

"Three more."

Summer grits her teeth, grip tightening around the loaded barbell lying across her shoulders. There's a faint sheen of sweat along her hairline, making the dusting of baby hairs stick to her skin. The ends of her French braids brush her chest as she sinks into a squat, ass absolutely tensing against her pale purple shorts.

Every part of her exudes power and strength. Ruthless determination. She's been pushing our training harder than ever this week, trying to make up for her fifth-place finish at Rocky Ridge—to punish herself a little for it, too, if I know her. But gifting me the view of a lifetime in the process.

I could happily die like this, I think. Standing in Brooks's home gym, just watching her body flex and release, her abs peeking out from where her shirt's ridden up. She's a perfectly packaged dichotomy—the softest heart wrapped in strength and a well-earned toned body.

More than once in the two days since we returned home, I've wondered if I've gone fully insane and completely imagined the events of that inn. Because why would Summer Prescott, in all her glory, ever let someone like me anywhere near her?

Let alone *in* her. Just a finger, but still.

Those minutes have been playing on a loop, like a translucent filter over my vision all week. No matter what I'm doing, where I am, who I'm with—it's all secondary to the sight of Summer's sun freckles up close. The curve of her Cupid's bow as she smiled at me. Her green eyes crinkling as she gave that soft laugh—*the* laugh, the one I misunderstood back in high school—and then squeezing shut with pure pleasure as I touched her.

The feel of her in my hands *haunts* me. Her body responded to mine as though, at least for one single blissful moment, she longed for me, too.

I've been dying for more. But she's been so down on herself about her score at the surf event and it hasn't felt right to press her on it. Still, there's a permanent stream of tension flowing between us since. The kind where you know something's coming—something major, inevitable—just waiting for the opportunity to present itself.

Not a matter of if, but when.

I rub a hand over my jaw as she comes out of her squat then sits back into another like it's nothing. And then again.

My head tilts, just watching her body move. "One more."

Summer releases the softest grunt. "What? That was three."

"No, it wasn't." *Yes, it was.* "One more, Summer."

She grumbles but does it. Dipping all the way down, then up. *Killing me.* "One more."

"Are you—" With a sound that's halfway between a laugh and a furious growl, Summer racks the bar and pivots to face me, gripping the metal hanging between us. "I've always known your ethics were shaky. But making your client squat for your own viewing pleasure? A whole new level of depravity."

She's teasing, but I can see it in the mirrors lining the wall behind her: the way she's arching her back, wiggling that little ass of hers. Leaning forward against the bar so that the tops of her breasts swell out of the low-cut neckline of her shirt.

Flirting, whether she means to or not.

I grip the bar, too, right beside her hands so that our pinkies touch. "If it's too hard for you and your delicate constitution, just say so. We can take it easy if you need to."

"*Please*—I could squat you in my sleep."

"Yeah?" I lean in so that my chest meets the bar, just inches away from her. It'd take nothing to kiss her. "Let's see it, Prescott."

No hesitation. She ducks under the bar and fists my shirt, driving me back to make room for herself.

A startled laugh leaves me. Summer circles my waist, bends at the knees, and hinges her hips, like she really expects me to let her injure herself to prove a point.

"Summer, are you insane?" I pry her away to find her laughing breathlessly, eyes closed, entire body shuddering even as she tries to wrestle out of my hold.

"Let me do it!"

"*Fuck* no!"

"Then admit you were making me squat to check me out."

"Oh, is that all you wanted?" She really is strong. When I wrangle her arms behind her and flip her around so that her back meets my front, it's with far more effort than I needed last weekend. "Of course I was checking you out. No one's got an ass like you do, Summer. No one moans quite like you do, either."

We lock eyes in the mirror ahead. Her laugh fades, but that playful spark still lights up her eyes. "That was a one-time gift from me to you. Savor it. Maybe put it in your diary so you don't forget."

"Good thinking." I brush her ear with my lips and she actually shivers. "Dear diary: Three days ago, my best friend begged me to tie her up—in a B&B hallway, no less—and then asked me to finger her until—"

She smirks. "Dear diary: Three days ago, I admitted to my best friend how desperate I am to push together her tits—her *perfect* tits, is what I actually called them—"

I nip the side of her neck. "Dear diary: Three days ago, my best friend let me finger her in a B&B hallway, and she's been replaying it so often that she's got my *exact* words memorized."

Summer's body melts back into mine. "How would you know that unless *you* were replaying it often?"

"Summer, love, if you think there's even a second of the day when I'm not obsessing over you to a near-debilitating degree, then you're not paying attention at all."

She stares back through the mirror. Eyes amused. Eyebrows crinkled in disbelief. Her entire backside pressing into me.

And I'm officially done playing this game of ours. The one where we pretend that nothing's changed between us. That I don't want to spend my every waking moment kissing her. That she doesn't look at me in a way that's very different than the way she does our guy friends.

Summer might not think I'm her dream man, but she wants me, and it's about damn time we stop dancing around that. I'm taking matters into my own hands. Making big moves on her Dream Man list, starting this Summer Friday.

With a kiss to her temple I release her, shoving her gently toward the squat rack. She catches herself on the metal bar, blinking at my reflection in the mirror, a little disoriented.

"Back to work, Prescott. And make it twenty reps, this time."

~~~~~

"Did you kiss?"

"No."

"Hook up?"

"No."

River bats his lashes, pouting over at me. "Aw, Parker. Did you finally get to hold your crush's hand?"

I resist the urge to hip check the kid into a nearby bush. We're half an hour into a light hike on the trail near Brooks's place, and as much as it would satisfy me to send River's smug smirk flying, I'm not even sure I'd be able to manage it this morning.

He's without crutches, looking stronger on his feet. Unbothered enough by our pace and the uneven terrain to be able to go in on me about the state of my relationship with Summer after witnessing our goodbye as they traded places in my morning schedule.

"I'm not talking about my dating life with you. You're a kid." I lead him up the path on a mild incline as we loop back around toward Brooks's gym. The dirt trail is lined with densely packed pine trees and otherwise deserted—I didn't know it existed until Brooks mentioned it a couple of days ago.

"I turn eighteen in a few months. And we both know you weren't an angel at my age."

"I'll have you know that I was a very responsible and studious seventeen-year-old. Focused on my education."

A laugh bursts out of River as we near a fallen log blocking our path. "I live in town. Have heard plenty about what you were like at my age, and *studious* is the last thing they called you."

River doesn't wince as he easily steps over the log, and a flood of pride pours into me, dulling my annoyance. Because *that*—having found a way to motivate this kid, who came to me all doom and gloom a few weeks ago?

No better reason to get out of bed in the morning.

It's what made me fall in love with this career in the first place— making an impossible situation feel possible, and then proving us both right. And if I've got anything to do with it, he's going to make that high school team come the start of the school year. Going to impress those scouts. Going to get recruited to a college very, very far away so that I never again have to endure the smirk he gives when he glances over at me.

"Maybe tone down the pathetic puppy thing when I'm around, then," River goes on. "You can't expect me to witness what I did this morning and not say anything."

"I wasn't acting like a pathetic—"

"Bye, Summer! Have a great day at work, Summer! I'll see you for dinner tonight, right? Text me later!" River bounces on his toes, enthusiastically waving at a pine tree in an exaggerated but not altogether false imitation of me.

"Have you called Macy yet?" I ask. River's expression turns vindictive. "Then I don't want to hear another thing about me and my girl."

"She's your girl now?"

"She is." River gives me a look. "All right, so she isn't my girl yet. But at least I'm talking to her, which is more than you can say."

We emerge from the hiking path right into the sprawling yard behind Brooks's house, a ranch-style mini mansion that puts my above-a-bar apartment to shame.

"That was a forty-minute hike," I tell River with a check of my watch. We round the house to the open garage doors leading to the gym.

"It was mostly flat and we were going at a snail's pace."

I fling out an arm to stop him in the driveway. All the joy he'd gotten out of teasing me seems to have evaporated. "That was a *forty-minute hike*, Nowak. Without crutches. Let that sink in for a second."

He gives me a half-hearted smile. "Nothing pinched this time."

"Fucking right, it didn't. And you know what? I will gladly let you give me hell about making eyes at my girl if it means you do it again tomorrow."

That half-smile turns full smirk. "Again, I'm compelled to ask: Your girl?"

I groan. "Way to ruin a moment."

River walks off toward the gym. "There was no moment."

"There was," I call, eyes narrowed on his back. "We were having a moment, and you know it."

His reflection in the wall of mirrors rolls its eyes. "I know nothing about a moment."

I turn at the sound of a car pulling up behind us, expecting River's dad, but it's a dark SUV coming to a stop in the driveway instead. The window lowers, and Noah waves me over from the driver's seat. I haven't seen him in a month, not since I got kicked out of my sister's house the night I made up with Summer.

"I was hoping to catch you here," he says when I come up to the window.

"That's ominous as hell. What can I do for you?"

Noah jerks a thumb at his gym bag in the back seat. "I just finished training at your last place of work. Happy to report that Don is still trying to ruin my off-season with more sessions than I probably need."

I chuckle, but there's nothing funny about it. "Good to know he's as useless as ever. I'm sorry I got you saddled with him when I left."

"Oh, don't be sorry. Be obliging." Noah's gaze swings across his windshield, looking into Brooks's gym. "Word on the street is you're running an underground training center here. You got room for another client?"

Chapter 29

Summer

"Hey, Dad! Just wanted to fill you in on how things went at Rocky Ridge. It was . . . well, a little tough if I'm honest with you. I'm not where I was a few years ago. I know, I know—it's exactly what you used to tell me. I'm in my head too much. But I really think that if you could get away for a couple of hours to come to the next one, I could do better? Having you there always helped, you know? Oh—and have I mentioned I'm trying to make the tour again? I forgot how much I used to want it, before . . . Anyway. Call me back if you can. I miss you."

~~~~

"That was a rough one."

Sliding back onto my board in the shallow, foamy water, I find a young blond girl grinning over at me. She's probably in her early twenties, wearing an adorable polka-dotted rash guard and matching swimsuit bottoms, floating on a board that looks like it's seen better days.

"Sadly, they're all rough ones these days," I tell her. She just witnessed me getting rag-dolled by yet another wave. I've been surfing every evening after work, hoping the repetition helps get me out of my head long enough to make it out of a barrel, in addition to my morning surfs with Parker. Which, lately, have come with a hefty dose of distraction considering the . . .

Let's just say I'll never look at a drawstring the same way again.

"You're Summer, right?"

"Yes!" I stare back at the girl, quickly trying to place her. "I'm so sorry, do we know each other?"

She shakes her head. "I'm Celia. My friends and I used to watch you compete growing up." She jabs a thumb over her shoulder at the lineup of surfers farther out, where two girls around her age eye us with interest. "You're surf royalty around here."

"Oh!" I give a small laugh. "That's very sweet, but you should've seen me at Rocky Ridge the other day."

"We were there. You did a snap in the third round that would've broken my back if I tried it. Not to mention it was your first event in years—can't believe how good you were. You're so inspiring."

"Wow, I had no idea I had such a fan club." I dust the shoulder of my rash guard, laughing, but something truly pleased blossoms inside me.

My gaze snags on a group on shore. There's a family of four standing out among the dwindling crowd. Two young kids are burying their father in the sand, laughing hysterically, while their mother reads on a beach towel. I picture Dad on his day off, doing exactly that with his twins, and my smile fades.

"Your family?" Celia asks.

I look down at my board. "I'm here alone. Reforming clinger, learning to enjoy solo time."

"Solo time I'm ruining."

"No, this is nice," I say with a smile. "It's part of it, you know? It's an individual sport, but the best thing about surfing is this." I gesture at the lineup. "The fact that you can be alone, but not *alone* when you're out here."

"Then I'm glad I worked up the courage to say hi." Celia gives an awkward laugh. "I've been chickening out for weeks."

"Have you really?" God, I'm so pathetically attention-starved that a lump actually rises in my throat.

You're surrounded by love, Sum.

It's foolish to have let Parker's words from that B&B take root in me, given the backlog of voicemails currently occupying my father's phone. But I so badly want to be the girl Parker sees when he looks at me—someone who's worth spending time on, occupying the background on a lock screen.

Sometimes, I close my eyes and simply picture the way he looked at me after we kissed. Think about us in those matching Hawaiian shirts. And I'll feel exactly that—worth the time.

I hesitate, nerves bubbling inside me. But I force myself to say, "If you girls ever feel like a snap tutorial, you could come find me. Anytime."

Celia's body jolts with such shock, she palms her board to steady herself. "Forget the tutorial. Wanna come surf with us?"

"Oh! Yeah—yes. Absolutely." A shaky laugh blows out of me. "Do you want to go ask your friends if they're okay with me crashing?"

"Are you kidding? They're going to *lose* it to be surfing with you. Let's go." Celia flattens to her board, leading me to the lineup.

I keep my eyes on her friends as I approach, a little embarrassed to have inserted myself into their group. But the girls wave at me—wide-eyed, as though this just made their whole day.

Really, they kind of just made mine.

~~~~~

I step out onto the busy cobblestones making up downtown Oakwood, the bell above the door announcing my departure from the local surf shop. After two consecutive nights of surfing and mini lessons with Celia and her friends, I decided it was time I venture back into town.

It's steaming hot for an evening, the humidity instantly making clothes feel damp against my skin. I hustle down the sidewalk toward my apartment, hat so low over my face that I only notice the familiar pair of shoes ahead a split second before I smash into their owner.

"Oh, I'm so sorry—*Summer?*"

I poke my hat a fraction up my forehead to find Shy ducking to get a better look at me.

"Shy!" I sweep her into a hug. "What are you doing here?"

"Didn't you see our messages? I'm meeting Melody and Zac at Oakley's—you were invited." With an impatient sound, she plucks the hat off my head, revealing the sidewalk and pedestrians I don't recognize out in droves. This influx happens every summer, between the tourists escaping the city's heat and those coming to watch Surf's Up.

"Why are you walking around practically blindfolded?"

"Same reason I'm not meeting you for dinner. I'm trying to be low-key. You know, on account of the harbinger of adultery thing."

I still haven't had the courage to visit Lisa and Jim at Oakley's, or Callie's shop, or to drop in on Wynn at the diner. Haven't had it in me to set the record straight about the situation with Denny, unsure if they'd believe me and not wanting to add them to the list of people who've let me down. They were, after all, part of what still made Oakwood feel like a home once my parents left.

"I'm sure people are over that by now," Shy says kindly, inching closer as a group of tourists edges around us on the sidewalk.

"Oh, you sweet summer child. If they're over it, then why did Jory Thomas keep gesticulating with his left hand while he rang me up at the surf shop just now?" She stares blankly. "His *left hand*, Shy. He was flashing his wedding band! And then there was Heather Sims asking her husband to fetch something from up in their apartment the second I walked by earlier. Like she expected me to jump him then and there."

"I can't stand small towns sometimes." Shy shakes her head. "What have you been up to these days? We haven't seen much of you."

"Oh, you know . . ."

Letting Parker tie me up in a B&B.

Developing a not-so-little crush on him, and simultaneously working my ass off to qualify for years' worth of travel without him.

"Little bit of this, little bit of that," I finish with a laugh. "Any-who! I've been meaning to pin you all down. I've almost got the details for Mel and Parker's birthday locked in—Zac offered up their place in the city. I saw the Sabres are playing an afternoon game that Saturday, which Park would love. And I've made us a reservation at the rooftop brunch spot Mels always raves about. You know the one I mean?"

"I think so. Sounds fun." Shy nods. "But how was Rocky Ridge?"

"What?" I squeak. I haven't uttered a word about last weekend—Parker or my competing again—to anyone. "Why do you ask?"

Shy gives me a funny look. "Why *wouldn't* I ask? You love that volunteer job."

"Oh, right." I fiddle with my brown paper shopping bag. "It was great. A raging success."

Her eyes narrow. "Summer."

"What?"

"Did something happen with Parker? I heard you stayed overnight." There's a warning in her face now. A very plain *don't you dare lie to me.*

Which is exactly what I plan on doing.

If there's one lesson I learned from the ordeal with Denny, it's that I need to see where things go with Parker before allowing any other excited voices into my head. She'd enable me like she has in the past. Letting me get ahead of myself over things that might not mean what my heart wants them to.

"Don't be absurd—what could possibly have happened?" I give a breezy laugh but her disapproving parent look is one hell of a thing. I'm a guilty perp, sweating under a harsh fluorescent light and my friend's apparent ability to weaponize silence. Shy doesn't say anything, just continues to stare at me so quietly, for so long, that a guilty stream of words push up my throat just for the sake of ending it. "It's me and Parker, for God's sake. We have boundaries and friendly parameters neither of us would ever dream of blurring with things like . . . God, I wouldn't even know, would I? Maybe, like, canceled rooms and drawstrings, dark nooks, or even—"

"Drawstrings?" Shy blinks, visibly working to keep up. Then her eyes go wide. "Did you two—"

"Keep it down!" I squeak, peering over my shoulder. "The last thing I need is to defend my poor decision-making to the entire county."

"How could this be a poor decision? It's *Parker*, Sum." Her smile takes over her entire face. "Haven't you ever wondered? What if this was always meant to happen?"

I hurry to beat back the thrill rising in my chest. I've *wondered* plenty in the past five days. We kissed, and it was incredible. We touched, and it was mind-altering.

But no conversations have been had to confirm that it was anything more than a fondle in a hallway, so that's the direction under which I'm going to keep operating for once.

It's for the best, anyway. I'm still well within reach of a qualifying spot for the Champions Tour, if I can get out of my head long enough to rack up more points. I let my heart hold me back once, put my ambitions on the back burner in favor of rescuing my relationship with Dad. Wrestling with unrequited feelings for Parker this time around won't do me any good.

"It's not like that—it was a heat of the moment thing. A tiny kiss." Shy looks about to say something, defend her excitement to the death, but I shake my head. "Please don't. I am the queen of getting my hopes up only to get slapped with a reality check. Trust me, I don't need you playing into it, too."

Shy takes my hands and squeezes them between hers. "But this is Parker we're talking about."

"Exactly. It would break me to be wrong about this one. Please, don't tell anyone else. I need to sort this out before you all start planning a wedding."

"All right." Shy's shoulders soften. She nods her chin at something behind me. "But I'm only letting this go because there's a very eager man parting a sea of tourists to get at you."

I turn to find Grant, my old head-volunteer, carving a path toward us on the sidewalk, eyes glued to me and a huge smile on his face. His dark, shaggy hair blows in the breeze. I glimpsed him at Rocky Ridge, but I haven't spoken to him since I bowed out of my volunteer duties to compete.

"Summer, I was wondering if I'd bump into you here."

"Well . . . here I am!" I wave at him. "What are you doing in Oakwood?"

"Helping Danica with your pop-up market. Divide and conquer, and all that." Grant drops his voice, leaning closer. "Between you and me, she's not quite as organized as you are."

My shoulders square. "So you're saying you miss your star volunteer?"

"Like crazy."

I glance at Shy, expecting to exchange a pleased smile at Danica's expense. But she's staring back at me, eyes wide. Trying to convey something I'm not quite grasping.

"Was that bad to admit?" Grants says with a small laugh.

"Why would it be?" I tear my eyes off Shy. "Please tell me the markets are earning enough for Wynn's repairs, at least?" I've been keeping an eye on the dilapidated building, and the lack of construction activity has had my heart hurting for Wynn.

"They're doing great. We handed over the first donation installment earlier this week."

Relief pours into me. Handing over the program to Danica had hurt, badly. But it's been nothing compared to the fear that we might've wasted an opportunity to do some good in the community. "Thanks for picking up my slack, Grant. I'm glad it's in capable hands."

"It was a fantastic idea." There's something a little sheepish about it, the way his fingers run through his hair. "So, listen, Summer . . . I was wondering if you were seeing someone?"

"Grant!" I rear back. "I had no idea you felt that way."

"How could I not?" He gestures at me. Shy gives a little sigh. "Obviously, I couldn't do anything about it before. The whole position of authority thing, right? But seeing as that's over . . . Can I take you out?"

My gaze flies across the street, skimming the apartment level of the strip and settling on Parker's living room window. I don't know what I'm hoping for. He isn't even home.

What am I supposed to say here, exactly? *Sorry, Grant. I can't go out with you even though you're a perfectly nice guy, because I can't stop fantasizing about my best friend who woke up one day deciding to drive me insane with flirting and kissing and a new pair of glasses which I secretly enjoy and it's all bound to blow up in my face when he eventually snaps out of it but I have a massive crush on him anyway and, oh, also, I can't go a single day without touching myself thinking about him and the way he sounds when he's turned on—*

And then I notice Shy. Staring at me with a knowing smile as I stared at Parker's apartment. My cheeks flush.

She's thrilled by my hesitation. So completely convinced that this is it for me—me and Parker, meant to be. My heart thrums, pleased by the very idea, and it's exactly what I didn't want.

No getting my hopes up. No letting my friends gas me up the way they had with Denny.

"Or I can cook you dinner at my place," Grant gently prompts me. "We can keep it casual. See where it goes."

Shy's smile grows with every second that passes. I can feel it. Her excitement seeping into me.

My panic spikes with it.

Grant is . . . nice. I don't have romantic feelings for him whatsoever but maybe this is just the thing to help slow the ones I do have for Parker. A distraction from the faint wedding bells singing in my heart, growing louder with every dimpled smile he gives me.

A casual, low-stakes dinner. I could handle that.

I force my brightest smile. "Okay. Let's do it."

Chapter 30

Summer

Mere minutes later, the sight of the first pink paper plane in my apartment has my stomach panging with regret.

I stare down the dim hallway, just inside the front door, straining my ears for a sign of Parker. Scrambling to figure out how to explain this date to him, as though I were doing something wrong by going on it. But my apartment is dead silent save for the sounds of the street below.

Still, I tiptoe up to the paper plane, unfolding it to find the words *Follow us . . .* in Parker's handwriting. The next plane, just steps away, is blank on the inside, but points to the remaining trail of folded pink Post-it notes. I follow them down the hall, past the kitchen, and into the living room which has been transformed into a scene right out of our childhood.

My mouth falls open as I take it in. The couch cushions and throw blankets have been rearranged into a pillow fort, the kind Parker and I first met inside.

We used to build these in the basement of his parents' old house every single weekend growing up. We'd hide in our self-made bubble, sneaking the rom-coms we weren't allowed to watch, but couldn't get enough of. Watching people get their happy endings while burrowed under a thick comforter, our arms and legs pressed together.

Heart thumping, I crawl into the fort. He's strung twinkle lights inside, over cozy piles of blankets and pillows. In the middle, another pink plane sits on top of a faded square of paper.

My type, is all it says.

I flip over the square. It's an old picture of the four of us I've never seen before. Parker and me in the middle, Zac and Melody flanking us. We're bathed in bluish light I recognize from our unsanctioned swim sessions, wrapped in towels and sitting on the tiled floor by the pool at our old high school. This was the night Parker had broken us in for a midnight swim, to get my mind off my parents' divorce.

And while Zac, Melody, and I smile brightly ahead . . . Parker is staring at me, the beginnings of a smile on his face as though he got distracted on the way to the camera.

My type.

I snap a picture of the photo and text it to Parker without preamble or follow-up, but the wordless demand is clear: *Explain. Tell me what this means.*

My phone lights up with a call right away, though I hadn't expected to hear from him. He should be at Brooks's, setting up for his first official session with Noah.

"Hi?" My voice is breathless, heart in my throat.

"Even then," he says quietly.

"What do you mean?"

"Even then, you were the most beautiful girl I'd ever laid eyes on."

I breathe a laugh even as something miserable twists inside me. "Shouldn't you be working? Especially now that you're out there poaching our clients."

"How pissed off was Don when Noah broke the news?"

"He was all fake smiles until Noah left. Then he stormed into his office and threw a muffin at the wall. I think he forgot we can see right into the room." His warm laugh against my ear has my stomach swooping violently. I flop back onto the pillows, staring up at the twinkle lights. "So, I found a pillow fort in my living room. Any idea where it came from?"

"A pillow fort? Weird." There's a smile in his voice. "We've been so busy with training, I thought it might be nice to bring back Summer Fridays. Put a rom-com on, see what we could get up to with a loose drawstring . . . You know, the usual." Parker makes a soft sound, and I picture him sitting down on a workout bench. "I left something on your bookcase."

"Oh?" I shuffle out of the pillow fort, gasping when I find a new box set of books on my shelf. "The *Hidden Moon* series! Thanks, Park. But you really didn't have to get me the whole set."

"It was the only way to get them with the sprayed edges. I thought they'd look nice on your shelves."

I flip over the box to find the purple page edges, dotted with crescent moons and little stars. "They're beautiful."

"If I'm honest, it's a little bit for me, too. I'm finding I have a lot of questions about alien sex."

I laugh. "I hear he's got three tongues in the third book."

"Well, shit. Good for him."

I run a finger over the painted edges. Parker's given me plenty of gifts through the years; we've sat in tons of pillow forts. But in the wake of our moment at the B&B, this feels . . .

Different.

"Safe to say I regret making plans," I whisper. "It could've been us and triple-tongue Tritus tonight."

"I'd make sure he was tongueless Tritus before he reached you," Parker says darkly. He pauses. "You have plans?"

"I'm . . ." I close my eyes, guilt and regret clawing at my insides. "I'm going on a date."

His end of the call goes so eerily quiet that I check it's still connected. It is, the seconds on the screen ticking by, the silence more stifling as they do.

"Who?" Parker asks softly.

"I bumped into Grant today. I don't know if you remember him, but he's—"

"I know who he is." He sucks in a breath. "You like him?"

"He's . . ." *Not you.* "Nice." I hold my breath, waiting for him to tell me *you're not going.* Hoping he'll say *go out with me instead.* But Parker only gives a thoughtful hum. "I'm going to cancel. I didn't realize you had this whole thing planned, and . . ."

"No, don't do that. You should go. On the . . ." He clears his throat. "With Grant. You always spoke so highly of him."

"Are you sure?"

"Very. You deserve it, Summer."

The pounding in my chest subsides, leaving acute humiliation. Where in the smutty alien romance did I think I was, hoping he would protest?

This is reality. One in which I'm friends with a man who's had decades to ask me out if he wanted to. And that's the thing about Parker: He's impulsive. Wears his mood on his sleeve, good or bad. And here he is, perfectly calm as I tell him about my date with someone else. While I'm standing here, foolishly hoping he'll tell me not to go.

I set down the books and rub a hand over my face. "I deserve what?"

"To be happy, whatever that looks like for you." I hear movement on his end of the call, then the sound of tires crunching on asphalt. "Noah's here. I'm sorry I made a mess of your living room. I just—I thought . . ."

My heart throbs at something in his voice.

Another long pause and I hold my breath, waiting for more. But the line goes silent.

Chapter 31

Parker

Mark Hartford was born in Norfolk, Virginia, to a trauma nurse mother and a college professor father. As a child, the boxer—

I slam shut the book on my lap, glaring down at Mark Hartford's unsmiling face like the celebrated boxer is the reason for the restless energy making it impossible for me to sit for more than a few minutes at a time before springing to my feet. Pacing to the window. Taking a peek at the apartment across the street.

Just casually. *Calmly.*

I'm just a guy checking that his oldest friend made it home safely, that's all. It's commendable. Respectable. What best friends do.

Somehow, Summer's apartment is still unlit, though it's been precisely forty-seven minutes since Grant picked her up for their . . . Fuck.

I can't even bring myself to call it a . . . Whatever.

Because Summer Prescott, my best friend, the woman I've been stupidly in love with for God knows how long, is on a . . . an appointment. With another guy.

I tap my phone to check the time again. Staring back at me is the picture from before the event at Rocky Ridge. Summer's hair is a mess, and she's got pillow creases on the side of her face. But god-damn does she look happy. As pretty as I've ever seen her. We look like a couple, leaning into each other. Grinning like idiots. Wearing matching shirts.

I thought I'd been doing the right thing by encouraging her to go on this . . . gathering. That I should simply focus on the things I have ownership of, like keeping a cool head. Finding my purpose in life. Following through on her dream man list, becoming someone who's worthy of her. And hoping that she chooses me at the end of it all.

Now, I think it might be the stupidest thing I've ever done.

I just . . . *want*. Her. Us.

The death of a man named Grant.

I've been going out of my mind pacing this apartment in between single paragraphs of Mark Hartford's biography. Imagining Grant's hands on her. Imagining him leaning in for a kiss. Thinking of—

Oh, thank fuck.

By the time I speed-read another paragraph and make it back to the window, Summer's apartment is lit up.

She's back. She didn't go home with him, they're not hooking up, and the relief is like nothing I've ever . . .

A bomb blows up inside me.

Framed in the window across the street is Summer, standing in her living room. As goddamn Grant walks up behind her, touches her shoulder, and hands her a beer.

I drop onto the sofa, trying to talk myself down. To be the cool-headed Parker she deserves. To be her friend, completely unselfish, letting her have her kicks wherever she wants to get them.

"You will remain seated," I coach myself. "You will remain calm." My knee won't stop bouncing. "You will—very slowly—get to your feet for the sole purpose of extracting a Mountain Dew from your fridge. You will take a sip and you will keep your shit together. You will return to this couch and get back to your book."

I get to my feet. Carefully, and with several deep breaths, I cross to the kitchen.

"Good. This is good," I praise myself, reaching inside the fridge. "See? This is what we call growth. You're having a relaxing night at home, with a refreshing beverage. And a riveting book."

I return to my living room, feeling proud as hell of myself. Shooting barely a glance out the window on the way . . .

Summer is still framed in the window. She's peering outside and I think she was looking for me because her body goes visibly still. Meanwhile, my heart tugs me right up to the glass, trying to get as near her as I can.

Why didn't I say something earlier?

I'd be over there now, basking in her smile. Holding her hand. Kissing her, maybe. Feeling whole even without all that, instead of the rapidly crumbling half human I am without her.

I lift a hand. It's meant to be a wave, but it turns into more of a reach. I watch Summer's shoulders rise with a breath.

She releases it almost angrily. And then reaches for . . .

Hell. Fucking. No.

She's drawing the curtains. And before I can even attempt to gather myself, to tell myself to *sit the fuck down*, I'm charging for the front door.

Chapter 32

Parker

In my defense, I find a way to grasp onto my last remaining shred of restraint and actually knock on Summer's door instead of barging in unannounced.

"Parker?" Summer's hand lands on her cheek, a physical manifestation of her shock.

I don't have very much to my name. But I'd give up every single thing I own just to be able to cup her cheek like that, whenever I want. To freely count the freckles dotting her soft skin. I want to exist in the crook of her neck, inhaling that floral scent. I want to kiss her again, so damn badly it physically hurts.

I lean a shoulder on her doorframe. She looks perfect as always, with her signature messy waves and glossy lips. Just so pretty, I can't help but smile. "Hey. I really missed you."

She chuckles, and it's a little dismissive. My stomach goes tight, thinking of those tense minutes on the phone. I should've said something right then and there.

I won't be making that mistake again.

"Summer? Anything I can help with?" Grant calls from inside.

I nod at the hallway behind her. "He seems nice."

"Yeah, he's—"

"Get rid of him."

Her lips pop open. "Excuse me?"

"You heard me." I lean in so close I can practically feel the fury building inside her. "Get rid of him, or I'll do it for you."

Her eyes narrow. "You've got to be kidding me. You *told* me to—"

I slip past her and kick off my sneakers. Her living room is back to normal. The only evidence left of my foolish attempt at our first date is the length of twinkle lights coiled into a ball, sitting on her bookcase.

There are two beer bottles on the glass coffee table. Grant sits relaxed on the sofa with an arm slung across the back, wearing a pristine pair of dark jeans, a polo shirt, and a look of surprise as I stroll into the room.

It goes from surprised to incredulous when I drop onto the seat cushion closest to his, so that his arm hangs over my shoulders. I yank off my hat, flinging it over his beer bottle like I'm at a carnival ring toss.

"I can't tell you how sorry I am to crash your date. But I didn't know where else to go." I heave a hopeless sigh, sinking into the cushion behind me and forcing contact with Grant's outstretched arm. Slowly, he retracts it. "I've been feeling really . . . ill."

The front door slams and Summer comes to a stop at the mouth of the hallway. "Parker, can I speak to you?"

"I'm so faint. And . . . hot. I'm overheating. I can't get my body temperature down. Grant, feel my forehead." I lean toward him. After a beat, and with a wrinkle of mild disgust in his face, he touches the back of his hand to my forehead.

"It feels fine—"

"But I'm so hot." I tug at the front of my shirt and waft myself with it. Summer crosses her arms. "And my throat feels like there's an army of fire ants living in it." I clear my throat as repulsively as I can. Grant inches away from me.

"Parker." There's an edge of warning in Summer's voice. I'm pretty sure she's going to lunge straight for my throat the moment I manage to get rid of this guy.

I widen my eyes in despair, keeping them on Grant. "And then there's the hiccups."

Grant stares skeptically. "You haven't hiccupped once since you—"

I hack a cough, making it sound as loud and painful as possible. Grant recoils into the sofa arm. "It comes and goes. Grant, I'm scared. What d'you think's wrong with me?"

"I don't know, man. Maybe it's a cold?"

Summer mutters something under her breath. I think I catch words like *murder* and *grave*.

"A cold with hiccups? Did I mention the hives?" I look around at Summer, who's shooting me absolute fucking daggers from where she's standing. I deserve a medal for keeping a straight face. "Isn't this what Don at the gym had a few months ago?"

Her nails bite into her upper arms as she very clearly battles the urge to throttle me. "I don't think—"

"No, it was. Remember? He was sick as a dog, just like this. Took him forever to recover." I turn to Grant. "He ended up making a full recovery, thank God. But Kendra caught it from him and died four days later."

Grant shoots to his feet. "I think I'm going to head out."

"Grant—"

"That's probably for the best," I tell him. "You never know with these things."

"I had a good time tonight, despite the . . ." Grant pauses in front of Summer. When he leans in, reaching for her, I perform an especially nauseating cough until he rethinks the foolishness. "I'll just let myself out."

I wave at him. "Bye, now."

With a parting look of murder, Summer follows him to the door. I strain my ears for any hint of kissing, but all I hear are a couple of hushed words before the door clicks shut and Summer marches back into the living room.

I sigh, settling comfortably into the couch. "Shall we put on a movie? We haven't watched *Sleepless in Seattle* in a while."

"Parker, what the hell?" Fury radiates off her as she reaches for a throw pillow and whacks me in the arm with it.

"Ow! Is that any way to treat your sickly best friend?"

"You aren't sick!" *Whack.* "You're an infuriating." *Whack.* "Cock-blocking." *Whack.* "*Ass.*"

The humor melts off my face. "You're telling me you were going to fuck that guy?"

Whack. "We were on a—"

"Don't say it." I take hold of the cushion and tug it out of her grasp. "Don't fucking say that word to me."

"He told me he's had a thing for me for three years." She wields the words triumphantly.

"Is that all?" I scoff. I've loved Summer Prescott one way or another all my life. But good for Grant and his little three-year crush.

"It's *romantic*," she insists. "You know what's *not* romantic?"

"Having a three-year crush and not asking you out because you volunteered together a couple months out of the year?"

"Telling me to go on this date, and then crashing it because you've suddenly decided that you're territorial." She throws out her arms. "You have absolutely no say in who I date or fuck, least of all when you keep making moves on me only to—"

I bark a laugh. "*I* keep making moves on you? Love, you're the one who asked me to tie you up."

"As though you didn't jump at the chance." Her glare turns derisive. "And you're the one who crashed my date."

"What did I say about using that word?"

"*Date.* The *date* I was on with Grant. Does that make you mad, Parker?"

She's trying to provoke me. Into leaving or making a move, I can't tell. "I'm not mad. I'm fucking furious."

I catch her wrist, tugging until she falls into my lap. She lands with the sweetest gasp, straddling me, her dress riding up. Watching the lust weave with that mean little look does something wicked to my body. Summer looks like she's in the mood to take a bite out of me. Tug my hair, rake her fingernails over my skin and make it hurt a little.

And fuck, that's all I want. All I need. My cock swells at the feel of her hips against mine. There's no way she doesn't feel it pressing into her thigh.

With an irritated huff, Summer runs her fingertips down my chest, settling her palms on my stomach. "Chocolate cake," she mumbles to herself.

"Beg your pardon?"

"You." She glares at the shirt beneath her fingers, as though speaking directly to my abs. "It's like living with a slice of chocolate cake for a shadow, making myself ignore it for years and years. And then I have a taste and suddenly it's all I can think of." Summer shakes her head at me. "Don't smile. Nothing you've done tonight warrants a smile."

"I couldn't disagree more." I rake back the hair on both sides of her face, tucking the strands behind her ears before settling my gaze on her lips. Perfect, plump, shiny from a swipe of her tongue. "Feels like the best decision I ever made."

She stares at me a quiet moment. "He asked me out and you didn't tell me to stay."

"He asked you out and you said yes."

"So what do you want from me, Parker?"

I withhold a laugh, sensing it would earn me another pillow beat-down. The list of things I'd like from Summer Prescott is a lengthy one, beginning with her assurance that she never intended to bed that moron, and ending with me on my deathbed at a hundred years old, with her wedding band on my finger and her sweet face telling me goodbye.

"I want to talk," I say instead.

"Bullshit."

Summer leans in and lays one on me. And this kiss, it's nothing like it was in that hallway, when she clammed up, let me take the reins until she found her footing and kissed me back. This time, Summer doesn't hesitate. Doesn't surrender control. She parts my lips with hers, tongue slicking against mine. Gets her fingers in my hair and goddamn, I've never felt anything like it.

It's surge after surge of fire through my body. Relentless, merciless flames that burn hotter with every scrape of her nails on my scalp. With every soft sigh and needy moan she unleashes against my lips. She pulls back to draw a breath and I'm an empty husk of a man. Then she breathes life right back into me when she sucks on my lip again.

I coax her up onto her knees so that she's kissing me from above, loving the feel of her owning me physically. Just like she owns my every waking thought and heartbeat. My past, with the way I unwittingly built my entire life around her. My future, and the way I want to become everything she wants in a man.

Summer holds the sides of my face, kissing me hard. Her thighs are bare, so soft underneath my palms. I squeeze them to keep from moving higher but it's a whole damn struggle. I want to fuck her, bad. But I also want to kiss her, just like this. No breaks until the sun comes up.

I seem to be alone in that. Summer pull backs, panting softly. "Still want to talk, Park?"

"Ah . . ." Her mouth tilts when my expression returns what I imagine to be a single question mark. My head is nothing but whooshing air and tumbleweeds. She's kissed the brain cells out of me. "Yes. Talk, I want to talk. To you. About things."

Which things, again?

"So talk, Park."

"Were you . . ." I mean to ask for crystal clear confirmation that I never had anything to worry about with Grant. That there was no plausible scenario where I'd find him skulking out of her building at the crack of dawn, because God knows I'd have stayed up all night, holding vigil for his blessed departure. But Summer flicks her hair over her shoulder and that floral scent drills a hole into my skull. And out pours whatever's left of my brain. "Goddamn it, Summer, I can't . . ."

"Can't what?" She presses wet kisses up my neck. I never thought this could feel so otherworldly. Every touch of those soft lips breaks me down until I'm delirious with want.

"That perfume." I take a handful of her hair, making sure she doesn't pull away before I've had my fill. "You smell like a wild garden. Like dusk and depraved sexual rituals."

"That's very specific."

"Do you understand what that perfume does to me? Do you have any idea at all?"

"I have an idea." She squirms in my lap, nudging the bulge insisting we do away with our clothes. "Is this what you sat me here to talk about? My perfume?"

"Yes." That's not quite right. My brain churns, desperately searching for clarity. "No. I want you to tell me you weren't going to fuck that guy."

"I wasn't going to." Triumph and relief surge through me.

"Why not?"

"Why did you barge in here to chase him away?" she counters.

We sit in a standoff, staring at each other until Summer cups the back of my neck, trying to kiss me again—rather, to absolve herself from answering.

I grab both her wrists and wrench her arms behind her back. That seems to piss her off but I know it turns her on, too. I remember exactly how much she shivered with need last weekend, when I'd bound her exactly this way. She makes a growl of frustration when I jerk out of reach.

"Tell me, Summer. Tell me what those greedy little growls mean." I take both her wrists in one hand and run a thumb over her nipple. "Tell me why these beautiful tits are begging for attention. Tell me that if you lifted that pretty pussy off my lap, I wouldn't find you soaking wet. Throbbing, begging me to fill you past your breaking point."

Summer grits her jaw. I'm dangerously close to her snapping but I can't help myself. I love goading her. Pushing her buttons like no one else can.

I sit back comfortably against the sofa, still trapping her hands. "Go on, Summer. Tell your best friend how bad you want to fuck him."

I'm not surprised when, with another angry growl, she wrenches out of my grip. Not at all surprised when she gets to her feet, tosses me my hat, and points to her front door.

"Get the hell out."

Chapter 33

Summer

Parker. Effing. Woods.

I've never met a more infuriating man. Anyone so adept at wea-
seling under my skin, raising my blood pressure.

He insisted I go on that date only to crash it. Who the hell does
that?

It doesn't matter that I had precisely zero intention of hooking up
with Grant, touching Grant, doing absolutely anything with Grant.
We'd gotten to the restaurant he picked out, saw it was shut down for
a private party, and after a stroll along the boardwalk, I invited him
over for a drink so that the night wasn't a complete wash for both of
us. As much of a dead end as it was, after the things Denny said to
me and the way Parker shut down after Grant asked me out, Grant's
attention felt . . . nice. Even if just for the night.

And in came Parker effing Woods. Territorial, yet unwilling to
admit to any sort of feelings for me.

I adjust my position in bed, growling up at the dark ceiling
when it doesn't help any. I'd been out for revenge with that make out.
Planned to rile him up, lead him an inch from the edge before telling
him to get lost while he begged me to finish the job.

What I failed to factor in was the state in which I'd be leaving myself in the process.

"Come on, you stupid thing. I just need one. One teeny tiny little orgasm."

Still nothing. With a sob of frustration, I stab my thumb at the toy between my thighs, killing the vibration and tossing it into the pile of equally useless silicone on the other end of the bed.

Five vibrators. I've tried *five*, and none of them have managed to perform the single duty they were put on this earth to do. I haven't had one shred of relief since Parker left my apartment hours ago, and I've officially ascended to fresh levels of rage.

And that rage has closed in on a single, infuriating, six-foot-three target.

All rational thought has left my body. I'm hangry. Hangry for an orgasm, and I'll be damned if Parker Woods gets his unperturbed beauty rest while I suffer across the street.

Screw that.

I toss the comforter off my body, pull on a pair of shorts. Grab my things, seeing red as I slam my front door on the way out. The main strip is dark and deserted—the mass exodus from Oakley's happened right around the time my third vibrator failed me. I march across the street and into Parker's building, practically stomping up the stairs to his front door.

Inside, Parker's bedroom door smashes into the wall from the force with which I throw it open. He lets out a shout and the shape of him jerks upright, reaching for his bedside table.

The soft light turns on, his alarmed gaze finds me. And he grunts when my projectile hits him square in the chest.

Parker squints at me, glasses on his bedside table. "*Summer? What the hell's going on?*"

"Do you know what that is?" He sorts through the sheets fallen around his hips, pulling free the purple, palm-sized vibrator I just launched at him. "That's my best vibrator. *My best one*. It's never let me down. And you know what it did for me tonight?" I throw out my arms, my purse dangling from a hand. "Absolutely nothing."

Parker stares at the vibrator, completely nonplussed. "And why are you—"

"And neither did this one." I shove a hand into my purse, fingers closing around another toy and then flinging it at Parker. "Or this one." He gets hit with another. "Or this one, or even *this* one."

Parker sits calmly as silicone missiles rain down on him. He's shirtless, his body mouthwatering and skin golden from our time in the sun. Hair rumpled in such an infuriatingly sexy way. How *dare* he look this good after being startled awake by uncooperative sex toys?

He reaches for the one by his hip, a sparkly pink approximation of a dick that only entered the rotation a couple of months ago. "Cute."

"Now's not the time for your little jokes, Parker." I march into the room, tossing my purse on the foot of his bed.

A slow smirk curls the corner of his mouth. "Is this what you've been doing since I left? Playing with your toys?" He picks up another one, a rose-gold suction toy. Clicks it on and examines it with interest.

Then it hits me, what I've just done.

The utter insanity of having charged across the street in the middle of the night to pelt my best friend with sex toys. I drop onto the mattress, facing away from him. A laugh bubbles out of me.

It's official: Parker Woods has broken me.

"You've done it. You've pushed me right past the brink of sanity and into the land of loopy, horny women who assault their inconveniently hot best friends in the middle of the night. I hope you're pleased with yourself."

"You think I'm inconveniently hot?"

He's so smug about it. I can tell without even looking at him.

"Of course, that's what you retain in all that. You know, I never asked for any of this. All I wanted to do this summer was focus on surfing, maybe have a little fun along the way. And here I am, emotionally and physically edged by my own best friend. Down a few orgasms. With a pile of broken sex toys."

"A little fun," Parker echoes. "And who, exactly, did you plan on having fun with?"

I snort, getting to my feet. "Why? So you can fake another disease to drive him away?"

"So I can convince you to pick me instead."

Parker's voice has gone low, and when I turn to look at him, I see he's lost all traces of humor. He's on his feet, his eyes doing that dark, lusty thing. The one that makes it impossible to move. Like he's pumped me full of lead, while every step he takes toward me has my heart pounding harder.

"You want fun, Summer? I'll give you fun. Say the word and I'll have you strapped to this bed until the sun comes up. Make you come so many times, and so many fucking ways, you won't even know where you are anymore. And in the morning, I'll send you off with a thoroughly fucked pussy and pretty marks around your wrists to stare at all day, until you're barging in here again. A desperate, needy mess at my door, begging for more. And then I'll fuck you all over again."

Parker comes to a stop right in front of me, forcing me to tip my head back to keep looking him in the eye. His body heat bridges the distance between us, licking at me, spiking my own temperature to unbearable levels. "That sound fun enough to you?"

A gust of air rushes from my lungs. "Have you always had a mouth on you?"

"It's something you seem to have inspired in me." There's nothing like the satisfaction of hearing that. Parker's gaze bounces from spot to spot on my body, trying to decide where to sink his teeth first. "All you have to do is ask."

This will probably turn out to be the mistake of all mistakes.

There's the risk of misplaced attachment and hurt feelings and destroyed friendships.

But my brain is rioting, my body a greedy mess. His lusty eyes, dark like the raging sea, will me to surrender. Demand the grand finale to the unbearable tension that's burgeoned between us.

We could do this. Survive this.

Just a little fun. Just once.

"You flirt a big game, Parker." I reach into my purse and pull out a bundle of coiled white rope, the kind we use to secure our boards to his car. I press it into the center of his chest. "Time to deliver."

Chapter 34

Summer

Parker's breaths aren't particularly loud, but they're like a chainsaw in my head. Harsh and goading, disintegrating the flimsy remains of my hesitation.

Then he tosses the rope on the bed, fists my hair, and with a tug our mouths crash together.

Instantly, it's mayhem.

He dips to cup my ass with his free hand and I'm climbing him, fingers clawing at his bare chest. Thighs working to hook around his hips, desperately trying to get closer. I thread my hands through his hair and tug in an angry demand.

With a groan, Parker lifts and shifts me until my pussy hits his cock. He grinds me against him as I pant and whimper against his lips. And then we're falling. No warning, just the *whoosh* of air as we cut through it, until my back hits the mattress. Parker hooks an arm around my waist and tosses me up higher on the bed. My nails graze the back of his neck, over his shoulders, scraping every part of him I can reach.

"Harder," Parker orders. He punches his hips to drive the point home, cock slamming into my clit through our clothes. All I manage in response is a desperate moan, digging my nails into his skin.

Parker bites my lip and I open my eyes to find his face contorted in ecstasy. Eyes pitch-black, brows furrowed. He reaches for my breasts. I hadn't bothered with a bra, but that doesn't seem to satisfy Parker any, because he fists the front of my shirt and yanks so hard I pop off the mattress.

"Take this fucking thing off." I struggle with the fabric, desperately trying to get it over my head. Parker loses patience, takes a nipple between his teeth before the shirt is even gone. He carries my weight as I wrestle with it. Once free, I'm dropped onto the sheets, again without warning.

I love it. I love how frantic he is, how he treats my body like it's durable, made for this. His skin is hot and soft and hard under my palms as my nails carve down his back, dig into his firm ass.

"More, Parker. Now." I reach for his waistband but he moves out of reach, dotting wet kisses down and across my stomach. He slides my shorts down, giving up on them once he catches sight of my bare pussy. They stay hooked around an ankle.

"Goddamn, Summer. You're so beautiful." His gaze rakes the length of my body, every inch of me laid out on his sheets. That familiar urge to cover up, to get the guy as naked and vulnerable as I am, isn't there. "I've thought about this for so long, I . . ."

He lays a hand over my stomach, watching his fingers spread wide. Like he's making sure I'm here and not some figment of his imagination. A laugh bubbles out of me, because he's acting like *so long* means years, and not the tension-filled weeks since our falling out.

Tonight, just for now, I'm going to let myself pretend that's exactly how he means it.

Years.

Parker settles on his elbows between my legs. My stomach pangs the moment I realize what he's doing.

"Park." Reaching for his hair, I try to pull him back up. "Parker, I can't—that doesn't work."

"Just warming you up. I'm going to suck on this pretty clit until you're good and soaked. You good with that?" He yanks his hair out of my grip and licks me, one long, slow stroke from entrance to clit that has me gasping. It's pleasure, but a little shock, too.

Parker pulls back just enough to meet my eye. *Are we okay?*

And . . . we are. The world didn't collapse. In fact, it seems to have opened up an entirely new wing I never knew existed—one painted ocean blue and smelling of pepper, hypnotizing in its appeal. Luring me deeper one step at a time.

"Don't stop," I whisper. I glimpse a dimple before Parker pushes his face into my pussy, sucking my clit into his mouth. I moan, arching off the bed. His hands grip my thighs, spreading them wide, and he's relentless against me. It's wet, loud, and a little bit mean as he pinches my clit between his lips, nips at it.

I'm already dripping. I can feel it, the wetness seeping out of my pussy, leaking onto my ass. He notices, and when he dips to lick my arousal from where it's dripped over my rear entrance, I all but buck off the bed.

I'm moaning and laughing at the ceiling, this breathless sound of disbelief and ruthless pleasure. I'm glad he's not easing me in, slowing the pace for my sake. I want him exactly like this—unforgiving and impulsive. Out of his mind for my body. Parker's fingers find no resistance as he works two inside me, pumping into me.

"So fucking needy," he murmurs, watching his fingers disappear inside me over and over. "Already soaked and ready, aren't you?"

I pant at the ceiling. "Parker, please."

"Please what?" His expression turns mocking when I simply glare down at him. "Come on, love. A wet pussy like this knows what it wants. Use your big girl words and ask for it."

I reach around blindly until my fingers close around the rope and toss it at him. "Tie me up, fuck me, and wipe that smug look off your face while you're at it."

The smug look stays perfectly in place—grows, even—but then he crawls up my body, kisses me, licking my own taste into my mouth, and I lose the will to fight him on anything.

"Winter," he murmurs. "That's your safe word. Say it and this stops. Don't and you keep taking it."

My heartbeat has to be audible. "I'm going to need a safe word?"

He ignores the question. "Move up the bed, Summer." I do what he says, scrambling to the very top of the mattress. "Arms over your head. Knock on the wall." He waits until I thread my fists through the bars on his headboard and rap my knuckles against the wall. "That's for when your mouth is full."

Oh, fuck. For the first time, I wonder whether I truly grasped what I'm getting myself into. Parker sheds his boxers, and I lift my head to have a good look.

Okay. Mhm. Definitely didn't grasp what I was getting into.

I soak him in as he kneels over me, this god that's existed at my side for years. The hard planes of his stomach, the deep V lines leading to an unobstructed view of the thick cock that's haunted my fantasies since that morning on his couch.

He's . . . utter perfection.

I can't wait to feel him inside me.

Parker thumbs my lower lip, lifts my head off the mattress as he shuffles farther up my body. "Suck on it while I tie you up."

I open wide with a greedy whimper. Parker pushes his cock into my mouth, dragging it over my tongue. He groans when I close my lips around him and suck. He's not all the way in, not even close. And at this angle, with my hands up over my head, I can't do much more than give him shallow pumps of my mouth. It's even harder once he releases my head to get to work on tying my wrists.

I strain to give him any kind of friction, letting my tongue do most of the work, dragging and swirling against the smooth underside of his cock. It seems to do enough. His breaths go ragged and he begins rocking into my mouth as he loops and cinches the rope around my wrists. He ties it tight, but there's enough length in the part of the rope that binds me to the headboard, allowing me—or, more likely, allowing *him* to move me around.

When he finishes, Parker angles himself to thrust deeper into my mouth, staring down, watching it happen. "That's so good. Such a hot fucking mouth, Summer."

Without warning, he pulls away. My body shudders, fingers finding the length of rope and holding tight in anticipation of him pushing inside me.

Instead, Parker lines up all five of my vibrators next to me.

"None of these work, you said?" He picks up the rose-gold one he examined earlier and turns it on.

Oh, fuck. "That one needs lube."

My jaw drops when he spits on my clit. "Good enough?"

He smirks at my expression and I'm done. Fucking feral. Toes curling, nails digging into my palms. Already regretting the bonds because all I want to do is tackle him to the mattress and sink onto his cock until we're waking up the entire street with our sounds.

Then Parker touches the toy to my clit. The suction takes hold and I'm gasping, moaning into the room. "Oh my God. *Park*."

His eyes roam my body as I squirm into his sheets. I wasn't sure what to expect exactly, but it's so *freeing*, being bound like this. Being kept close, wanted, hoarded by the man who's been stealing my heart for weeks. My mind melts blissfully as the toy sucks on my clit, but I keep my eyes on Parker, living off the wonder in his face as he watches me.

My body has been primed for hours, since our moment on my

couch, so it takes no time for searing heat to rush down my legs, to coil around me, yank my back off the mattress. "I'm gonna come," I say urgently. "Parker, I'm gonna come, I'm gonna—"

He adjusts the toy ever so slightly and I'm shuddering, crying out, yanking at the rope, trying to grip onto something as the orgasm rocks through me. I stay like that for what feels like eternity, crunched up as far as the restraints allow before crashing back down onto the bed.

Parker just made me come. Holy shit.

Parker Woods just made me come, and it was . . . incredible. Not even the slightest bit weird.

"Well, aren't you just pretty as fuck when you come." Parker places a wet kiss on my clit, tossing away the suction toy. "And that one seems to work just fine."

I give a shaky laugh. "Just put your dick in me, already."

Instead of a reply, I hear a click, a steady buzz. He's got another toy between his fingers, a U-shaped one that he pushes into my pussy. With his eyes on my face, Parker twists it in small increments, looking for—

"*There.* Oh, right there." The rope strains when I forget I can't simply reach down to make sure he keeps the toy's position. He does so without my help, though, and then places the outer curve of the pale blue silicone over my clit. It's sensitive after the first toy, but the ache dissipates quickly.

Hands now free to roam, Parker smooths his palms up and down my thighs, watching my chest rise and fall rapidly as the toy pulses inside me. "What do you do with your hands when you use this one, Summer?" My eyes squeeze shut; I'm too overcome with bliss to muster words. One of his hands slides up my body, closes around my breast. "Do you play with your tits?"

I nod and he pinches my nipple, dipping to suck the other into his mouth. And God, oh God, it's so much better than doing this alone. Even better when I hear Parker's muffled moan and lift my head to see that he's let go of my breast to stroke himself.

"Don't come. I want you inside me," I demand. "Parker, I swear to God."

"Don't think you're in a position to issue any threats, love." He yanks at the rope. Cinches it tighter, forcing my back straight. "Are you on birth control?"

"Yes. And I've been checked after . . ."

"Me, too." He kisses me, absolving me from having to bring the last guy into our perfect, raunchy bubble.

Then he reaches between my thighs and hits the button to strengthen the vibration. A strangled shout escapes me. All I can do is lie here, shuddering with pleasure, watching him stroke himself. The sight is so incredibly hot that the tight pull inside me grows, and before long I'm coming again, pussy clenching on the vibrator.

"Look at that." My hips squirm, the sensitivity on my clit turning unbearable until Parker removes the toy. "Works like a charm."

I moan, pushing my cheek into his sheets. They smell amazing, like him. "Enough. You made your point. Please, just fuck me before I can't anymore."

"But I'm having so much fun playing with you." Parker takes hold of my hips and the world spins. I land on my stomach. He yanks on me again, positioning me on my knees with my ass in the air.

"I don't know if I can." I try to lift onto my elbows but my body is already fatigued, wound tight, and I collapse back down onto my cheek. I've never been able to make myself come more than a couple of times before the sensations become too much to bear.

Something broad and smooth touches my entrance. I barely glimpse my sparkly vibrator before he's shoving it inside me. "*Fuck*."

He withdraws it nearly all the way out before slamming it back in. God, that feels incredible. A perfect, blissful relief from the pain in my clit. "So wet, Summer. Look how easy I can fuck you with this."

And then I hear another buzzing sound, look down just in time to see him move my black bullet vibrator to my clit.

"No, no, no, no." It's pointless. I haven't used my safe word. And if he did stop, even through the pain, I'm fairly certain I'd beg him to start again.

Parker pumps the dildo into my pussy hard enough that I grip the bars on his headboard to keep myself in place. This one takes longer, more effort from him, but when Parker sinks his teeth into my ass cheek, biting hard, I'm coming with a desperate wail I've never heard come out of me before.

"Attagirl." Parker withdraws both toys as soon as I collapse onto my stomach. He rubs my back, strokes the hair off my cheek. Kisses my neck. "So good, Summer. You're doing so good. One more."

"No more. I can't," I moan, letting him flip me onto my back. He picks up the last remaining vibrator, the purple one, my favorite. But the sight of it, three orgasms deep, exhausted and hurting, makes me snap my legs shut.

"Poor thing," he taunts. He wraps his fist around his cock. "I was gonna let you have this. But if you want to quit . . ."

"Wait. *Wait.*" The rope tenses as I try to lunge for him. "Please. I want it."

He chuckles. "Thought you might say that."

I don't even have the energy to snap back at him. Parker plants a hand by my head, using the other to coat the tip of his cock over my dripping pussy. I bite my lip, waiting, heart pumping, and . . .

Nothing.

Parker hovers over me with a line between his brows, eyes fixed on a point above my head, even when I shimmy my hips. There's a quip on the tip of my tongue, ready to tease him for clamming up after all that talk. But then his eyes meet mine, suddenly so soft and unexpectedly vulnerable it steals my breath.

"Can I untie you? Please."

I manage a nod. At once he's reaching over my head, pulling me free. Rubbing and kissing at the red lines the rope left in my skin, before placing my open palms on either side of his face.

Just like that, this feels like anything but a middle of the night mistake.

The way Parker looks down at me is so intentional, the kiss he presses to my mouth so sweet. My heart swells so big it fills my entire chest. When I stroke over his cheek with my thumb and Parker leans into the touch, eyes closing, my heart threatens to burst altogether.

Years.

"I want you," I whisper. Every part of my body already tells him so, but I need him to know it.

He pushes inside me, and we're both gasping together, eyes on each other. I give a breathy, shaky laugh, because me and Parker, like this? I think it's exactly where I'm supposed to be. Always should've been.

"Fuck yeah," he breathes, cupping my cheek. "Goddamn you feel good, Summer. I can't take it."

"*You* can't take it?" I gasp another laugh when he thrusts just a little deeper. He's barely inside me and I feel stretched thin. Physically. Emotionally. "I'm the one who can't do this."

"You can. Look at me and breathe." He takes my jaw in a massive hand. "Let me in, Summer. All the way in."

All the way in. Something tweaks in my head, brain scrambling to read between lines like it loves to do, desperately searching for any scrap of deeper meaning.

Parker sits up, holding my hip and pressing soft circles on my clit with his other hand. He watches himself ease into me until he hits resistance. Pulls back and moves in again, a little bit deeper this time.

"I wish you could see this. You're soaking the sheets. Trying so hard to take me."

I try to get a look, but it's impossible to do while relaxing my body. "I want to see." It comes out like a petulant whine and I don't even care. I'm boneless, mindless, barely human anymore as my body succumbs to the pleasure of his cock sliding into me. "Park, I want to see. Use my phone."

Parker's gaze snaps to mine. "You want me to film us?"

All I do is sob an impatient response. Chuckling darkly, he reaches for my purse at the end of the bed. I close my eyes, no longer capable of expending the energy required to leave them open. My only indication that he's located my phone is the feel of his body rocking deeper into mine, sending sharp bursts of heat down my legs the farther he gets. It's amazing. He's so filling, the perfect amount of painful.

"Almost there," he says gruffly. I circle my hips to help him along and he groans. "Summer, baby, I'm not gonna last. You're too tight. And you've tortured me, watching you come so fucking hard, over and over."

"Whose fault is that?"

"You're so right." He's over me again, kissing me. A final, hard snap of his hips and Parker surges inside me, hips flush with mine, moaning into the room. "This is so fucking right."

My brain insists there's subtext here, but then Parker pulls back, shoves back in, and I'm too busy shuddering into his sheets to focus on much else.

"Open your eyes." Parker props my phone against a pillow, hits the play button. And *holy shit*. It's us. A perfect close-up of his smooth cock working its way inside my pussy.

"Oh my God," I pant, watching him fuck me as he actively fucks me, kissing my neck. I've never experienced anything as hot as this in my life. "Parker, I think I'm gonna come again."

His hips pick up the pace, knocking into mine, shoving the breaths from my lungs. "Do it. Please. I wanna feel you."

Parker reaches around, and I know what's coming even before I hear a click and the resulting vibration. The purple vibrator touches my clit just as his thrusts turn merciless. My eyes are stuck to my phone, watching his cock disappear inside me. But the moment I feel that first surge of heat, my gaze finds his.

His hair falls over his forehead, damp with sweat, and his every muscle bunches with effort as he fucks me. When the orgasm slams into my wrecked body and I clench around his cock, he groans so loudly it's surely woken the neighbors.

"*Summer*, fuck." His mouth falls open, and not a moment later he's coming inside me, slumping and shuddering against my body. The video on my phone has ended, the screen gone black.

I'm exhausted. Sore. A sweaty, sticky mess, but nothing dims the euphoria coursing through me. A laugh escapes me. "Oh my God, we just did that."

Parker breathes his own laugh into my neck. "We just did that."

He's moving already. Kissing me gently, whispering how well I did, how proud he is, as he strokes the sweaty hair off my face. My eyes close. I'm loving everything about the gentle way he handles me now, wishing I could have it forever.

He starts to crawl off the bed but I reach for him, nails digging into his wrist. "Don't go. Please, can you just . . ."

He doesn't question it, doesn't insist otherwise. Parker settles back into bed, tucking me into him. "I'm not going anywhere, love. Staying right here."

Relief pours into me. My eyes shut, brain starts to drift, and the moment Parker sets my ear right over his beating heart, I fall asleep.

Chapter 35

Summer

Thump thump thump thump.

It's the second time I'm waking up like this, cheek pressed to my best friend's chest, his heart beating into my ear. Last time, the impromptu sleepover drove me into a confused, lust-addled spiral. And while there's plenty of lust to go around this morning, skin-to-skin the way we are, there's no confusion to be found.

It's Parker who caused the delightful soreness between my thighs, his lips that made mine swollen and sensitive. He put the faint red marks around my wrists, cold hard proof that last night wasn't a figment of the copious fantasies that've haunted me since our first kiss.

Careful not to wake him, I shift onto a pillow, craving a better look at him like this: peacefully asleep, hair a mess. I brush the thick strands off his face, trail a finger down the bridge of his nose, just because. My heart threatens to explode just from the sight of him so at ease with me like this.

I stare into his gorgeous face, wishing I could see into his head. Is he feeling this way, too? Will he forgive me for lying about the tour?

In which world could I plausibly leave town now, when it feels like I'm on the verge of the very relationship I've longed for my entire adult life?

Is there a reality where I could go and he'd simply . . . wait?

"Hey." Parker's soft voice, thick with sleep, startles me out of my head even as the questions continue to pile up, a new one added to the mix by the second. His palm touches my cheek. "Thinking too hard this early in the morning."

I search his sleepy face. "Last night."

A dimple in his cheek. "Yeah."

"It was . . ." *Everything I've ever wished for.*

"Yeah." He's stroking his thumb over my cheek, gazing at me with sleepy eyes.

Is it too much to hope for that he means it in exactly the same way I do?

This is foreign to me. Having all these questions and feeling suddenly unable to speak them out loud to Parker of all people—and *now* of all times, when we're lying naked together with nowhere to hide.

But asking them would mean admitting that I've lied to him. And after last night . . . blame the delusional girl in me, but I don't want to ruin the magic.

"I think I should go," I say slowly. Get some space, some perspective, and figure out how to talk to him about all this.

His brows pull together. "Okay."

I slide out from under the sheets before I can think better of it. Parker sits up, watching me search for last's night clothes. My chest pinches at the neat way he's laid out my vibrators on his nightstand.

He brought every single one of my sexual fantasies to life, simultaneously demolishing every insecurity brought on by the men before him. And that there should be the deciding factor, shouldn't it?

There's no way I can leave town now. Not if there's a chance this thing between us is real.

I sweep everything into my purse and face him. He looks almost exactly as he did when I woke him last night. Bare-chested, covers around his hips. Visibly confused. Except I can see the red lines my nails scored into his shoulders before he bound me.

"Well . . . thank you. For the . . ." I clear my throat. "Sex."

Thank you for the sex? What in the awkward morning after is the matter with you?

Parker doesn't say a word. Doesn't take his eyes off me. But I think I see something like amusement flair in them before I flee.

~~~~~

I keep my chin tucked as I cross the street at a damn near run, hoping this doesn't look like the walk of shame it absolutely is because . . . *thank you for the sex?*

Peak shame. Peak first-, second-, thirdhand embarrassment.

No recovering from this.

"You'd better hope you make that tour now," I mutter to myself as I race up the steps of my walk-up. "Or you'll have to assume a new identity. Grow a mustache—a beard, even."

In my apartment, I dump my purse on the table by the door. Run my fingers through my disheveled hair. I can feel the ghost of Parker's fingers tangled in it while he angled my mouth just right before sliding his—

My blood heats when I spot my phone on the table. Oh my God—I didn't just fuck Parker. We filmed ourselves last night. Like a pair of rabid, horny teenagers.

I swipe at my screen, tapping to the video with a shaking hand.

The still is enough to get my clit throbbing—it's me, stretched out on Parker's sheets, legs thrown open with Parker between them.

"Summer Freya Prescott, you cannot be serious," I mutter to myself. "You're not really about to—"

I hit play. Dig my teeth into my lip as Parker's cock sinks inside me. Whimper at the sound of his groan, and I can't help it. I reach between my legs, dragging a finger over my clit—

A knock at the front door has me jumping out of my skin.

"Open up, Summer."

I slap at my screen, make it go black. Open the door with shaking hands to find him there—Parker dressed in a mouthwatering pair of sweats and a T-shirt, his hands braced on either side of the doorframe. My pussy clenches, furious at his interruption and demanding he right his wrongs.

Parker looks down at me in the same measured way he had in his bed, mere minutes ago. "You done yet?"

My heart thunders. "Done what?"

"Freaking out."

"No, actually." I jerk a thumb over my shoulder. "I was just about to go drown myself in the shower over the *thank you for the sex* thing. Give me a couple minutes and I'll be right with you."

"Now you're rescinding the appreciation? Not very polite."

Parker steps into the apartment and kicks the door shut. It's like he's walked through a veil at the threshold, wiping away the mild-mannered man I've had all morning. Sheer starvation pours from his eyes as they bounce over every inch me. Like he's just endured years without the feel of me and he's sick of waiting for more.

He makes a winding motion with his finger. "I vote we fast-forward through the freak-out. We've got more pressing matters to deal with, don't you think?"

"Like what?" His eyes land on my mouth. Something hot bursts in my chest. "That's what you came here for? To offer me more sex?"

Parker takes my face in his warm hands. "First, I came to make sure we're okay. Are we?"

I can't speak for myself on an individual level, considering *thank you for the sex* and the fact that he nearly just caught me watching our sex tape. But I nod. Even with the questions that pulled me from his bed, nothing's ever felt more *okay* than this—Parker holding my face, smiling gently down at me.

"Good." His thumbs brush my cheeks. "Second, I came to tell you how unbelievable you were last night. All of you. Your body is to die for." His thumb presses down on my lip. "This mouth is to fucking die for. Your sounds—your *sounds*, Summer. I'll be thinking about last night on my deathbed."

A smile tugs at my mouth, the typical post-hookup nerves fading. "Definitely came for more sex, then."

Shallow dimples pop in his cheeks. "Are we doing it again?"

"I don't know. Is that really a good idea?" I'm asking us both, fingering my wrist. I can feel lingering traces of last night's rope. "It's so messy, Park."

He lifts a brow. "I seem to recall you were the one begging for my—"

I clap a hand over his mouth. "You really can't help yourself, can you?"

He licks my palm. I release him. "I heard a great analogy the other night—what was it?" His face scrunches. "Oh yeah: It's like finally having a bite of that chocolate cake, and—"

Collecting my phone, I start heading down the hall. "*And* you just guaranteed you're never getting another bite again."

"Too bad. Really was a great cake. Best bite of my life."

I stop dead, stomach swooping. Biting down on my lip and staring at my toes, trying not to smile so pathetically big before turning back around.

"Well." I fiddle with my phone, happy butterflies dancing inside me. "That really shouldn't have come as a surprise—"

A moan fills the hallway.

My moan.

Then the very obvious sounds of skin hitting skin, and—

"*You're too tight. And you've tortured me, watching you come so fuck-ing hard, over and over—*"

My fingers fumble over my screen, killing the video that'd still been cued up. Silence rings around us and it's official: a beard and a new identity won't suffice.

"Hey, Sum?" Parker leans his hip against the table. "Whatcha watching?

I can't do it—I can't look at him. "Some guy sent me his sex tape. It's not very good though."

"Is this why you hurried out of bed?" Parker steps closer and tips back my head, forcing eye contact. A smirk tugs at his mouth. "Were you touching yourself watching us fuck, Summer?"

"Hardly." I raise my brows. "It was boring. Vanilla. Could never get me off—"

I gasp when he throws me over his shoulder. Parker strides into my apartment, straight to the couch, and drops me onto the cushions just as roughly as he'd handled me last night.

"Prove it," he says, snatching the phone from my hand. He places it on the coffee table, propping it up against a stack of books before dropping into the seat next to me. "Play it here and now. Watch it to the end without touching yourself. Without making a single needy sound. I dare you."

The obvious answer is no. Maybe to kick him out of my apart-ment, for the second day in a row. But he looks so completely smug, pleased to no end with himself, and nothing ever gets me going like that does.

"What do I get if I do?"

"I'll leave you alone. Never mention last night again, just like you pretend you want me to." He smirks when I scoff. "But if you don't? You're going to spread your legs then and there, and let me fuck

you until the sun sets. And again tomorrow. And the day after that."
Parker sinks lower on the sofa, lacing his fingers behind his head. "It's
win-win, really. I'm considerate like that."

I eye his profile. "Like a friends-with-benefits situation?"

"Call it whatever you want." He nods at the phone. "Now, play it.
I'm dying to see your pussy again."

I fire up the video before I can think better of it, sit back, and
cross my arms tight across my chest.

In an instant, I know I'm at a complete disadvantage. Just watching my calf muscles flex in response to Parker brings me back to last
night, the toe-curling perfection of feeling him stretch me. The camera work is rough at best, unsteady as Parker thrusts and draws back.
But it only intensifies the ache in my pussy, remembering how frantic
he'd been with me. How I could feel his desperation to touch me
everywhere, experience as much of my body as he could, like he didn't
believe he'd get to again.

Our sounds fill my living room. Panting, groaning, gasps and
moans. The creak of his bed as he fucks me.

I rub a hand over my chest, push the hair off my neck as I
threaten to overheat. My clit throbs when the camera flicks upward,
over my body, capturing the way my breasts bounce with every perfect shove of Parker's hips. He has a hand on my hip, holding me
firmly in place as though I weren't tied to his headboard, completely
at his mercy.

"Un-fucking-believable. Look at you, Summer," Parker rasps beside me. I glance over to see that he's hard and leaking, staining the
fabric of his sweats. His eyes are glued to my phone, where the video
has panned back down my body. Another thrust and his cock is halfway inside me.

Unbearable. This is utterly unbearable.

A soft groan has me tearing my eyes off the video again. Parker
now grinds his palm over himself. When he notices me looking, he

tugs down the waistband, freeing his cock. Uses the moisture to stroke himself until he's gasping for air.

Fuck. I'm clamping my jaw so hard it hurts, digging my nails into my palms so deep I must be cutting into my skin. I want it so badly— the relief of pressing on my swollen clit, and the sheer high of feeling Parker fuck me hard and fast.

"Summer, baby, just do it. Pull down those shorts and play with your pussy. We both know you're dying for it."

"No way." My voice is shaking. I catch myself squirming into the couch and force myself to stop.

On my phone, Parker rocks into me another inch, withdrawing to the tip. Back in, just a little deeper, and out again. I swallow hard, sweat breaking along my hairline. Listening to myself pant and moan as he fucks me. Hearing Parker's hand stroke his cock beside me, and it's too much—so much I know I'm about to burst into flames. Die, here and now. Needy and stubborn.

I close my eyes, hoping it helps, and then—

"Summer, baby, I'm not gonna last. You're too tight—"

That's all it takes. The gravelly sound of Parker's voice fills the living room and I'm whimpering, falling back against the couch cushions.

It's like firing a starting pistol.

The sound barely leaves my mouth before Parker slides to his knees on the ground, so fast he jostles the coffee table, sends my phone and the stack of books flying. My legs are thrown open, hips are lifted, and I don't care to pretend, play it off. I palm my breasts through my T-shirt, pinching my nipples as Parker rips off my shorts and panties. He hooks my legs over his shoulders and groans into my pussy without a single preamble.

I cry out, light bursting across my vision. I don't know how I went from death to ecstasy in two seconds flat. But it's so Parker, wasting no time dancing around what we both so clearly want.

Parker sucks on my clit, pausing only to bring my hands to his hair. "Pull on it." When I do, he nips my clit and grunts, "Again. Harder."

He groans loud, face contorted in pleasure. He licks a line from clit to ass, and I gasp a laugh at the ceiling, because of course he would. Trust Parker to go all in, this early in the morning.

"I love your pussy, Summer. Feels good. Tastes good. I could stay here forever."

I'm moaning, scraping at the seat cushions as his tongue attacks my clit, delivering sharp, steady bursts of pleasure. His fingers push inside me, curling, hitting that perfect spot he'd found with my toy last night. But in this new world where I know what it feels like to be fucked by Parker, to feel his weight against me, all it does is tease me.

"Fuck me. *Now*, Parker," I beg. He makes a sound of denial, finger-fucking me with abandon, and I nearly give in, loving every second of it. "*Winter*. Winter, winter, winter, please, just fuck me."

With a disapproving growl, Parker peels away. His face is *soaked*, chin and cheeks glistening with me. Without thinking, I dart forward and lick at his lips, kissing it all away, tasting myself on him.

"Told you, you taste good," he whispers. "Selfish little Summer, keeping that sweet pussy to herself all these years. The lengths I'd go to keep tasting you . . . You have no idea."

I smirk. "Is this how I can keep you in line when you piss me off? Drop my pants just to make you shut up?"

"That's how you guarantee I never stop trying to piss you off. May as well go skirts only. No panties. Open access."

"That's not sounding too bad at the moment."

I slide off the couch and into his lap. Parker takes fistfuls of my ass and lifts me, and we're both moaning when I slide down his length. I brace myself on his shoulders and circle and swivel my hips, working him inside me as we both watch.

"I'll never get sick of this." He grunts. "Seeing us together. The feel of you, Summer. Too good to give up."

I can't do more than whimper my agreement, but I feel his words seeping into my love-starved skin. Once he's as far in as I can take at this angle, I lift, drop back down, and this is it: heaven. Right here, in my mess of a living room. I squeeze my eyes shut, forgetting where I am, not caring how loud I'm being or which unbecoming sounds are making their way out of my mouth. This is me and Parker. My favorite person in the world, my safe place. A gentle tremor racks my body as I rock over him, and my eyes spring open.

"Park, I think I'm going to come." My voice is urgent, disbelieving. In all the madness, I'd forgotten about the toys sitting in my purse by the door.

"I felt it." He reaches for a fistful of hair and pulls me in for a hard, messy kiss. "Keep going. Use me. Take whatever that perfect cunt needs from me."

We stay like this, kissing and fucking. Simultaneously pulling back to smile at each other because it really is so good. I didn't know it could feel like this. There's no pretense, no playing it cool or trying too hard. No wondering if I'll ever see him again after giving it up.

Just me and Parker.

Parker meets my thrusts, fucking into me while my fingers scrape down his back with enough pressure to make him groan. He reaches for my clit, rubbing firm circles, and I really think . . . Oh my God, I really do think I'm about to . . .

He makes a sound of acknowledgment, like he knows and refuses to back off it, now that it's in reach. "Come on, Summer. Come for me just like this and I promise I'll make the next time even better. However you want it."

"Next time?" I'm breathless.

"And the time after that." He kisses me. "And the one after that." Another kiss. "And every single time after."

In the end, it's his words that do me in. The promise of more.

White-hot heat bursts inside me and I'm coming, crying into the room. The movement of my hips stutters before Parker grips them and shoves me back down on his cock. He's ruthless, fucking me through my orgasm, drawing it out. And when the bite of my nails into his back turns punishing, when I whisper for him to come inside me, Parker goes off. Neck arching, brows pulled together.

I stare at him in wonder, basking in his pleasure, wanting to re-member this exactly so that I can pull it up whenever I need a lift.

I did that. I made him feel that good.

Parker collapses on the floor, taking me with him. I slide off him, and we both gasp as he slips out of me. He throws an arm over his eyes, working hard to regain his breath.

My gaze travels to the ceiling. "I can't believe I came."

"I can." There's a dimple peeking out from under his arm.

I smirk. "Because it's you, with your massive unit and pussy prowess?"

"Because it's us, Summer. We were always going to be magic." He rolls, landing over me on hands and knees and burying his face in my neck. "Tell me we can keep doing that."

"You won the bet, didn't you?"

"It's not good enough. I want you to want me back."

I hesitate, even while knowing I couldn't bring myself to stop at two. Painfully aware that I'm planning to jet around the world for the next year, hopefully the one after that, and that fresh feelings like these might be too new to stand the test of world travel.

But my feelings for Parker have been a runaway train for weeks. And for however long he wants me, however long this lasts, I want to keep doing this.

I want him to keep holding me like this, like I'm the only one who matters.

"We keep it to ourselves," I say quietly. I need to figure out what the hell Parker and I are doing, and where the hell I'll be this time next year, before letting any other excited voices in my head.

Parker chews on the inside of his cheek. "Yeah. All right. But I have a condition, too—no more running out of bed in the morning."

"We should set boundaries. I should sleep in my own bed—"

"No. You sleeping anywhere but next to me after we're together is a hard limit for me. If you can't commit to that, then I don't think I can do this."

My heart leaps. "Committing is the stuff of relationships, Park."

"Like I said: Call it whatever you want. I'm not letting you love me and leave me." He sits up, shoving the hair off his forehead. "Now, come on. I've never fucked in a bath before."

"You're not done?"

Parker lifts a brow. "Can you get up and walk on your own?"

"Yes, Park," I say with a laugh. "Pretty sure I can walk to the bathroom."

"Then I'm nowhere near done with you."

Chapter 36

Parker

"Tell me what happened."

"No."

"Tell me what happened or my pinched nerve will inexplicably reappear and I'll make you bridal-carry me through town."

I glare at River, who's keeping pace with me as we jog around the wooded bend that links Brooks's private street to the rest of Oakwood. He glances back all innocent looking, but the little shithead is fighting a smirk. He's got a radar on him, too—the same way he somehow detected a shift between me and Summer after Rocky Ridge. He's convinced he caught me giving her a look this morning, and has been nagging me like an incessantly annoying kid brother since.

There were obviously looks. Though I'm not sure which one he happened to catch.

Maybe it was the *I can't wait to fuck you later.* Or the *please love me back, I'm dying a slow death every minute you don't.* Or was it *what's the minimum required time I need to wait before begging you to marry me?*

"You realize I'm not a child, right?" River continues. "I know what it looks like when two people are f—"

I shout before he can finish that sentence. "No, none of that. I'm not discussing that with you."

His smirk grows, even as he's panting. "I never said I wanted to discuss it—all I wanted was confirmation, which you so kindly just gave."

"Fine. Things with Summer have . . . progressed. In a good way. A great way, in fact."

It's not exactly what I'd hoped for when I set my heart on earning Summer. But it's been enough to have me floating through the past week. She's got me fully indoctrinated. Completely convinced that this is all I'll ever need for the rest of my life. Me and Summer. Fucking. Surfing. Eating. Fucking some more. Reading in bed together, then listening to the hums she makes in her sleep, her face pressed into my chest—when I can let myself believe that, with a bit of luck, time, and a few more items checked off her dream man list, she could love me one day, too. Would let me have this forever.

And if that fails, I'll simply fuck her to a delirious state, then make her promise to marry me before she comes to her senses.

"Figured that was the case, now that I don't have the human equivalent of Eeyore training me. I'm . . ." River's voice stalls, and I watch him struggle with words as we pass a row of bait shops. "I'm happy for you. That's all. You seem . . . good, lately. I figured your girlfriend had something to do with it."

Girlfriend. I don't correct him. Instead, I let the word float into the universe, sending a wish after it.

"River Nowak. Who knew you were so sentimental. Deep, *deep* beneath the surface."

We come to a stop at a bench. River slumps into the seat, bracing his elbows on his thighs. He draws deep breaths while I wrench off my hat to push the sweaty hair off my forehead.

"Was it hard, getting started with physical therapy?" Despite the question, River's gaze sweeps the street with his usual apathy.

"I'm not sure I understand. I haven't had an injury requiring therapy since I played college ball."

He sighs like I'm being dim on purpose. "I meant *working* in physical therapy. Rehabbing athletes. Do you like it?"

I drop onto the wooden bench. "I wasn't sure I did for a while. But yeah, I do. It's nice heading home at the end of the day knowing I made a difference in someone's life."

"Do you think it's something I could do one day?"

He's still checking out our surroundings, the picture of indifference, but I hike a knee on the seat to face him. "I thought your plan was to make it to the league?"

"It is. But I've been thinking about what you said before—about having more than one plan."

I try match his nonchalance despite the inner burst of satisfaction, knowing anything else won't get me very far with River. But damn if hearing him talk like this, planning for his future, doesn't feel gratifying. "If it's something you decide you want to do one day, I'll do whatever I can to help. We can make sure you're getting the right credits in college."

"Okay. Whatever."

"And what about Macy? Have you reached out to her?" River's eyes narrow, but I'm not teasing him. "River, that was a three-and-a-half-mile run we just did. You haven't touched your crutches in weeks. What else are you waiting for?"

"I keep thinking about asking her out . . . and her saying no." River glances at me. "I know I'm being a chicken shit. You don't have to say it."

"I definitely think you are. But I get it. Whatever this is with Summer . . . I'm not sure she feels the same way." I stare down at my open palms. "She doesn't want to tell anyone about us."

River drops his face into his hands. "Why is this stuff so hard?"

"If it weren't hard, it wouldn't be worth having."

And I mean that. For now, I'll take what I can get of Summer. I've got a foot in the door. And in the meantime, I'll become gainfully employed. Figure out a five-year plan, somewhere to live where the main perk isn't being able to judge the busyness of the bar below. And I need to learn how to fry an egg without setting off the smoke alarm.

"Good morning, you two. Not a bad day for a run." River stiffens as Wynn Sheffield, diner owner and blueberry donut purveyor, approaches us with a grin. He's wearing a dusty pair of shorts streaked with what looks like plaster.

"Hey, Wynn. How are the repairs coming along?" I ask, trying to save River from conversation. I can feel him shrinking into himself, and fuck if my heart doesn't ache for him. It can't be easy, running into the owner of the business his car destroyed in that storm.

"I'm on my way back there now—the new floors are finally getting put in. Did you know Danica Klein set up a fundraiser for the diner?"

Fucking Danica Klein. Of course she's taking credit for Summer's idea. I bite my tongue, remembering the promise I made Summer not to get involved in her issues with the town.

Wynn's gaze swings over to River. "I've been hoping to run into you, River."

River manages a split-second glance at Wynn. "Oh."

"I haven't seen those crutches of yours in a while," Wynn continues. "I'll tell you, nothing makes me happier. I'm glad to see you doing better."

River's shoulders ease when he sees the man grinning down at him. "Thank you. That's . . . nicer than I deserve."

Wynn's smile falls. "Nonsense. I've known you since you were a baby. Why would I want otherwise?"

You've known Summer since she was practically a baby, too.

My knee bounces compulsively, body trying to expend the

sudden buildup of energy within me, dying to leap into action. *Don't get involved. Do not get involved.*

Thankfully, a car pulls up to the curb behind us. River's dad calls out for him from the open passenger window.

"I better go." River flashes a tentative smile at us before adding, "Thanks. To both of you."

Just like that, my buffer's gone. And I know I promised Summer. I *know* I did. But the injustice of it all is eating away at me, and—

"It wasn't Danica." The words fly out of my mouth before I can stop them. "The fundraiser was Summer's idea. She set it all up."

The surprise in Wynn's face fades fast, like now that he thinks about it, this version of events makes a whole lot more sense. "Is she all right? I haven't seen her in months."

"She's Summer. Puts on a happy face, but the gossiping destroyed her. You should see the way some people have been treating her—it's her parents' divorce all over again, except now she's the bad guy."

Wynn gives a frustrated sigh. "I never believed that for a second, not that she's given me the chance to say so. She runs the other way every time she catches sight of me."

"Can you blame her? Ninety percent of town *did* believe it—and all of them should've known better. It's no wonder she'd assume you did, too."

Wynn looks out toward the diner. "I suppose that's fair. But some of us miss her very much."

"Then maybe try a little harder to show it. Give her a reason not to expect the worst," I tell him. When Wynn gives a contemplative nod, I decide to push my luck. "If you happen to be in the mood to start—or to pay it forward for the donations? I might have an idea as to how you could."

～～～

A couple of hours later, I'm heading home from an impromptu cooking lesson at the diner. I reek of bacon but feel like I've got a decent grip on various methods of cooking eggs, after several failed attempts—enough to try my hand at making breakfast for Summer in the morning, and convince Wynn that giving me nightly cooking lessons going forward won't be a complete waste of his time.

Summer wants a man who cooks. So, fuck it. I'll become a man who cooks.

My phone goes off just as I'm nearing my place. I pull it out to find Brooks's name lighting up the screen.

"If this is about the mess I left your gym in this morning, rest assured that I'll clean it up in due time. Also, lay off the security cameras, you creep."

Brooks chuckles. "There aren't security cameras in the gym. But you might want to start thinking about getting your own training space."

Fuck. I've been dreading this day. "How long until you want me gone?"

"I don't care if you stay. But I figure once you hear this, you'll want something a little more formal than my house." There's barking on his end of the line, and Brooks takes a moment to talk his dog down before coming back to me. "I just got a call from my GM, who wants to know if you'd ever agree to let them ship players on our injured reserve to work with you in Oakwood."

I stop dead in my tracks. "This better not be a joke."

"It's not. You fucking earned it." I can hear the smile in Brooks's voice. "Are you in?"

Chapter 37

Summer

"Hey, Dad! I got your text. I didn't realize you've been planning a family vacation—Mexico sounds amazing! I'd love to come; thanks for inviting me! It's just that . . . well, remember how I told you I was competing in Surf's Up? The trip would overlap with the final event in a few weeks. Any chance we could reschedule to a little later this summer? Totally okay if you can't, of course. But I guess it means you won't make it to watch me, huh?"

～～～

"You're up early."

Parker glances at me as I hike myself up on the bathroom counter. He's brushing his teeth in just a pair of sweats, hair still a wreck from sleep, and I'll never understand how it is that he manages to look so damn delicious before the crack of dawn.

"Needed to get a head start on a few things before our surf." He rinses his mouth then reaches for the toothpaste, applying some to my own toothbrush and handing it to me. His eyes linger on my bare thighs, barely covered by the T-shirt of his I stole when I rolled out of his bed. "How'd you sleep?"

"Like a baby," I say around my toothbrush. "Nothing like a handful of orgasms to knock you out, you know?"

"More than a handful by my count." His smile goes lopsided before he bends to wash his face.

It occurs to me that I've never watched him like this before: Parker with his full guard down, letting me in on a moment he only ever has in private. It might be the single most intimate thing I've ever sat through. Maybe my favorite thing about this new version of us.

I reach for his towel hanging off the counter. He smiles when he resurfaces and sees it in my hands, and stands obediently still as I pat him dry, my toothbrush stuffed in my cheek.

Parker squeezes my thighs. "Why're you smiling at me like that?"

I run my fingers through his unruly hair, but it's a lost cause. The stubborn strands stay charmingly ruffled. "I've never seen you wash your face."

"And that's something worth smiling about?"

"It feels . . ." *Anything but casual.* I lean over the sink to rinse my mouth. Parker gathers my loose hair and holds it out of the way for me. When I finish, he wipes a lingering trace of toothpaste from the corner of my mouth.

Perfect. Like we always should've been like this.

"Like us. But different," I finish. It's ineloquent and incredibly obvious, but it's the best I can do without carving open my chest and letting him see for himself the excitable butterflies he unleashed the night of our first kiss. They're stronger now, after weeks of flight. And since our first night together, they take barely a hint of a dimple to get started.

Just watching Parker wash his face has sent them in a tizzy.

I'm dangerously close to tumbling over an emotional line I don't think I can ever come back from. All I can do now is turn myself over to the hope I've done my best to renounce since my last attempted relationship.

Hope that he's feeling these things, too.

Hope that I'm not getting way ahead of myself.

Hope that I'll make the right call when it comes to the next few years of my life.

"Us but different," Parker echoes. He leans in, presses his face to the side of my neck, and inhales deeply. I must still have traces of the perfume he seems to like so much. "You're saying I was right about the sleepovers?"

I laugh. "About that—you do know you can *buy* a body pillow, right? I'm not technically required to be here."

"But then you wouldn't have this." He kisses that spot on my neck. Instantly, I'm whimpering, melting into the mirror behind me. He nips my lip next, then sucks it between his. "Or this."

My eyes fall shut, fingers sinking back into his hair. "So the sleepovers are for me, then?"

"No. They're absolutely for me." He drops to his knees and yanks me to the edge of the counter, wrenches up his shirt so that it gathers at my hips. "No better reason to get up than this."

"*Fuck.* Yes." My head falls back against the mirror when he licks all the way through me, then clamps his lips over my clit and sucks with an absolutely flawless pressure. "The sleepovers were a genius idea."

~~~~~

An hour later, I'm thoroughly fucked, sore, and late for our morning surf.

The sun is already beginning to brighten Oakwood's main strip, but it's still early enough that it's deserted but for us. Parker cinches the rope tying our boards to his car, then reaches for the phone dinging in his back pocket. It's Brooks blowing up his phone, which he's been doing more than usual for the past couple of days. But Parker hasn't been particularly interested in enlightening me as to why.

I've let him keep his secrets, seeing as I've been holding on to a few of my own.

I unzip my backpack in the passenger seat to check that I remembered to pack a fresh stick of sunblock. "How's Brooks doing?"

Parker swipes away from his messages. "He's all right."

"Have you said anything about us?"

"No, I promised I wouldn't." He looks me over. "Is that why you've been quiet in the group chat lately? You worried they'll figure it out?"

Between sleeping with Parker and the potential tour—not to mention the fact that I haven't even mentioned to our friends that I'm competing again—I've been keeping it to short, non-incriminating answers in our chat. Shy's been messaging me periodically since I ran into her in town, but she's started to get the hint after days of evasive answers.

"Partly." I toss my bag into the back seat and lean against the side of his car. "But it's mostly because I can't find a moment alone these days. There's this guy always hanging around, begging to take my clothes off. Poor thing; it's like he hasn't gotten laid in years."

Parker yanks on one of my braids. "Or maybe you're just that good a fuck, Summer. Ever think about that?"

"Meanwhile, you're . . ." I make a wishy-washy sound. "We'll get there eventually."

Parker gives a solemn nod. "Excellence does take practice. And lots of it." There's a tender edge to his smile, even more so when he takes my hand. "I used to dream about this with you."

I laugh. "Oh, I remember that dream. Vividly."

"Not that dream. Well . . . *definitely* that dream, believe me. But also . . ." He stares at our intertwined fingers. "Let me cook for you tomorrow."

"Is that a euphemism I'm not aware of?" He's the one person in town who might be a worse cook than me. "Code for bending me over and stuffing me like a—"

"Summer." Parker's smile tilts to the right. Amused, then sympathetic the longer he looks at me. "You really don't have a clue, do you?"

The way he looks at me has my stomach tumbling. "A clue about what?"

He squeezes my hand. "Dinner. Tomorrow night. My place."

"Okay." The word wobbles out of my mouth. "Why are you acting like we've never had dinner at your place?"

"Because it's never been a—"

"Oh God." My gaze darts over his shoulder to find Wynn Sheffield marching down the sidewalk toward us. It's the first time I've properly seen him in a while—I've been avoiding him since the public showdown with Denny.

Snide remarks from the people I'm not close to are bad enough. Hearing them from Wynn? It would crush me.

I slip my hand from Parker's and step toward his car. "Should we go? We should go. Quickly, before he gets here."

"Sum, come on." He takes my wrist. "Why are you hiding? You've done nothing wrong."

"You know what? You're right. Screw running." I roll back my shoulders. "I'm—I'm standing my ground for once. In fact, he's the one who should run the other way. All I ever did was try to help with the diner!" I step around Parker just as Wynn takes his final steps toward us. "If you've come to make some sort of pointed commentary like the rest of this town—"

"I thought you might like something to eat before your surf," Wynn cuts in. He eyes me carefully. Steps closer and offers a sleeve of blueberry donuts. "They're still warm. Baked them fresh for you."

"Oh." The rush of adrenaline fizzles away, leaving confusion in its wake. I take the donuts.

"I know you want your space—we've gotten the message." Through my surprise, I sense something a little sad in Wynn's voice. "But I wanted to say thank you. I know you're responsible for the fundraiser."

My brows fly up my forehead. Parker mutters something unintelligible and shuffles away to check the ropes securing our boards to his car. "Danica told you?"

"No, not Danica," Wynn says. More muttering from Parker. This time, I catch the words *this town* and *mouths shut*. Tentatively, Wynn reaches for me. Squeezes my shoulder. "We hope you're well, Summer. Don't stay away too much longer, you hear?"

He hurries off before I can speak. Almost like he's afraid of what I might say.

Then he glances back, sees me looking, and gives me a gentle smile. Almost like he doesn't hate me, judge me at all.

Almost like he misses me. *Me.*

I clasp my cheek, staring after Wynn. "Parker?"

"I'm sorry. I know I promised not to say anything. But I heard Danica was taking credit for the donations, and you deserved to have Wynn know how much you care about him, and care about this town, and . . ."

Parker trails off when I toss the donuts into the bed of his Jeep and throw my arms around him, burying my face in his chest. "Thank you."

His arms enclose me. A palm at my lower back, the other in my hair. "You're not angry I got involved?"

"Did you throw a punch?" He shakes his head. I inhale his peppery scent, holding it for a long time. "Then I'm not angry, Park. Not even close."

~~~~~

Floating in the ocean an hour later, I stare down the horizon while Parker watches this morning's surf footage on his waterproof camera.

Something feels different today.

There's a pretty set of waves approaching, growing higher as it builds momentum. The kind you'd die for mid-heat when you're down in the score and desperate to make up the points. The kind younger me, who was so sure about herself, would go after with everything she had. Without fear that a single wave might change the course of her life for the worst, disrupt the relationships she held so dear.

I miss that me.

I really want her back.

"I'm doing it," I announce.

"Yeah?" Parker eyes the approaching wave, understanding right away. "Fuck yeah, you are. Let's see it, Sum."

I flatten to my board before I can overthink it. He does the same, heading for the shore, getting into position to record it. I brace myself as the wave catches up. It's a big one, a perfect barreling wave that sends water arching over me before I've even sliced all the way down its face.

Water thunders around me. My legs tremble. It's a protest from my heart, telling me to kick out, quit. For once, I refuse.

Maybe it's the quiet domesticity of my morning with Parker. The fresh blueberry donuts, or Wynn's simple touch to my shoulder. Maybe it's Parker having my back, or holding my hand out in the open—in the middle of Oakwood, for anyone to see. The nightly surfs with Celia and her friends, reminding me of every reason I longed for the tour in the first place.

Or maybe it's the foreign kernel of anger mixed with the cutting hurt inside me, at the text my dad sent earlier. A whole family vacation planned. Clearly inviting me as an afterthought. No acknowledgment that the trip overlapped with a competition he *knows* I'm surfing in.

Who the hell does that?

I shift my weight, stalling as the barrel envelops me completely. Oh, fuck. *Yes yes yes*, I can do this—

And yet . . . Dad *did* invite me. I should be grateful, shouldn't I? It's a step in the right direction.

If I'm not around, how long until Parker finds another hand to hold out in the open?

My chest constricts, panic overtaking me. Just ahead, the tube opens up to a view of the coastline. It's the closest I've come to allowing myself to complete a barrel since I started competing again. I'm physically strong. Feet so solid on my board. Almost there.

But I picture it—making the tour and Parker falling for someone else while I'm all the way across the world. Dad hosting family dinners I wouldn't be around to attend. Out of sight, and completely out of mind to everyone back home.

My breaths start coming in shallow, rapid bursts, as it hits again—the inner war that overtakes me whenever I'm hidden within a tube of water.

My brain screams at me to stay on my feet, to surf the way it knows I can. Ride the barrel, rack up the points, make the tour. Easy. Just like I've always dreamed.

But my heart begs me to quit, disconnect from my board. To stay put, here at home. I'm too forgettable to leave.

I drag as deep a breath as I can into my lungs and kick my board out from under me, falling back into the water and letting the wave punish me for it.

Coward.

When I resurface, Parker is already nearly at my side. He slides off his board and meets me in the water, pushing away the hair stuck to my face as I regain my breath.

"You okay?" He helps me grasp my board, then holds on to its other side so that we float together. "Did you lose your balance again?"

You absolute coward.

I can't look him in the eye. I'm furious with myself, but I think I also might be crying. It's hard to tell with salt water already streaking down my face.

"Love, it's okay." He squeezes my hand before sliding his camera's strap off his arm and settling it between us, clicking until I appear on the small screen. "You have this. You were so close this time. Look."

He replays the footage—mostly just a barrel moving toward shore—and then, at the very end, a peek of yellow at the mouth of the tube. Parker shakes his head at the camera. Pure awe despite the supposed wipeout that followed. "You were right there, Sum. You almost made it out."

He throws back his head and howls wildly at the sky. Then surges over my board and plants a hard kiss on my mouth.

A shaky laugh tumbles out of me at his palpable excitement, even as shame overtakes me.

You absolute, self-sabotaging coward.

Chapter 38

Parker

Abandoning my new cookbook—a gift from Wynn after a week's worth of semi-successful cooking lessons, featuring an impressive stack of blueberry pancakes but an overcooked, rubbery roast chicken—I pull up the instructional video I took yesterday and prop my phone on a bottle of olive oil.

I try to let muscle memory take over, and slice through the herbs like Wynn does on-screen. But the leaves are wet and sticking everywhere—to my knife, my fingers—until the result is a sad sprinkling on the chicken sitting in a pan on my kitchen counter, surrounded by chopped carrots. On the stove, tomato sauce bubbles away next to a pot of water waiting to be boiled.

Wynn had me convinced I could pull off a pasta dinner for tonight's Summer Friday. And it might've been that his vote of confidence overinflated my ego a touch, because I decided to give the roast chicken another shot, too.

Summer's dream man would put in the effort.

Since Brooks's first call, I've had meetings with everyone from the heads of the Rebels' training and medical teams, to higher-ups in the front office. I've spent all week outlining a business plan for my very own rehabilitation clinic, and signed the lease on a space just this morning.

The me of a few months ago, who felt caged in by my own life and obsessed over all the ways I fell short, never would've imagined an opportunity like this. All I can think about now is telling Summer she was right. That if I'd given up the way I wanted to, stayed in bed the way I wanted to, I wouldn't be on the precipice of a dream I'd never even let myself have.

Hence tonight's dinner date.

It's a *thank you for believing in me*. An *I love you*. A *couldn't have done it without you*. An *everything I do, everything I am, it's to be worthy of you*.

Also, it's an opportunity to grill her on how serious she is about marrying someone with dark hair, because I'm not sure I could pull it off.

I yank open a drawer and pull out a spoon, checking my distorted reflection in the back of it. Could I pull off dark hair? Maybe I should try it.

My front door swings open, bouncing off the wall in the hall and startling the spoon out of my hand.

"Park." Summer groans. "I cannot begin to tell you how sore I am from today's workout. I had to crawl up the stairs just now. Preston Wembley down the hall definitely thinks I'm possessed. Which I suppose is an improvement on *homewrecker*, but not by much."

"Shit, she's early," I mutter to myself, hurrying to sweep the vegetable scraps into the compost bin under the sink.

"Parker, did you hear me? I think you have to tell Herb we're skipping tonight's swim. Otherwise, you'll be diving to the bottom of the pool to retrieve me, and . . ."

Summer pauses in the mouth of the hallway. She's dressed in the tiniest, most agonizing frayed denim shorts, an oversized T-shirt hanging off a shoulder. Her loose waves flick as she stares around the kitchen while I hold my breath.

"Wow, Park." She gives me a curious smile. "That smells amazing. What are you making?"

I breathe a relieved laugh. "Pasta sauce. I still need to put the noodles on. I'm making roast chicken, too."

"Oh, good." She nods, eyeing the aluminum dish on the counter with relief. "That should be enough food for everyone."

"No one else is coming. It's . . ." *A date.* "Summer Friday."

Summer doesn't seem to have heard me. She drifts toward the dining table on the far side of the island, trailing a finger over its surface and smiling down at the pink glitter she collects, left over from my T-shirt crafting for her next surf event.

I don't know why I'm so suddenly nervous about this. Our first real date.

Possibly, it's because I'm not exactly sure she's realized yet it's a date. But we'll get there.

Her gaze lingers on the flowers sitting in a vase, and then the ones still in their brown paper wrapping. She tugs on a rose petal. "Flowers?"

"For you."

Her gaze flicks to me. "There are two of them."

"You spend so much time here, I thought you could have one in both places. Yours and . . ." *Ours.* "Mine."

"Oh," she says softly. Summer floats to my side in the kitchen, eyeing the roast chicken and the wonky herbs atop it. Then turns to me, head tipping all the way back as she searches my face. "What happened to the guy whose signature dishes were burnt toast and soggy microwaved rice? How are you even pulling this off?"

"Wynn's been helping me out with cooking lessons this week."

She rears back. "That's what's kept you busy after work? Cooking lessons?"

"More or less. It's something I've been meaning to brush up on." She squeaks when I pick her up by the waist and set her down on the counter, caging her in with a hand on either side of her. "Wine or Diet Coke?"

She glances at the flowers, cheeks flushing the most subtle shade of pink. *Come on, Summer. Add it all up. Flowers plus dinner equals . . .*

"Wine, please," she whispers.

Attagirl.

I open a fresh bottle of red. Her smile is timid when I hand her a glass, then clink it with mine. We take our sips with eyes on each other and it feels exactly the way I hoped it would. Us but different.

Us but better.

"Parker, I think I screwed up." Summer carefully sets down her glass, and when she looks at me again it's with a healthy dose of guilt. "I bumped into your sister earlier and she asked what we were up to tonight, so I mentioned you were cooking. It all sort of snowballed from there, and . . . everyone's coming. Here. For dinner. Tonight."

Oh, fuck me.

Summer eyes the flowers again while I silently beg the ceiling to crack open and bury my humiliated body. It's the pillow fort night all over again. I'm half expecting her to tell me *everyone* consists of a mass crowd of irritatingly nice surfer dudes she amassed throughout the day.

"Define *everyone*."

"Your sister and Zac. Shy's bringing Rosie." *Better than surfer dudes, at least.* "And . . . your mom called Mels to say they were driving through town tonight. Your parents will be here in an hour." *Worse. Absolutely worse than surfer dudes.* "Should I try to disinvite them?"

"No, that's . . ." I clear my throat. "I'm making enough food so . . . why not, right?"

I should've known better.

If there's anything Summer's better at than overthinking, it's brutally misreading romantic signals. She managed to turn a *let me cook you dinner at my place* into a dinner party with my mother as the guest of honor.

She watches me chop through more potatoes. "Silly me, coming over early to help you cook when I use my oven as shoe storage. You're really putting me to shame with all this." She tucks her hair behind her ear, and it's a little self-conscious. "He mocked me for it."

Denny. I know she's thinking of the list of every supposed reason she's single—*used to be* single, as far as I'm concerned. I'd love nothing more than to bury him alive.

"That guy couldn't know the first thing about being marriage material, Sum. It'd be like taking savings advice from a bank robber." I cut through a fresh potato. "The only insulting part of him bringing up your oven storage is the fact that you took credit for the idea, when it was mine to begin with."

Summer pauses, wineglass at her lips. "What?"

"It was my idea. Don't you remember your closet crisis a couple summers ago? You had a meltdown trying to decide which pairs of shoes to donate when you ran out of room at home." I sat with her all day, helping her sort them into *keep* and *donate* piles as she got increasingly upset to be losing so many beloved pairs. I suggested the oven when she couldn't decide between two pairs of similar-but-supposedly-totally-different pink heels, and we spent a good while filling it while laughing our asses off.

A smile tugs at her mouth. "I totally forgot about that."

"Besides," I say with a shrug. "Maybe I'm learning how to cook so you'll never have to."

"That's . . . kind of the hottest thing anyone's ever said to me." She gives a little laugh, eyeing the ball of cooking twine as I start unwinding it. "And what's the occasion for this . . . dinner?"

I take my time trussing the chicken, letting my nerves settle. This feels like the first proper step in the big picture plan, making Summer see me as someone worth her time. I put the pan in the oven, and wash off my hands before turning back to her.

"Brooks called last week. His coaches want to work with me to rehab anyone who ends up on the Rebels' injured reserve." Summer's hand flies up to her cheek. "I signed the lease on a new clinic space this morning."

"*Parker*. Are you kidding me?"

"I asked the same thing. Can you believe they'd trust me with something like that?"

"*Yes*. Absolutely, I can." Summer takes my shoulder, shaking me gently. "How are you so calm right now? This is huge! And so deserved—you've worked hard at this for years. It was only a matter of time until someone took notice." She hops off the counter, turning in a frantic circle on the spot. "I can't believe you didn't tell me sooner. I could've brought champagne—a cake! There's still time! Where's my purse?"

I laugh, tugging her back by the belt loop before she makes it too far across the kitchen. "You're all the celebration I need, Sum."

"But . . ." She blinks around the kitchen. At the pasta sauce on the stove, the wine. The flowers. Then up at me, in a way she never has. Like she's seeing me for the first time. "Parker, look at you. You're cooking. Starting your own business before the age of thirty."

"I'm thirty in two weeks."

"Don't do that—don't downplay the accomplishment. This is major. Life-changing, and it couldn't have happened to a better trainer. A better person." She takes my shirt in her fists and tugs, like she's willing me to see it her way. "I'm so proud of you."

I let her validation wash over me, sink all the way in.

She beams up at me. "It's like you're a whole different man overnight. Who are you, and what have you done to Parker Woods?"

I tuck her hair behind her ears and cup her face. "Turns out, all I needed was the right motivation." She goes quiet. Points at her own chest in a silent question. "Yes, love. You."

Summer shoots up on her toes and kisses me hard. She clings to my hair and pulls me in, then changes her mind and shoves me back into the counter. Fucking hell, she's been plenty enthusiastic in the two weeks since we started fucking, but being manhandled by her like this has the blood pouring straight to my dick. She trails kisses along my jaw, down my neck, as her fingers fumble with my belt.

I groan into the apartment. "Summer, baby, we have to stop. Or my family will walk in on things that'll put them in therapy for years."

Her whimper is soft and her arms fall at her sides. "I don't think I've ever been so jealous of a chicken."

I bark a laugh. Lift the cooking twine off the counter. "Cause of this?"

"You're telling me it didn't cross your mind to use it on me, even for a second?"

"Better question would've been whether I've managed to think of something *other* than using it on you." I taunt her with the twine. "Come on, then. Hop on that dining table and let me eat you for dinner instead."

She backs away with a laugh in her eyes. "Don't come near me if you can't finish the job before they get here."

"Don't go shy on me now. What was it you said a couple months ago? You wanted to be edged to the point of insanity?"

"I thought we agreed never to talk about that."

"Summer, come on. I would never agree to something so ridiculous." She backs away. I take a step toward her. "You wanted me even then, didn't you? Naughty girl, thirsting for your best friend."

She's fighting a laugh. "Please shut up."

"Bit rude." I lunge for her and she squeaks, makes a run for it around the kitchen island. But I grab her by the waist and haul her to the dining table. She's laughing so hard she's not making a sound. "Rude girls get punished, Summer." I trap her between my body and the table. Wrangle her arms at her front and bind her wrists together. "They get tied up and feasted on until they're screaming, and then they get left high and dry until they apologize."

She yelps when I sit her ass on the table. I love the look of this woman a lot of ways: Bold Summer, focused on a wave. Timid Summer, cheeks flushing bright. But I'd die to keep her looking exactly like this, always—blissed out, happy, laughing uncontrollably.

"They'll be here in half an hour—"

"Let them come. Let them see what you do to me." I scoop her ass off the table just to grab a handful through her denim shorts. "This ass. It's been teasing me half my fucking life." I nip her lip as she continues to laugh. "You think that's funny? Causing me physical pain every time you show up in these tiny shorts?"

"These shorts do it for you, Park?"

"These shorts. The leggings and the ridiculously tiny dresses. Watching those goddamn swimsuits ride up on the beach. My entire life with you is an exercise in self-control, and I'm running dangerously low."

She snorts with laughter when I flick open the button on her shorts, but lifts her hips to help me slide them down her thighs.

"Spread your legs. Let me see you." My Summer doesn't argue. She props her heels at the edge of the table and slides her panties to the side. I drop to my knees, kissing up her thighs. "I could spend the rest of my life like this."

She breathes a laugh. "On your knees for me?"

"On my knees, tongue-deep in this sweet cunt." I take over holding her panties. "Push your fingers inside."

It takes a little effort with her hands bound, but she pumps two fingers into her pussy, gasping into the room.

This is what I love most about the new us—our ability to go from uncontrollable laughter to moans in the span of a heartbeat.

Us but better.

The front of my jeans goes painfully tight watching her fuck herself. The next time she pulls out, I join a finger with hers and we sink into her pussy together. She moans but it's nothing compared to my groan, the feel of her making me damn near delirious with want. That's how we stay a while. Fingering her together as her breaths become increasingly desperate.

I kiss up her thigh, inching toward her pussy, licking and nipping on the way. Summer rocks her hips, offering herself to my tongue. I lean away, sliding our fingers out of her, too.

"Parker," she says sharply.

"Summer," I say with an innocent smirk. I inch forward again, swipe my tongue a single time over her clit before moving back.

Her eyes go wide. "You're really going to play this game now? Make me sit through an entire dinner without coming?"

"Baby, it's how I'll be surviving this dinner. Knowing you're sitting right there, pussy soaking through your panties. So desperate for an orgasm, counting down the seconds until you get my cock. It'll teach you a lesson about letting people crash our night."

"Fine. Mission accomplished." She nods at the front of my jeans, where my cock strains painfully against the stiff fabric. "Take off your pants. Let me take care of you, unless you plan to greet your mother like that."

"Nice try."

Summer cries out when I dart forward to suck on her clit, just for a second. Something absolutely furious flashes in her eyes before she tips back her head. Whimpers like she's in pain. "Parker, take off your pants. Please?" Her voice goes breathy and soft. "I really want to suck on you. Just a little bit?"

My cock throbs. "Don't do that—"

She slides off the table, and Jesus, she drops to her knees. Looking up at me with wide, hopeful eyes. "Please? Are you really going to make me beg for this? You have no idea how often I lose focus, all day at work. Dying to touch myself, just thinking about you like this. About how good it feels to lick your cock, how good you taste on my tongue—"

My abs clench. "*Summer.*"

"How sexy you sound when you're coming down my throat. And I swallow every drop, don't I? Just like a good girl—"

The fake-as-fuck doe eyes disappear when I wrench open my belt and shove down my jeans. I take a fistful of her hair and pull her in. "Make it good."

She doesn't hesitate. My groan echoes around us when she sucks me into her mouth, pulls back to drench my cock with spit, opens up even wider. Just the sight of her like this, on her knees, working me with her tongue, sends me careening toward the edge.

Her bound wrists slip between her thighs and I almost black out. It takes a little shifting around but I feel the exact moment she gets her fingers inside herself. She sucks on me harder, in a fucking frenzy, gently rocking on her fingers.

"That's so good, love. So perfect." My legs are unsteady but I lean back just to get a better view of her. "I wish you could see yourself like this. You're a fucking dream."

Summer backs off me only long enough to mutter, *phone*. With a groan and a silent thank-you to whichever entity brought this precious woman into my life, I reach for her phone on the counter behind me. It takes a few tries to hit the record button, and then I keep the camera trained on her while she bobs over me ever harder. Putting on a fucking show.

"What do you want with these videos, huh? You gonna watch them and play with your pussy whenever I can't do it for you?" Summer whimpers around my cock, furiously fucking her fingers. "Nah, you wanna know what I think it is? You like having hard proof of how crazy you make me. Get off on knowing I'm desperate for you. Would get my life together for you. Then blow it up all over again just for a single, flimsy chance at hearing that little whimper you make right before you come."

Her eyebrows crinkle, eyes squeeze shut, and fuck me. I know I started all this just to mess with her, but seeing her so close has me gently brushing the hair off her cheek.

"There you go. Make yourself come. Let me hear it."

I fist her hair and hold her mouth still, letting her focus on herself. She bounces over her hand, grinding her thumb over her clit and trembling like a leaf as her orgasm builds. Her whimper is muffled but it's everything I dream about at night.

Summer rides her fingers until her soft shudders subside. She's flushed when she looks up at me. Toys with my cock with her tongue, reaches for me with her glistening fingers—

The shrill beeping of the fire alarm fills the apartment.

My chin whips toward the kitchen, where a steady stream of smoke leaks from the oven.

"Oops." Summer gives me one last, merciless lick, then smirks up at me. "Guess you'll be the one desperate at dinner."

I toss away her phone and yank her to her feet. Crush my mouth against hers. "I'm gonna wreck you tonight. Start praying for your pussy."

She laughs. I stuff my aching cock into my pants and wash my hands, pulling the tray from the oven.

"*Fuck.* I forgot to tinfoil the chicken." The skin is burnt to a crisp. And when I stir through the pot on the stove, I find the pasta sauce has burned at the bottom.

Not sure Wynn would've approved of the mid-cook blow job break.

The front door opens in the hall, laughter filling the apartment.

"Parker?" Melody calls from the hallway. "Preston Wembley just asked if you need the number for pest control. Whatever you're cooking is wafting down the hall, and he's worried."

In a panic, I wheel around to find Summer yanking on her shorts with her hands tied. I hurry over and wipe at the wetness around her mouth. Comb my fingers through her hair as quickly as I can.

"It smells a little like the liver stew we had up north last year, Brian. Do you remember?" My mom's voice is the most effective cold shower I could've asked for.

The cooking twine around Summer's wrists falls to the floor just as my sister appears in the kitchen. Melody's gaze sweeps the room, taking in the utter destruction of the forgotten meal around us. "This should be interesting."

Chapter 39

Summer

"Well, Park. This wasn't what I expected when I heard you were cooking, but it was probably for the best."

At the dinner table, Melody pops the last of her French fries into her mouth, courtesy of the emergency takeout that Parker ran down to get at Oakley's. His poor chicken is still intact in its platter on the stove, completely undercooked but burned on the outside, while I scrub at the globby remains of the pasta sauce coating its pot at the sink. Parker stands at the counter with me, filling the dishwasher while I rinse. His family, plus Shy and Rosie, lounge around the table.

"Actually, the food looked quite fantastic before we got to talking," I say in Parker's defense. Behind the coverage of the kitchen island, he slides his foot to touch mine. "The disaster was completely my fault."

"Melody, you're being too hard on your brother," Caroline says. "It was a lovely meal that brought us together as a family."

I smile down at the pot in my hands.

I know I'm not supposed to get ahead of myself. But between the flowers, the dinner, the making me come so hard my life actually flashed before my eyes, I'm almost certain that tonight was a date that I ruined. And yet, the night turned into something just as good.

I can't remember the last time I had a family dinner.

I pass the pot to Parker, who crouches to load it in the dishwasher. "For the record, I regret nothing. You, on the other hand . . ."

I smother a laugh. He spent the entirety of dinner shifting uncomfortably in his seat. Threatening sexual comeuppance with his eyes, while I gave completely exaggerated, satisfied sighs. Maybe trying to rile him up, just a little. Inspire him to draw out my inevitable punishment.

I hand him a plate. "Is there an end to that sentence?"

Parker looks up at me. "How's this one: The second they go, I'm strapping you to that table and having my way with you all night, like the perfect little fuck doll you are."

My eyes dart around the room to make sure no one else heard. Parker pinches my ass. I swat his hand away, but he laces our fingers and squeezes. So does my heart.

"Well, isn't this the picture of domestic bliss?" We disentangle when Shy wanders over with a couple of plates.

I shoot her a warning glare. She's been sending me gleeful looks all night, whenever Parker and I so much as glance at each other.

"How long are you in town, Caroline?" I ask before she can get going.

"Just for the night," she says between sips of the homemade kombucha she brought. "We've got a wedding in Virginia the day after next."

"Anyone we know?" Parker asks.

"Oh no, we're not guests. Did we never mention your dad got ordained?" Caroline gestures at her husband with the glass bottle, the liquid swirling dangerously close to the lip. "*The Traveling Officiant.* Gained a nice little following online."

I look over at Parker. He shakes his head. Leans in and whispers, "Order of business when they leave: titty fuck, followed by an internet search."

"Promises, promises," I whisper.

Caroline takes another long sip of her drink. "We've made a bit of a business of it. Show them, Brian."

Brian pulls out his phone and I feel Parker stiffen at my side. Melody and Zac do the same from across the room.

"Prepare yourself," I whisper to Shy. "Brian Woods doesn't say much, but whenever he does, it's . . ."

Brian hands his phone to Zac, while Melody tentatively leans in to have a look.

"Fuck!" Zac jerks away from the phone, almost fumbling it. His panicked gaze bounces from his in-laws to Rosie obliviously playing in the living room. "I—I mean, *wow*. You—you're—it's . . ."

"Dad," Mel wails, ripping the phone out of her husband's hand, who's gone alarmingly pale and is now staring at the wall with unfocused, horrified eyes. "Why are you naked in these pictures?"

I dig my nails into Parker's arm, trying to contain myself.

"Oh!" Caroline exclaims. "Did I not say they were weddings on nudist resorts? Dad's a big hit with them. Besides, we made sure to paste stars in these pictures, over his—"

"*Mom*." Parker flings an arm toward Rosie. "There's a child in the room."

"*My eyes*." Mel sobs into her hands. Meanwhile, Shy has melted into my other side, laughing hysterically.

Caroline holds out the phone. "Summer, darling, do you want to see?"

"*No*," Parker practically shouts.

"No, *thank you*." I give him a pointed look, before beaming at his parents. "I'm sure you officiate lovely ceremonies, Brian."

"Kiss-ass," Parker mutters, bumping me with his hip. He takes a dish from me, chuckling to himself. And it does feel domestic. All of this.

Tonight has felt like a dream that eighteen-year-old me might've had, hosting my husband's family for dinner. And what a blessing it would be for *this* to be my family. To have two of my closest friends as a sister and brother-in-law. To have Caroline and Brian Woods, who opened their home to me when I was three, as parents.

Then there's Parker. If I'd have told myself that I'd be falling for him one day, I wouldn't have believed it.

I can't for the life of me remember why that is.

He's transformed from lost boy to a man who makes my heart pound just by standing next to me. And what I wouldn't give to be that lucky, one-in-a-million girl. Who fell for my best friend, my person, and had him fall right back. Forever.

If you stayed, you might. You could have all of it.

My muscles tense in protest, the way they do whenever my heart urges me to quit on a wave. Give up on the idea of the tour. And with my next event just a few days away, I'm running out of time to decide what I want.

Go and lose this.

Stay and lose me.

The déjà vu is haunting. I gave up surfing for love once. Have regretted it ever since.

"Since we have you here," Parker says now. He glances at his sister and Zac, who's still staring blankly at the wall, then around me to Shy. "What's the plan for next weekend?"

I nearly fumble the plate I'm holding. I nudge Parker's foot but he gives me an oblivious dimpled smile.

"What's happening next weekend?" Shy asks.

"Summer's event. She doesn't surf until mid-morning, but we'd need to arrive first thing to get her ready," Parker says. The apartment goes silent, except for Rosie who's wandered into the living room and is playing with the TV remote. Undeterred, Parker reaches on top of his fridge and produces a glittering TEAM SUMMER shirt, showing it off. "I made us all T-shirts."

Melody's gaze swings from the T-shirt to me. "I thought you were just volunteering."

Parker makes a confused sound. I avert my eyes and tuck my hair behind my ear. "Didn't I tell you? I'm competing this year."

"Well, that's wonderful!" Caroline exclaims. "You have such a knack for surfing, darling."

"You definitely didn't tell us." The news seems to have resuscitated Zac, who now looks at me curiously. "Are you trying to qualify for the tour again? I never understood why you gave up on that—you were so close to making it the last time."

"God, no!" The words slip out before I can stop them. "It's a simple matter of good old-fashioned revenge."

"Revenge?" Shy says slowly.

"Yeah. Why should Denny get to win that prize money when it can contribute to my retail addiction instead?"

"Her next event is next Saturday, at Crystal Cove. Just half an hour away," Parker says slowly. "We could all go together. Maybe Brooks and Siena can catch a flight—"

"No, don't put that on them. It's too short notice." I muster the courage to look at him, but it's to tell him to *drop it* with my eyes. "But if the rest of you want to come, I'd love to have you. No pressure, though."

Melody's face falls. "Sum, I really wish you'd have said something sooner. We've just invited Zac's coaching team to a dinner at our place in the city. It took forever to get the date lined up."

"My parents are away, and Max is training at the base for the next few weeks," Shy says softly. "I don't have anyone to watch Rosie. Sum, I'm so sorry."

I wave away their long faces despite the sinking feeling in my stomach. It's not as though I have the right to be disappointed. They only just learned I was competing. But, in a way, it only validates the reason I kept it from them in the first place.

I spend enough time hoping Dad will make it. I couldn't add my friends to the list of impending disappointments.

"Of course, I totally get it! It's not at all a big deal, which is why I didn't mention it in the first place. This is just something silly I'm doing. So not worth the effort."

But Caroline claps a hand on the table, making her kombucha splash in its bottle. "Nonsense! We could make it back in time. Couldn't we, Brian?"

Brian lifts his phone off the table. "If we leave immediately following the ceremony. Let me check the schedule."

"That's so . . ." My hand drifts to my cheek. I can feel the hope rising within me, even as I beg it to stop. "That's really so sweet. But you don't have to do that."

"No one *has* to do anything in life. We'd love to join you, darling."

A proper lump forms in my throat. Brian leans over to his wife, indicating something on his phone. They start talking logistics, and I use the opportunity to quietly excuse myself. I can feel Parker staring as I head down the hall, diverting to the guest room instead of his at the last second.

Eyes stinging, I sink to the edge of the bed and pull my phone from my back pocket. I adore their enthusiasm, whether they really mean it or not. But all it's done is set a glaring spotlight on the most noticeable absence in all this.

SUMMER: Hi, Dad. Have you been able to give more thought to Crystal Cove next weekend?

For once, Dad's reply comes quickly.

DAD: Hey, Sunshine. Meant to text you sooner. Turns out the twins have a soccer tournament. I'm sorry I'll miss you. I know you'll do great.

The pit inside me crumbles wider, deeper. And I unravel. I'm sobbing and hiccupping. Face soaked, nose running. The bedroom door creaks open and Parker slips inside, shutting us in.

"Love." He heads straight for me, kneels at my feet at the foot of the bed, and gently grips my thighs. "I'm so sorry, I didn't know you hadn't told them about Surf's Up."

I try to steady my breath. "He's not coming."

"Your dad?" Parker catches a tear dangling at my jaw. "Is that why you didn't tell anyone? You were worried they wouldn't come?"

"He's my dad. If he won't come, why would anyone else?"

"Because they adore you, that's why." He looks up at me with the saddest smile. "Because you're worth better than what your father is giving you, and I hate—*hate*—it. It breaks my fucking heart, Summer, every time I think about it."

I sob and his eyes go damp. "I've been trying so hard ever since he left town. I chose him over Mom, and she stopped talking to me because of it. I don't understand what I ever did to deserve this from him."

"Nothing, love. You did nothing—this is all him, I promise you. And the worst part is that he's made it impossible for you to see how deserving of better you are—how *loved* you already are." Parker releases a shuddering breath, blinking rapidly as he reaches for more of my tears. He tips his head toward the bedroom door. "Just listen to them out there."

It's muffled by the door and half drowned out by the sounds of whatever Rosie's managed to play on TV. But I can hear them— Caroline and Brian still conferring over their travel schedule, as though they really mean it. Really think they're going to make it back in time for me.

And they sound . . . *excited* by it.

It emboldens the hope as it battles something ugly inside me. The ruthless, insidious voice whose job it is to remind me of who I am, and where I stand in this world.

I'm Summer Prescott. Only child. A stranger to her parents. Perpetually single. Not worth the time, the effort. Not wife material.

Forgettable.

It's the reminder that had me retiring from competition years ago, when Dad told me he was leaving town. The one that torments me now, every time I try to surf through a barrel, give my all to a wave.

"You really think they'll come?"

"My parents are batshit, certifiably crazy, Sum. Especially about you." Parker scoops me into his arms and sits me on his lap on the bed. He buries his face in my hair. "I'd bet my life on it."

Parker lets me shift around to press my ear over his heart. What had been a foreign sound to me mere weeks ago now serves as absolute proof—so long as this heartbeat is nearby, I'm never really alone.

Sensible Summer should know better than to let her hopes soar. She's been the last priority enough times to know this probably ends with her disappointed on a beach.

She's not in the room anymore, though.

Here, in the safety of Parker's arms, drenched in his soothing peppery scent and with his steady heartbeat in my ear, I'm wishful Summer. As close as I've ever felt to the me from before, who had dreams, a family, and expectations, and the belief that she was worthy of it all.

We sit there a long time, in comfortable silence. Eventually, I frown at the bedroom door. "Did . . . did your mom just ask Mels whether Crystal Cove is *clothing optional*?"

"Fuck my life." Parker throws himself back onto the bed, taking me with him. "Remind me to pack a spare outfit in case my dad shows up with his star-covered bits on display."

Chapter 40

Parker

"Those bastards," my mom mutters under her breath from where she sits beside me on a massive beach towel with Dad at her other side.

Her blond hair has become increasingly bushy with the day's humidity, and like Dad and me, she's damn near soaked through her shirt. Still, Mom leans toward the ocean, propping her sunglasses on top of her head to give herself the clearest view. We managed to claim prime seats nearly at the edge of the rocky outcrop curving around the small but packed beach making up Crystal Cove. The spot brings us as close as possible to the action in the water, the long, steady wave wrapping around the coastline below.

"What happened to the no swearing rule?" I ask distractedly. Summer paddles back toward the tip of the outcrop after riding a seemingly mile-long wave that sent her flying in the opposite direction. The lengthy waves meant more paddling today, and she must be exhausted.

Mom peels away the hair sticking to her neck, fanning herself from the heat. It doesn't help that our TEAM SUMMER glitter T-shirts are on the thicker side. "Those judges had the gall to give

Summer a seven-point-two on that last wave. As if! She deserved sixty points at least."

I chuckle. "You can't score higher than a ten in surfing, Mom, but I appreciate the enthusiasm."

After a week of refusing to acknowledge my parent's attendance today—trying, I think, to manage her own expectations—Summer had been a tearful mess when we'd spotted their RV rolling through town this morning. She'd insisted on packing us a picnic basket full of snacks and the best kombucha Oakwood had to offer as a token of unnecessary-but-effusive gratitude, that my parents accepted with identical befuddled looks.

I've spent the past several months resenting my parents for the lack of structure they instilled in my life growing up. But they really did me one better, didn't they?

They taught me the proper way to love. Because, as far as they're concerned—and what Dave Prescott so clearly fails to understand—when it comes to your people, you show up. No matter what it takes.

We watched Summer out-surf her competition in her first heat. And again, in her second. It was a near-miss on her third, but she managed to pull through to the next round. She's been surfing strategically, holding out for the perfect wave—long enough to show off the extent of her skills, but not quite big enough to form a viable barrel.

Today's plan appears to be *I can't wipe out if there's no barrel.*

I still can't figure out what's happened to her ability to surf them, but she's gotten away with it in the earlier rounds, where she easily out-skilled her competition. Racked up enough points to put her in a good position in the overall series standings, still within reach of that prize money. Except, same as at Rocky Ridge, it's starting to catch up with her. She's only ahead by two points in this quarterfinal heat, and there's fifteen minutes left.

Summer floats on her surfboard, eyeing the endless stretch of rolling water at her back. By late afternoon, the clear sky has turned a deeper, more vibrant blue, with the sun sitting right above her. Her bright pink rash guard and the red jersey on top stand out against the deep blue ocean, like there are two balls of light illuminating the world.

Maybe just illuminating mine.

I pull out my phone, itching to capture her like this. In her natural habitat. Her happy place. Through the camera lens, I can make out the salt water pouring from the ends of her French braids, the gray tint to the slope of her nose from the sunscreen she wears. Her fingers delicately skim the surface of the water at her sides, like she's caressing it. Making nice with the ocean, sweet-talking it into delivering a winning wave.

Summer looks toward the shore, making eye contact through the camera lens. I point to my chest, shifting the phone so she can see the glitter letters written there. I don't know how much she can really make out from where she floats. But she gives a soft smile and I snap a few pictures.

There it is. Photographic evidence that my own heart beats outside my chest.

I send the best ones to the group chat, which immediately lights up with excited texts for Summer, and a stern one to me from Siena, demanding videos from the day. Helpfully, she follows it up with *We all know your phone is maxed out with them. Don't be stingy.*

I send them forty-three videos of Summer, and I'm not even embarrassed. What the hell else is the point of all that digital storage?

Mom leans into my side. "She feels the same way. You do know that, don't you?"

Hastily, I make the screen go black. "Feels the same way about what?"

"My darling son, I can hardly remember a time before you were in love with her." She turns to give me a proper look. "And she feels the same way."

"How do you know?" My heartbeat stutters. "Has she said anything to you? About me?" I nudge my glasses up my nose, aware that I'm babbling like a desperate idiot but unable to stop. "Does she talk about me, ever? Has she said anything to Mels, maybe, or—"

"Take a breath." Mom places a gentle hand on my shoulder. Beside her, Dad laughs softly to himself. "She's not said a word about it to me. But a mother has a seventh sense for this kind of thing, and I've known that sweet girl nearly as long as I've known you. I'm not sure what you're waiting for, Giggle Bear. Will you really continue letting her live without knowing the kind of love she's always had by her side? When the poor girl keeps looking for it in unreliable places?"

I've never known Mom to be a beacon of wisdom. But here we are.

"I think you meant a sixth sense."

"Oh, no. My sixth sense is for telling exactly when your father is in the mood for—"

"*Mom.*"

"Pancakes," she finishes with an innocent smile, linking arms with my dad.

I laugh, wiping a hand down my face. "Actually, I'm going to tell Summer tonight. I wanted her to get through today. Didn't want to throw her off."

I've spent all week rehearsing it—a real, proper *I love you*. One she couldn't doubt, could never deny, because God knows it'll be her first instinct once I finally tell her.

Tonight, at my place. I'll draw her a bath after a long day of surfing. Light the dozens of candles I've stashed in my closet, cook the steaks marinating in the fridge. And I'll tell her.

I've been overflowing with nerves all week. But I've done everything I can to hedge my bets—have checked off nearly her entire dream man list, and I don't want to wait anymore.

Mom beams at me, touching my cheek. "I'm so proud of you."

I hug her into my side. "Thanks, Mom."

In the water, Summer's focus has settled back on the horizon. Her opponent, Devin Flynn, paddles back after his last barrel ride.

"Here we go," I mutter. Our mornings in the water haven't done much for my surf skills, but I have got a better read on waves. There's the right kind of tension in the water coming toward her.

Summer flattens to her board and starts paddling aggressively. The wave takes shape fast and *tall*, at least a couple of feet bigger than any I've seen her surf today. Still, her every stroke in the water exudes willpower. The water draws up, so fucking steep, taking Summer with it. She pops up and tips over the lip of the wave.

There's absolutely nothing hotter than watching Summer surf. Her sheer athleticism, the way her body works to maintain its balance, the confidence with which she carves her board through water. She's extraordinary. Strong and graceful, making it look easy as breathing.

When she catches air on the first section of the wave, the crowd erupts in enthusiastic cheers. She's moving fast, braids whipping behind her as she attacks the next section. I think she's eyeing another aerial as her board starts to ride back up the face of the wave, but then the water arcs wide over her, crashing white onto itself.

Oh, shit. She's going to do it.

I hold my breath as Summer disappears behind the white curtain. I've got my phone in a vise, watching the water move, waiting for her to emerge on her board at the other end of the barrel.

She doesn't.

My stomach sinks when she resurfaces closer to shore seconds later, swimming toward her yellow board floating a couple feet away.

"You know, I was a little worried when she decided to compete."

The world's most punchable voice draws my focus off Summer, and onto the world's most punchable face.

Denny stands at the edge of our beach towel, staring out at the ocean. His hair is still soaked from his previous heat. Yet another victorious one that's kept him at the top of the event and series leaderboards.

My parents look around at him. Wordlessly, I refocus on Summer.

"I thought there was a chance she'd give me a run for my money for my spot on the tour," Denny continues. "Well—not *my* spot on the tour, because, well . . . I am *me*, after all." He laughs. I suck in a deep breath, forcing my fists to relax. "But that second qualifying spot, maybe. I thought I'd have to spend the next year avoiding her around the world, you know? But it doesn't look like that'll be a problem. Too bad for her."

"She doesn't care about the tour." I don't know why I'm even bothering with him, but it appears that no amount of self-reflection this summer can keep my visceral hatred for him out of my voice.

"Doesn't care about the tour? It's the whole reason she's competing. I heard it straight from her own mouth."

"No, you didn't," I mutter. "This is so tired. Take her rejection like a real man and leave her alone—you've done enough."

"But she was telling Harriet Young all about it at Rocky Ridge." A mean smile curls Denny's lips the longer I silently stare up at him. "Was plenty enthusiastic about the tour then."

I don't want to believe him. I *don't* believe him. But, for some reason, my heart picks up speed.

"She said something about it always being the plan. Traveling with her dad? Which I found weird, to be honest, seeing as he so clearly doesn't care about her." My ears start to ring. Mouth goes dry. "Did she really not tell you?"

My stomach goes so tight, I feel a little ill. Summer's sitting on her board, looking in the opposite direction, but I study her distant figure as though it'll help me detect Denny's lie. Nothing—not a single cell in my body wants to believe a word out of that bitter dirtbag's mouth. And yet . . .

The way she clammed up at dinner, when Zac asked whether she was trying for the tour.

"Giggle Bear?" Mom's voice sounds like it's echoing through a dark tunnel.

This—*this*—is the real reason she's pushed our training so hard, isn't it? It has nothing to do with prize money, or getting back at the sadist now gleefully staring at me. She's trying to qualify for the fucking Champions Tour—the one that'll be her ticket out of town for the next year.

And I'm the idiot who didn't see it coming. Who's spent the past couple of months foolishly trying to earn her, win her over. While she's been planning her great escape.

My brain is in overdrive, connecting dots I should've linked from the start. They meld into a heavy chain that loops around my lungs and squeezes hard, making it difficult to breathe. She lied to me, kept this important thing from me, and it's the worst betrayal of all. We've always been in it together. A ride-or-die pair. The realization that we've been behind the wheels of two entirely different cars for months, speeding in opposite directions—probably for the first time ever—is the worst dagger she could've dug into my chest.

Driving down the coast with the top off my car, ocean air whipping through my hair. Worth getting out of bed for.

Starting football drills with River tomorrow morning at the high school.

I hunt for any remaining sliver of light.

Summer grinning from ear to ear after qualifying for the tour. Finally getting to live out the dream she's had for as long as I've known her.

The thought bursts through the dense fog in my head and I grab onto it for dear fucking life.

"You know, I always thought it was funny you finally went for her, after all that time." Denny's voice plucks me out of my own head. "And here I thought *she* was the desperate one."

I spring to my feet.

"Mind your manners, young man. Where were you raised?" My mom's voice is sharp, aimed at Denny as I step up to him.

I drop my voice so only he can hear. "You wanna know what's even funnier? The fact that I actually owe you one, bud."

Denny cringes, hopefully feeling every inch of our height difference. "The hell are you talking about?"

Back then, Summer had promised her dad she'd get her education before jetting around the world. But then we'd graduated, and she'd insisted on applying for a job at the rehab center. And I'd been . . . relieved. Too co-dependent, too scared to be without her, to question why she suddenly lost all desire to compete.

I don't need Summer any less today than I did then. But I am capable, this time, of making sure that the woman I love takes a proper chance on herself. If she wants to make the tour, I'll damn well make sure she does. No matter how bad it'll crush me to watch her leave.

"I'm talking about you being the reason I finally woke up and realized what I had right in front of me. My dream woman, my future wife, the mother of my children. I hate that it took your pathetic ass to help me figure it out, but I've never been more grateful for anything in my life."

I say all this mostly to get it off my chest. I don't know whether it'll ever come true, now especially, but it feels good to get the words out.

Speak them into existence, in case the universe is listening and wants to give me a hand.

Then I bend at the knees, putting me at eye level with Denny. "But just so we're clear? You go near her again, and I'll destroy your life beyond repair with a fucking smile on my face." Denny flinches when I raise my hand, but all I do is give him two gentle taps on the jaw. "Say hi to Allie for me, yeah?"

Chapter 41

Parker

"Park, are you sure you're okay?"

Summer grabs my wrist as I reach for the doorbell at Melody and Zac's city town house, before I can officially kick-start this torturous weekend.

Since Crystal Cove, I've dreaded my thirtieth birthday weekend for reasons entirely different from the ones that haunted me months ago. Now, it's about the miserable idea of having to keep my hands off Summer in front of our friends. Holding in the *I love you* I couldn't get out after finding out about the tour. Keeping to myself that I know all about her grand plans, so that I don't ruin what's supposed to be a celebratory weekend for me and my sister.

Summer finished in fourth place at Crystal Cove, now sits in third place in the overall Surf's Up standings, and I keep going back to it— the night she decided to enter. She'd been in shambles over the things Denny said to her. I can't figure out whether she wants to make this tour because she wants *it* or because she wants to escape the solitude of home.

I catch Summer's hand in mine. "I'm all right. Are you?"

She blinks up at me, a slight wrinkle in her brow. "Why wouldn't I be?"

Is it really possible?

Has she really not grasped that I'll be following her around like a puppy desperate for her attention for as long as she lets me?

That if she ends up alone, then so will I?

We'd be alone together and, to me at least, that's far from a sorry ending.

"You've been so quiet all week." Her gaze darts to the windows framing the front door and, satisfied that we aren't being watched, she wraps her arms around my middle. "Are you bummed out about your birthday? The fact that you can't call me your cougar anymore, because we'll finally be the same age again?"

"I'm hanging on to those five months of difference with all I have, Prescott." I stare down at her stunning face—the bright green eyes, the single freckle hidden in her hairline. *Just tell me, here and now. I'm always on your side.* "Come on. Kiss me before the vultures get in the way."

She pushes up onto her toes to kiss me, laughing when I don't let her pull away. Every press of my mouth to hers is a silent wish, a prayer.

Love me back.

Tell me the truth.

Go, but don't let me go.

"Parker, we're two hours late to your own birthday weekend." Because she woke me up by climbing on top of me, and I refused to let it end. She's in a fit of giggles now, the breathless kind that makes me smile even as I continue to attack her with kisses. "I planned this party—the decorations are in my bag."

The door handle rattles. We spring apart just as it swings open, revealing Siena in a pair of white denim overalls with a nasty-looking green cocktail in her hand.

"I knew I heard something out here. Summer, I missed you!" The girls leap together, squeezing each other. "Thank God you're here—

Zac put me on cocktail duty. Look at this drink, it looks like we're sipping on phlegm."

Summer grimaces at the glass. "Don't fret, your resident mixologist is here and ready to go."

I clear my throat, injecting Siena's bright tone into my voice. "And Parker! I missed you, too! Oh, and happy birthday!"

They laugh, finally acknowledging my existence. Summer's shimmering eyes linger on me, dipping from my glasses to my dimples.

How can you look at me like that, then walk away like it's nothing?

"Oh my God, you're sleeping together." Our heads snap forward to find Siena's free hand clutching her chest. "You horny little devils. You're totally sleeping together!"

"Gross, Cee." Summer recovers quickly, shuddering in apparent disgust. And I know she's just pretending, that she doesn't mean it, but in my current state it stings. "That would be equivalent to sleeping with . . . *Brooks*. Don't even want to picture it."

"Hey—I am *great* in bed." Brooks marches into view, eyes narrowed on us. He nudges his fiancée. "Tell them, babe."

I raise my hand. "I'd like to be excused from that conversation."

"And I'm really not the audience for it," Summer says.

Siena pats Brooks's chest, who's still glaring at us both. "Eyes on the prize, Attwood. Your besties are banging. Trust me, I've got a radar for this kind of thing."

Brooks turns an inquiring look on me, but I don't give him anything.

Summer shrugs. "The radar's gone wonky, Cee."

"You're really trying to tell us there isn't even a teeny-tiny, itty-bitty little thing happening here?" She points between us. Summer shakes her head. I die a little more inside.

Siena breaks into a radiant, truly frightening grin. One that threatens a whole lot of suffering at the hands of a woman apparently incapable of letting horny little devils lie. She steps aside, letting us into my sister's house.

"We'll see about that, shall we?"

~~~~~

They're all in on it.

All of them.

After Siena gleefully announced that I'd be sharing a room with Noah, and Summer with Shy—dashing any hope of sneaking into each other's beds—Summer and I returned to the kitchen from our designated rooms to find it filled with not-so-covert stares.

But nothing—*nothing*—prepared me for the game they decided to play this weekend.

I was expecting some light teasing. For them to wedge themselves into every single second of alone time Summer and I managed to scrounge up.

Instead, all weekend, this scheming group of so-called friends have made it impossible to *avoid* Summer.

Seating us together at the birthday dinner Zac planned for Friday night. Quickly occupying every armchair and sofa cushion back at home but the one right beside me, forcing Summer to sit mere inches away. Giving us bedrooms right across the hall from each other, skyrocketing the temptation.

I've found myself wishing for the aforementioned teasing, which would've been only half as excruciating as existing in such proximity to Summer without touching her. Kissing her. Begging her to tell me why she's kept her secret from me.

They're trying to catch us in the act. To clock even the tiniest hand graze. A too-long stare. And I'm suffering from the worst physical and emotional blue balls of my entire existence.

324 Ellie K. Wilde

"You all right over there, Woods?" Sadistic joy pours from Siena's eyes. She surveys me from her spot sitting on the island in Mel and Zac's kitchen on our final evening in the city.

For a moment I pity Brooks, who must never get a restful night's sleep with this viper lying next to him. But then I catch him chortling at his fiancée's antics, and I no longer feel bad in the slightest.

"Yeah, Park. You're looking a little . . ." Melody wobbles on her feet, trying to come toward me but thwarted by the copious Summerpolitans she's had tonight—the bright pink, incredibly strong cocktails Summer mixed up. Zac catches my sister around the waist before she knocks into the island, chuckling to himself.

"Pouty," Mel finishes with several seconds of delay, smoothing down her hair.

"Why would I be pouting? I'm here celebrating my birthday with my very kind, very *supportive* friends." Glaring, I toast them all with my glass—including Noah sitting at the round kitchen table and Shy who's pouring herself a fresh Summerpolitan. Summer is upstairs fetching my sister a sweater, giving my aching skin a reprieve from her proximity.

"We *are* kind and supportive," Mel insists. "Even if there's really nothing going on, consider this . . . a gentle nudge in that direction. Some innocent meddling."

Something occurs to me. I narrow my eyes at my sister. "Was it you? Did you cancel the second room at Rocky Ridge?"

Melody blinks. "Which second room?"

"Hold up—are you telling us that you and Summer *shared a bed* that weekend?" Siena turns gleefully to Brooks. "I told you they're doing it."

I get to my feet, sliding my now-empty glass across the counter. "Believe it or not, we're perfectly capable of sharing a bed without doing anything in it."

Technically true. I fingered her in the hallway.

Noah deliberates over my point. "I guess that's possible—"

"No, it's not," Melody and Siena say together.

Siena jabs a thumb over her shoulder. "Brooks and I were stuck sharing a room while we were still fake dating, and we absolutely—"

"I don't need to hear about it."

Mel nods in earnest. "And I was stuck sharing a tent with Zac before *we* got together, and we totally—"

"I definitely don't need to hear about *that*." I hear Summer's footsteps upstairs, crossing the landing. "Can we all just . . . lay off the meddling for one damn minute?"

"No," Zac says with a cheerful smile.

"Oh, Parker, relax. It's just a bit of fun. Here, have another drink." With a suspicious twinkle in her eye, Shy crosses the kitchen with a fresh Summerpolitan, glass extended toward me.

Then she stumbles and the pink liquid goes flying out of its glass, soaking the front of my shirt. "Oh, *oopsies*!"

Siena claps a hand over her mouth, stifling a laugh.

"Come on, Shy," I groan, dabbing at my shirt with a napkin, but it's hopeless. The entire cocktail got dumped on me. I catch Shy exchanging a look with my sister.

"Honestly, Shy, you are so clumsy!" Melody hurries forward just as Summer's footsteps bounce down the staircase. She reaches for the hem of my shirt. "Quick, give that to me. It's going to stain if I don't get it in the wash."

"*What?* What the hell, Mels—" I swat my sister's hand but she persists, working the shirt off my body. Either I'm more buzzed than I thought or she's alarmingly strong for someone so damn small. Melody manages to wrestle the shirt completely off me.

"Mels? I wasn't able to find a white sweater, but this gray one is probably safer considering everything you've had to drink . . ."

I turn, following the sound of Summer's voice, only for her to slam face-first into my bare chest. Something soft falls to our feet— probably the sweater in question, though I'm too preoccupied by the excruciating feel of Summer Prescott pressed into my naked upper body to check.

Dimly, I register a loud, collective gasp behind me. But Summer's effect on me is instantaneous, like a fiery geyser coming to life. Tripling my temperature when she surfaces from my chest with lust-filled eyes.

"Hi," Summer whispers with a smile. Then she blinks, remembering our surroundings, and staggers away from me with her hands held aloft like she's just run them through mud. "Ew."

"*Ew?*" I can't stop myself from biting back. "Really, Sum? *Ew?*"

She sweeps Melody's sweater off the ground. "Why are you standing around shirtless, you weirdo?"

"That's a question for your friends." Friends who've all gone suspiciously silent. I turn around to find all of them gaping at me. "What? What now?"

"Oh my God," Summer whispers. I wheel back around to find her now staring in horror.

"Jesus Christ, Parker." Brooks wipes a hand down his face.

"*What?*" I scan the room. Zac's and Shy's smug looks, Melody's dismay. Noah's breathless laughter. "Somebody spit it out."

"Summer," Siena singsongs. "Any idea what happened to Parker's back?"

My . . . oh, hell.

The fingernail scrapes that've decorated my back since the first night Summer and I fucked.

Summer tips her head as though genuinely considering Siena's question. "No idea, but I'd strongly consider a tetanus shot if I were you, Park."

"It was a . . ." I reach for the soaked shirt in Melody's hands, throwing it back on. It reeks of cream soda, and sticks to my skin. "I got into a scrap with a . . . stray cat."

Every single person in this kitchen rolls their eyes. Summer's is accompanied by a look that says, *really? That's the best you can come up with?*

Glaring at them all, I jab a finger at Shy. "You. Pour me another drink."

Chapter 42

Summer

"Hey, Dad. It's Summer. I've been tied up with my friends all day, didn't see your texts until now. No, I'm definitely not making your trip to Mexico. Anyway . . . Talk soon?"

~~~~~

My fingers skim the wall to keep myself oriented in the dark.

I follow the sounds of stuttering snores belonging to Noah and the soft, sleepy breaths I recognize as Parker's toward the bed at the far end of the room.

It's just past midnight, officially his birthday. We all crashed tonight after an early morning and a long day in the sun, and I know I'm risking being found out, but it's the same as it was back before I knew what it was like to kiss him.

I'm possessive of Parker. Hate the idea of not being the first to wish him a happy birthday. Especially when he's not been himself all week.

He's kissed me plenty, still insatiable in bed. He's training me harder than ever and blushing adorably whenever Tritus's three tongues make appearances in our current read of the *Hidden Moon* series. But there are moments when he doesn't think I'm paying attention where the dimples smooth over. His eyes glaze over, deep in thought.

He keeps worrying over a crumpled sheet of lined paper, but all I ever catch are check marks and scribbles before he notices me watching and stuffs it back into his pocket, slapping on a smile.

I've let him keep his secrets because it's not as though I'm not keeping some of my own.

"Park, wake up," I whisper, squinting into the dark. My knees hit the edge of the mattress and I reach out, touching his clean-shaven cheek and stroking down his neck.

Wait a second—

Noah's shriek pierces the silence. I squeak, stagger backward, slamming my elbow into the wall. The lamp at the far side of the bed turns on and Parker pops up behind Noah's panicked figure.

"Sum?" he mumbles, reaching for his glasses on the nightstand.

"What the *fuck*, Summer—"

Parker leaps across the mattress and claps a hand over Noah's mouth, cutting off the rest of his shouting. "Pipe down, Irving. You'll wake up the whole house."

I bury my face in my hands, sliding down the wall. "Oh my God."

Noah mumbles something under Parker's hand.

"She wasn't feeling you up. She thought you were me." Parker's gaze darts my way. "Right?"

"I saw a big shape in the bed and thought . . ." I look between them. "In hindsight, Noah is quite huge—"

"*Hey*. I'm huge," Parker protests. His eyes narrow at the sound of muffled words from Noah. "Don't start. Can I trust you to keep it down?"

More muffled words and Parker releases him. There's a smirk plastered on Noah's face. His voice goes high-pitched. "'There's nothing going on between us.'"

"That better not be an imitation of me," I say weakly, getting to my feet.

"It was Parker, actually." Noah grunts when Parker tosses a pillow at him. "Well, to what do we owe this midnight surprise, Summer?"

"I—well, I wanted . . . ." Parker's no help whatsoever—he's laughing quietly to himself, watching me stutter.

"I see." Noah wags his eyebrows. He rolls off the mattress and springs to his feet, reaching for his phone on the nightstand. "Well, I'm sure you won't blame me for not sticking around. I'll take the couch. You kids have fun—use protection."

"Irving," Parker calls as Noah reaches the door. "Thank you."

Noah salutes us before slipping into the hall. Parker takes me in properly for the first time. "Why are you fully dressed?"

I reach for his jeans slung over an armchair in the corner and toss it at him. "Because I'm taking you out, birthday boy."

~~~~~

Parker's fresh champagne glass clinks against mine. The server who's been overseeing our night heads back into the inner bar, leaving us on the otherwise deserted rooftop terrace.

It's a cozy space nestled in a quiet neighborhood of semidetached brick houses, with lush trees lining the sidewalk below. The terrace is lit with Edison bulbs strung over a handful of unoccupied couches and tables and an unmanned bar toward the back.

I planned this night for us several weeks ago—not exactly what we're used to back at Oakley's, but close enough. I've got Tritus and his tongues, Parker's got a new autobiography, and we've been picking away at appetizers since we arrived.

"I can't tell you how much I missed doing this with you," Parker says, sipping on his drink.

"Been too long," I agree. I stack our books off to the side of the table, pushing our food out of the way. When I look back at him, Parker is staring at me with the same contemplative look he's worn on and off all week.

"A lot's changed since the last time," he says slowly.

I nod, smiling, and then my stomach pangs when I realize he's frowning. But he doesn't add anything, so I reach into my purse and pull out his gift. I wrapped it in the most obnoxious pattern I could find, and he opens it to see two equally horrendous matching Hawaiian shirts folded one on top of the other.

Parker huffs a laugh, watching me pull mine on. "I can't decide if this is a punishment, after what I told you."

"Hate to say it, but they've grown on me. You did this to yourself." With a shake of his head, he slips his arms into the sleeves. I sweep aside the wrapping paper, unearthing the second part of his gift. "Now this."

Nudging up his glasses, Parker slides the scrapbook closer. I've been putting it together little by little for months. Unearthing pictures from my own collection, and from the boxes of Parker's childhood things stacked in his spare bedroom.

Still, when Parker flips it open to reveal a fading picture of the two of us as kids, there's an unexpected bursting in my stomach. We're three years old, on the day we met. I'm dressed in pink denim overalls with lopsided pigtails. He's in tear-away trackpants with blond hair falling into his eyes. We're smiling inside a pillow fort at day care, blankets piled on our laps, sitting shoulder to shoulder.

Parker rubs at his chest, staring down at the book. "Well damn, Prescott. You really should've prepared me for this."

I tuck into his side, and he flips through the next few pages. Toddlerhood, then kindergarten, all the way through junior high. Our hair grows, legs get longer. Teeth go missing, braces come on and off. Parker's skinny frame fills out, my suntan deepens. Drastic changes within just a few years, yet there we are, still shoulder to shoulder.

Another page and we're in high school. Creased pink Post-it notes accompany nearly every picture now, starting in our freshman year. Sitting cross-legged under the bleachers at school after cutting out of class, together at the end-of-summer parties Zac used to throw at his grandmother's house. There's a picture from Parker's first football game, him in full gear, me in a spare jersey of his. He'd left it in my locker earlier that day, with a paper plane that said *How many touchdowns do you want tonight?*

I'd told him three. He'd scored me four. And when I'd teased that I was his lucky charm, he'd shaken his head. *Not luck. Motivation,* he'd simply said. The touchdown requests became our game-day ritual all the way through college.

Parker smooths his thumb over a photo from our senior prom. We're dressed to the nines, dates who aren't each other flanking us as we pose for the picture side by side. The month prior, he'd flung a paper plane at me in class after I'd admitted that I suspected my date had only asked me to prom to spite his ex. *What color's your dress?* his note says.

I'd rolled my eyes when he showed up to prom in a tie just a shade lighter than my pale pink dress. Pointed out that his own date was wearing green. But secretly, I'd loved knowing I was the other half of a marked pair.

Parker grows increasingly quiet as he flips through the book. The surf events, football games, college parties, and Summer Fridays. Mundane workdays and trips with friends. Walking down Melody and Zac's daisy-lined wedding aisle, our arms linked. Some of my favorite moments through our decades of heartbreak and triumphs and fumbling through life together, and I stare at the pages holding my breath, as though I hadn't made them myself. Like I'm a spectator to my own story, dying to know what happens next.

And seeing it like this . . .

Parker reaches the final page of the scrapbook. It's us, smiling at the camera in matching Hawaiian shirts the morning of the Rocky Ridge event. Just hours after our first kiss.

It's a cliff-hanger, a *dot dot dot*. An unfinished sentence at the end of a page. The arrow on a compass whipping about, searching for north.

I clasp my hands, realizing they're shaking. I thought this would be a fun way to reminisce. Share some good laughs, bond over the most meaningful friendship I've ever had. But now I feel as though I just brandished insistent, conclusive evidence of something else.

I've always wondered how Parker so easily gets under my skin.

But I think it's because he *exists* under my skin. Burrowed in me so deeply as a child, then grew into me, his soul molding to mine along the years. Filling cracks. Reinforcing weak points. Invading my space when I get too comfortable, pushing me to spread in new directions.

He's part of me in a way that, if I were ever to try cutting him away, would make me less me. Like punching out an apple's core, and trying to pass it off as whole.

Parker sits perfectly still. Not saying a word, just staring at that final picture.

"So, that's . . ."

It, I mean to say.

Real love, I want to say.

Isn't it? For weeks, this thing between us has felt out of the blue. A freak accident. A mistake he'll come to regret. But, on display from beginning to end like this, leading up to that first kiss . . .

It's hard to imagine there was ever another outcome for us.

A soft cough has me glancing at Parker. He's still staring down at the scrapbook, throat working on a swallow.

I tuck my legs underneath me and face him. "Parker."

"Seeing it laid out like that . . ." Parker's breath shudders. He tips back his head to stare at the sky. I run my fingers through his hair, gently scraping at his scalp. "I can't believe it took me so long to figure it out."

"Figure what out?"

A tear trickles down his cheek. I wipe it and place a kiss in its place.

"I am so—" His breath catches and he clears his throat almost angrily. Jaw clenching. A breath in. A breath out. And then he looks at me with those deep blue eyes, tortured, beseeching. "I've been so in love with you for so long, Summer. And I've been kicking myself for months, thinking about how many years I wasted pretending I wasn't. Letting you think that I didn't. Wondering how things could've been different, where we might be, and everything we'd have if I'd realized it sooner, but—" He places an open palm over the scrapbook, then over his chest, fingers spread wide. "I wouldn't change a single second of us. I love you and I'm exactly where I want to be—exactly where I was always supposed to end up. And I know that you're not, and that's . . ." His fingertips dig into his chest as though clenching his splintering heart, trying to hold it together. "I guess I'm just hoping that whatever your life looks like for the next few years—wherever you are—there's still a place for me in it."

Heart pumping hard, I lean into the cool leather back of the couch. Questions form, their letters scrambling into new ones so fast that I close my eyes, trying to keep up with it all. *So in love with you. Years. Pretending. I love you.* "Wherever I am?"

"I know about the tour." My eyes fly open. The blatant hurt in Parker's face is a kick to the stomach. "And I'm so pissed off you didn't tell me. That you'd lie to me, and that I'd learn about something so important from someone so insignificant."

"Who?" Parker tips his head in a look that says *who do you think?* My shoulders fall. I reach for him, clasping his wrist. "I'm so sorry. I wanted to make sure you were in a good place, and wouldn't . . . I wanted you to be better before I told you. And then everything happened between us, and I didn't know how to anymore."

Even now I'm torn on the conversation—want to backpedal several steps, start with a different question, examine a different angle. *So in love with you for so long.*

But Parker forges ahead. "And the solution was to . . . what? Sneak out of town this fall without a word? Send me a picture of yourself from across the world saying, *Guess what, Park?*"

"Of course not. I was waiting for the right moment."

His eyes try to look through me. "Why are you leaving?"

"At first, I thought it might be a fresh start after everything that happened, between *him* and the people in town. But the longer I've been back in it, competing . . . I've spent my entire adult life clinging to people and to this place. And wanting to mean something to everyone, to the point where I lost the thing that meant so much to me. I never planned to spend my whole life in Oakwood. At least, not until much later."

"I know that—you should've left years ago."

"Well, it doesn't look like I'm going to qualify anyway." I slide my hand into his palm. *I love you and I'm exactly where I want to be.* "Maybe it's for the best."

A line forms between his brows. Parker scans me, leaning back as though he requires a better vantage point. Nerves tug inside me because he's holding my hand but not *holding* it. Less in that sweet way between lovers confessing their feelings. More like a man trying to hang on to a skittish animal.

"What's going on with your barrels?" Parker asks abruptly.

I knew it wouldn't take him long to figure it out. That the moment he had the full picture, he'd know.

He'd know, and he'd call me on it, and he'd try to talk me into something I'm not sure my heart is ready to take on. Maybe, if I'm really honest with myself, it's why I kept the tour from him in the first place.

"Is that really what you want to focus on? You've just said all these really big, incredible things. Shouldn't we talk about that?"

"We are talking about it. What's going on with your barrels, Summer?"

Humiliation forces my face to heat. "There's nothing wrong with them. I can ride a barrel in my sleep."

Not a hint of surprise in his face. "So why aren't you?"

"Because I can ride them in my sleep. And if I did . . ."

"You'd win. Right? You'd make the tour and have no more excuses to stay back in Oakwood. You haven't been failing—you've been quitting." When I don't answer, Parker leans in, determined to press the issue. "Have you been falling off your board or jumping off it?"

My nose stings. "It's not technically as simple as *jumping*—"

"Fuck," he breathes, his fingers tunneling through his hair. I know he's kicking himself for not seeing it sooner—every shred of evidence he's probably adding up in his head now. "This whole time?"

"It's stupid, right? Wanting something so badly and then making sure you can't have it?" I whisper, staring beyond him at the high branches of a tree on the street below, leaves dancing in the breeze. I wipe my tears impatiently. "I can't make myself do it. I've been dreaming of that tour since I was a kid, but I'm alone enough as it is without adding several thousands of miles between me and the people I do have. What's going to happen when I'm not around to make sure no one forgets I exist?"

Parker surprises me by laughing softly. He points at the scrapbook. "How can you put this together, and still think like that? How can you look at me now and still say that?" He reaches for my hair, toying with the end of a braid. "You cut me off earlier this summer. I came crawling back to you. You hid this from me, made me feel like a fucking fool, and here I am, telling you that I love you. You flinch every time I say those words—have you noticed? And still, I'm saying them again: I am in love with you. Be here. Be across the world. Love me. Hate me. I don't care. *You* are what I want. *You* are where I belong. I'll keep crawling back to you, no matter where you go."

"A year is a long time away."

"Twenty-seven years is even longer."

"But it's not the same anymore. This thing with us, it's so new. Look how easily those twenty-seven years have flipped within a matter of months. Who's to say it won't flip all the way back over the course of a whole year?"

"Do you want it to flip back?"

"*No.* I love the way we are now. You're everything I've ever hoped for." I take his hand in both of mine. "I think I'm going to stay."

"I don't want you to stay just because you think we won't last otherwise. I'm telling you, we will. And it's not just about us." Parker sits back, pulling out of my grasp and draping his arm over the back of the low sofa. "Let's take me out of the equation for a second. Because for someone who loves love, you really go out of your way to deny you're completely surrounded by it."

"My parents—"

"Your mother doesn't even deserve to be in this conversation. And with all due respect to your dad, neither does he. It fucking kills me to see how hard you work for his attention, only to get scraps back."

"That's exactly my point."

"That's exactly *my* point—you're so busy chasing those scraps that you don't even see what's in front of you: real, lasting love that's begging for *your* attention. My sister and our friends, who want to be involved in your life. You've got people in town waiting for you to stop avoiding them. My parents, who rushed back home from whatever-the-fuck naked wedding they were at, to show up for you last week.

"Summer, I'm sorry about your dad. Truly." He cups my cheek as though trying to pour his apology into me. "I know it's nothing like the relationship you wish you still had with him. And it doesn't even come close to what you deserve. But you're sitting here, telling me you're worried about leaving town because you think no one will care, yet you're the one pushing everyone away. You've taken the words of a known cheater—who couldn't possibly know *anything* about what it means to show up well in a relationship—and held them up as evidence that you'll be alone forever. And at a certain point, you need to decide: Are you ready to let yourself be happy?"

I rear back, feeling gut-punched by his words. "That's a little harsh, isn't it?"

"It's the truth, isn't it?"

I take in the calm in his handsome face, the relaxed set of his body despite the tension sizzling between us. Parker, who's always loved who I've loved, hated who I've hated. Blindly followed me through every flight of fancy. Now challenging me in a way he never has.

And the longer my brain scrambles to form a counterargument, the more I think he might be right. I've known I've been pushing away my friends. Not telling them about Parker or competing—none of that was an accident. But maybe I've also been begging for attention in places there's no longer any to find. Like a dog clinging to a poisonous bone, despite its insides decaying further with every bite.

"You think I should give up on him?" My heart chips just thinking about it.

"Love, he's your dad. I'd never tell you what to do there. All I want is for you to see what's in front of you. What you've always had, rather than what you've been missing."

I'm sitting so tensely that my shoulders ache. Parker beckons me closer with a finger. I hesitate, but when I lean in, he takes my chin between his fingers and kisses me softly.

It's short, perfectly sweet. An everyday kiss you give someone you love before running out the door in the morning. I can't tell whether it's the warmth of his fingers on my face, or the simple fact that he's kissing me in the middle of an argument instead of building walls or growing distant. Maybe it's that he's putting me in my place for the first time ever. It could even be the way the string lights above us hit the blue of his eyes that's made me realize it, but . . .

I've always been someone who falls hard. Lets my emotions sweep me offshore, pull me under. Throw me around like the harshest of waves, with no say in the matter. Until finally I surface, disoriented. Gasping for breath and paddling desperately for land.

Falling in love with Parker didn't feel anything like that.

There was no earth-shattering moment, no cataclysmic strike of lightning that set my life ablaze. Loving Parker feels like the fog clearing after a storm. The stillness of the ocean after a hurricane. It's living through the worst day of my life and then slipping into a warm bed back home, with French braids in my hair and paper planes to make me smile.

The most natural thing in the world.

I love him back, and it's everything I wished for through the bad dates and broken relationships. But I have no idea how to let myself have us, and then leave him behind with only a hope that he'll still be here waiting for me if I go chasing the other things I've wished for and gave up on too quickly the first time.

"I'm scared. I don't know if I can have both."

Of course, he understands. Parker gathers me into his lap, buries his face in my neck. "You already have me. Have had me from the moment we met. You just have to believe that you're someone worth keeping."

I hang my head. "How do you do that? Know exactly what I'm thinking?"

"I've always been fluent in Summer Prescott. It's my favorite language." He inhales deeply. "I think I was made for you."

Made for each other. There's not a doubt in my mind.

The door at the far end of the terrace swings open, a chorus of "Happy Birthday" breaking the delicate silence. Servers approach us with a candlelit cake, grinning wide.

Parker startles, blinking around our surroundings like he forgot where we were. I take his hand and press three kisses to his palm, hoping he translates that, too.

By the look of his dimpled smile, he does.

Chapter 43

Summer

DAD: Hey, Sunshine. Sorry to hear about Mexico. You up for a family dinner the weekend we're back? Been a while.

SUMMER: How about we regroup when you're back? Have a good time.

~~~~~~

"Oh *fuck*, Summer."

Parker traps my wrists behind my back, watching my hips roll on top of him, taking his cock as deep as I can, as quiet as I can. "Yeah, like that. That's so good."

I hang my head, jaw clenched tight to keep my noises in check, trying not to wake the rest of the town house. After the bar, we went for a long, quiet walk down city streets in our matching shirts. Not saying much of anything, and kissing quietly under streetlights. The sun was just beginning to peek over the horizon by the time we made it back. We fucked quietly, fell asleep. Drowsily reached for each other, went another round, and passed out again.

I love you and I'm exactly where I want to be.

As much as I love our friends, I wish we weren't here. Wish we were back home, in my bed or Parker's, able to spend all day just like this. Wrapped up in each other and ignoring every decision looming over me. With the event at Pine Point just five days away, I'm running out of time to figure out where I see myself for the next year, and beyond. And what it means for us.

Parker yanks me down to kiss him, thrusting up into me. "Are you going to come now, Summer? Can you let me feel that pussy clench around me?"

"Yeah." He adjusts the vibrator on my clit—he'd packed it for me himself, and if I wasn't already out of my mind in love with him, that surely would've done it. He's looking at me like I'm actively ruining his life, then building it back up just to wreck it all over again. And since our moment on that terrace, every little touch, look, kiss feels amplified to a monumental degree.

I feel them down in my bones.

"Attagirl. Hold this." I take over holding the toy and Parker flips us over. His cock fills me again with a single, rough thrust that shoves me up the bed. I clamp my jaw shut, scraping fingers down his back so hard it has to sting. His entire body jolts, and his pace grows more frantic. He covers my mouth and fucks me harder, rougher, every thrust sending a flash of light across my vision. I burst, eyes squeezing shut as the orgasm rips through my body. The sound I release into his palm is a pathetic, stifled wail, which becomes a gasp as Parker shoves himself inside me one last time before he comes, teeth sinking into my shoulder to muffle his own sounds.

"Did I hurt you?" I whisper, tossing away the vibrator then rubbing my palms up and down his back as though to erase the angry red marks. But I mean the question the other way, too—*did I hurt you by not saying it back? Because I love you in a way I could never undo.*

Parker kisses me hard. "It hurt in the best way. Shower with me?"

"I should sneak back into the other room before anyone notices."

With a kiss to my shoulder, then my forehead, then the tip of my nose, Parker rolls out of bed and heads into the adjoining bathroom. He returns with a damp cloth, cleaning me up before helping me up and settling behind me on the bed.

I've been so in love with you for so long.

"Let me fix your hair before anyone sees you. You're a mess, Prescott." I tip back my head, letting him work French braids into my hair.

Just say it back, you coward.

"Park?" He makes a soft sound of acknowledgment. "I . . ." My mouth opens and closes. The *I love you, too* snags on the jagged mess of my insides like it has every time it's tried to make its way out since last night. "I can French braid," I blurt instead.

Parker goes still. "What?"

Maybe it's not an *I love you*, but it's the one secret I thought I'd keep from him forever. The single tendril of longing for my friend that I ever allowed myself over the years.

I turn my chin as far as I can without disrupting his work. "I know how to French braid. My dad taught me years ago, long before he left town. But then I saw you watching those tutorials, and . . . I pretend I don't know how, because I like it when you do it."

Deep down, I think I've always known what it meant to let him braid my hair—I never would've asked the same of Zac or Brooks.

Parker's surprise melts into the sweetest smile I've ever seen. Soft, a little shy. "I'm . . . going to pretend you don't know how to braid. If that's okay with you."

And then we're both quietly laughing. Two bandits who've caught each other in the midst of an identical heist, confessing to crimes against the platonic friendship we always swore we had.

Parker dots soft kisses along my shoulder and heads into the bathroom. Looks back as though to check I'm really there, that *that* really happened, before shutting the door.

I get out of bed, stuffing my toy into his duffel bag and fishing my clothes from the tangle of sheets. My shirt is barely on when the bedroom door bursts open.

"Rise and sh—*iiit.*"

Screeching, I drop to my knees, obstructing my lower half from view behind the bed. Brooks staggers into an equally startled Zac before they both wheel around to face the wall.

"*What the hell*, guys," I shout. "Ever heard of knocking?"

Brooks throws up his arms as though he's being arrested. "I thought this was Noah and Parker's room!"

"It *is* Noah and Parker's room," Zac says.

The bedroom door across the hall swings open. "Has anyone seen Summer? I don't think she slept here last night."

"She's in Noah and Parker's room."

Another door opens. "She's *where?*"

"It's Parker's room, technically. They kicked me out last night," Noah calls, footsteps thundering up the stairs.

Siena's laugh tinkles from the other end of the hall.

I shuffle and stumble, getting my shorts on before rising to my feet. Catching us in flagrante delicto isn't how I'd have chosen for our friends to find out what Parker and I have been up to this summer.

The doorway is now packed with them. A solid wall of nosy friends all trying to peer around the other, get a good look at the sideshow.

Siena nudges Brooks out of the way, clearing a path into the room and looking absolutely thrilled with herself. Shy and Melody follow her in.

"Would anyone believe me if I said it's not what it looks like?" I try.

"*No,*" they all say together.

The bathroom door flies open.

"Love, have you seen my glasses?" Parker freezes, squinting at the scene before him. He's fully dressed, which I suppose is a blessing.

"It's not what it looks like. I had . . . a health emergency. The cat scratches—I think they're infected—"

"For the love of God, please stop." Siena bounces down on the end of the bed. "She has beard burn on her neck."

Parker looks over and mouths *I'm sorry.*

I feel the weight of fourteen eyes on me as I choose my next move. I've spent all summer dreading this moment, hiding my growing feelings for Parker until I had complete clarity as to the direction of our relationship.

I don't feel any less confused about my future, after last night. But how could I keep hiding Parker? He's as good a man as they come. Wears his whole heart on his sleeve.

He deserves to be claimed. Flaunted. Adored loudly.

I reach for his glasses on the nightstand and slip them on him myself. When his brows lift in pleasant surprise, I press up onto my toes and kiss him.

A symphony of sounds fills the room—happy sighs and snickers and an *aww* I recognize as Shy's. And then—

"I *told* you it would work!" Melody stares gleefully over at Zac, who's rolling his eyes but also trying very hard not to laugh. She holds out a hand. "Pay up, Porter."

"You know what? I'm not even mad at it." Zac plucks his wallet from his pocket and forks over a fifty-dollar bill.

Parker narrows his eyes. "What the hell is this?"

"Retribution." His sister neatly folds the cash and pockets it. Lifts a hand to her ear as though holding a phone, makes her voice higher and brighter. "'Hi! This is Summer Prescott. I'd like to cancel the second room on my reservation—'"

My jaw drops. "*You* canceled the second room at Rocky Ridge?"

Siena throws herself down on the mattress, curling up in laughter. "Oh, you tiny, evil genius." She sobers suddenly and springs upright. "You guys totally fucked on this bed, didn't you?"

I wince. "A little bit."

"Really, Mels?" Parker cuts in. "Canceling a room? You know, the fact that you can't mind your own business—"

"Hypocrite," Zac coughs.

Brooks shrugs. "Personally, his meddling worked in my favor."

"*You're welcome*, Brooks," Parker says, glaring at Zac. "Besides, I already told you: Nothing happened that weekend. No kissing. Especially no fondling. We simply had a good night's sleep, and—"

"Stand down." I pat his arm. "You're a terrible liar."

"And I believe the words you're looking for are *thank you*," Melody says. "Look at you now—Summer, we're going to be sisters!"

Sisters. Family. I could have one again if I stayed—

"Let's all take it easy." Parker's palm brushes the small of my back. "Your meddling is exactly why we kept this quiet to begin with, and we'd appreciate some space to figure things out for ourselves."

Unintentionally, I make eye contact with Siena, whose now-confused gaze flicks over from Parker. "All right." She strides over to Parker and drags him to the door by the wrist. "Everyone without boobs, *out*. Now."

"But—" Brooks starts to protest. Siena single-handedly manhandles the guys into the hall, slamming the door in their faces. She turns to me, pointing to the end of the bed. "Sit."

Reluctantly, I do so next to Shy. "Why does it feel like I'm in trouble?"

"Because we've now all gone a good couple of months without speaking to you properly, and I, personally, have had enough of it." She plants her hands on her hips. "Anytime we talk, you make it about us, or the weather, or the new shade of pink you've painted your nails."

"We miss the way it was before," Melody chimes in. She sits cross-legged on the floor. "You complaining about your job. All your volunteer work. We miss hearing about the guys you're dating, the dragon-shifters you're reading about, and how good the waves were on your morning surfs. You tell us nothing about what you've got going on anymore. And suddenly you show up here, and you're sleeping with Parker. And lying about it like we can't see what's right in front of us."

"Don't you think we would've loved to know about this, Sum?" Siena adds. "To be there for you, be excited with you? I mean, you're *Summer and Parker*. This is huge."

Guilt nags at me even worse than it did last night, when Parker pointed out the very same thing. But my relief is even stronger— knowing that they've noticed me pulling back, cared enough to discuss it among themselves, and then to sit me down and deliver the hard truth.

I pick at the frayed edge of my denim shorts. "Is it better or worse if I say that Shy already knew?"

Siena wheels around to her best friend. "You traitorous little—"

"I was sworn to secrecy," Shy cries. "Besides, I barely knew. She mentioned something about a drawstring once and then refused to speak of it again."

"A drawstring?" Melody's face scrunches in confusion. Then clouds over in disgust. "Okay, I did *not* need to know about that."

Siena pats her shoulder. "My thoughts exactly, Mels. How utterly depraved!" Then she cups a hand around her mouth and stage-whispers to me, "Tell me all about it later. Every detail."

God, I've missed them so much.

And having them here, beaming and sitting happily in my company, has the weight of this summer—my falling out with Parker, the shift in our relationship, and my falling flat on my face in love with him—bubbling up inside me. I hiccup a breath, nose stinging, tears pouring before I can stop them.

"Oh, honey." Siena sits next to me, tucking me into her side. Shy takes my hand. Mel shuffles closer to give my knee a reassuring squeeze.

"It's been really confusing. It felt like he came out of nowhere and for a while I didn't know how to wrap my head around it. And I finally have this thing I've been so desperate for, for so long. With the best person I could've asked for. And I'm terrified I'll make a mistake."

"How could it be a mistake?" Shy says softly. "You know everything about each other."

"I don't think *we're* a mistake—I'm worried I'll ruin it by leaving. Or *not* leaving, and then regretting it for the rest of my life."

Siena eyes Melody, who gives a small shake of her head. "Leaving where?"

I swipe at my tears. "I entered Surf's Up to qualify for the tour. To travel and make a career out of competing, the way I always planned."

The room goes very quiet.

"Well, that's . . ." Melody swallows, combing her fingers through her hair. "I'll be honest, it's not ideal for me. You're only allowed to go if you agree to weekly calls. At a minimum."

"We're going to need that in a written and signed contract," Shy adds.

"Come on, you two. You're ignoring the bright side." Siena gives a shimmy. "Obligatory group trips! This'll be fun."

The other two perk up at that, and they all dive straight into planning mode—locations and flight routes, overlapping breaks from work.

"Maybe you could start now?" I ask, before I can think better of it. "My next event is on Saturday, and I'm sorry it's such short notice but I'd really love it if you came to support me."

"Awkward," Siena singsongs. "We're already coming—I've got a boat set up to give us front-row seats in the water."

"My parents are coming, too," Melody says. "They haven't stopped raving about your last event."

My eyes prickle again, gratitude overflowing my system. "That means so much to me."

"And about Parker . . ." she adds. "He would want you to be with him *and* go."

"I know."

"He loves you so much," Shy says.

"It's mutual." I fiddle with a braid. "I feel so lucky to have him. I don't want to lose it."

"Luck had nothing to do with it, Sum. That's my brother for you—once he decides he wants something, there's no getting it out of his head." Melody nudges my foot with hers. "He's a pest like that."

I laugh. But my stomach flutters at the very thought that my falling in love with Parker had been part of some grand, romantic plot to get the girl. One of our rom-coms come to life.

"Summer?" Siena says after a few minutes. "Are those . . ."

She takes my hand, splitting the stack of braided string bracelets I've taken to wearing to cover the faint marks around my wrists. She breaks into a smile. Shy laughs. Melody retches.

Flushing, I adjust the bracelets. "So, funny story—the other day, Parker took in a stray cat . . ."

Chapter 44

Parker

"Where the hell are you taking me?"

I pick up the pace when River and I reach the hill in the road, neither answering nor slowing down until we're at its peak, where I ease us into a cooldown pace.

"Relax, Nowak. Have I ever led you astray?"

"The old you? No. *This* guy?" We reach flat ground and come to a stop. Hands planted on his hips, River pants at me with even more suspicion. "You're in a weird mood. Happy one second. Looking like you've been hit by a truck the next."

I don't answer, but he isn't wrong. Since our weekend in the city, I get to stroll down Oakwood's streets holding Summer's hand for anyone to see. Get to kiss her in front of our friends. And then she goes to work, or over to her place, or duck-dives through a swell in the ocean, temporarily disappearing from view. And it feels like a possible glimpse into the years ahead, my whole heart far from home, bouncing from country to country. Living an entire life without me, after decades at arm's length.

The separation anxiety is at an all-time high.

My only comfort is the thought that, if she chooses to do it—surf the way I know she can—she'll be embarking on the adventure that I know has called to her ever since she got her first board.

River follows my lead as we round a bend in the road. I'd never live it down if I admitted it to his face, but I want to see him happy. Which is why we're running in Baycrest instead of Oakwood this morning, weaving around its winding main street until it opens up to a view of the bay. It's not until we hang a right at the end of a parking lot, our backs to the boardwalk, that I brace myself for—

"Parker, what the actual hell?" River halts the moment the flower shop comes within view, looking like he's either seconds away from socking me or diving behind a nearby trash can. "How do you spring this on me? I look like a fucking mess. I'm sweating, and my hair's overgrown—"

River makes a move to turn around, away from the shop, but I step in his path. "It's time, Nowak. Enough excuses—we made a deal earlier this summer, and I've come to collect."

"How did you even figure out she works here?"

"Macy's dad coaches the women's softball team at UOB. We've crossed paths." I take him by the shoulders. "Listen to me, River. You can try to get every little piece perfectly in place, and she might slam the door in your face anyway."

His eyes grow in alarm. "Is that supposed to be a pep talk?"

"Yes." I chuckle. "Because there's every chance the opposite happens. You go in there, tell her how you feel. And if you're lucky, she'll ask what took you so long. It doesn't matter if things are perfect. What matters is that you tried. Put yourself out there. Gave her the chance to tell you one way or another."

River rubs at his face. "I don't know if I can."

"A couple months ago, you were on crutches and thinking you'd never come off them. But you tried, anyway." I straighten out his shirt for him. But because we're us, always going to jab at each other, I add, "What happened to your balls, Nowak?"

He glares. "My balls are fine."

"Prove it." I check my watch. "I called ahead to check. Macy's shift started ten minutes ago."

"And you said there was no reason to be suspicious." He eyes the shop over his shoulder. "Can you at least . . . Just don't leave, okay?"

"You got it. I'll be right here."

River nods. Over and over, staring at me while working up the nerve. Then he turns on his heel and marches into the flower shop.

I follow only as far as the large windows by the flower display outside the shop. Far enough to give him privacy. Close enough to pick up the pieces if this goes south.

There's a young girl behind a workbench toward the back of the shop, chin tucked as she clips flower stems, long brown ponytail spilling forward. She hasn't noticed River striding toward her.

Already, I'm damn proud of him. But then he must say something, call her name maybe. Macy's gaze darts up. She breaks into a wide, unmistakably happy smile and rounds the workbench to hug him.

Relief hits me smack in the chest, as though I'm standing in River's worn-in sneakers myself. I really didn't want to be wrong about this.

I lean my weight against the flower display, just watching them together. He's grinning wider than I thought he was physically capable of, then laughs at something she's saying. Loud enough that I can hear it from outside.

I let the happy sight wash over me. I did that—I got that kid off crutches, got him out of his own head and into the waiting arms of the person he loves.

And I've just figured out exactly how to do the same for Summer.

Chapter 45

Parker

That Friday evening, Summer stops dead just ahead of me with her yellow surfboard held over her head.

"You did not," she says, voice hushed. I catch up to find her staring, mouth ajar, at the pale-yellow camper van sitting on the edge of the beach at Pine Point. She'd groaned when I insisted on parking my Jeep farther away from the rocky section of the ocean that causes the barrel waves this spot is known for—which I'd used to lure her here after work.

Now, though, Summer turns her wide eyes on me. "I thought we were here for a last surf before tomorrow."

"We are. But I figured we could hang around overnight, since you start bright and early."

She forges ahead, bare feet sliding in the sand in her excitement.

Call it manifesting, call it playing pretend. I want to give her a taste of a day down the road. When she'd be doing this very thing across the world, and I might fly out to do it with her.

Maybe I also wanted to make sure no one crashed our Summer Friday this time around.

Summer leans her board against the side of the van and lets

me slip off the straps of her backpack before she bounces inside like a kid at Christmas. I came to set it up earlier today, loading it with the requisite pre-bed reading material and stocking the fridge. There's a family-sized bag of chocolate-covered almonds and cans of Diet Coke—her favorite post-fuck snack—waiting on the nightstand.

Summer climbs onto the bed—a mattress of questionable quality lying on an elevated platform at the back of the small space. She shuffles to the double doors at its other end, throws them open to a view of the beach, then flops onto her back.

I lean against the doorway, grinning as she sighs up at the paneled roof.

"Best Summer Friday ever," she declares.

"I got you something." Ducking my head under the low ceiling, I uncover her gift where it leans between the seats at the front of the van. A shiny, brand-new surfboard in the exact model and shade as her current one.

I sit next to her, placing it across our laps. Then I flip it over to reveal the artwork on its underside.

"*Parker*," Summer gasps, a palm meeting her cheek. It's our surf spot at Crystal Cove, where we've spent every morning for months. Swirls of blue make up the water spanning nearly the entire length of the board. The curving outcrop is on one end, lush with trees; the tiny squares making up Summer's favorite beachfront bungalows sit on the other. The sky is countless shades of burnt orange, the setting sun hovering over the edge of the ocean.

"It's beautiful."

Summer's fingers trace along the cursive words painted over the artwork. *Team Summer, here and across the world.*

I reach for my phone and snap a picture of her beaming at the surfboard. The clicking sound has her looking around.

She shoots me a teasing smile. "You and your pictures."

I shrug. "It's a long life, you know? I want to make sure I remember the good parts at the end of it all."

"Me staring at a surfboard is a good part?"

"*You* are the best part."

~~~~~

Over the next few hours, Summer surfs while I float along nearby, waterproof camera trained on her. We meet the people in the camper van parked next to ours, a boyfriend-girlfriend pair of surfers competing in tomorrow's event. Summer takes to the other woman so quickly that we pool our dinners and end up cooking burgers on the small grill attached to the back of their camper. We sit eating together in the sand, and it feels like we might be on one of Summer's tour stops on a Tahitian beach or the Australian coast.

I can't say I really connect with this lifestyle. I'm too partial to my things, my bed, my people. But I can understand the appeal of it for someone like Summer, who so easily makes friends, and who'd exist in the ocean if biology allowed it. For my parents, too, who thrive in new experiences.

It's bittersweet, seeing her so in her element. Knowing it'll take her away from home. Her first adventure without me. But feeling, deep in my bones, that it's an experience she's meant to have.

We sit on the roof of the van now, just the two of us, as the sun sets. Summer got increasingly quiet after dinner, when her new friends turned in and the beach started to empty out. She stares at the horizon with unfocused eyes, legs swinging over the edge of the roof.

"Thank you for doing this for me. It was fun." She leans back on her hands, French braid flipping over her shoulder as she looks at me. She gives a small smile when she catches the expectation in my face, waiting on her to say whatever I sense she's working up to. "The other night, what did you mean by *so long*?"

"I meant I've been in love with you for years."

To my surprise, she doesn't deny it. "But when did it happen?"

"I don't know. And believe me, I wish I did." I stare out at the now-quiet beach. There's an aging couple walking hand in hand along the shore, and I can't help but hope we'll be there one day. Me and Summer, taking on yet another stage of life together. "I would've caught that moment in a jar, held on to it so I could relive it whenever I needed to. Because knowing us, it would've been a good one."

She smiles softly. "It must've been big. The time we all snuck into the drive-in after hours in high school, and I figured out how to get the projector working?"

"No way—it would've been something like this. You and me, just existing together. Easy. Nothing to it, but it's like the whole world pauses." I wind an arm around her waist and tuck her close. "I've loved twenty-eight versions of you, Sum, one way or the other. I couldn't tell you when *that* kind of love became *this* kind of love, but I think that's the point. Falling for you was the most inevitable thing in the world for me. It was always going to be you—just took me a while to realize it."

She rests her head on my shoulder. "Earlier this summer, when I first kissed you. Did you know?"

"I knew when you iced me out and I lost all semblance of direction without you."

"That was the night I realized I could love you."

My entire chest squeezes, her words like a zap to the heart, sending it into overdrive. Every frantic pump shouting, *Do you? Do you? Do you?*

"What if I wanted this—all of it?" She gestures at the beach, the camper, her hand settling on my thigh. "If I left . . . would you wait?"

"I'd be counting down the seconds, waiting for you to come home." I take her hand, press her open palm over my heart. "And you'd stay right here. Where you've always been."

Summer's fingers grip my shirt. "How could you know for sure? We've never really been without each other. Not like that."

I swing my legs onto the roof of the van. "Come on, let's go in. Let me explain it to you in a way you'll understand."

She's confused but follows me inside, dropping into the van from the skylight and landing on the mattress with a bounce.

I slam shut the doors at the opposite end of the bed. "Clothes off."

Summer blinks, then hurries to peel off her tank top and tiny denim shorts. "Unexpected turn, but I don't hate it."

Once she's naked, I grip her hips and spin her around so that she lies face down on the bed, gasping into the sheets. I tug on her hips again so that she's on her hands and knees, unable to take my eyes off her as I undress. Bent over, already glistening, greedily squirming that ass in the air. That visible rush of adrenaline as her body trembles, waiting for whatever I give her.

The first lick is all for me, lapping her from one entrance to the other, collecting every bit of her I can without going anywhere near her clit. She whimpers into the room.

"Can you—That was . . ."

I slip a finger inside her, just teasing her. "Where do you want my tongue, love?"

She makes a frustrated sound, squirming her hips again. "Parker."

"Here?" I spread her cheeks, thumb circling her other entrance. Greedy girl that she is, she thrusts her hip back, demanding more. Goddamn. I give her what she wants, licking, swirling my tongue, making her squirm and gasp.

"Holy shit, I actually think I'm going to . . ."

Summer reaches for her clit. I let her go a while, rubbing circles over herself as I lick at her. Until she's really shivering and her breaths become nice and labored. That's when I pull away, and rip her fingers from her pussy.

I flip her onto her back. "None of that tonight, Summer."

"None of . . ." Summer swallows, panting and blinking hard, completely disoriented. "Why'd you stop?"

"Told you: I'm explaining it in a way you'll understand."

"And that involves not letting me come?"

"Yes." I reach for my backpack on the ground by the end of the bed, pulling out the length of rope I brought just in case the mood struck. I yank her upright. "Grab your elbows behind your back."

With greedy eyes, she does, and I get to work binding her upper arms to her sides, wrapping and crisscrossing the rope around her torso.

I dip to press a kiss to her clit just to piss her off. She clamps her jaw shut, gaze now petulantly stuck to the ceiling. That is, until I line up my cock at her pussy. I rock just inside her, groaning at the hot, wet feel of her. Goddamn, her body is heaven.

Made for this. Made for me.

I push her legs up as high as her flexible body allows, sitting back so that I can see every throb and clench of her pussy as I slide into her fully, then pull all the way out.

"*Parker*." Summer whimpers in protest, face twisting in agony.

"Yeah." I tap her clit. "That feeling you have right now? Where everything hurts, your body begging for something it can't have? That's what it's like for me when you're not around." I lean in and kiss her deep, fingers clutching the sides of her throat, holding her in place as I sink back into her pussy with one long stroke.

"Oh my God," she gasps against my mouth.

"And this—the way it feels when I fuck you?" I thrust into her in shallow strokes. "That's how it feels to be with you, Summer. I'm alive. On a different fucking planet."

Her eyes close, brows draw together as she surrenders to the feel of us together.

"You and me?" I thrust hard, all the way in. "It's the kind of high you kill for." Another thrust that has her crying out. "Ruin your life for." Another thrust. "Burn it all down for. You get it yet?"

Her face melts, eyelids go heavy. I kiss her until she's gasping for air, shuddering beneath me, and pull out of her just as her back begins to arch.

"*Fuck*, Parker," she sobs as her orgasm recedes. "You're going to kill me."

"So will you. Do you get it yet?"

She growls at the ceiling. I kiss her hard, then slide off the bed. "Then sit tight. It's about to hurt, love."

I lift her phone off the tiny kitchenette, punching in her passcode and smirking when I see she's got our videos organized into a neat little folder. Fucking her for the first time, her mouth around my cock in my kitchen. The night she begged me to record myself jerking off. The morning she rode me in the driver's seat of the Jeep after a surf.

It's all there, undeniable evidence of us. The way I love her, would destroy my body to give her whatever she wants. The way she needs me back.

I set it on autoplay and prop up the phone against a pillow by her head.

Summer inhales a soft breath, mesmerized by the video like it's the first time she's seen it. She squeezes her thighs together, giving her clit some friction as she watches.

I wrench apart her legs and settle between them to keep them spread.

"Parker, *please*."

"Relax, baby. Enjoy the show."

She turns to glare at me, lips parting when she sees me stroking myself. Fury and undeniable exhilaration pour from her eyes. I can't help but laugh, leaning down to bite her lip.

"You're cute when you're needy. I ever tell you that?"

I turn her chin toward the phone when the next video starts—I'm in my bathroom, shirtless, sweats pulled down, phone trained on the mirror. Stroking my cock. Thinking of her and losing my fucking mind over it, as though she were in the room with me.

"Fuck, you're so hot," Summer whispers, eyes glued to the screen. "You're torturing me."

"You've got me wrapped around your finger. How can you not see it?" I lean down to kiss her neck while she watches me pump into my fist. "Look how hard you make me. I was thinking about you. Your pretty smile, the way your ass looks in a swimsuit. The way you sound when you come. And—"

My groan fills the van when I come in the video. Summer trembles, looking more distraught by the minute.

"Do you get it now, love? How bad it'll hurt to be apart from you?" I run a thumb over her nipple, take the other in my mouth. She cries out something unintelligible. When I hover over her again, her face is contorted in agony. "You make me want to be the best version of myself, someone who's good enough to have you. You make me feel loved, and safe, and like things will get better no matter how wrong they go. All I want is to do the same for you. No matter where you are. For the rest of my life."

Her expression morphs as I speak. Pain to frustration to desperation as wetness gathers along her lashes. "You do the same for me," she whispers.

I stroke her cheek. "So, do you get it? You go, and I'll be here. Missing you. Wanting you. You don't have to be here for me to love you."

Summer inhales a shuddering breath. "What if it goes wrong? Our relationship, down the drain. A whole friend group ruined. Half of them are related to you—they'd choose you, and then I'd really have no one left."

"*I'd* choose you. You're either ending up my wife or my best friend—both, if I'm lucky. No matter which way this goes, it's you and me. I would choose you."

Tears pour from the corners of her eyes, and I hate it—loathe seeing her cry. But these are the tears of a woman who's maybe—*finally*—starting to understand.

I kiss her, slow and soft. Flip us so that I'm sitting, settled against the wall of the van, and bring her down onto my cock.

"Oh fuck," she cries. She's still bound, off-balance, so I do the work for her. Lifting and dropping her; filling, then emptying her. The relief in her face is vulnerable, so sweet. She brings her lips to mine. "Thank you. Thank you, thank you."

My laugh is more of a breath, because the feel of her is so perfect I could die like this. And then she's coming so hard that her lips freeze over mine.

"Attagirl." I scatter kisses all over her face. "Take another one. You earned it. Such a sweet, patient girl."

I reach between us. It takes barely a few strokes and she's coming again, whispering my name, kissing my neck, thanking me over and over as if she wasn't the best thing to happen to me. Then she begs for another one and we come together, limbs tangled, skin slick with sweat.

Later, when we're cleaned up and thoroughly ruined, Summer lies with her head in my lap as I read out from her book. She pauses with a handful of chocolate almonds on its way to her mouth and says, "I'd choose you, too. If it all went wrong, I'd choose you."

A fist closes around my heart. "There was never another choice for me."

She nuzzles into me. "You flying out to watch me compete."

"Is that a formal invitation?"

"Every stop. Whenever you can."

I smile down at her sleepy face. "Worth getting out of bed for."

Chapter 46

Summer

Hours later, I stare up at the moonlit paneled roof of the camper van.

Parker's soft breaths tickle my neck. He fell asleep about an hour ago, holding me tightly to him, my back to his chest. Making good on his promise to keep me close, in his heart, even in his sleep.

Halfway into the final chapter of our *Hidden Moon* book, my dad sent a good luck text for tomorrow, alongside a family photo of them enjoying a day on the beach. It's everything that's made me feel like I could disappear, sink to the very bottom of the ocean outside this van, and it would take ages for someone to notice.

For once, I don't feel that way.

The nonstop stream of messages in our friends' group chat, co-ordinating their arrivals tomorrow, is a buoy thrown at me. The sight of Caroline and Brian's RV, now parked a few rows down from ours, a life vest hugging me tight. The feel of Parker's beating heart against me a sturdy rope, tethering me to safety.

I don't want to give up on my relationship with my dad. But what has it brought me recently, other than heartache and feelings of crippling insignificance? For years, it ripped the joy out of the thing I loved most. Derailed every single plan I had for myself in favor of staying desperately put in a place where he could easily find me, once it was finally my turn to have him again.

Tonight, in this cramped, overheating camper van, I decide that I'm done waiting for my turn. I want to go into tomorrow, into the future, without the deadweight of broken hope holding me back.

Sitting up, I stroke a finger over Parker's stubbled cheek. "Park?"

His eyelids flutter. As though he were hovering on the edge of consciousness, just waiting to be called back to me. "Love?"

"Can you do something for me? Can you just hold my hand for a few minutes?"

He sits up, laces our fingers.

I reach for my phone on the nightstand and dial. My father's voicemail greeting fills my eardrum. The one I've got memorized.

The one I shouldn't know by heart.

"Hi, Dad. It's Summer." Parker shuffles closer, his body tense as though ready to jump into a brawl with me. "Do you remember what you used to tell me when I was younger, before I'd compete? You'd take me by the shoulders on the sand, tell me to close my eyes. 'Big, big breath, Summer,' you'd say. 'I love you no matter what. I'll be right here, waiting for you.'"

I close my eyes and I'm back there again. The first time he said it to me at thirteen, knees bent to bring us at eye level. His green eyes near-identical to mine.

Tears fall down my cheeks, because this is the last kind of call I ever imagined making. I'd believed him with all my heart—*I'll be right here, waiting for you.*

"Maybe you thought that I'd always be here waiting for you, too. That our bond was self-sufficient, that you didn't need to look after it, or me. That you could call me in and out of your life whenever it suited you. But God, what you've done to me for the past few years? I wouldn't wish feeling so damn irrelevant on my worst enemy." Parker's warm hand around mine is my courage. My sanity.

My dream of something better. "I'm calling to tell you that I'm finally done waiting. Done making excuses for you. Done trying to make you see me. You won't be hearing from me again. And I'm not leaving this message hoping you'll call me, or try to change my mind. I'm leaving it for me—a clean break."

Something heavy lifts off my chest at the words, as though my heart needed to hear it to believe it. That it could finally release the piece of itself that belonged to him, waiting for him to reclaim it. And offer it to people who'd cherish it the way it deserved to be.

"I'm blocking your number. If you ever want to talk . . . I'd say you know where to find me, but I don't plan on being here to wait around for you anymore." I take a breath, filling my lungs to the brim, then releasing it all. "Bye, Dad."

With shaking hands, I hang up. My rough sobs fill the van as I block and delete his number, curtailing the temptation that I know will come at my lowest points.

Parker holds me tight. Lets me soak through his shirt. Lets me shuffle around to press my ear right over his beating heart.

Thump thump thump thump. My favorite sound in the world.

He strokes my hair, whispering *I love you so much, that was so fucking brave, I'll always be here, right here for you, Summer* as I cry myself to sleep.

Chapter 47

Summer

The scoreboard at Pine Point sits partway between the beachy shore covered in spectators and where I currently float in the water—ignoring, as I have for the past ten minutes, the blond man sitting on his own board a few yards away.

I've managed to avoid Denny since the event at Rocky Ridge, while knowing, deep down, that this was bound to happen, eventually. Me and him, head-to-head in the water.

It's the first heat of the day, and that scoreboard isn't nice to look at. It's been all bad luck since I got in the water—lackluster waves, and even more mediocre surfing. Every time I've managed to pull ahead of Denny's highest scoring waves, he's made up for it on his next turn.

He's still sitting pretty in first place in the overall series scoring, while my third-place standing makes me the weaker surfer between us.

On paper.

A good first round would set me up for the rest of the day. It would mean eliminating Denny from this event. His overall score would take a hit, and mine would skyrocket if I can manage to put my whole effort, my whole heart into surfing today.

I stare off to where spectator boats dot the water, finding the large sailboat where my friends sit with their legs dangling over the ship's side. Caroline and Brian Woods wave at me enthusiastically. At the very end of the row sits Parker, Hawaiian shirt fluttering in the breeze, phone trained on me.

The words TEAM SUMMER glitter from all their chests. And my heart squeezes tight at the sight.

"Are the old ones paid actors?" Denny's voice is taunting. "Don't your parents avoid the hell out of you?"

It's hard to be bothered by him with a literal boatload of people here for me, just like they said they'd be. Without taking my eyes off them, I give Denny the finger.

And I swear, Parker's smile goes wider.

He moves his phone out of the way, pointing at the TEAM SUMMER on his chest like he did moments before I got into the water.

Here and across the world, he'd said, echoing the words on my new surfboard.

All my life, I've operated under the assumption that Parker is, well . . . Parker. Bound to me by sheer virtue of how deeply intertwined our lives have been since the moment we met. And in many ways, I've made sure we stayed intertwined. Moving into an apartment across the street from his, convincing him to give up every Friday night for me. I always assumed that, one day, he'd meet someone and make his merry way out of my life like everyone else had.

We've been tangled up together our whole lives, but what if it wasn't by force, but by fate? What if I'm one of the lucky few who gets to say that they've been loved by the same person through every single version of themselves, through every single phase of life?

It's improbable. A pipe dream wished for by every lover of love like me. And yet, when I burned down our friendship earlier this summer, there it was rising from the ashes as something even better.

Unbreakable.

It's time, I finally decide. Time to welcome the love I do have, from wherever it comes. To choose myself, and trust my people to stay my people, no matter where I am.

Team Summer, here and across the world.

With a breath, I tear my gaze off the boat and fix it on the horizon. I thread water through my outstretched fingers, arms floating at my sides. *I'm ready whenever you are.*

Minutes later, I spot a gorgeous set of waves forming in the distance.

Seconds after, I ride my first barrel.

~~~~~

"Darling girl, we are so proud of you." Caroline squeezes me so tightly a breath actually gusts out of me.

I should've been better prepared; since the judges announced my win at Pine Point and second-place finish in Surf's Up, guaranteeing my spot on the Champions Tour next month, she's hugged me and gushed over me whenever we've come within range. Which, given the close quarters of Parker's apartment and the bodies currently filling it, has been occurring at ten-minute intervals.

"Thank you for being there for me." I hug her back, so damn grateful for her and every person here to celebrate with me.

A deep sense of peace overcame me as the water flung me out of that first barrel, still on my feet and feeling stronger than ever, in every way. By the final heat of the day, any lingering doubt that this was what I was meant to do had vanished. And it wasn't just because of the final standings—it was seeing my own euphoria mirrored in my friends' faces. It was the happy tears that Parker hastily brushed away when his sister started teasing him.

These aren't people who'd forget me.

This is family, one who chose to love me a long time ago. Who chose to keep loving me even while I kept them at a distance this summer.

My gaze wanders over Caroline's shoulder. Melody, Siena, and Shy are laughing together, replenishing the snack table. Parker sits on the couch between Zac and Brooks, with his dad nearby. They seem to be arguing about something, and over the low music and the sounds of the girls laughing I hear the words *completion percentage* and *receiving yards*.

Parker's eyes flick across the room mid-sentence, finding me without trying. Dimples pop in his cheeks. My stomach bursts with pleasure, then pinches with preemptive longing.

I can't believe I'm about to go months at a time without that smile.

Caroline draws away, noticing where I'm looking. "Did you know Brian and I are high school sweethearts?" She nods when I tell her I didn't. "Since we were thirteen. We went to different colleges, and it was . . . not the easiest thing in the world, if you want the truth. Experiencing this exciting, life-changing thing without my best friend—my safety net. Made me prouder of every independent victory, though. And every reunion was that much sweeter."

"I'm nervous," I admit. "I'm a grown woman suddenly realizing how little I've done on my own. He's always been right there, you know?"

"You're both more than ready—look how far you've come in a matter of months. Together, but as your own people, too." Caroline's smile is kind, but then she catches sight of something over my shoulder, and her lips purse together. "In fact, this may be your first opportunity to practice."

I turn to find Callie, Wynn, and Lisa inching slowly toward us in Parker's kitchen, a whole spectrum of emotions written over their faces: Callie stern. Wynn cautious. And Lisa beaming at me, face brighter than the overhead lights.

"I can stay, if you'd like backup," Caroline whispers.

"That's okay. I can handle them."

With a smile at me, and a warning look at the trio now approaching me, Caroline heads into the living room.

"Hi," I say cautiously. "What are you doing here?"

"Parker mentioned something about a party." Lisa's smile doubles. "You were fantastic today. We were all so proud."

"I didn't know you were there. Why didn't you say anything?"

"Same reason we haven't seen you properly in months. We wanted to give you your space." Callie gathers me in her arms before I can wrap my head around their words. "But for God's sake, Summer. Please tell us you're done avoiding us."

"There was more gossiping than I could stand," I whisper into her shoulder. "I swear, I didn't know what he'd been doing."

"Of course you didn't." Wynn shakes his head disapprovingly. "Small-town nonsense. Some people will believe anything."

"We've all been so sick about it," Lisa adds. "And we've refused to serve that boy every time he's come into Oakley's since."

My eyes prickle. I squeeze Callie back. "Thank you."

Again, Parker's eyes connect with mine unprompted. There's a barely perceptible rise in his brow, a silent question to me as he studies our scene. I nod and he relaxes.

He mouths *love you*. And keeping the *I love you, too* to myself is a whole fight. I'm happy for this party but longing for later. When we're alone again and I can tell him exactly what he means to me.

How no amount of distance over the next year, and any year beyond that, could undo us. How I'll find the stormy blue of his eyes in every ocean, hear his laugh in every thundering wave. How his belief in me will power me through every surf, and the thought of a tomorrow where we're together again—no matter how far away—will be all the strength I need to get out of bed on my hardest days.

Brian wanders over, inquiring about the diner, and I take the opportunity to excuse myself for a breather. I shut Parker's bedroom door behind me and flop face-first on his bed, inhaling his peppery scent off the sheets. I'm going to have to steal his bodywash.

I pull my phone from my shorts, about to text him to sneak away to meet me, when I notice a flash of white in my periphery.

I reach for the crumpled sheet of paper on his nightstand, standing out against the neatly stacked autobiographies and a spare pair of glasses sitting in its case. It takes me a few blinks to understand what I'm looking at, even though the title should make it obvious.

Summer's Dream Man

It's the stupid list we'd put together earlier this summer. I haven't thought about it since, but it seems Parker has. There are scribbles all the way down the paper. A slash of ink crossing out the words *has dark hair* that makes my heart sink. A check mark beside *can cook* that has tears of pride forming.

At the very bottom, an address I vaguely recognize is written in Parker's messy scrawl next to *owns a home*.

"Oh, Parker." I want to say that I can't believe he's done this, obsessed over this silly list. Methodically worked through it, giving me everything I once said I wanted from a partner. But of course, he's done this.

When has Parker ever not given me his all?

At every turn, every phase of my life, he's been exactly what I needed. The raucous boy befriending the timid only child at day care. The rebellious teen coaxing me out of my misery after my home life blew up. A man who's shown me what I've been missing, the way I've always dreamed of being loved while chasing after boys all my life.

I throw myself back on the mattress, holding the mangled paper to my chest. I'm going to marry that man one day.

The bedroom door swings open. Melody leads Siena and Shy into the room.

"There you are," she says. "Everything okay?"

Wordlessly, I hold out the list. They gather around me on the bed, eyes flying over the sheet of paper.

"Marry him. Bear his children," Siena orders. "Use that rope of his to muscle him down the aisle if you have to."

"I'll help," Shy adds.

I laugh. "I was just thinking the same thing."

Melody flings herself down next to me, throwing an arm over her eyes. "Thank *God*. He's your problem now."

I bounce to my feet and head for the door, suddenly unable to spend a single second more at this party. "Do me a favor? Tell my problem to meet me at my place in ten minutes."

Chapter 48

Parker

Follow us . . .

The pink paper plane note in my palm is the first of several lining a path down the hallway in Summer's quiet apartment. She's got them laid out in the same formation I did for her weeks ago.

Last time, it had been for the first of our failed dates. When another man swooped in and claimed her before I had a chance to. One of the worst gut-punches of my life, on what had eventually turned out to be one of the best days of my life.

"I'm gonna be honest, Sum. The déjà vu is a tad worrisome," I call out. "Last time this happened, I had to chase away a surfer dude with no idea how to take a hint."

I hear her quiet laugh. *The* laugh—the nervous one she gives me sometimes—that has me thinking that I might be on the verge of the newest best day of my life.

Heart pumping madly, I follow the paper planes toward the end of the hall. By the time I catch sight of the pillow fort lit up with twinkle lights, my pulse is so rapid that I go a little lightheaded.

I crouch at the mouth of the fort, peering inside to find Summer lounging on a pile of blankets. "Fancy seeing you here."

Her face falls. "Oh, this is awkward. I was expecting a different guy."

"Then move over—this is the perfect hiding spot for an ambush. He'll never see me coming."

She laughs and I crawl into the tight space so that we sit side by side. So close together that all I smell is that mind-numbing floral perfume. Between that, the verging on heart failure, her win today, and the way the green in her eyes shimmers under the twinkle lights, I'm a moment from death. Happy as can be.

Until she winces and says, "Park, we need to talk."

"Buzzkill," I mutter, poking her side.

She smothers a smile. "I've been thinking a lot about this whole relationship thing, and . . . You know I've got a lousy history with guys. So if I'm really going to do it again, it has to be with the right man. One who's exactly what I'm looking for. I won't settle for less."

My eyes narrow. "Not convinced I like where this is headed, but go on."

"All I'm saying is that I have very strict criteria." With a breath, she pulls a square of paper from the back pocket of her denim shorts. I think I'm seeing things when she unfolds it to reveal the words *Summer's Dream Man* at the top, because last I saw that list, it sat on my bedside table. But this list is neater—her loopy writing all over it. No check marks and no scribbles damning the shade of my hair.

Summer clears her throat. "First of all, he'd need to look damn good in a Hawaiian shirt. And he'd wear them just for the sake of making me laugh."

I'm the one who laughs then. Every gasp of air fills me with something that feels oddly like helium, until I'm floating, barely touching the blanket-covered floor.

"This dream man, he'd be the type to ride for the people in his life, no matter how long they've been in it. Like . . . following me blindly into a ridiculous revenge scheme, without ever making me feel small or stupid about it—even when I hurt him in the process. He'd spend his summer bonding with a kid he didn't know. Take the time to understand him past surface level, and he'd care enough to make that kid's life better in every possible way. He should have an in with local security guards, just in case we're looking to break some rules—"

Another laugh bursts out of me. "Would you do that? Break some rules?"

"With him, I would. Because he'd make everything feel safe, like nothing bad could ever happen when he's around. And if it did, he'd do anything he could to make it stop hurting. He'd . . . he'd be the kind of man to take cooking lessons for someone he loves, who'd put effort into bringing the best version of himself to a relationship. He'd be brave enough to lean into his feelings, no matter the risk to his heart. He'd have big hands—"

"Huge," I stage-whisper. "Huge hands."

She smiles. "He'd have huge hands and light brown hair."

I clutch my chest. "Thank God."

"He'd push me to grow. Challenge me to want more whenever I settle." Summer swallows, her smile turning watery. "He'd be self-less enough to let me go, even though I know he doesn't want me to. And I'd spend every single minute away missing him. Craving him. Wishing we were in the same place. Me and him, just existing together."

Summer folds up her list, clasping it in her fingers. Put together like that, it sounds like she's talking about someone else—someone so different than the person I was just months ago. Who didn't know where he was headed, could barely look after himself, didn't even have a proper read on his own feelings for the most important person in his life.

Only to find that the pieces of what I wanted were already there, waiting for me to see them. Fight for them, shape them into a life better than I could've dreamed of having. With a golden, indestructible thread running through it all, beginning to end—me and my Summer.

She hasn't taken her eyes off me. "Know anyone who fits the bill?"

"I might."

"Well, he's too late. It would never work out." Summer heaves the most aggrieved sigh. Tosses away the list and climbs into my lap, taking my face between her hands. "Turns out, I'm in love with my best friend."

A bomb goes off inside me—warm and fizzy and filled with hot-pink glitter. I let the grin fall from my face. "You're in love with my sister?"

Summer nips my lip. "Yeah. You think I should go for it?"

"I think she'll stay away from you if she knows what's good for her." I lift my chin, kissing her softly. "Say it again. Please?"

"I love you, Parker. More than I know what to do with. But I promise I'll spend the rest of our life together coming up with new ways to show you."

This must be it—the feeling Summer chases with every wave. The pure euphoria of putting yourself at the ocean's mercy, just praying you survive, and landing on your feet; of handing your heart to the love of your life, just praying she'll keep it, and earning hers in return.

It's no wonder she's making a life out of it. I'll be chasing this feeling for the rest of mine.

Summer searches my face. "I saw an address on your list. Are you leaving your apartment?"

"Eventually. There's a plot of land on the beach at Crystal Cove. I figured it'd be a good way to stay busy while you're away. Give you somewhere nice to come home to, whenever you're ready."

"It's funny to think we'll all have gone by the time I'm back. We were the last ones left in town." Her words are a soft, shaky whisper. Homesickness in every syllable. "I'm going to miss you so much."

I bury my face in her neck. "A house on the beach one day. Worth getting out of bed for."

She nods. "You hiring me at your clinic once I retire from surfing. Worth getting out of bed for."

I gulp down her perfume. "A kid?"

"I think so."

"Dog?"

"Several." Summer pulls back to look me in the eye. "And even if none of that happens . . ."

"You and me, just existing together." I wipe away her tears. "Worth getting out of bed for."

Summer slides off my lap and settles beside me. I pull out my phone and snap a picture of us. It's a near-mirror image of the one from the day we met in that pillow fort, twenty-seven years ago, beaming at the camera.

If only I knew then what I do now—I was a kid with my whole life ahead of me. And my entire world sitting right beside me.

Summer hums at the phone, eyeing the picture. "It's not quite right. Let's take another one."

This time, she grabs the front of my shirt and pulls me in at the last second. Kissing me hard for the camera.

Epilogue
Parker

It's mid-afternoon by the time I weave a path through the thick crowd lining the beach in a tiny Portuguese fishing town.

I ignore the grumbling as I shoulder my way to the very front, as close as possible to the water without outright wading into the ocean. Don't even bother with the guy in the distressed bucket hat trying to kill me with a glare when I step around him, obstructing his formerly clear view of the half-formed barrel just ahead, and the surfer disappearing inside it.

He can kick rocks, for all I care.

Endless flight delays mean that I've already missed two of Summer's heats today. Worse yet, I still have to endure another fourteen minutes and eleven seconds before feeling her skin against mine again. Seeing her smile in person. Kissing her for the first time in two and a half months, our longest stretch apart since the Champions Tour kicked off in the fall.

Every day since, I've been gulping down any little drop of her I can. Calls, texts. The live streams and recordings I find of the surf events I've missed, with my nose practically touching the screen. As though, by some miracle, it could transport me to wherever she was.

None of it has. The only thing still tethering me to my humanity is the immeasurable joy plain on her face whenever we video call. Her excited, mile-a-minute chatter as she fills me in on her day and recaps her best wave. Her breathy moans as she comes, not taking her eyes off me through the phone.

Between the steady stream of clients coming through the clinic and finalizing our plans for the beachfront bungalow before we break ground next month, I've tried to keep myself distracted. I've been counting down the minutes until the end of the football season, when I can take an extended break to travel with Summer for a blessed few weeks before heading home to get River into playing shape for his first season of quarterbacking at UOB.

I'm jostled around. Bucket Hat is trying to make foolish moves to regain his position in the sand. Maybe spotting the glitter on my chest and the obnoxious pattern on my open shirt, and thinking I'm easy prey.

I take my eyes off the water just long enough to give him a cutting stare. "Back up. This is my spot now."

He retreats several long steps.

The crowd roars when Summer emerges from the barrel. Feet still planted on her board, barely a hair out of place from her ponytail.

See her? I want to tell them. *She chose me.*

Summer rides out the last of the wave, then slips into the shallow, foamy water. She scans the crowd as the judges announce her score. I wave at her. Unnecessary, given the atrocity I'm wearing. The clashing colors on my Hawaiian shirt draw her gaze. She starts paddling toward shore, eyes stuck to me. The crowd murmurs, probably confused as to why she's now on land when there's still ten minutes in this heat.

Summer rips the leash off her ankle. Abandons her board and doesn't stop until we collide in a tangle of arms, her legs wound around my waist.

Everything. I have everything I'll ever need right here in my arms.

Summer's palm cups my cheek. Slides down my neck and stops over my pounding heart. "You're here."

"I'm here. I missed you so much, Summer—"

She crushes her mouth against mine, moaning loud enough for anyone to hear. Fingers threading through my hair and holding tight. It takes me a minute to remember where we are, what she's supposed to be doing. When I do, I break away. I try to set her down but she triples her grip on me.

"Summer, baby, with all due respect, what the hell are you doing?" I push away the wet strands of hair clinging to her cheek. "You're supposed to be surfing—"

She cuts me off with another kiss. "I'm way ahead in the score. Let the other guy think he has a chance before I keep crushing his spirit."

I love every version this woman, but this one especially. This is a Summer who knows exactly who she is, what she's capable of. Exuding confidence. Completely in her element.

"You know what?" I say, pulling her back in. "It's the polite thing to do."

~~~~~

The house is bursting with noise.

It's our third year in our beachfront bungalow, but our first hosting our family for Christmas. Low carols filter from the speaker system, a scream I recognize as Macaulay Culkin's streams in from the TV in the living room. My twin nephews squeal as their uncle Brooks and pregnant aunt Siena entertain them, Siena's mom laughing happily as she watches on. I can hear my sister groaning at our own mother, who's rambling at Zac about something or other.

"You hiding from your mom?"

Strong arms wrap around my middle and Summer presses her

face between my shoulder blades. I grip her arms, squeeze her back as best I can.

"I thought I'd get started on cooking—it's Christmas brunch. A big deal. Can't screw it up."

"Park, it's seven o'clock on Christmas Eve," she says with a laugh. "So again, I ask: Are you hiding from your mom?"

"Abso-fucking-lutely I am, and I blame you. That woman does not need wine."

Summer unravels from me and leans against the counter. Since retiring from competitive surfing at the end of last summer, she's chopped her hair to a sexy-as-hell chin-length that constantly requires me to check myself or risk ripping off her clothes in company.

Her smile is soft but her eyes glint with mischief. It's exactly the way she looked at me on the French Polynesian beach where we eloped two years ago. As though she were the one getting her way. But it'd been me who took one look at her upon my arrival in town and decided I was done living without her as my wife.

All it took were some well-timed orgasms to get her to agree.

"What's got you looking so pleased with yourself, Woods?" I ask, nudging her chin.

She tucks her tousled hair behind her ears. "I want to give you your Christmas present early."

My stomach bursts, a whole swooping feeling that actually draws my hand to my middle. Because I know my wife better than I know myself. And she isn't looking at me like that for the sake of a pair of socks.

"Summer." There's already a lump forming in my throat, burning in my eyes.

With that breathy, nervous laugh, she reaches into her back pocket and places a test on the counter. I don't need to look at it. Don't need to see anything but the joy and mild terror in her beautiful eyes to know exactly what it says.

There's been no shortage of practice over the years, but it took us a long time to decide we wanted this. For a while, we didn't think we'd get to that point at all—Summer eventually started flying home between tour events, but she wasn't ready to give it up altogether. And I'd developed my own affinity for world travel, meaning we were country-hopping every time I could pull off an extended break from the clinic.

It was on one of those trips several months ago, watching the sun set on our boards in the Indian Ocean, when she turned those green eyes on me and simply said, "Should we?"

And here we are again, on the precipice of another grand adventure. Another phase of life, together.

"Did your life just flash before your eyes?" Summer asks with a laugh.

"Yeah, it did." I dry my cheeks, rest my forehead on her shoulder. Inhale the perfume I made her swear she'd never stop using. "Looks like it'll be a good one."

~~~~~

I'm slow getting through the final chapter of my book, unable to keep my eyes on its pages for long.

At the other end of the bed, Summer is curled around a pillow, humming sweetly in her sleep. Our six-year-old son lies between us, little arms flung overhead, after a brutal two hours of trying to coax him back to bed after a nightmare. The dog snores soundly from the foot of the mattress. It's hard, looking away from my favorite view in the world.

I reach for my phone and quietly snap a picture of them together.

There's a framed photo on the nightstand beyond my wife, a forever-favorite of mine. Me and Summer, ten years younger. Kissing in a glowing pillow fort in her old apartment in town.

So much has changed since then. We've traveled the world, built a thriving business together. We've fought and we've loved, made a home and a family. New lines mark our skin, a few gray strands streak through our hair.

And yet, every day since feels the same as it did when we took that picture. Same as it always has with Summer.

I'm still just a kid with my whole life ahead of me. And my entire world lying right beside me.

Acknowledgments

One of my favorite things to do at the end of a first draft is to read through the earlier books in a series and re-experience my characters before they became leads in their own story. It's been so much fun to see Summer and Parker as best friends who love to roast each other in *Only in Your Dreams*, then ones who wonder about each other in *Only Between Us*, to leading such a vulnerable story while maintaining the teasing edge that makes their friendship so much fun to read about. I hope you loved their story as much as I do.

I may have been the one to write the words, but it took a heck of a lot of people to have made it possible to share their story. First and foremost, thank you to every reader and bookseller who picked up, raved about, and reviewed *Only in Your Dreams* and *Only Between Us*, and to those of you I got to meet at events over the past year. Your support of my work means that I get to keep writing more stories, and I couldn't appreciate you more for it.

To my husband, son, and family for the unwavering support and for making me feel so cool for having this career even though I'm a greasy-haired, stress-ridden troll while in my writing cave. Doing this would be impossible and pointless without you in my life. To Jillian, for letting me vent when I need to, and giving me laughs and pep talks when I need those. My mental health would be in the toilet without our friendship. To Shelby, Lauren, Chris, and Vanessa, thank you and thank god for your early eyes and feedback on this story.

To the team at Folio, especially my agent, Lauren. Thank you for being a champion of my stories and for mastering the art of the gentle "calm the f**k down, Ellie" when I toe the ledge.

To the wonderful teams at Atria and Simon & Schuster Canada, thank you for giving this series a home. To my editor, Melanie, thank you for being so cool when I declared that I was going to rewrite the entire second half of this book even with a looming deadline. Also for the multiple brainstorm sessions, letting me brain dump in your email inbox, and for co-parenting our problem children Summer and Parker until they became characters that did more than make me want to pull out my hair. Your work on this story made all the difference, and I'm so grateful for it. Thank you also to Elizabeth, Camila, Zakiya, Chloe, Natasha, and Mackenzie for everything you've done to make sure this book does more than gather dust on shelves.

Saying goodbye to the Oakwood Bay series and its characters is so bittersweet, especially because it's one that changed the trajectory of my professional life. I'm grateful to everyone who touched all three of these books, and for the characters themselves, who taught me so much about patience, perseverance, and who I am as a writer.

About the Author

Ellie K. Wilde is the author of the Oakwood Bay and Sunset Landing series. She dreams up love stories with a lot of heart and the kind of spice that makes your knees shake. She writes male leads with big personalities and sweet, cinnamon roll insides, and women who discover they're just as tough as they wish they were. Visit EllieKWilde.com, sign up for her newsletter at EllieKWilde.com/newsletter, and follow her on Instagram and TikTok @EllieKWildeAuthor.

Return to Oakwood Bay

For a spicy, small-town, brother's best friend, second-chance romance "packed with sizzling tension, heat, and sweet, swoon-worthy moments" (Peyton Corinne, *USA Today* bestselling author) with Melody Woods and Zac Porter.

For "undeniable chemistry, page-turning tension, and authentic emotions" (Grace Reilly *USA Today* bestselling author) in this steamy, whip-smart, fake-dating sports romance between Siena Pippen and Brooks Attwood.

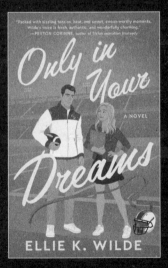
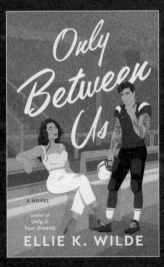